P9-CBE-657

MASSACRE IN BEIJING:
CHINA'S STRUGGLE FOR DEMOCRACY

BY THE EDITORS
OF TIME MAGAZINE
WITH AN INTRODUCTION
BY NIEN CHENG

Edited by Donald Morrison

A TIME BOOK

DISTRIBUTED BY Ⓦ WARNER BOOKS
A WARNER COMMUNICATIONS COMPANY

This Warner Books Edition is Published by Arrangement with
Time Incorporated
Time & Life Building
Rockefeller Center
1271 Avenue of the Americas
New York, N.Y. 10020

Cover Design: Robert Potter
Text Design: H. Roberts
Cover Photo: Ron Dean, ABC News

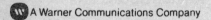 A Warner Communications Company

Printed in the United States of America

First Printing September 1989

First Edition

10 9 8 7 6 5 4 3 2 1

ISBN Number 0-446-68000-1

CONTENTS

Map of Beijing   iv

Foreword   v

Map of Tiananmen Square   vi

Introduction   1

1. The Battle of Beijing   17

2. "Mr. Democracy and Mr. Science"   71

3. The Road to Reform   97

4. "Long Live the Students!"   123

5. A Cry Heard Round the World   161

6. The Crackdown   193

7. China's Future   235

A Chronology   252

Who's Who in China   262

A Glossary   268

Index   272

The Authors   278

Peking
University

0   1 mi.

B E I J I N G

Dongzhimenwai St.
to airport

Forbidden
City

Zhongnanhai
Compound

Military
Museum

Fuxingmen
Overpass

Tiananmen
Square

Diplomatic
Compound

Muxidi
Bridge

Xidan
Intersection

Changan
Ave.

Jianguomenwai
Overpass

Qianmen

Yongdingmen
Bridge

Temple of
Heaven Park

FOREWARD

He stood there. The shooting had not yet stopped when, in broad daylight, a man in a white shirt and carrying a duffel bag stepped into Beijing's Changan Avenue and faced down a column of lumbering tanks. He put up his hand, and the lead vehicle ground to a halt six feet in front of him. "Why are you here!" he shouted at the silent steel bulk. "You have done nothing but create misery. My city is in chaos because of you." The lead tank swiveled on its treads and tried to go around the man, but he stayed in front of it. The tank tried to turn in the other direction, but again he blocked its path. Finally the man's companions, who had been watching in frozen horror, ran into the street and pulled him to safety.

The image of the man in the white shirt stopping a row of tanks is destined to become one of the century's most inspiring, most unforgettable icons. For one moment a lone citizen had thwarted the armed might of a government. That brief encounter sums up an epochal event in modern Chinese history: the rumbling, menacing state is halted in its tracks because the people stood in its way, and because the state stood in theirs. Thousands died as a result of the 1989 crackdown on China's pro-democracy movement. But so did the notion that the Chinese people are a silent, apolitical mass unwilling to stand up to their government.

This is the story of that confrontation.

—D.M.

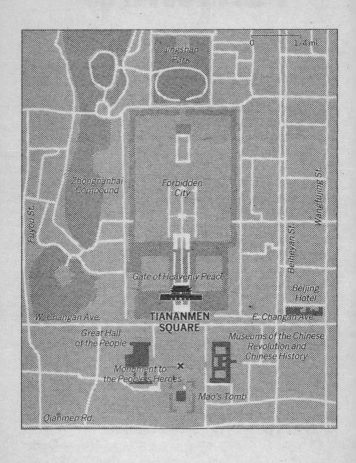

INTRODUCTION

On Aug. 16, 1988, in a moving ceremony at the Statue of Liberty, I took the oath of allegiance and became an American citizen. I felt immeasurably proud and happy. In the five years I have lived here, I have already grown to love America and its people. Then, on Nov. 8, I got up very early to vote in the presidential election. It was the first time in my 73 years that I had the opportunity to vote in a free election. For the rest of that day and many times afterward, I thought of the significance of that simple act. I felt it was such a great privilege, something enjoyed by those who are truly free. And I recited to myself again the oath I had taken: "I hereby declare, on oath, that I absolutely and entirely renounce and abjure all allegiance and fidelity to any foreign prince, potentate, state or sovereignty of whom or which I have heretofore been a subject or citizen. . . "

I said to myself, "Yes, I am now an American. I have exercised my right to vote as a citizen of America. China and the years I spent there belong to a page of my life that I have now turned. I will stop thinking about it."

I felt lighthearted, as if a heavy weight had been lifted from my shoulders.

For weeks and months I hardly thought of China. But one night when I switched on the television news, I saw unarmed student demonstrators and ordinary citizens being mowed down in Beijing by soldiers with automatic weapons. My heart filled with anguish. Tears rolled down my cheeks. Then I knew that although I had become an American citizen, my Chinese heritage remained with me still. The past came back in a flood of memories, for I had lived in Communist China for 31 years, and I know the Communist regime. I was there from the beginning.

Early one morning in May 1949, after a quiet night following days of hearing gunfire, I opened the front gate of my house in Shanghai and saw a group of young Communist soldiers sitting on the sidewalk. They wore straw sandals and faded khaki uniforms. Their faces were deeply tanned and their eyes bloodshot and glazed. They seemed very young, no more than 18. They were gazing intently at nothing in particular, as if in a trance, their faces devoid of any expression.

I did not know then that soldiers of the Communist army, before an engagement, always received a few days of intensified political indoctrination in an isolated spot, cut off from all outside contact. They would listen to lectures by officers, chant slogans and pledge devotion to the cause and their readiness to die for it. They would also express their love for the party and the leader, and their hatred for the enemy. They did all these in a group so that everyone could get into a highly emotional state together. By the time they were sent into battle, they would have attained an exalted sense of their mission and be in a state of hysteria, with no other thought than their task to kill. The soldiers I saw on the TV screen reminded me of those I had seen on that first day of the Communist occupation of Shanghai.

The year 1989 was to be an important year for the aged leaders of the Chinese Communist Party. Exactly 40 years ago, after 28 years of hard struggle, they gained control of the whole of China and founded the Chinese People's Republic. Now in their 80s, they are unlikely to be around to celebrate the 50th anniversary. For 40 years they have enjoyed absolute power over the Chinese people. They have seen the government they created recognized by nations of the world, including great powers at first skeptical of its legitimacy. And they have seen the guerrilla forces they led become a modern army with nuclear weapons. On the personal level, the state-controlled economy provides them with a life-style comparable to that of Kings and Presidents. Their privileges are extended to their families and relatives for at least three generations. They regard the country as their own property, to be governed in the way they deem fit because they fought for it and won. They see the people as men and women to be made to obey and work for whatever project they want accomplished.

Under their rule, the Chinese people suffer great hardship and have no freedom. From cradle to grave the party controls their lives. Which school to go to, which subject to study, where to work, what rate of pay: all are decided by the party. It intrudes into people's private lives with advice and regulations on marriage, having children and divorce. Indifferent to personal suffering, the party makes awful mistakes. A sculptor is forced to make tiles, a musician is made to teach language, a talented scientist has to become an accountant, and so on. Husband and wife are often sent to different parts of the country to work and are allowed to meet once a year on "marital leave." Only when they retire can they make a home together. In every Chinese city there is a severe housing shortage. It is commonplace for a newly wedded couple to live with their in-laws, sharing a room with a partition.

Everybody belongs to a work unit. The party secretary of the unit personifies the party and must be obeyed unconditionally. He or she can have a person arrested and has the right to suggest a suitable sentence. The people are allowed to write letters to the government with their grievances, but their letters are routinely forwarded to the party secretary of their work unit. Once a young woman said to me, "Of course I am afraid of Chairman Mao in Beijing. But I am more afraid of the Chairman Mao of my work unit."

The only people who can escape such arbitrary treatment are the children of senior officials. They attend special schools, are given well-paid jobs of their choice and are never separated from their spouses. Often spacious apartments are kept empty waiting for the leaders' grandchildren to grow up and marry. Above all, no matter what they do, children of senior officials cannot be touched by law, just the same as their parents. Under their leader Mao Zedong, the Old Guard launched one political movement after another, singling out one group of people at a time for political persecution. They set up labor camps and created political prisons. Millions of people have perished, disappeared, been exiled or put in prison simply because of their family origin, economic status, foreign connections or religious affiliation. Others were executed for opposing the Communist Party or criticizing the leadership.

Most of the Old Guard were peasants with no education who joined the party and the army at a young age. Their knowledge is the practical experience of fighting men and the doctrines of a simplistic form of Marxism translated from Soviet text. They share a deep mistrust of scholars. Habitually they view educated people as potential enemies. The party's declared policy toward intellectuals as stated in Mao Zedong's writings is to reform their political thinking, make use of their knowledge and reform their political thinking again *(gaizao, liyong, zai-*

gaizao). What they succeeded in doing was to make liars of the Chinese people. They detest intellectuals because intellectuals are brain workers and they can think, and the Old Guard can't bear people who can think.

Among this group of aged leaders, Deng Xiaoping was a little different. He had lived in France in the early 1920s and was a radical student. Together with Zhou Enlai and several others, he joined a Marxist study group that was incorporated into the Chinese party. During most of his career, he served in the army as a commander or political commissar. During the war against Chiang Kai-shek's Kuomintang in the late 1940s, he was appointed by Mao as political commissar of the combined forces of the 2nd and 3rd Field Armies. In that capacity he directed the important campaign to cross the Yangtze River and capture the Kuomintang capital of Nanking and the industrial city of Shanghai. Because of his close association with the People's Liberation Army for so many years, a number of senior officers who had served under him remained loyal to him.

During the Cultural Revolution, Deng Xiaoping was ousted from his position as General Secretary of the party and denounced as the "No. 2 capitalist roader." To justify the encouragement of individual initiative and free markets, he had remarked that it didn't matter whether a cat was black or white. As long as it caught mice, it was a good cat. For that he was accused of reviving capitalism and punished by being made to work as a common laborer. In April 1973 he was rehabilitated largely through Zhou Enlai's intercession with Mao. Zhou was ill with cancer, and he wanted Deng Xiaoping to succeed him as Premier. Deng was eventually appointed Senior Deputy Premier and Chief of Staff of the army. To ease Mao's concern that the regional commanders had become too powerful as a result of the army's role during the Cultural Revolution, Deng devised a plan to have the commanders moved around without allowing them to take their troops with them. After Zhou Enlai died, Deng was again ousted by the Gang of Four. He did not make a full comeback until 1978, when his Old Guard comrades supported his return to power.

A decade of Mao's Cultural Revolution had thoroughly discredited the Communist Party. China was in a state of political disintegration and economic stagnation. Deng decided to revitalize the economy and thereby recover the party's prestige. At the same time, to ensure orderly succession after his death, he did not take the position as Chairman of the Communist Party but appointed his longtime protégé Hu Yaobang to that job. Deng also picked reform-minded Zhao Ziyang as Premier. The two younger men were charged with the task of carrying out Deng's policy of "opening the door to the outside world and invigorating the economy internally."

Deng's policy of economic reform was accepted by his Old Guard comrades with reluctance and a great deal of misgiving. But his personal prestige was such, and the condition in the country so desperate, that they could not oppose him. However, they watched every measure taken by Hu and Zhao closely, finding fault with the two men at every turn.

To carry out economic reform and attract foreign investment, Hu and Zhao had to rely on the country's educated élite. Many intellectuals and technocrats were promoted to responsible positions; others were recalled from labor camps and hastily rehabilitated. For the first time since the Communist Party came to power, a person with talent and education could hope for a place of honor in society. But the prejudice against intellectuals was deeply rooted in party tradition. With the Old Guard entrenched in Beijing, the local party bureaucrats, whose only qualifications were loyalty to the party leadership and an ability for witch hunting during political campaigns, resisted reform and blocked effective changes in work methods and personnel. Whenever a well-trained person was appointed to a senior position or became a manager, the party bureaucrats would isolate him by making up rumors and spreading gossip to sabotage his work and make his life unpleasant.

While rural reforms between 1979 and 1984 were largely successful in increasing agricultural production and improving living standards, urban reforms encountered major obstacles. Disunity in the workplace between the intellectuals carrying out reforms and the old bureaucrats compounded the difficulties. Reluctance to dismantle the state-owned sector of the economy while desiring to encourage small-scale private enterprises resulted in two kinds of economic operations coexisting side by side. This situation created confusion as well as tempting opportunities for corruption.

Guanxi (connections) became the most important word in the Chinese vocabulary. Without *guanxi* little could be done. People with the right connections laid their hands on state-subsidized materials intended for state-owned factories and sold them on the free market to make huge profits. Using their connections with state-owned factories, they obtained manufactured products in short supply and sold them on the free market. Sons and daughters of senior officials had the best connections, so they got richest. Sometimes, even officials who were not corrupt had to resort to *guanxi* simply to get their jobs done or to obtain the materials needed to keep their factories in operation. Among reform-minded officials and intellectuals there was a gradual realization that a state-subsidized price system and a free-market price system could not exist together, and that a state-controlled economy and a free-market economy were incompatible. If reform was to succeed, China had to abandon socialism, accept capitalism and carry out political reform to relieve the people's frustration and resentment.

The most successful part of Deng Xiaoping's economic reform was the open-door policy. The world wanted to help China in its effort to break out of isolation and restructure its economy. Technical assistance and loans were given by international organizations. Billions of dollars worth of joint-venture investments from Hong Kong Chinese and foreign businessmen poured into China. Tourists arrived in ever increasing numbers, earning China $2 billion in 1988. There were frequent cultural exchanges. Young people came to study and to teach English. Communist China was seen as a friendly and civilized place. This image was largely created by the intellectuals and reform-minded officials, who dealt with the outside world because of their superior language skills and technical know-how.

Foreigners seldom saw the other important people of China: the members of the Old Guard. The Old Guard looked upon political reform as heresy and betrayal, regarding the free association between China and the outside world as dangerous. They feared the contamination by Western values, especially the concepts of democracy and sexual freedom. In 1983 they launched the "Anti-spiritual Pollution Campaign," aimed at the reformists and intellectuals. But the campaign fizzled because Deng Xiaoping did not give it his wholehearted support. The reformists scored a temporary victory.

In 1988 the economic situation worsened. Zhao and his economic advisers were blamed for their tentative experiment with price reform: they had released a few items from government subsidy and allowed them to find their price level in the marketplace. The inflation rate accelerated. People cashed in their savings in waves of panic, buying to preserve the value of their money. The People's Bank ran out of banknotes. The shops ran out of goods, and inflation rose. Life for those on fixed incomes became unbearable. When a delegate to the People's Congress urged the government to raise the pay of professors to the level of waiters at tourist hotels, Premier Li Peng said the professors should find subsidiary jobs to earn additional income. University students then appeared outside the congress meeting hall with shoeshine equipment, offering to shine Li Peng's shoes so they could earn money for their professors.

In China there are said to be three Communist parties: the official one, the "geriatric party" and the "princes' party." Li Peng, the adopted son of the late Premier Zhou Enlai, was the first member of the princes' party to gain a senior position. He grew up in the revolutionary base area of Yan'an (Yenan), where he enjoyed the protection and privileges of his family's rank. After receiving his education in the Soviet Union in the 1950s, he worked without distinction in a series of technical posts. The Old Guard pushed him into the position of acting Premier in November 1987, and he was confirmed in the job a few months later. They expected Li Peng to use his office to undermine Zhao Ziyang, who had become General Secretary of the party, in his effort to bring capitalism to China. The Old Guard could not disagree with Deng Xiaoping's economic reforms openly, but they could try to destroy the men who were working to carry them out. Hu Yaobang had already been ousted. That left only Zhao Ziyang.

In early 1989 rumors began trickling out of China that another round of power struggle was imminent and that the Old Guard was pressing Deng Xiaoping to remove Zhao, blaming him for inflation and the failure of price reform. It was also rumored that Deng was hesitating to dump Zhao because of the impending visit of Soviet leader Mikhail Gorbachev on May 15.

The year 1989 promised to be a particularly important one for the students at Peking University, for it marked the 70th anniversary of the May 4 Movement, which originated from a demonstration by students protesting the government's concessions to Japan at the Versailles peace talks. The May 4 Movement was the prelude to the founding of the Chinese Communist Party two years later. In 1939 in Yan'an, Mao Zedong designated May 4 as China's Youth Day. Since then it has been routinely celebrated by the students.

Peking University students were preparing to hold a parade to celebrate the movement's 70th anniversary and renew the call for democracy, which was still unrealized, when they received some disturbing news: Hu Yaobang, the deposed General Secretary of the Communist Party, had died suddenly while making an emotional speech urging the party leadership to curb corruption in its ranks. To the students Hu was a sympathetic figure. He had spent years working with young people in the Communist Youth League before becoming General Secretary. In December 1986, when students demonstrated for democracy, Hu had refused to take repressive action against them. For that he was denounced by the Old Guard and lost his position. In addition, despite the atmosphere of official corruption and nepotism, Hu's family members kept themselves above reproach.

To mourn Hu's passing, the students decided to move their demonstration ahead by two weeks. They paraded with banners eulogizing Hu and laid wreaths at the Monument to the People's Heroes in Tiananmen Square. They also demanded that the party assess Hu's life work fairly. They were joined by students from other universities in Beijing. As May 4 approached, students came out in increasing numbers calling for democracy.

Support for the students grew. Citizens of Beijing lined the streets to cheer them, brought food and drinks for them and joined their ranks to demonstrate. In spite of a news blackout in the official press, students and other citizens in cities outside of Beijing learned by word of mouth of the demonstration. People responded by organizing their own and were quickly joined by the general populace. The atmosphere was upbeat. The demonstrators believed they had a good chance of persuading the government to improve. People across the country were united in demanding changes in the political system and a greater voice in their own destinies. At one stage the number of demonstrators in Tiananmen Square was estimated to be 1 million. I felt elated and hopeful because the Chinese young people seemed to have been transformed by the open-door policy and contact with foreigners who had come to China, and by books and periodicals. They behaved in an organized and restrained manner.

The students demanded to be received by a senior official of the government, preferably Li Peng, to whom they wanted to present their petition. But their request was ignored. The students began a hunger strike. After a couple of days the number of hunger strikers grew to 3,000. The young people lying in the broiling sun focused the attention of the world on Tiananmen Square. When the scene appeared on international TV programs, it touched the heart and stirred the conscience of the world.

Zhao made a visit to the hunger strikers. He was followed by Li Peng, who finally agreed to meet with the student leaders. They gathered in the Great Hall of the People, but both sides were arrogant and uncompromising, and the meeting led nowhere. Not long after, Deng and the hard-liners made final their plans to use force. Martial law was declared. But the students did not leave the square.

For days no further action was taken. Top government leaders disappeared from view. The atmosphere at Tiananmen Square relaxed, and the hunger strikers took food on doctors' orders. But the quiet in Beijing was merely the quiet before the storm.

Mindful of his humiliation during the Cultural Revolution, Deng Xiaoping took a serious view of the demonstration and tried to suppress it in April before the workers had even joined. But opposition from the army, the party and the press delayed his actions. Deng saw the outpouring of popular sentiment for the students as a threat to public order, the Communist regime and his personal power. He decided to crush the demonstration with brutal force.

Foreign journalists in Beijing faithfully reported the events at Tiananmen Square. The world was shocked by the violence seen on TV screens and recounted in newspaper and magazine stories. The crackdown seemed so vicious. It offended the conscience of civilized people everywhere and was condemned by the world family of nations. I felt terrible. I was heartbroken. It seemed that the ten-year effort had gone down the drain. I really believe the relationship between the party and the population is now worse than after the Cultural Revolution. Then they alienated the intellectuals. But this time they alienated the workers and the masses.

The old men in the Communist Party leadership, including Deng Xiaoping, appeared on Chinese television to congratulate the soldiers for a job well done. Even before the bloodstains were washed away, large-scale arrests were being carried out. Workers who took part in the demonstrations in Beijing, Shanghai, Chengdu and other cities were executed. Zhao was put under house arrest pending investigation of possible criminal activities. Close associates were taken into custody. Wanted lists of student leaders and intellectuals were published. Some were quickly arrested.

The distinguished American writer and journalist Stanley Karnow said to me, "This was not the worst, only the worst that was seen." I agree with him completely. Certainly more people were executed during the land-reform movement and the Suppression of Counterrevolutionaries Movement of 1950-52. And in the Antirightist Campaign of 1957, probably more intellectuals were put into prison and labor camps than the eventual figure this time. As for the Cultural Revolution of 1966-76, the official statement said that 100 million people were affected adversely. The unofficial estimate is that 1 million died

because of persecution and factional fighting. In his nearly four decades in power, Mao Zedong launched nine major political movements, and each time a large number of
people suffered imprisonment or death. But the world
knew little or nothing about them. This time the world
was there to record everything, thanks to the news media.
And television brought the horror right into our homes.

This was the first time in the history of the Chinese
Communist Party that the People's Liberation Army was
used to carry out repression. Even though millions had
been victimized during the political campaigns of the past
four decades, the killing was always done by the police
and those members of the masses who were given temporary power. Having the army fire at unarmed civilians
will have far-reaching consequences. Already it has destroyed the traditionally harmonious relationship between army and people carefully fostered by Mao. It has
also opened the way for the Communist government to
degenerate into a military dictatorship.

The man who played a prominent role in the crackdown and stood by Deng throughout was Yang Shangkun, the President of the People's Republic. Of all the
Old Guard, he is one of the most robust. Beside holding
the largely ceremonial post of President, he is also the
Permanent Vice Chairman of the Military Commission.
During the Cultural Revolution, he was accused of planting listening devices in Mao's home.

With Zhao Ziyang and his team purged, reform of
China's economic structure has suffered a major setback.
Deng Xiaoping and Li Peng will try to increase efficiency
and productivity in the factories by imposing more political indoctrination of the workers and tighter control by
party bureaucrats—the same methods that had been used
before the Cultural Revolution. They will also limit the
profit of individual small businesses by increased taxation. Many businesses will close. The already tiny private
sector of China's economy will shrink. Deng and Li will

try, however, to keep China open for foreign businessmen and tourists because the country needs foreign investment, loans, and earnings from tourism. Some foreign businessmen and international agencies may indeed be willing to bail out the current regime. Others may want to ponder the image of the massacre at Tiananmen Square before they decide that the government values prosperity over ideology.

The tragedy at Tiananmen Square and the setback suffered by the prodemocracy movement greatly saddened me. When I heard about the arrests, I thought about the prison cell I stayed in, the torture. In the end a large number of the young people will be sent to labor camps, and that will be terrible. But I take comfort in the knowledge that many on the wanted lists have escaped arrest. Their ability to remain at large demonstrated the fact that many people are willing to risk their own safety to hide them. This tells me that the current leadership has indeed lost the people's support. All members of the Old Guard are in their 80s. Within the next five years or so their ranks will be thinned by age. In the meantime, simmering discontent will be driven further underground. People will seek expression of their anger in covert resistance: sabotage, slowdowns at the workplace and absenteeism will become common. The economy will suffer, and there will be hardship. That in turn will create more discontent. When the power of the Old Guard is weakened by death, the power of the people will erupt again. Deng Xiaoping claimed that the crackdown was needed to restore stability. On the contrary, the result has been even more tension. Real stability can come only if the people are happy and have hope for their future. Only a democratic system of government can ensure that. China must make a choice, to go into capitalism or socialism. What they have now is two systems shuffling along side by side. Another fundamental point for China is that it must have some laws and the laws must be applicable to everybody. Official privileges outside the law should be abolished.

Perhaps the massacre in Beijing will unite the people even more and bring the day of democracy nearer. My grief is that so many fine young lives have been so ruthlessly sacrificed. As for the parents who have lost their children, I weep for them, for I know well how they must be suffering.

Nien Cheng
July 31, 1989

CHAPTER ONE

THE BATTLE OF BEIJING

JUNE 2

For days, many of Beijing's 10 million residents had slept fitfully. Ever since the first giant student demonstrations in Tiananmen Square on April 16, following the death of China's reform-minded former Communist Party General Secretary Hu Yaobang, the warm spring air had carried a heady fragrance of excitement. The new mood was one part exhilaration, one part uncertainty and a large dose of fear. Not since the Communists came to power in 1949 had there been such huge protests in the Chinese capital in favor of freedom and democracy. Not since teenage Red Guards turned China upside down in the first three years of the 1966-1976 Cultural Revolution had young people so unceremoniously disrupted normal life in the city. But the Cultural Revolution's chaos had been deliberately fermented for political purposes by China's Communist Party Chairman, Mao Zedong, and it was he who decided when the demonstrations would end. Now, on the night of June 2, 1989, nearly two weeks had elapsed since an angry Premier Li Peng had declared martial law in sections of Beijing. During this period, China's military commanders had embarrassingly failed to get their troops anywhere near the center of Beijing.

For the few hundred students still camping out in army tents in the center of Tiananmen Square, the sense of victory was mixed with a feeling of disquiet. True, convoys of troop-laden trucks that had entered the city when martial law was declared had been turned back to the outskirts by vigilant citizens determined to protect "their" students. Crowds of shoppers, off-shift workers and students corralled the troops in their trucks, lectured them on the need to "love the people" and respect democracy, plied them with cigarettes, refreshments and food, then, almost condescendingly, sent them back in the direction they came. Even at the Beijing railroad station, where thousands of troops from the suburbs and distant provinces had later tried to disembark, students seemed to have succeeded in blocking them. Was it really possible that the 3.2 million–strong People's Liberation Army—the world's second largest military force, obedient to Communist Party leaders who were themselves hardened by years of combat and civil war—would meekly succumb to civics lessons by 20-year-olds and hectoring by middle-aged housewives?

Some of those 20-year-olds dozing and chatting in the insurrectionary Tiananmen encampment may have believed so—especially the out-of-town students, who had poured into Beijing in the last days of May and now outnumbered the increasingly weary local students. For the newcomers, the atmosphere of the square was intoxicating. Pennants and flags from campuses all over the country fluttered bravely from atop the lines of tents in the stiff spring breeze. The Goddess of Democracy, a 30-foot statue of plaster-covered Styrofoam, faced north toward the portrait of Mao Zedong on the Gate of Heavenly Peace. The statue was surrounded by a circle of blue and white pup tents provided by Hong Kong supporters of the prodemocracy movement. Piles of garbage, make-shift tents, student leaders and Western television crews had long since taken over the upper balustrade area of the Monument to the People's Heroes. Student marshals prevented crowds of well-wishers and passersby from ducking under a barrier rope on the bottom level. Large banners strung across the monument indicated the new boldness that was infecting students, and indeed all of China's intelligentsia, in the past seven weeks. CONVENE THE NATIONAL PEOPLE'S CONGRESS, IMPLEMENT DE-MOCRACY, DISMISS LI PENG, BRING AN END TO MAR-TIAL LAW, they said in huge yellow letters on a red background. Lower down, another message declaimed, WE ARE ON HUNGER STRIKE, WE PROTEST, WE CRY OUT, WE REPENT. Even jaded Western journalists could not but be touched by the naive optimism of China's youth at Tiananmen Square.

The more experienced among Beijing student leaders, however, were nervous. Among them was Uerkesh Daolet, 21, a Uighur education major at Beijing Normal University who was better known by his Chinese name, Wuer Kaixi. A dynamic, elflike figure, Uerkesh had been voted out of the leadership of the Autonomous Students' Union of Beijing Universities, in part for proposing to end the occupation of the square on grounds that the military was about to take it over by force. Chai Ling, an electrifying orator also from Beijing Normal University, had taped a tearful interview with ABC News announcing that she would go into hiding because the entire protest movement, she prophesied, would soon be put down in a bloodbath. Other Beijing students were concerned about a more mundane matter: the "movement," as they called their occupation, was so physically fatigued that it was in danger of breaking up.

JUNE 3

Not long after midnight on June 3, word swept

through the square that the army was on the move again. Convoys of trucks had been spotted in the north of Beijing, in the south and in the west. Oddest of all, thousands of soldiers, unarmed and wearing khaki pants and standard white shirts, were attempting to jog in ranks ten abreast down Changan Avenue, from a starting point in Tongxian County some six miles away from Tiananmen. From the opposite direction, trucks and military buses were gingerly approaching Tiananmen with the rifles, ammunition and other equipment that the jogging troops would need when they reached the city center.

In no time, students and sympathizers on bicycles and motorcycles roused Beijing's by now politically savvy citizenry. People swarmed in their shorts and undershirts out of apartment blocks and the city's *hutongs* (alleyways) to surround the invading forces and demonstrate the same extraordinary "people power" that had kept the military at bay for the previous two weeks. Road blocks of hastily commandeered buses and trucks were set up at key intersections. At the Yanjing Hotel, on Changan Avenue three miles to the west of Tiananmen, the first group of marching uniformed soldiers was surrounded by crowds and searched for weapons. Some of the military vehicles were overturned by citizens on the Yongdingmen bridge in southern Beijing. Out west at Muxidi, where the dead straight Changan Avenue crosses a canal in its sweep from west to east, tires of military trucks were slashed. If the army wanted a fight, it now had a justification for one.

7 a.m.

The last body of foot soldiers, who had jogged into the city, retreated eastward down Changan. Sweaty, exhausted and in some cases weeping, they presented a pitiful sight. They had run a gauntlet of invective, abuse, argument and even physical assault on their way into the city. Many had become separated from their officers and were completely disoriented. They had been halted at 3 a.m. just in front of the Beijing Hotel, a sprawling block-long complex east of Tiananmen Square. Most were teen-age peasant recruits who seemed quite unsure why they had been sent into the city. "We came here to restore order," a soldier told the crowd that had surrounded his unit on the eastern part of Changan. "We were obeying orders. Beijing people don't understand us." Crouching in the road nearby, a woman retorted, "We do under-stand you. We do not need you here."

Some of the soldiers were cruelly mocked by the crowds who tried to block or taunt them as they moved into town. In some cases refreshments were thrust into their faces as they jogged or staggered along. On both sides—army and citizenry—nerves were stretched taut by the bizarre, cat-and-mouse approach that the military seemed to be taking toward implementing the martial-law decrees.

Now, by first light on June 3, an ominous souring of relations between the people of Beijing and the army seemed to be setting in. No one had attempted to steal guns or ammunition from the army on any of the mili-tary's previous forays into the city, and the troops them-selves had in general been treated correctly, sometimes quite well. By 7 a.m., though, students and young work-ers outside Zhongnanhai were smashing their way into two military buses filled with AK-47s, light machine guns and crates of ammunition. "We are peaceful stu-dents who love our country," shouted a young man with a white headband. "Why must the People's Army threat-en the people with guns?" As for the isolated pockets of troops hemmed in at intersections and overpasses around the city, the crowd was not in a mood merely to lecture them. In some places, soldiers were stripped almost na-ked, chased or struck by angry citizens. Other injured troops had difficulty getting to hospitals as mobs deflated or slashed the tires of military ambulances.

Incidents such as these were used by the authorities to justify the mobilization of the army. "Beginning in the small hours of June 3," said Beijing Mayor Chen Xitong in a statement released after the massacre, "a band of counterrevolutionary thugs incited some people to illegally set up roadblocks, steal the troops' arms and equipment, destroy and burn military vehicles and stop and block martial-law troops from taking up their positions." Time and again, continued the mayor, his charges wildly belying the facts, "they frenziedly stormed Zhongnanhai, the Great Hall of the People, broadcasting stations and other key departments, and looted shops."

Wisely, the student leaders had anticipated government attempts to provoke violence, and had kept tight control over their own rank and file, lest they unwittingly abet them. In Chai Ling's taped account, smuggled out of China to Hong Kong one week after the massacre, she described how the military had tried to bait the dissidents. "Several army trucks were put deliberately in our hands," she said. "In the trucks, there were weapons and soldiers' coats." On learning that protesters were helping themselves to the contents of the truck, student leaders took action. "We handed all the weapons to the Public Security," she stated. "We still have the receipt."

By the time Beijing had eaten its early breakfast and set off to work June 3, its people came upon some startling scenes throughout the city: disabled military buses and trucks, their windows smashed and their tires deflated; barricades of buses, trolleys and commandeered trucks parked across intersections; and pockets of demoralized soldiers, some of them injured, either trapped by intransigent crowds or wandering around aimlessly in small groups, trying to find their officers. Chinese student leader Wang Dan commented on this latest in a series of military fiascos: "The awareness of the public was very high. That was the reason they couldn't get us."

But "they" had not stopped trying. The efforts of China's military leaders to penetrate the city had foundered ignominiously so far, but there was no sign at all that the overall strategy was going to be modified. Meanwhile, the first fatalities from the army's latest push occurred. A jeep that formed part of a nine-vehicle convoy racing into town from the east in the early hours of Saturday had skidded out of control on the rain-drenched streets and run into four pedestrians. Three were killed, one of them dragged along under the jeep's bumper as the driver struggled to bring his vehicle under control. When the jeep careened to a halt, the driver jumped out and tried to get away, but was caught and barely escaped a severe beating at the hands of an enraged crowd.

Until that moment, the seven weeks of swirling demonstrations in China's capital had produced only a handful of injuries and not a single known death. Hours later, China Central Television came forward to accept blame for the incident, saying that the jeep had been borrowed from the police for a film being prepared for the 40th anniversary of the founding of the People's Republic. But the semi-apology did little to soothe angry emotions. An ugly genie seemed to have been let out of the bottle.

On Tiananmen Square, the morning hours of Saturday passed by much as they had during the previous week. One thing was new, though. In a khaki army tent on the upper level of the Monument to the People's Heroes, a new hunger strike was under way. It had started the previous afternoon, and was something of a last-ditch effort by student organizers to rekindle the enthusiasm for protest that had characterized the prodemocracy demonstrations during the first few weeks. Though all four strikers could be considered intellectuals, none was a student. The most prominent of them was Hou Dejian, a well-known songwriter and vocalist who had dramatically defected to Beijing from Taiwan in 1983. The other three were Liu Xiaobo, a lecturer in the Chinese department of Beijing Normal University; Zhou Tuo, a lecturer in sociology at Peking University; and Gao Xin, former editor of the Beijing Normal University *Gazette* and a Communist Party member.

Hou had been ambivalent about becoming so visibly involved in the student demonstrations, though he had actively supported them from behind the scenes. The strike was scheduled for 72 hours, but Hou's recording schedule in Hong Kong required him to limit his own involvement to 48 hours. He agreed to take part, he told a friend in Beijing Friday, because he saw no other way to keep up the momentum of the protest movement. "The problem with Chinese intellectuals," he said, "is that they are all talk and no action. That is the reason I think I should do [the hunger strike]."

At a Friday press conference, the four strikers had told journalists that they had four "basic slogans." In light of the violence that descended upon Beijing less than a day later, they make interesting reading today. "1. We are not against anybody and do not let hatred and violence poison our fight for democracy. 2. We are all responsible for our own past backwardness. 3. We are Chinese citizens. 4. We are not seeking death, but a real and better life."

Hou and his three fellow hunger strikers sat inside the darkened tent Saturday as throngs of student supporters and the just plain curious crowded up to a rope on the lower steps to gape at the scene. White-clad medics occasionally came and went, ensuring that none of the four was in medical danger. From different parts of the square, loudspeakers relaying prodemocracy sentiments from student leaders kept up a cacophony over the heads of the thousands of young people, sightseers and even occasional foreign tourists threading their way through tents and parked bicycles.

On Changan Avenue on the north side of the square, there were far more bicycles than usual, meandering along to look at the mayhem from the early morning hours. Normal traffic had a hard time moving. Vehicles traveling west across the square, in fact, were diverted by traffic police south in front of the Great Hall of the People. West of the square, Changan was now closed for a few blocks because the avenue was still obstructed by the weapons and ammunition buses that students had broken into earlier in the morning. Glass and rocks littered the street, and Beijing's bicyclists wove slowly in and out of groups of pedestrians who also wanted to see the latest evidence of the clash of wills between the army and the people. Further west along Changan, there were still isolated groups of soldiers trapped inside, or alongside, their trucks, and subjected now to almost constant barracking and harassment by the cocky citizenry.

2 p.m.

The students and the curious youth of Beijing bicycling slowly from one bottleneck to another might have thought at this point that life could possibly continue in this manner almost indefinitely: the army would try, the citizens would react, the army would try again, the citizens would stop them a second time, and so on until, perhaps, the government stepped down.

But two things had changed. First, as Beijing's inhabitants would find out to their horror later, a military plan was already afoot to crush the prodemocracy movement with full lethal force. Second, both China's military and the People's Armed Police, who are under the control of the Ministry of Public Security and the Defense Ministry, had become almost paranoid about the busload of weapons and ammunition that had been broken into earlier in the morning just half a block away from the main entrance to the Zhongnanhai compound on the north side of Changan Avenue. What might happen, the authorities worried, if the peace-loving students lost control of the situation and mobs of angry workers tried to storm the political heart of Beijing with AK-47s and machine guns?

The bus the authorities most worried about was at Liubukou, where Fuyou Street intersects Changan, on the western end of the Zhongnanhai block. Shortly before 2 p.m., loudspeakers operated by the army broadcast orders for students and ordinary citizens to return the guns and ammunition they had taken from the smashed bus and hand over the bus itself. In the milling crowd, there were jeers and snickers. Suddenly, at 2:10 p.m. fear swept through the thousands of people around the buses. Wearing helmets and wielding nightsticks, some 3,000 People's Armed Police stormed out of Zhongnanhai's main entrance and blocked off Changan Avenue. They then tore into the crowd around the Liubukou weapons bus. Rocks were thrown, people started running and tear-gas shells were fired directly into the crowd. It was the first known occasion in the 40-year history of the People's Republic that tear gas had been employed in Beijing against the city's inhabitants. Later, an angry student showed an American reporter a discarded tear-gas shell stained with blood where it had smashed into someone. "Metak 38m MN-05" was written on the shell casing.

For several minutes the crowd fought back. But the Armed Police displayed greater resolution than security forces had at any time in the seven previous weeks of demonstrations. Men, women, young and old were clubbed or smashed open by tear-gas canisters if they got in the way. Ambulances roared up, sirens wailing and blue lights flashing, to remove the first casualties of the battle for Beijing. Furious now, young people gathered up any bricks and rocks they could find to hurl back at the riot police, who seemed to be changing the equation in the struggle. The crowds thickened and began smashing street lamps and the windows of army buses parked on the south side of the street. Several rocks were hurled at the very gate of the Zhongnanhai compound.

Overwhelmed by numbers, the riot police fell back down Fuyou Street, finally taking refuge inside Zhongnanhai via the compound's west gate. Possibly fearing that the crowds might attempt a frontal assault on Zhongnanhai, about 40 soldiers with clubs came out of the main gate and stood shoulder to shoulder in front of the entrance. Though jeered and insulted, they made no effort to attack the swirling mobs in front of them. A young rock thrower who came too close to the gate was smashed to the ground by the troops before managing to wriggle free and make his escape.

3 p.m.

Within less than an hour, a large crowd had surrounded a military bus at the Xidan intersection, one long block to the west of Zhongnanhai along Changan. The bus, containing military supplies and weapons, held about 80 troops. The crowd lectured the troops, admonishing them not to kill the people. For their part, the soldiers replied politely that they were only following orders. Later in the day the bus remained at the intersection but all its windows had been smashed. Inside, the frightened soldiers had stuffed bedrolls into the windows to keep out the mob. After the massacre, the bus was found empty and burned.

Meanwhile, a new locus of tension between troops and students had come into existence outside the western side, that is, the back, of the Great Hall of the People. Just as the People's Armed Police were surging out of Zhongnanhai, 2,000 or so helmeted and backpacked troops had come marching out of a ground floor side entrance to the Great Hall, which has long been known to have underground passages that connect it with the Zhongnanhai compound on the other side of Changan. The troops may have been secreted into the Great Hall via Zhongnanhai, and it is possible that they had even made their way to Zhongnanhai itself via Beijing's underground network of bomb-shelter tunnels built under the orders of Mao Zedong in the late 1960s. Foreigners had occasionally been shown a glimpse of the tunnels, one of which was entered through a secret, electrically operated sliding door in a clothing store on Da Sha La Street. The tunnels were said by Chinese officials to extend for miles under the city's streets and to be capable of protecting much of the city's population from all but a nuclear direct hit.

The Great Hall troops may not have intended to proceed very far, but from the perspective of the Tiananmen students and the Beijing citizenry now supporting them, the only obstacle separating them from the square was the Great Hall itself. The soldiers were already worryingly close to the political heart of the prodemocracy movement. Within minutes, thousands of students and citizens had gathered from the square and nearby streets to block the movement of the soldiers, who were from the 67th Army. Two city buses were also driven up and parked near the Great Hall, cutting off the soldiers from Changan Avenue. Thousands of people now surrounded the troops, who were instructed by their officers to sit down on the sidewalk and the roadway in the shade. There was a lot of shouting, and many young men climbed atop the commandeered buses for a better view and to observe the troops more closely. When an American network camera crew arrived on the scene, the crowd cheered lustily.

But it was already a hot day, and the officers were in a sour mood. As some of the students pushed too close to the edge of the sitting troops, some of their commanders took off their belts and swung them into the students' faces, drawing blood and infuriating the crowd. Groups of students, in turn, would from time to time snatch a helmet from a sitting soldier and run off with it, to a roar of delight from those nearby. On Tiananmen Square for much of the afternoon, students triumphantly wheeled around flatbed bicycles with trophies of their various confrontations with the army mounted atop them: helmets, I.D. cards, officers' caps, even an occasional rifle.

5 p.m.

Spectators on the western steps of the Great Hall watched the slow-moving confrontation between the crowd and the Hebei troops with interest, occasionally shouting insults up at staff workers who were looking out of second-story windows in the hall. "Li Peng, step down!" was one popular demand hurled upward in unison by a group of young people. Then, impatient at the ugly reaction of the belt-wielding officers, angrier members of the crowd picked up stones and began throwing them into the ground floor compound areas of the Great Hall, smashing windows in a small guard booth and in the hall itself. A few students with headbands tried to reason with the troops and their officers, and white-coated students from the Beijing Union Medical College set up a temporary first-aid station right in a patch of the roadway amid the besieged troops. Bloody-faced students continued to stagger out, victims of the belt buckles of an increasingly angry officer corps.

The rising anger of crowds at intersections along Changan all the way to the Military Museum of the Chinese People's Revolution was now being expressed in rock throwing at People's Armed Police and several government buildings. Windows were smashed not just in the Great Hall, but also in the Propaganda Department of the Communist Party Central Committee and the Ministry of Radio, Film and Television. Several guards at these buildings, as well as at Zhongnanhai, had by late afternoon been injured by flying rocks.

One reason for the crowd's fury was the violence

employed by the riot police attempting to clear Changan in front of Zhongnanhai and to recover the blockaded weapons and supply buses. A woman caught by riot troops at the Xidan intersection in mid-afternoon, for example, was kicked to the ground by five policemen, then beaten with truncheons as one held her hair. Nearby, a man was cornered by three policemen who beat him about the face and chest for a full minute before letting him go. His face and upper body streaming with blood, he staggered off, barely conscious.

News of these ferocious incidents flashed back and forth from crowd to crowd in a one-mile radius of Tiananmen Square, along with scattered and panicky accounts of yet another troop movement in some part or other of the city. Around 5 p.m., several hundred young workers donned their yellow construction helmets and headed for Tiananmen with makeshift pikes and clubs, as though preparing for a violent confrontation with the military. A crowd of about 1,000 ordinary citizens, meanwhile, pushed down the wall of a construction site near the Xidan intersection and made off with tools, bricks, reinforcing bars and anything else that seemed usable as a weapon.

To the beleaguered authorities of both Beijing municipality and the Communist Party Central Committee, the new developments were the stuff of every Communist leadership's nightmare: the "people" turning against the "people's leadership." Though the prodemocracy movement had meticulously avoided any public attacks on the Communist Party, or indeed upon socialism itself throughout most of the long weeks of escalating protest, such self-restraint was evaporating fast. The June 14 official government report on the massacre asserts that Tiananmen loudspeakers in the hands of the Autonomous Workers' Union were broadcasting appeals "to take up arms and overthrow the government." It is unlikely that the union was saying anything of the sort, but it is possible that some individual workers were calling for extreme action against the authorities. Some of the many worker and student rallies proceeding on the square in late afternoon had their own independent bullhorns. Who knows what was said in the flush of antipolice anger?

Words, though, are seldom merely words in the dense legal mythology of Communist power. Even a whispered yearning for weapons by a hunger-striking student in the corner of a dark tent would have been seized upon as evidence of anti-Communist intent. For the martial-law authorities in Beijing, whatever insurrectionary sentiments were publicly voiced around 5 p.m. at Tiananmen Square on Saturday seemed to serve as the judicial trigger for much that happened in the next few hours.

The Plan

Just how many troops were outside Beijing may never be precisely known. Nonetheless, a source in close touch with the White House throughout the crisis said flatly that there were as many as 350,000, drawn from all seven of China's military region commands. Deng Xiaoping had summoned the regional commanders to a meeting in Wuhan to obtain their support for the crackdown. Western intelligence was not privy to those confidential discussions, but once the troops began to actually enter Beijing, it was a relatively simple matter to keep track of them. Makeshift tactical orders were being transmitted by radio in the clear, without scrambling or encryption. As a result, U.S. intelligence agencies using satellites could listen in on radio communications right down to the battalion level.

Deng himself was kept informed of all the major troop movements and decisions, and had insisted that elements of all Chinese military regions take part in the final crackdown on the students. This was a precautionary measure both to prevent the emergence of an all-powerful military warlord should the military operation prove a striking success, and to spread the responsibility among as many units as possible should it be a failure. On his return from Wuhan, Deng remained in the Beijing area for a few days, but then left once more, on May 28, for the Yellow Sea resort of Beidaihe. Equipped with comfortable villas for the use of high Chinese officials on vacation, Beidaihe had several times in the past served as the locale of important Chinese policy gatherings when Deng—and before him Mao Zedong—needed to forge agreement at high level in a less formal and more confidential setting than was possible in Beijing. During the last days of May and the first one or two days of June, Deng presided over the planning for the military operation and double-checked the political allegiances of both his military commanders and the political leadership at Politburo level. Deng, despite his semi-retirement in 1987 from day-to-day administration, still held the one vital lever for controlling political power in the People's Republic: chairmanship of the Central Military Commission.

The last details in place, Deng evidently returned to the Beijing area before June 3. He did not, however, go back to his official residence. Instead, he went to the Western Hills, where some senior party officials have villas in a well-guarded area away from the prying eyes of foreigners or ordinary Chinese. A temporary military command post appears to have been set up nearby when the assault on Beijing began. It is possible that most of China's top leadership still considered loyal to Deng also met there, until it was apparent that the military would gain the upper hand in Beijing. Then, on June 6, three days after the crackdown began, the martial-law authorities moved the tactical military command post into the Great Hall of the People.

Even with a determined effort to involve every major military region in the Beijing assault, Deng left nothing to chance in his delegation of authority. His primary conduit was President Yang Shangkun, who, along with the already disgraced party General Secretary Zhao Ziyang, was a vice-chairman of the Central Military Commission. Yang, in turn, was related by blood or marriage to at least three of the key personnel entrusted with completing the takeover of Tiananmen Square:

• His son-in-law, Chi Haotian, chief of the general staff of the P.L.A. and thus the one man in a position to coordinate all military deployments within China.

• His younger brother, Yang Baibing, chief of the general political department of the P.L.A.

• His nephew (and Yang Baibing's son), Yang Jianhua, commander of the 27th Army, a unit within the Beijing military region that is based in Shijiazhuang in Hebei province.

The detailed operational planning of the troop movements into Beijing was in the hands of Chi Haotian, whose final instructions from Deng Xiaoping could probably be summarized as follows: use whatever force necessary to complete the suppression of the student movement. As Chief of Staff, Chi bears major responsibility for the violence unleashed upon Beijing's citizenry by his troops. Yet he almost certainly hoped that firepower would not be necessary during the operation. For one thing, there was profound unease throughout the officer corps at the use of the military for purposes of political control. For another, China's field commanders, like the field commanders of virtually any other regular army in the world, probably dreaded the prospect of subjecting their troops to the serious logistical problems of moving around within a densely populated city, and especially of exposing them to the fury of the aroused and politically radicalized populace.

In retrospect, it is obvious that the operational plan to take Tiananmen Square envisaged the use of a tough and heavily armed field army as a last resort. None of the military units deployed in the initial probing forays into the city on the night of June 2 had been provided with ammunition. Some of them, as noted earlier, did not even have weapons. There were sound military and political reasons for that caution. The 38th Army, based at Baoding, 90 miles from Beijing, was composed of officers and troops native to the Beijing area. A number of the students demonstrating in Tiananmen Square had even done their reserve training in the 38th. Many officers of the unit had relatives or friends who were students. Politically, the 38th Army may have been the P.L.A. unit most sympathetic to student arguments and thus least psychologically suited to carry out the task of suppressing them. In fact, tanks from the 38th Army were used early on in the approach to Tiananmen, but they were not armed and their turret-mounted heavy machine guns were never used against demonstrators. Several unit commanders were later reported to have been removed, and some even executed, for refusing to move aggressively against Beijing. Had any of their soldiers been armed, these officers might have turned the guns against the troops that were prepared to suppress the population.

Low motivation was apparent in other units brought into the vicinity of Beijing from China's seven military regions. From Chengdu in Sichuan Province, home of Deng Xiaoping, came elements of the 70th Army; from Shenyang, elements of the 40th and the 65th (with the 65th containing some troops from Inner Mongolia). From Datong came elements of the 28th Army. These units, as well as others that have not been identified, formed part of the military stranglehold that Chi Haotian hoped to put into place on the center of Beijing during the afternoon and evening of June 3. Some had made their way to Beijing by road, but the bulk of troop movements evidently took place by air, with the Nanyuan military airfield south of Beijing being heavily used in the final hours before the June 3 assault. As for the Chinese air force, responsible for troop movement by air, there were repeated though unconfirmed reports that its commander, Wang Hai, had been opposed to the initial declaration of martial law in Beijing. "The air force had nothing to do with this," Wang Hai supposedly said when the scope of the Beijing massacre became apparent.

It is not clear exactly how many of China's armies were in place around Beijing when the final assault took place, but it could have been as many as ten, even if not all were at full strength. Besides the 27th, 28th, 38th and 65th, there were divisions or smaller units from the 16th, 17th and 69th. To add real combat muscle to these forces, at least one regiment of the 15th airborne division, from the Wuhan military district, was also on hand.

Troops from most or perhaps all of these units were involved in the military occupation of Beijing that took place once Tiananmen Square had been taken. But one field army behaved with particular ferocity and brutality on the night of June 3-4: the 27th Army under the command of Yang Jianhua, Yang Shangkun's nephew. Some of its troops had been recruited into the army only as a last resort to avoid prison sentences. Many were combat-toughened veterans of China's 1979 battle with Viet Nam. The men of the 27th, generally older than the teen-age recruits who had so dismally failed to penetrate Beijing in convoys or in jogging units, were mostly of peasant background, and they seemed to feel nothing in common with the young people of the Chinese capital. No doubt because of their presumed impermeability to propaganda blandishments within Beijing proper, they were entrusted with the task of ensuring that, whatever else happened, China's military would secure a tactical victory on Tiananmen Square.

Chi Haotian's plan called for the 27th to be held in reserve to the east and west of the city, in case other units failed to secure the square and real shooting was needed.

But the unfolding operation was a lengthy one, additionally complicated by uncertainty over which troops would be able to reach the center of Beijing from which axis of approach. From the south, for example, troops moving toward Tiananmen from Nanyuan airfield had a more difficult task than those scheduled to make the approach from the west or the east. That is because none of the north-south streets of Beijing offer the broad and uninterrupted axis of approach to Tiananmen provided by Changan Avenue. Navigating through crooked intersections around the Temple of Heaven Park, troop trucks and armored personnel carriers were easily blocked by commandeered buses and other vehicles in the Yongdingmen area, south of Tiananmen.

On Dongzhimenwai Street, which leads into Beijing from the airport, a convoy of some 50 trucks was finally halted around 5:30 p.m. when students and local citizens overturned a vehicle and completely blocked the relatively narrow road. As the crowd grew and citizens surrounded the halted trucks to talk to the troops within them, several buses were placed across the main Dongzhimen intersection to prevent any further efforts to bring in troops from this sector.

6 p.m.

A strange quiet now came over the center of Beijing, as though each side in the approaching clash was sizing up the other. There were still thousands of people and bicycles in and around Tiananmen Square itself. Changan remained closed off in front of Zhongnanhai. But there had been no more tear gas or fighting since early afternoon. Behind the Great Hall of the People, crowds of students and citizens continued to hector each other and clash in small ways with the thousands of troops hemmed in on the roadway. Nonetheless, it now seemed clear that the soldiers were unlikely to attempt any aggressive action for the remainder of the evening. Pockets of stranded troops and trucks continued to fidget amid humming crowds in different parts of the city, though with little sign that violence was about to erupt.

Meanwhile, the authorities in Beijing were preparing to warn the city that matters had now reached the point of no return. At 6:30 p.m., the municipal government and the martial-law authorities issued a new emergency statement. Broadcast repeatedly on radio and television, it called on residents of the city to "heighten their vigilance" and to stay off the streets and away from Tiananmen Square. Workers were urged to stay at their jobs or remain in their homes. The students in the square almost certainly paid little attention to the emergency statement, any more than did Beijing residents caught up in the all-consuming task of keeping the army at bay. After all, had not there been one "serious warning" after another ever since the original martial-law declaration on May 20? Why should this one be any different?

The tear gasings, beatings and other injuries on Saturday afternoon had all occurred in the vicinity of Zhongnanhai. Yet it was the presence of fully armed troops so close to Tiananmen Square that seemed to have students and citizens most worried. The belt lashings inflicted on some of the students by officers went on intermittently until evening, and sometimes bricks and bottles were thrown back and forth. Whenever things seemed to be getting out of hand or the troops looked as though they were about to fight back, the crowd would shout out in unison, "Don't fight! Don't fight!"

8:30 p.m.

Suddenly the orders seemed to have changed. At about 8:30 p.m., some 2,000 men clambered to their feet, formed up in ranks, then marched uneventfully back into the ground-floor gate of the Great Hall from which they had originally emerged. At least one crisis now appeared resolved. Perhaps others might be defused in the same nonviolent way.

That was not to be. Possibly as part of the decision made around 5 p.m. by the martial-law authorities, new waves of troops began surging into the city along whatever axes were not already blocked. When about 40 trucks filled with troops came down the first ring road to the Jianguomenwai overpass, just two miles to the east of the square along Changan, they were also stopped by citizens. This time the soldiers sensed the mood was not at all friendly and clutched their rifles nervously. Some of the crowd clambered over the halted trucks or tried to disable them by removing parts of the engines. As diplomats brought their families out onto the balconies of the Jianguomenwai foreign compound to watch, a tense standoff developed.

Meanwhile, the military was not giving up. Yet another contingent of about 1,200 men, helmeted and armed, had somehow approached undetected along Qianmen West Road, just to the southwest of Tiananmen. Once again, thousands of young people streamed toward it from the square, which was now illuminated brightly by the floodlights on huge lamp standards surrounding Tiananmen. An articulated bus, jammed to capacity with young people, 50 to 60 of them perched dangerously on the roof, lurched out of its temporary location in front of the eastern steps of the Great Hall—that is, facing the square—straight toward the intersection of Qianmen West with the square itself. As TV crews turned their own lights on the bewildered and hemmed-in troops, the bus shuddered to a halt diagonally across Qianmen West, the newest sally in the people's guerrilla traffic blockade. Harangued, squeezed between the crowd and obviously exhausted, the soldiers waited passively for new orders against a background din of shouts, the tinkling of bicycle bells and the now more sinister, consistent *ee-aw, ee-*

aw of arriving and departing ambulances. Finally, the officers ordered the men to line up and march back down Qianmen to the west. As they did so, there was a roar of approval from the crowd, which once again drifted back to the square.

Not long after this, yet another group of troops, this time unarmed, tried to double-time into the square from the east. It is not clear from where they had come, but they were literally collared by hundreds of angry citizens just in front of the Beijing Hotel. Several of the soldiers were beaten on the spot, while others retreated north.

Probably no one in Beijing at this moment could have grasped exactly what was taking place all over town. Great caravans of trucks, with armored personnel carriers behind them, lay backed up along at least four axes into town: east along Changan; west along Changan (with about seven miles separating the two main pincer arms of the approaching 27th Army); south along Yongdingmen Street that, for about seven long blocks, heads due north into Qianmen guarding the south of Tiananmen; and from the airport to the northeast. Tires had been slashed, bottles and rocks thrown and the troops often beaten up and chased away from their trucks. Commandeered city buses and trucks had been jammed into dozens of intersections by angry and frightened citizens in the desperate hope that they would somehow keep the army out of the city center. Broken glass, rocks and pieces of brick covered the usually litter-free streets in the center of the Chinese capital.

Yet the military was inexorably closing in, coiling itself for the final strike against the prodemocracy movement. As if temporarily flitting in from another universe—though he was probably at the Western Hills command post at this time—Premier Li Peng appeared on television late in the evening to give a speech on environmental problems. He had not been seen or heard from in public for nine days.

In Tiananmen Square, the final target of the advancing troops, an eerie calm prevailed. Several thousand students and their supporters were milling around, listening to speeches, catching snatches of news from around the city from the student-controlled loudspeakers, gazing at the Goddess of Democracy or at the tent containing the hunger strikers on the Monument to the People's Heroes. BBC senior correspondent Kate Adie remembered being impressed by the confident mood of the bystanders. "It was a real atmosphere of a Saturday night on the town," she recalled. "It was not tense. There was a sort of I-think-we've-done-it feeling."

Hawkers selling meat on skewers unconcernedly plied their trade in the southwest of the square, not far from the malodorous assemblage of temporary outdoor toilets. Couples wandered about, hand in hand. A ceremony—small but, in the context of the prodemocracy movement, important—was unfolding. Yan Jiaqi, then the director of the Political Science Institute of the Chinese Academy of Social Sciences, was delivering a speech in honor of the formal opening of the University of Democracy, a sort of unofficial colloquium of Chinese academics who support political and social pluralism and want to expose Chinese young people to the underlying philosophical concepts. (Yan, a supporter of Zhao Ziyang, later escaped from China and took his campaign for democracy education among Chinese abroad with him.) His remarks were brief, as befitted an evening that was still rapidly unfolding. When he finished speaking, firecrackers were set off to honor the occasion. They were the last nonlethal explosions heard in Beijing that night.

10 p.m.

The killing began less than four miles west of Tiananmen Square, along Changan. Without warning, the 27th Army opened fire on demonstrators at Muxidi

Bridge. That landmark, over a canal that drains the lake in Yuyuantan Park, a few blocks to the north, is the second last major bridge before Changan reaches Tiananmen. Earlier in the evening, it had become a junkyard of trolleys and buses as group after group of citizens had sought to make the way into the city center impassable. West of the bridge, long lines of trucks and armored personnel carriers (APCs) abelonging to the 27th waited impatiently to move on.

Shortly before 10 p.m., the troops were given the order to clear the obstacles, disperse the crowds using whatever means necessary and keep moving. First, teargas shells were fired into the crowds, and soldiers with truncheons ran forward on foot, beating anyone who got in the way. The troops ran around or between the blockading buses, looking for people to hit. Then, infuriated, the crowd rallied and started fighting back, hurling rocks and bottles at the soldiers and forcing them to retreat. Molotov cocktails started smashing into the buses and the troop trucks trying to nudge forward. Some youths brought rugs from nearby apartments, doused them with gasoline, placed them on or in the buses and ignited them, attempting to create a wall of flame through which the incoming troops would have to move. As the rain of bottles, rocks and Molotov cocktails intensified, the first shots rang out. At the beginning, the troops did not seem to be shooting at people so much as over their heads, but the distinction quickly vanished. Within minutes, AK-47 barrels were lowered and bodies began falling on Changan Avenue and on the side streets nearby.

The troops pushed forward again and the crowds once more fell back. Heavy equipment was moved up to push the burning buses and trucks out of the way. This too was attacked. So were municipal fire trucks that were summoned to douse the blazing buses but that had to retreat when they themselves became the targets of a withering barrage of fire bombs and rocks. Gas tanks exploded and the sky turned into an orange inferno sliced through by occasional tracer bullets. "Fascists! Fascists!" the crowd chanted after a volley of gunfire would crackle and ricocheting AK-47 rounds smashed into walls, pavement and people.

As the advance proceeded, one troop truck or APC after another was set on fire. Within an hour of the assault on Muxidi Bridge, twelve army vehicles had been burned out in a four-mile stretch of Changan. Meanwhile, virtually every military vehicle crawling slowly into the city from the west had to fight off attacks by Molotov cocktails. The troops themselves were no longer aiming simply at rioters but in virtually every direction where there was a crowd of people. Ordinary citizens were cut down in apartment buildings lining Changan. In Nos. 22 and 23, residences reserved for senior government officials or retired party leaders, there were several deaths and injuries, including at least one official at the vice-ministerial level. An old woman was struck in the head and died instantly while she was cleaning her teeth. A travel agent from Oregon staying at the nearby Minzu Hotel watched the carnage in disbelief from his balcony, but he had to duck as bullets smacked into the hotel near his room. He was then warned by public-security officials that anyone observing the scene from the balcony might be shot at.

The warning was no bluff. When the American went downstairs into the lobby, plainclothes officers from the Ministry of State Security darted into the hotel and shot in cold blood a Chinese who had taken refuge there. The body was dragged across the carpet, leaving a dark stream of blood in its wake. Shortly afterward, army sharpshooters took up positions in several of the Minzu Hotel windows, firing both into the street and into buildings they suspected might be used by demonstrators to fire on the army. After the military had taken complete control of the city, the authorities repeatedly maintained that some of the automatic rifles and machine guns stolen from army buses early Saturday morning had been used against the military coming into the city. That was possible, though there was no independent evidence to support the assertion.

Firing from trucks and in the street, the incoming troops were now aiming low. As a student near him was hit in the leg, Associated Press correspondent John Pomfret heard the youth cry out as he collapsed, "Live fire! Live fire!" Many of the students were slow to grasp that message, though blood was now thick on the street and sidewalks. Determined pedicab or freight bicyclists were frantically pedaling back and forth to nearby hospitals with the latest victims of the mayhem. The cacophony was uninterrupted: deafening volleys of AK-47 rounds, the heavy pop of tear-gas canisters, the crunch of metal against metal as tracked military vehicles pushed blazing wreckage out of the path of the incoming trucks and APCs, the downpour of bottles and rocks smashing into military vehicles and immobilized buses, shouts of anger and abuse at the troops, screams of the wounded, the wail of ambulances and the *whoomph* of gasoline explosions.

Just east of the square, several thousand people had gathered on and around the pedestrian overpass at the intersection of Dongdan Street and Changan. There was no violence or shooting here, but three rows of buses had already been parked across the avenue to block any vehicles coming in from the east. The crowd, aware of the fighting now going on west of the square, clearly expected the troops to come into town from the east at any point. John Landy, New Delhi bureau chief for United Press International, was surprised to come across about 800 soldiers, surrounded by crowds who were now screaming at them, sitting in the middle of Beijingzhan Street, the broad road leading perpendicularly off Changan to the Beijing railroad station. The soldiers were armed with automatic rifles and had obviously been there a long time. But they looked befuddled and unsure of themselves. Landy and some journalist colleagues, exhausted from a long day's reporting, ducked into a Korean restaurant in an alley off Beijingzhan Street. The proprietor offered the reporters beer, food and soft drinks. The vague presence of attractive young women in the background soon became apparent to the reporters: in the midst of the battle for Beijing, they had wandered into a brothel.

11 p.m.

Back at Muxidi, the battle was raging. Incredibly, the troops had made little forward progress. Pierre Hurel, a correspondent for the French magazine *Paris-Match*, watched as a noncommissioned officer stood up in a jeep and bellowed at his troops through a megaphone, "Charge, you bunch of cowards! Clear away all that!" Some of the soldiers then hurled strange grenades that exploded as they hit the ground but failed to produce much noise. As the troops charged clumsily forward, the crowd briefly retreated, then regrouped amid a new hail of bottles and rocks from all across the road. "Fascists! Fascists!" the crowd kept shouting as a group of four students, stripped to the waist and standing to face the soldiers alone in front of a blazing barricade, banged together the poles on which the scarlet banners of their universities were flying. Around 11:30 p.m., Hurel watched in astonishment as hundreds of new troops jumped out of trucks backed up along Changan and riflemen coolly fanned out to take up firing positions against the stone throwers. Next to Hurel, and close to the canal flowing under Muxidi Bridge, the T shirt of a 15-year-old exploded in red as an AK-47 round smashed into his chest. From behind a tree, Hurel caught sight of the army sniper leaning against the side of a bus and calmly taking aim again. As Hurel took off with the screaming crowd away from the deadly volleys, a bullet slammed across his lower back, drawing blood but miraculously missing both his kidneys and his liver. After a quick swig of bourbon and some stitches inserted by a German doctor, the journalist went back to the streets.

Hurel, like the majority of Western reporters, had concentrated on the fierce fighting along the western sector of Changan as the 27th Army slugged its way toward Tiananmen Square. The focus made sense. As the Chinese authorities would later admit, more than 300 military vehicles—tanks, trucks, APCs and jeeps—were "obstructed or besieged" along Changan Avenue west of Tiananmen. But the convoys trying to approach the city center from Nanyuan airfield in the south were having a nightmare too. The intersections were obstructed by buses, trucks, bicycles, even furniture. Moreover, the narrower streets in this part of town made it easier for demonstrators to attack the trucks at close range. Dozens of trucks and APCs were hit by Molotov cocktails and burned. The troops fired at the demonstrators, and shortly before midnight some of the fiercest encounters anywhere in the city were taking place on the roads north from the Temple of Heaven. Journalists observing events from balconies on the upper floors of the Beijing Hotel watched orange machine-gun tracer fire crisscrossing the sky about half a mile south of the square. Several civilians were shot down not far from the Kentucky Fried Chicken franchise south of the square.

JUNE 4

The four hunger strikers in the tent and the other students still gathered around Tiananmen Square's Monument to the People's Heroes had begun to hear reports of the killings that had been taking place at Muxidi to the west. A young woman covered in blood came rushing from Changan and spoke in a loud emotional voice to the students and supporters gathered around the monument. The bloodstains were not her own, she explained, but came from wounded victims she had helped carry away from the line of fire. Her listeners were horrified. Some students nearby had armed themselves with makeshift bamboo spears, and several workers had already banded together to resist the military with whatever puny weapons they could find. But political scientist Yan Jiaqi, still perhaps hopeful of some miraculously peaceful end to the day's violence, appealed for a conciliatory approach. "If the soldiers leave Beijing," he said, "we can forget the rest [of what they have done]."

What "rest"? his listeners may have wondered. The indiscriminate shooting, the beatings, the headlong destruction wrought by advancing Chinese troops? One of the most gruesome events of the night was about to occur a few miles east along Changan, where some 40 army trucks, each with about ten soldiers, had been blocked on the Jianguomenwai overpass for nearly four hours. They had tried to move onto Changan from the ring road, which passes under the overpass in a north-south direction. More than 5,000 students and citizens had gathered on the bridge, and they had already pushed seven of the trucks, complete with troops in them, onto the middle of the overpass to serve as an obstacle for military convoys that might be coming from the east. Just after midnight, a lone armored recovery vehicle—essentially a tank without a turret that is used to tow disabled armored vehicles—roared eastward toward the overpass from the direction of Tiananmen, though no one was quite sure where it had started. As the crowds scampered to safety, the driver managed to negotiate the narrow space still left between vehicles on the overpass, then roared toward the Jianguo Hotel, a popular, Western-managed watering hole conveniently close to the Jianguomenwai and Qijiayuan foreign compounds.

Then, to everyone's amazement, the vehicle swung

around and headed back toward the overpass. As it approached, it accelerated to about 50 m.p.h. Once more the thick crowds on the overpass scattered to either side of the road. Less fortunate were the students and soldiers sitting and squatting atop the trucks in the middle of the overpass. This time the armored recovery vehicle made no effort to steer through the parked trucks. Crunching relentlessly over hastily abandoned bicycles, it smashed at full speed into one of the parked army trucks. That vehicle toppled instantly, sending flying from its canvas roof about a dozen soldiers and civilians who had been perched there discussing the immorality of the army's assault on the square. One of the civilians, a short young man with matching pale jacket and pants and black cotton shoes, was smashed into the pavement with such violence that his brains spilled out on the road. The body lay curled in a pool of blood for four days before the military finally allowed its removal. A soldier with a serious head injury was quickly placed on a flatbed pickup truck and taken to the hospital, still clutching his AK-47 rifle.

The crowd reaction to this ramming of one military vehicle by another was immediate. "This is the most terrible scene I've ever seen in my whole life," said a visibly shaken Mao Xiangdong, 25, a former computer salesman. "The leaders don't care about our lives at all." Angry groups from the crowd then dragged several of the frightened and equally horrified soldiers, all from the Shenyang-based 39th Army, out of the trucks to view the civilian corpse. "Look at what they've done to your brother!" one screamed. "How can you bear this?" A third kept shouting, "Shameless! Inhuman!" Several of the troops unashamedly started crying as the crowd pleaded with them to abandon their positions. "Down with Li Peng!" the crowd chanted. "Burn Li Peng to death!" Beside the truck not far from the bridge, a tall, lean Chinese man in his 60s lectured a junior officer sitting in the passenger seat of a truck. "I was a soldier for

40 years," he bellowed in a thick, provincial accent. "Watching what you've been doing these days, I cannot find any place to hide and cry. In 1949, when we moved into Beijing, the people offered us water to drink. Can you expect them to do the same now?"

Joe Kahn, a reporter for the Dallas *Morning News,* was following the murderous armored recovery vehicle on his bicycle as it careened down Changan back toward Tiananmen. Just after the vehicle left the scene of the ramming on the overpass, it crushed a row of abandoned bicycles by the roadside and seriously injured an old woman who was too slow getting out of the way. Then it vanished as mysteriously as it had first appeared.

Just minutes earlier, not long after midnight, a lone APC had broken through the obstacle course along Changan into Tiananmen Square from the west, roared across the north of the square, then disappeared in an easterly direction. Less than half an hour later, another APC rolled into the square, this time from the southeast. It drove north alongside the museums of the Chinese Revolution and Chinese History, then hit a metal barrier that the students had erected for the purpose of halting just such vehicles. It stopped momentarily, got its tracks caught, then tried to back away. But the crowd was onto it in a fury. Smashing metal bars against its side and further entangling its tracks, the mob then piled clothing and other material atop the hull, doused it with gasoline and set it on fire. When some of the students objected that the driver would be incinerated if he was not permitted to get out, the crowd shouted back, "It's okay. He's not a human being." The driver and whoever else was inside the APC quickly burned to death. The vehicle, No. 003 painted in white atop the camouflage pattern on its hull, was the first Chinese military vehicle to come to a halt in the square, and the first to be destroyed.

Not long afterward, another APC came up from the south toward Changan. A bus was driven into it to prevent it from moving back toward the west. Then it too was set afire, but the crew jumped out. They had barely got a few yards from their blazing vehicle before being set upon by the mob and savagely beaten. An American student who was close to the incident and tried to prevent the mob from killing the soldiers was himself badly beaten. An hour later the APC was still burning. The fate of its occupants was unknown.

Other youths in the crowd were trying to pull down or otherwise disable the remote video cameras mounted on lamp standards up and down Changan Avenue in the vicinity of the square. Their instinct was correct. Footage from the cameras, which had been installed ostensibly for traffic monitoring, was later screened again and again on television by the authorities, both to construct an image of the prodemocracy demonstrators as wanton rioters and to identify those the authorities sought to arrest.

1 a.m.

As the truck and APC columns from the south fought their way toward Tiananmen, laying down a blanket of tear gas and rifle fire, the first regular infantry troops moved into the square from the south. They were sweaty and exhausted, and many of them were injured. They slumped down to rest in front of Chairman Mao's Memorial Hall. But they had little respite. Crowds quickly formed, and a rain of bottles and rocks fell upon them. Some of the soldiers were badly injured in this new barrage, but there were apparently no medics among them, and it was impossible for military ambulances to get through into the square. A squad of riot police that arrived to clear away the mob came under a deadly hail of bottles and rocks.

By now, however, troops were beginning to move into the outskirts of the square from all sides. Several hundred of them, armed with long sticks but equipped with neither rifles nor bayonets, came into the square from the southeast. They walked between the Museum of the Chinese Revolution and the Hong Kong material supply station, a temporary assemblage of tents and tables on the square that Hong Kong students had been using as a base to supply the material needs of the prodemocracy students. Hong Kong students who watched the soldiers walk by to take up positions in front of the museum said they looked calm and unwarlike. Some of the troops, they reported, even promised not to harm the students in the square. There was handshaking between the two groups. It may have been the last gesture of friendship of the whole night between the People's Army and "the people."

Now the noise of the hard fighting along the western portion of Changan was becoming threateningly close. Paul Caccamo of Garden City, N.Y., who was teaching English in the northern city of Changchun, had come into Beijing two days earlier. He left the square at the north end around 12:30 a.m. and moved with some Chinese friends toward where the noise of strife was loudest, about a mile away to the west. "Suddenly the crowd in front of me halted," he recalls. "I thought the troops in front of us would move and turn back. There was this faith in the People's Army. Some people even told me that the soldiers were using only plastic bullets. The people in front of me had linked arms. But the soldiers facing them were kneeling down and were spraying the crowd with bullets. In the first second, everybody turned and ran. I thought I was never going to stop running."

Eventually, a Chinese grabbed Caccamo by the arm and told him he could stop: the immediate danger was past. A man came up to him and shouted, "Foreigner, foreigner, come and look at this!" "I walked over to where he was," Caccamo says, "and there on a bicycle rack was an 18-year-old girl with a bullet through her chest. That changed my mind about everything."

As the crowd retreated to another intersection

blocked by buses, there were frantic shouts to set the vehicles on fire. But the troops were moving fast now and had already jogged around the buses and were taking aim again at the swirling mob in front of them. Caccamo and several Chinese raced down Fuyou Street, next to Zhongnanhai, but a squad of the troops followed, shooting indiscriminately. Caccamo dived to the ground. When he thought there was a safe moment, he sprinted to the Zhongnanhai wall. Looking round, he saw dozens of bodies lying in the street. Some of the victims were probably still alive, but he could not stop to check. He and many others raced north to escape pursuit.

Meanwhile, BBC's Kate Adie had persuaded her driver to leave the relative safety of the Palace Hotel and circumnavigate the Forbidden City. After midnight, this was the only reasonably safe way to approach Changan Avenue to the west of Tiananmen. The car took the first ring road and approached the overpass at Fuxingmen. Long before reaching it, Adie was surprised by the number of roadblocks that citizens had put up at almost every major intersection. The car stopped some 400 yards from the overpass, and Adie and her crew got out to take a look. "We couldn't believe it," she said. "The whole of the top of the overpass on Changan had blazing trucks on it. Soldiers were silhouetted against them and were firing at people. There were heavy trucks and APCs pushing through. We were at the bottom of the exit ramp from the ring road and were crawling on the grass. I saw about five people fall to the ground nearby. Others were just standing there in disbelief. There were a lot of people who didn't seem to realize how lethal the shooting was."

At the intersection of Xidan and Changan, four buses were on fire. There was hand-to-hand combat all around the intersection, with the demonstrators and units of the 27th Army mingling in a furious, running melee. A Chinese photographer of the liberal intellectual magazine *Nexus,* was aiming her camera at the scenes of violence around her. A junior officer approached her from behind and shot her in the back with his pistol. The bullet passed through her body and left a gaping wound in her stomach. Astonishingly, she survived.

Just west of the intersection, the mob began rocking an officer's jeep and succeeded in overturning it. Furious, the officer crawled out and fired several times into the crowd, killing four people. When he had stopped firing—either for lack of ammunition or because his gun jammed—the mob jumped him and beat him to death. Then they stripped him, castrated him, slit open his stomach and disemboweled him. They hung his body by the neck against the side of a gutted city bus, an officer's cap placed contemptuously on his disfigured head. A crudely written slogan placed near the corpse read, "The people will be victorious."

At about the same time, near Qianmen, another officer fell into the hands of the enraged mob after shooting several women to death. He too was beaten to a pulp, then hung by the neck from the overpass at Qianmen and the eastern side of Tiananmen. Other soldiers caught by demonstrators after assaulting civilians were thrown from overpasses, set on fire, castrated or thrown into Beijing's canals. In an attempt to vilify the demonstrators, Chinese television for several days subjected its audience to grisly shots of the disemboweled Xidan officer. Even nearly two weeks after the massacre, it was airing horrifying footage of incinerated cadavers of soldiers literally being shoveled out of the charred remains of burned out trucks and APCs.

Tracer fire over the square was becoming almost constant. Gunfire was lapping at the very edges of Tiananmen from the south, particularly around the Kentucky Fried Chicken franchise, and the western end of the square on Changan. Nick Griffin, a correspondent with Asia Television in Hong Kong, decided with his crew that the monument, stuck in the middle of the square, was both a dangerous place to be based and a difficult spot from which to observe the swirling current of events. So along with his team of two cameramen, two reporters, a technician, his boss and a personal assistant, Griffin moved to the side of the square just south of the Great Hall and climbed to the roof of the public lavatory. "It gave us a great view of Tiananmen," he said.

What he saw was not encouraging for the students. Some 5,000 troops had infiltrated the square from the south, in addition to those already resting on the ground by Mao's Tomb or lined up with sticks in front of the museum. The crowds shouted, "Leave, leave, you mustn't kill them [the students]!" But the troops marched impassively down the side street at the south end of the Great Hall, then entered the large building. Later, along with other troops already inside the Great Hall, they were to emerge through the main doors on the east front and move down the steps into the square. Meanwhile, ambulances were coming and going into the square to pick up critically injured demonstrators who had been treated at a temporary first-aid station. Many of the wounded had serious gunshot wounds and were close to death. Volunteer Chinese doctors from nearby hospitals, as well as medical students and some medics from Hong Kong worked in desperate conditions—no running water, no proper medical supplies, no sterilization—to save what lives they could. "These are the children of China," a Chinese physician told a Western reporter. "I will be the last to leave." If he was, he almost certainly suffered the fate of several Chinese doctors in the square, who were bayoneted or shot to death as the 27th Army advanced.

Perhaps no group in Beijing behaved more heroically during the night of June 3-4 than the doctors who worked to save lives and limbs in the hospitals close to the center of Beijing. Several doctors from the Beijing Union Medical College Hospital and other institutions took turns providing basic first aid on the square. Many were either killed where they were working or arrested for allegedly assisting demonstrators.

The hospitals quickly turned into scenes out of Bruegel or Hieronymus Bosch as the dead and wounded were carried in—sometimes on stretchers, sometimes on bicycles, sometimes even on doors converted in desperation to portable beds. The dead were often dumped unceremoniously into side rooms because the hospital morgue was already overflowing and the staff had no time to cope with people who were no longer alive. The BBC's Kate Adie, like several Western reporters, found her car and driver at one point swept up in a desperate effort to get wounded Chinese as rapidly as possible to medical care. She recalls, "I came to a section of the crowd that was shouting 'hospital!' There was a woman with her brains hanging out, dying. We took her and a man and a female relative to the Children's Hospital, got her out of the car and raced in. The place was heaving with action. We realized we were in a procession. There were people on bicycles, on park benches, on tricycle rickshas. Park benches, with wounded people on them, were being carried directly into the operating theater. I went into one theater and found, at a quick estimate, that there were 30 people lying on the floor. All of them had major gunshot wounds, to the head, the body, the legs, everywhere.

"A man with a two-way radio seized me. Chinese escorting me around shouted 'Party man! Party man!' and hustled me away from him. There were 30 to 50 people brought in in the first 20 minutes there, and the doctors and nurses were in a state of rage. There was no confusion in their minds as to what had happened. They were screaming with sheer outrage."

A few hours later, after returning to the Beijing Hotel to telephone her broadcast to London, Adie took her crew to the Beijing Union Medical College Hospital, the largest and best-equipped medical facility in the vicinity of Tiananmen. "The operating theater was on the third floor," she recalled. "The surgeon was saying, 'We just can't cope. How many have come through here? Hundreds. But you must be careful.' A middle-aged woman, an official, started screaming at me, and the students with me screamed back at her. Then they took me to another room and pointed out to me a Xinhua News Agency reporter with a serious head wound. A lot of people were unconscious. There was no treatment being given. Two days later they told me that many doctors and nurses had been shot on the square. There was a struggle around me between the party people and the students. All the people were shouting, 'Tell, tell, tell the world!' "

Dr. Michael Mueller, an American physician who was in Beijing at the time, was told by Chinese medical friends that at least nine doctors had been killed helping the wounded in and around Tiananmen and that several doctors had been beaten up inside the hospitals by troops who came in looking for wounded students. "They were very scared," Mueller said of his Chinese colleagues. Chinese physicians and nurses told Western reporters that the troops in a few instances pulled life-support systems away from seriously wounded patients, then struggled with doctors who tried to interfere. Some Chinese medical personnel were almost certainly killed inside their hospitals. As for the corpses, the hospitals at first refused to permit relatives to see or collect them. But at some hospitals the crush of angry relatives was so great that the authorities had to relent. Still, many hospitals kept their cadavers for days afterward, under instructions from martial-law authorities not to reveal the number of dead they held.

1:30 a.m.

It was only a matter of minutes before the 27th Army would burst through the final barriers with tanks and APCs and occupy Tiananmen Square. Some students and even teenagers were sharpening tent poles and other crude pikes. Other demonstrators were donning surgical masks against the anticipated tear gas. A few formed what they called "daredevil squads," which would, they hoped, attack the troops in needle-like guerrilla actions around the city.

All evening long, the war of the loudspeakers had continued, with the more powerful, party-controlled amplifiers repeating the martial-law warnings to people in the square to disperse or else accept full responsibility for any physical harm they suffered. The less powerful student loudspeakers broadcast defiant accusations of military brutality and recordings of the *Internationale,* the socialist anthem.

At precisely 1:30 a.m., a chilling new order came booming from the government speakers. "A serious counterrevolutionary rebellion has occurred in the capital this evening," it declaimed ominously. Many of the students flinched at the word counterrevolutionary, a deadly accusation in Chinese Communist parlance. It had not been previously used in government descriptions of the prodemocracy protests, but its currency now meant only one thing: the army would be pitiless in its suppression of the protest. The announcement continued: "Rioters have furiously attacked soldiers and robbed them of their weapons and ammunition. They have burned military vehicles, set up roadblocks and kidnaped officers and men in an attempt to subvert the People's Republic of China and overthrow the socialist system. The People's Liberation Army has kept an attitude of restraint for some days. However, the counterrevolutionary rebellion must now be resolutely counterattacked. Residents of the capital should strictly abide by the specific regulations as provided by martial law and cooperate with the soldiers to safeguard the constitution and defend the security of the socialist motherland and its capital. The personal safety of anyone cannot be guaranteed if he disregards this warning. He will be held responsible for all the consequences."

The announcement was repeated over and over. As the official voice began to blend with the furious noise of the army breaking into the square, the students responded with an appeal of their own. "Do you still have a conscience?" their loudspeakers asked the troops beginning to pour into Tiananmen. "We are all Chinese."

Other demonstrators were driving buses back and forth on the north side of Changan in front of the Gate of Heavenly Peace while the students inside tried to figure out what to do with them. One bus was driven directly into the narrow tunnel in the middle of the gate and parked with deliberate awkwardness at an angle from one side to the other. The driver seemed intent on protecting the students in the square from being attacked by motorized units possibly concealed within the ancient courtyards of the Emperors. In another, almost suicidal maneuver, one driver smashed his bus right into the front of the first convoy to reach the square. As a result, the tanks and APCs ground temporarily to a halt just 100 yards west of the square proper. Behind them were several helmeted troops.

Quickly, military snipers started running along the wall of the Forbidden City, shooting as they went, and taking up positions to protect the north flank of the 27th Army as it prepared to enter the square proper. There were still thousands of people in the square, though none seemed to know exactly what to do. The headlights of armored personnel carriers, tanks and trucks were gleaming malevolently in the blackness, as though hunching up for a final pounce.

About 100 yards in front of them, a thin line of students and workers, arms linked, stood defiantly, waiting for the military to make the next move. Then the rattle of automatic fire was heard, and several in the front line of demonstrators crumpled to the ground. Shooting now seemed to be going on from several points on the northern side of the square. There was a constant to and fro of flatbed bicycles and tricycle rickshas coming and going with the wounded, blood dripping onto the street, or in some places left thick upon the ground. Ambulances continued to make their way through the crowds to the center of the square or to the first-aid tent not far from the Goddess of Democracy. Several ambulances arrived at nearby hospitals with bullet holes in the doors.

The most militant of the demonstrators fought back, with little effect on the relentless advance of the soldiers. Molotov cocktails bounced against some of the APCs. Rocks were hurled through the air toward the west, where the bulk of the armor and troops still held itself coiled for the final push. But most of the crowd now ran in terror from the volleys of AK-47 rounds that smashed back and forth in front of the gate.

2 a.m.

Soon there was almost constant firing in the northern part of the square, most of it by troops moving eastward to block access along Changan. But while the crowd that had been herded east by the incoming troops had given ground in the square, it still contained thousands of demonstrators. More firing broke out. More people dropped, bleeding, to the street, and the panic-stricken demonstrators began to disappear up north-south streets leading off Changan.

To Hong Kong correspondent Nick Griffin, watching from his perch on the roof of the public lavatory south of the Great Hall, what was frightening about the newest wave of troops entering the square in his vicinity was their demeanor. "They looked doped up to their eyeballs," he recalled. "They were waving their rifles around. When civilians would grab at them, they would nod as though spaced out." Other reporters who had seen the 27th Army up close on its way down Changan found chilling the manner in which some of the soldiers were smiling as they discharged their rifles. These impressions lent currency to a persistent rumor that the men of the 27th had been given amphetamines before their final thrust into Tiananmen. The most commonly relayed account was that the troops had been told they needed immunization against the poor hygiene in the square, and were then given either injections or tablets. There was no official confirmation of those reports.

Not far from the square, Michael Fathers, Asia editor of the British daily newspaper *The Independent,* was set upon by 27th Army troops. "Several soldiers broke ranks and ran to me, punching me and kicking me," he reported. "There was pure hatred in their eyes. They pushed me into a kneeling position and had another go at me, whacking me across the back with their rods and kicking, always kicking, until I fell over. They pulled off my spectacles and crushed them." Added Fathers: "If this is the People's Army, God spare China."

Dozens of APCs were now grinding across the square from west to east, taking up positions facing south. With them came more helmeted troops, assault rifles at the ready. Amazingly, a bus filled with young demonstrators went speeding westward against the flow of the crowd straight into the advancing APC columns, evidently determined to help stop the military onslaught. From their increasingly dangerous perches on the top level of the monument, Western camera crews recorded the scene as riot police boarded the bus as soon as it stopped, dragged out the driver and other occupants, and began beating them with long truncheons.

Light machine guns were now being set up on tripods on the north and west sides of the square, and Tiananmen was already hemmed in by troops on three sides. Only to the south was there room for crowds to come and go. The gaps were rapidly being filled here too, as more and more soldiers came in from the convoys that had by now broken through by the Kentucky Fried Chicken store. When some people in the large crowd still in the northern part of Tiananmen started shouting, "Strike! Strike!" the troops fired directly into them.

Bullets began thudding into the upper stories of the Beijing Hotel, which offered a clear view of Tiananmen to several Western camera crews inside. But that vantage was not safe. People on the hotel's balconies spotted army sharpshooters on the roof of the Ministry of Public Security building across the street. Military snipers seem to have occupied other high points in and around the square. Some Beijing Hotel occupants were warned by public-security officials that they would be shot at if they came out to watch what was happening. Whenever the cacophony of rifle fire would let up a little, though, another sound would filter up to the balconies, the sound of the screams and groans of the wounded and the incessant torrent of abuse shouted at the troops.

3 a.m.

By now, Changan Avenue between the Beijing Hotel and Tiananmen Square had been cut in two by several lines of soldiers who sat or knelt sullenly, aiming their rifles toward the angry and taunting crowds. The crowds moved back and forth on foot or on bicycle between stalled buses and other vehicles dragooned into service as barricades by angry citizens. In the square, a few thousand students and workers were left, boldly taunting the incoming soldiers with shouts of "Fascist!" and hurling insults at Li Peng. The student loudspeakers were responding to the endless government repetition of the martial-law warning with news of the casualty situation.

In the south of the square, troops were putting together a perimeter toward Qianmen, trying to keep people away from the Great Hall. Many of the troops had bayonets fixed on their AK-47s, lending a sinister new dimension to their growing numbers. In the tents closest to the edge of the square, most of the students roused themselves from sleep and other activities and moved closer to the monument. Surprisingly, Hou Dejian, the Taiwanese vocalist and hunger striker, was still there with his companions. Around 3:30 a.m., he succeeded in negotiating with a senior officer in the square a moratorium on a full-scale military assault, pending a student vote to withdraw from the square peacefully. The officer agreed to allow additional time before clearing the square.

But Hou had little room for maneuver among the remaining students, workers and sympathizers close to the monument. An hour earlier Chai Ling, the spellbinding student orator, announced to her fellow demonstrators over the public address system that those who wished to leave could do so. Yet even this declaration had intensified disagreements among the remaining protesters. Hou and Beijing Normal University lecturer Liu Xiaobo, two of the four hunger strikers, took turns appealing for calm and nonbelligerence through the student-controlled speaker system. But when they convened a meeting of student representatives in one of the tents, one faction favored a quiet withdrawal from the square while another insisted that everyone should stay until death.

Several students had prepared Molotov cocktails, and one group had a rifle and a machine gun captured from troops the previous morning. A student organizer later explained, "One worker held on to the machine gun with one hand and brandished an iron bar with the other. He swung against anyone who tried to wrest the gun out of his hands. But we patiently explained that, yes, he could mow down several soldiers, but it would be at the cost of several hundreds of us getting killed too. Finally, he relented and we had the gun removed from the square."

4 a.m.

The initiative was hardly with the students now. As the government-controlled loudspeakers kept up their ominous warnings, the bright street lights, which had burned every night during the student occupation of Tiananmen, were suddenly and without warning extinguished. It was 4 a.m. There was a brief and dramatic silence before a spotlight came on and illuminated thousands of helmeted soldiers with mounted bayonets coming out of the Great Hall and taking up positions in front of the building, ready to move into the square. "They filled out the whole parking lot," recalled David Schweisberg, U.P.I.'s Beijing bureau chief. "Their uniforms and bayonets were glinting. Immediately, the students played the *Internationale* on their speaker system and began singing it. Some of them lit fires around the monument. Otherwise, it was pitch dark. Then people seemed to come back into the square from side streets and joined in the singing of the *Internationale*. It was eerie."

The lights came on again at 4:39 a.m. APCs were rumbling into the center of the square, heading for the tent city that had occupied that area for weeks. At the same time, there was a great burst of gunfire all over the square, most of it, at first, apparently over the heads of the people. Suddenly, a great fear seemed to take over most of the remaining protesters still in the square, and a large exodus began, all of it to the southeast, where the troops had kept an exit corridor open. Over a loudspeaker, Hou Dejian explained why he and the other hunger strikers, who were now essentially the leaders of the remaining protesters, were willing to quit the square. "We're not afraid to die," he said, "but we've already lost too much blood."

About ten APCs had started rolling into the tents now, smashing them flat and destroying everything in them. On the west side of the square, the thousands of troops from the Great Hall also started moving in, forcing anyone in their pathway to move, bayoneting some who resisted or were not moving fast enough, beating and occasionally shooting others. Students later claimed that several of their number had been crushed to death in the tents by the APCs. The authorities denied that charge, but given the fury of the assault it is likely that some people did die beneath the tracks of the vehicles.

5 a.m.

Chinese commandos in camouflage uniforms surrounded the monument with AK-47s and drawn pistols and issued a three-minute ultimatum for people to leave. Most of the remaining demonstrators took heed and moved quickly away from the monument to the south. Others, though, hesitated and were shot on the spot. At exactly 5 a.m. a sudden and unexplained burst of artillery and heavy machine-gun fire was heard from somewhere south of Tiananmen. Within ten minutes, troops were pouring into the center of the square from all directions. The attack forced the several hundred students who remained either to flee to the corridor still left open, where student marshals were guiding their comrades to the safety of side streets, or to face near certain death.

By now firing was continuous in the vicinity of the square, though it was difficult to be sure exactly from which directions it was coming. Over the loudspeakers, students called on the ordinary citizens of Beijing to do what they could to stop the troops. Nonstudent crowds in the square area responded by trying to block the intersections leading into it. Despite plaintive appeals for calm, some demonstrators continued to hurl Molotov cocktails at incoming APCs, and two were set alight on the outskirts of the square. As many of the students trickled out of the square, they chanted, "Down with fascists! Down with violence!" Others flashed the V sign and shouted "Go with us!" at applauding Beijing residents.

At the eastern end of the square, ambulances were no longer being permitted through the defense perimeter set up by troops across Changan Avenue near the Beijing Hotel. Thousands of young people were angrily milling around about 75 yards from the sitting soldiers. Many people were shouting "Fascists!" and "Beasts!" From time to time, a group of troops would stand up, or adopt a kneeling position, and fire straight at the most provocative looking knots of people, felling several and sending the others scurrying for cover.

What happened in the next hour or so is difficult to piece together, but it is almost certain that this is when the most deaths occurred in the square. At about 5:15 a.m., a convoy of eight tanks, 21 APCs and more than 40 trucks crammed with troops roared down Changan Avenue, past the Jianguo Hotel and across the Jianguomenwai overpass toward Tiananmen. Despite the absence of other traffic, it took them 15 minutes to reach the square. They had to smash through low railings, disabled buses and piles of debris left on the road by Beijing citizens to try to slow down incoming units. At 5:30 a.m., the tanks crunched at high speed past the Beijing Hotel and into the square. The tanks led the convoy, chiefly because they were the only vehicles capable of plowing through the burned-out buses and piled-up construction equipment that still blocked Changan at the intersection with Wangfujing Street. As they stormed by, the lead tank smashed over the last main obstacle on the street, a small construction dozer that forced the front of the tank up into a 30° angle. The dozer was split, and a pathway was cleared for the APCs and trucks.

As the tanks roared on, the sound of machine-gun and automatic-rifle fire from the trucks was constant, and some of the APCs started emitting noxious clouds of tear gas. Despite the danger, young men were still crouching in front of the wall of the Forbidden City, hurling rocks and bottles vainly at the fast moving vehicles and howling with rage. But the tanks kept moving toward the square, and it was probably just after 5:30 that one of them knocked over the Goddess of Democracy statue. Grainy government television footage aired several hours later showed a single tank toppling the statue amid signs of desolation and destruction in the surrounding parts of the square. Most of the shooting from the incoming trucks seemed to be aimed in the air, though citizens were still being killed and injured as the convoy came through. Then at 5:45, there was intense machine-gun fire either from the northern end of Tiananmen Square or from inside the Forbidden City. Tracer fire also continued to arc through the sky, and the occasional heavy boom of a tank or artillery round punctuated the night.

6 a.m.

The last of the students staggered out of the square. Even then, though, they were not safe. As they walked, arms linked, down Qianmen Road, several were chased by APCs. As many as eleven people were crushed as they tried to make their way first west, then north to their universities. Several dozen students were shot at point blank as they approached Changan Avenue on their way north on Beixinhua Street. Eyewitnesses said the gunfire was ferocious for several minutes. Other students in the street were crushed against walls by APCs.

Back on the square, the army was mopping up. The number of corpses may never be known, or what happened to them or to the unfortunates who were wounded and could not be evacuated. There were persistent reports soon after the massacre that flamethrowers and blowtorchs were used to incinerate piles of dead on the spot. Other reports asserted that several of the casualties were removed from the square and taken west along Changan in military trucks. Some versions had it that the dead were taken to Babaoshan Revolutionary Cemetery, one of the few large crematoriums in Beijing, and that the bodies were immediately cremated. Other stories spoke of a mass incineration of corpses out in the Western Hills within the military-security zone.

In the official effort to rebut charges of indiscriminate shooting in the closing minutes of the military attack on Tiananmen, political officer General Zhang Gong asserted that "there was no single casualty on the square." It is conceivable, though unlikely, that in the central part of the square around the monument, there were no fatalities during the period in question. Too many reporters, other foreigners and Chinese, however, witnessed volley after volley of gunfire directly into crowds on Changan on the edge of the square, and heard furious fusillades within the square during the time in question, for the government claim to be taken seriously.

Dawn

As the sun came up on June 4, citizens of Beijing who were unaware of the night's chaos awoke to a shocking sight. Spirals of black smoke were rising over several parts of the city from burning military and civilian vehicles. Dozens of intersections were littered with the carcasses of burned-out buses and trucks, with rocks, bricks, smashed bottles, half-demolished construction equipment, discarded shell casings, and pedestrian and bicycle guard rails dragged into the street and then twisted into baroque shapes by the tracks of onrushing armor. A smashed bus still burned near the Wangfujing and Changan intersection. It had not been used as an obstacle to the military but as a makeshift ambulance. Toward the west along Changan, destruction was still taking place. Bold groups of citizens were systematically destroying APCs that had either parked or stalled during the slow move eastward into the city the previous night. Before long, the line of burned-out APCs near the Minzu Hotel looked more like a national military debacle than what the authorities termed, early Sunday, as their "initial victory" over the "scum of society."

The army later acknowledged that 364 military vehicles—tanks, trucks, APCs, jeeps and military buses—had been destroyed in the furious hours of combat with unarmed civilians in the center of Beijing. Authorities claimed that some 1,000 troops had been killed or injured. Some Western military attachés put the figure higher.

In any case, the killing of civilians was still continuing, now in broad daylight. Near the Beijing Hotel along Changan, group after group of civilians would come within 50 yards of the sullen lines of troops guarding the square and taunt them. Then, provoked to the point of anger, an officer would give an order and a volley of AK-47 rounds would fly, sending the crowd scrambling once more and leaving another dozen or so bodies on the street. A particularly vicious round of gunfire at 10:27 a.m. left dozens of people littering the surface of Changan. Several rounds also hit the Beijing Hotel, where a handful of Western reporters had managed to elude the room searches conducted earlier in the morning by angry public-security officials. Alexis Feringer, a graduate student at Tufts University's Fletcher School of Law and Diplomacy and working temporarily for Cable News Network, carefully observed every major event from her eleventh floor Beijing Hotel balcony from late Saturday night until early Monday morning. Her notebook indicates six incidents of troops firing into the crowds on Sunday: at 10:55 a.m., 11:53 a.m., 12:10 p.m., 1:10 to 1:15 p.m., 2 p.m., and 3:20 p.m. On each occasion, there were casualties. Meanwhile, Chinese military helicopters were landing and taking off from Tiananmen Square at almost five-minute intervals, probably helping evacuate the seriously wounded from Tiananmen.

How many civilians died in the battle for Beijing?

How many civilians died in the battle for Beijing? No one may ever know the precise figures, even if the regime in China were to change and a truly honest investigation were conducted. Children were killed holding hands with their mothers. A nine-year-old boy was shot seven or eight times in the back, and his parents placed the corpse on a truck and drove through the streets of northwest Beijing Sunday morning. "This is what the government has done," the distraught mother kept telling crowds of passersby through a makeshift speaker system. A similarly gruesome traveling atrocity exhibition was arranged by students at the pro-democracy Political Science and Law College of China. The cadavers of five students who had been crushed by APCs after leaving Tiananmen Square early in the morning were packed in ice and carried in grisly pomp from university to university in northeastern Beijing.

Workers were shot bicycling to factories, old people died in their apartments as bullets thudded into the building. Students were crushed even on Sunday morning by APCs roaring west along Changan. Moreover, many bodies may never be located. Aside from isolated soldiers thrown into canals or the question of the dead on Tiananmen Square, some corpses were dumped into rooms in buildings that had no connection with hospitals. Mitch Presnick, of Centerville, Va., a graduate student at Peking University, was taken surreptitiously into a building in northeastern Beijing and shown several corpses—all of student age—lying on tables. He never discovered where they had been killed, or what the bodies were doing there.

U.P.I.'s David Schweisberg called several Beijing hospitals for a body count for the first three days after the massacre and added up a total of 321 dead—until the hospitals refused, under government pressure, to give out any more figures. Officials of the Chinese Red Cross reported that 2,600 died, but then they too were ordered to keep silent and to deny that they had ever given out such figures. The mayor of Beijing announced that more than 1,000 army personnel had been killed or wounded in the street fighting, but he made no mention of civilian casualties, which, it stood to reason, would have been greater. A courageous announcer for Radio Beijing's English service told listeners that "thousands" of protesters "had died in the tragic incident" and called upon the people of all countries to "join our protests against the barbarous suppression of the people." Several minutes later, another version of the same news item was broadcast, and the announcer who had read the first bulletin was never heard again on the radio.

The *Far Eastern Economic Review* reported that Beijing hospitals queried by its correspondents had come up with a total of about 700 deaths. At the other end of the spectrum, Beijing-based Soviet correspondents reported privately to their editors that they estimated the number of dead to be close to 10,000. Experienced East European diplomats who specialize in Chinese affairs also seemed to find this figure comfortable.

In all probability, the total number of civilian dead in Beijing during the 24-hour period beginning around 10 p.m. Saturday, June 3, was between 1,000 and 5,000. The number of soldiers killed was probably in the scores or low hundreds.

Whatever the number, all were the victims of what can only be called a massacre. All died because of efforts by a reactionary regime to stop the clock on political change in the world's most ancient continuous civilization. As a youthful leader told a Western correspondent shortly after the taking of Tiananmen Square: "Our calls for democracy have reached the living rooms of a largely apolitical people. Now, at least, they know that there are such things as democracy and freedom and that they too deserve them."

CHAPTER TWO

"MR. DEMOCRACY AND MR. SCIENCE"

To say that life in China is exciting is to put it fairly ... think of kids in our country from 14 on taking the lead in starting a big cleanup reform politics movement and shaming merchants and professional men into joining them. This is sure some country.

> —American philosopher-educator
> John Dewey, 1919

The quest for democracy is the essential thread that pervades the entire history of China in our century.

> —Belgian sinologist Simon Leys, 1989

In the 70 years between John Dewey's excitement at an earlier student reform movement in Beijing and Simon Leys' sad reflection on the crushing of the most recent one, China has never ceased to amaze. During those turbulent decades, when the country experienced the birth of the Communist movement (1921), invasion by the Japanese (1937-45), civil war (1946-49), Communist victory (1949), the Great Leap Forward (1958-61), the Cultural

Revolution (1966-76) and the reforms of Deng Xiaoping (1979-?), most foreign comments about China were tinged with sadness and dismay. The country seemed simply ungovernable during much of the century. Even in those brief interludes of order and especially during the rule of the Communist Party, from 1949 until the present, the country has often seemed bent on self-destruction.

But 70 years is a mere instant in the measure of China's history, which stretches back continuously for close to 5,000 years. An enormous body of Chinese literature existed for centuries before the philosopher Confucius (551-479 B.C.) first enumerated the ethical and social ideas that were to guide Chinese society for two millenniums. In the Mediterranean, the emergent republic of Rome was still struggling with the Carthaginians when the Great Wall was built, during the reign of the Chin dynasty Emperor (221-206 B.C.). Europe was still in the Dark Ages when the greatest of Tang dynasty poetry was being written, in the 8th century A.D. As for Marco Polo (1254-1324), his stories of a country where black rocks (coal) were burned, money was made of paper and people ate noodles were simply not believed on his return to Europe.

Only after 16th and 17th century Jesuit scholars visited China, lived there and began sending back reliable accounts of what they saw did Western knowledge of China emerge from the forests of fantasy to the broad plains of established fact. At this point, European intellectuals idealized the country as a land where scholars ruled and reason prevailed in the affairs of state. The 18th century French philosopher Voltaire asserted, "One does not have to be an enthusiast for the achievements of the Chinese to recognize that the constitution of their empire is the most excellent the world has ever seen, and the only one based on patriarchal authority."

Voltaire's praise, though overblown, was typical of the respect China was accorded by the principal exponents of the European Enlightenment. Ironically, the China so admired by 18th century European intellectuals was passing through the golden age of order and learning in the Qing (Ching) dynasty and was moving steadily into a period of decline (1775-1911) characteristic in Chinese history of the waning years of a "dynastic cycle."

The Chinese themselves were acutely conscious of these cycles and deeply superstitious about them. China's traditional ethical and governmental system was known as Confucianism, deriving as it originally did from the philosopher Confucius. The basis of the system was thought to be five human relationships, three in the family (son to father, wife to husband, younger brother to elder brother) and two outside (subject to ruler, friend to friend). Though Confucius himself paid little attention to such metaphysical religious issues as God and heaven, the fully evolved Confucian ideology in imperial China spelled out a precise theology of relationships between ordinary Chinese and heaven. The Emperor of China, in whatever dynasty, was thought to be the "Son of Heaven" and was responsible for ordering the affairs of humankind in conformity with the will of heaven. The Chinese did not believe in a precise communication of heaven's will to mankind in the manner of biblical revelation. They held that the signs of heaven's approval of a particular dynasty or ruler—the "mandate of heaven"— were order, peace and prosperity. Conversely, when war, disorder, famine and natural catastrophes abounded, both educated and uneducated Chinese began to believe that a particular dynasty had lost the mandate of heaven. The belief would then become a self-fulfilling prophecy, as internal rebellion or external invasion would bring in new, vigorous rulers to restore the kingdom and, above all, the ethical conduct that Confucianism regarded as essential to good rule.

Until the late 18th century, China's Confucian system and dynastic cycles had proceeded with remarkably little interference from the outside world. The very name for China, Zhongguo (Middle Kingdom), signified the center of the known human world. True, the Mongols had invaded China in the 13th century and constituted the ruling dynasty when Marco Polo traveled there. In addition, the Qing rulers were not Han Chinese, the country's major ethnic group, but came from Manchuria in northern China. But it was not until the end of the 18th century that China suddenly found itself rudely encroached upon by the commercial ambitions of modernizing Western powers, at a time when its own internal structure was deteriorating through overpopulation and increasingly corrupt and ineffective administration.

The American Revolution was one of the impulses that led to China's forced encounter with the modern world, for it unleashed the commercial energies of the new republic into all parts of the globe. The American trading ship *Empress of China* sailed from New York to Guangzhou (Canton) in 1784 and set a pattern for a lucrative New England trade in silk, tea and porcelain. The new wealth created by the Industrial Revolution in Britain inspired a demand for these luxury items, while the increasingly influential bourgeois class of entrepreneurs and manufacturers urged the British government to help them find new markets for their goods. But when Lord Macartney, an envoy dispatched by King George III to China to urge fewer restrictions on British trade with the Chinese, arrived in Peking in 1793, the Emperor responded in a way that typified Chinese arrogance toward the outside world. "Our celestial empire," he said, "possesses all things in prolific abundance and lacks no products within its own borders. There was therefore no need to import the manufactures of outside barbarians in exchange for our own produce." The American John Quincy Adams, later to be President, lambasted "the arrogant and insupportable pretenses of China," and declared it "a noncommercial empire."

The much desired Chinese luxuries could be purchased by Westerners only in the port of Guangzhou in the south of China and then only for silver. In fact, the first silver coins ever used as currency in China were Mexican dollars introduced by Americans. The British East India Company, which had a British monopoly on China trade until the 1830s, at first balanced trade by shipping Indian cotton to Guangzhou to sell to the Chinese, but later, undersold by northern Chinese cotton dealers, had to pay for its Chinese goods with silver, a financial burden the company soon found insupportable. To remedy the problem, it then resorted to a trading device more familiar to the late 20th century: drug smuggling. The narcotic opium was grown in India, transported aboard British ships to Guangzhou, then smuggled ashore for lucrative sale by corrupt Chinese go-betweens. The trade grew so rapidly that China's own supply of silver began to be drawn down and opium addiction became a social plague that eventually wrecked the lives of millions.

Until the advent of opium, educated Chinese had little clear idea of how backward their country was, much less of what being modern meant. What awoke them was their defeat by the British in the 1839-42 Opium War, in which they unsuccessfully attempted to bring an end to the drug trade. The war ended with the Treaty of Nanjking (Nanking) in 1842, which forced China to open five coastal cities for open trade with the West: Fuzhou (Foochow), Xiamen (Amoy), Ningbo (Ningpo), Shanghai and Guangzhou. That treaty-port system was greatly expanded and refined during several more decades of military humiliations at the hands of the Western powers. The system served as a constant reminder to the Chinese of Western technological and political superiority and conversely of China's vulnerability to the outside world during the age of imperialism. Yet the treaty ports came to provide windows into the West for curious and entrepreneurial-minded Chinese. Under the legal protection of extraterritoriality—by which Westerners and Chinese within the treaty ports were not subject to Chinese law—ordinary Chinese could study Western manners and Western science, digest Western ideas, and even look into Western religion. Thus China, which for millenniums had looked down on all foreigners as barbarian bearers of tribute, was exposed to a forced encounter with the rest of the world that was to change its own ideas of politics and governance.

Initially, it was Christian ideas that created a major crisis inside China. A young member of the Hakka minority in Guangdong (Kwangtung) province, Hong Xiuquan (Hung Hsiu-ch'üan) (1814-64), in 1836 picked up a Christian tract in Guangzhou during one of many unsuccessful efforts to pass the examination needed to become a member of China's ruling scholar-gentry class. Falling ill in 1837 after another try at the examination, Hong had a vision in which he later understood himself to be the younger brother of Jesus Christ entrusted with the task of establishing the Kingdom of Heaven on earth. His newfound sense of mission won converts among family and friends, as well as a ready audience among impoverished and dispossessed groups in South China. By 1850 Hong had enough followers to embark on a full-scale rebellion against governmental authority. For the next 14 years, his rebel movement, which called itself the Taiping Tianguo (Heavenly Kingdom of Great Peace), devastated huge parts of central China and led to the death of as many as 30 million people.

Though Hong's ideology left no permanent imprint on China, it had profound resonances during the Communist movement of this century. Taiping Tianguo called for the brotherhood of man, community of property and equality of the sexes. The fact that huge numbers of illiterate Chinese responded to these ideas, which were completely alien to Confucian precepts, was an ill omen for

China's traditional imperial ideology as it faced unprecedented challenges at home and abroad.

Many Western missionaries at first welcomed the Taiping movement, believing it to be a genuine Christian phenomenon. But as the rebels became increasingly mercenary and cruel in their depredations, both missionaries and Western secular officials turned against it. For one thing, the Western powers now needed stability in the Qing empire after imposing yet another set of humiliating and unequal agreements on the Chinese in 1858 and 1860 with, respectively, the Treaties of Tianjin and Beijing. The rebellion for many years threatened the security of the foreign-controlled International Concession in Shanghai. But in addition, leading Chinese officials were beginning to grasp how vital it was to adopt some measure of Western skills in order simply to prop up the ailing dynasty.

But the thinking remained shortsighted. Almost all educated Chinese critics of their country's misfortunes deemed the solution to them to lie in moral regeneration and renewed social discipline rather than institutional change. It was a pattern of response to be repeated again and again during China's search for modernity, right into the Communist era. Typically, the Chinese thought that Western industrial and weapons skills could be adopted by the country without bringing alterations to any of the nation's social or political substructures. One prominent commentator on the need for modernization, Feng Guifen (1809-74), put it this way: "We have only one thing to learn from the barbarians, and that is strong ships and effective guns. . . . The intelligence and ingenuity of the Chinese are certainly superior to those of the various barbarians; it is only that hitherto we have not made use of them." Feng further advocated "the use of the barbarians' superior techniques to control barbarians."

One measure of how out of touch China was with the rest of the world is that the imperial court did not decide to send a diplomatic mission abroad until 1867. Ironically, the first envoy was actually an American, Anson Burlingame, who led a Chinese official delegation to the U.S., Britain and Russia. Burlingame did much to dispel the Chinese conviction that foreigners were united in wanting only to despoil China. Meanwhile, under the slogan of "self-strengthening," China allowed an interpreters' school to be established in Peking by foreign missionaries in the 1860s. The institution, which became Tongwen College and included science among its subjects, was to become an important conduit for Western ideas among educated Chinese. Other missionary schools, not just in the treaty ports, but after 1860 in the interior of China, challenged China's young people with a vastly different view of the world from that described in the Confucian classics. In the 1870s, China sent its first batch of young people abroad—to the U.S.—to study at first hand what the outside world was about.

The knowledge and ideas these young students brought back, along with that acquired in the missionary schools, was bound to strike at the roots of China's traditional sense of cultural identity. Yet that identity itself was being ever more forcefully challenged from outside by the demands for commercial, cultural and diplomatic concessions imposed on the country by the Western powers in the last decades of the 19th century. In 1897-98, the Germans seized Jiaozhou Bay in Shandong province for a naval base; the British demanded the lease of Weihaiwei for similar purposes, along with de facto control of the Chang Jian (Yangtze) Valley; Japan won a sphere of influence in Fujian province opposite Taiwan, which Japan had annexed after defeating China in war in 1895; and the French grabbed Zhanjiang (Kwangchow) Bay in Guangdong province, in the far south. The threatened dismemberment of China provoked a crisis of confidence at the imperial court, and led to one of the most extraordinary episodes in modern Chinese history: a 100-day period of radical, modernizing reform in 1898.

So desperate was China's national plight in the late 1890s, under the constant pressure of the Western imperial powers for more concessions, that the cry for reform finally reached the Chinese imperial court. An outstanding Confucian scholar, Kang Youwei (1858-1927) proposed a complete transformation of China's educational system, a constitutional monarchy and the vigorous development of domestic and foreign trade. Kang was possibly the last great creative thinker in the Confucian tradition, and he still believed it was possible to reform and save China's two-millennium-old system of rule.

In June 1898, the 27-year-old Guangxu Emperor received Kang in person in Peking and gave him full powers to implement his ambitious program. In just over three months, later referred to as the "Hundred Days," edict after edict issued forth from the Chinese capital calling into being the new reform order. But the pace of the program was too frantic and the opposition to the new order too well entrenched. Kang was unable to secure military support to block the antireform efforts of the dowager Empress Cixi (Tz'u-hsi), who was the Emperor's aunt. Then she herself moved, pulling off a palace coup against the Emperor, who remained a prisoner until his death in 1908. She ordered the arrest and subsequent execution of many of the reformers and their supporters. Kang, along with other key pro-reform intellectuals, escaped to Hong Kong, in a manner eerily prescient of the escape from Beijing of prodemocracy reformers in 1989 after the Tiananmen massacre. Kang and other activists in his movement eventually took refuge in Japan.

With reform now blocked, nationalist resentments at China's condition exploded in a fanatical antiforeign revolt originated by members of a secret society called the Society of Righteous and Harmonious Fists, but irreverently dubbed by Westerners the Boxers. In 1899, foreign missionaries and technicians were attacked and murdered all across north China. The legation quarter of Peking was under siege for nearly two months until foreign troops were able to break through and relieve it. In reprisal, the major powers imposed punitive financial reparations on the Qing court and demanded the right to station foreign troops all the way from the port of Tianjin to Peking itself.

Far more important, in the long run, was the foreign insistence that the Confucian examination system be abolished by 1905. For hundreds of years, the examinations had determined which Chinese could become members of the scholar-gentry class that ruled the country. Since knowledge of the Chinese literary classics was a prerequisite for succeeding in the tests, perpetuation of the system during the 19th century virtually guaranteed that China's scholar-gentry would provide the most entrenched opposition to institutional reform and to the new ideas coming in from the West through the treaty ports. Some scholars, like Kang Youwei, recognized the need for reform but believed it could be accomplished within the ethical and social traditions of Confucianism. Even toward the end of the 19th century, though, most Chinese intellectuals would have subscribed to the formulation of a conservative reformer, Zhang Zhidong (Chang Chih-tung), who originated the terse epigram *"Zhongxue wei ti, xixue wei yong"* (Chinese learning for the essence, Western learning for practical application). An intriguing modern-day analogy to this debate over "essence" and "practical use" is the effort of China's Communist leaders to implement economic reform without touching the political ideology and institutions that underlie the rule of the Communist Party in China.

Pressures for far-reaching change in China in the first decade of the 20th century had reached the point of no return. The conservative reformers, however well intentioned and admired by the foreign powers, had proved unable to restore the vigor of Confucian rule. At the same time, they had been unable to stand up to the arrogance of the foreigners. The Boxers had demonstrated the intensity of Chinese national feeling, but their principal supporters were reactionary members of the gentry and the court who were uninterested in institutional change. New ideas for China would obviously have to come from outside the country, and those would be unlikely to offer anything less for the Middle Kingdom than some form of revolution.

The principal breeding ground of such new ideas was Japan, home to some 8,000 Chinese students in the early years of the century. It had not escaped the notice of inquisitive Chinese that Japan had modernized itself with dramatic success in just a few decades after the American Commodore Matthew Perry had forced open its doors to the outside world in 1854. Japan had even defeated China decisively in a war over control of Korea in 1895. After Japan's crushing victory over Russia in the Russo-Japanese War of 1905, Japan's prestige among Chinese intellectuals disgusted with their own country soared even higher.

Tokyo, meanwhile, provided a safe haven for the activities of one of the chief ideologists of the 1898 reform, Liang Qichiao, who had escaped there after the debacle of the Hundred Days. Liang advocated, among other things, a union of the Asian races against the white, an idea that grew out of the intense resentment of Chinese at Western imperialism. His views were then spiced with an additional measure of radicalism provided by Russian anti-Czarist revolutionaries—especially anarchists—who found refuge in Japan after the abortive 1905 attempt at revolution in Russia. Chinese intellectuals concerned for their country talked less about reform and more and more about revolution.

Yet the man who came to embody such sentiments

and who is today revered as the father of modern China was neither an anarchist nor a racist. Instead, he was a Western-trained Chinese Christian physician who had received his early education at an Anglican missionary school in Hawaii. Sun Yat-sen (1866-1925) had spent the first twelve years of his life in a village 40 miles from Guangzhou on the South China coast. He was thus familiar at first hand with the backwardness and superstition of life in China's countryside. His ideas, nevertheless, were profoundly influenced by his Western education. Even when he decided, in the mid-1890s, that the Qing dynasty could not be reformed but must be completely overthrown, his notion of the China that would replace the traditional world of Confucius and empire was of a fundamentally Western character. "Where did the idea of revolution come from?" he once asked a large Protestant audience rhetorically. "It came because from my youth I have had intercourse with foreign missionaries. Those from Europe and America with whom I associated put the ideals of freedom and liberty into my heart."

Sun Yat-sen's views evolved over his lifetime. When he first started out on his revolutionary career in the 1890s, he was influenced by the ideas on liberty of John Stuart Mill and on land reform of Henry George. By the end of his life, he began to show the heavy influence of Marxist-Leninist thought, introduced into China by Soviet advisers to the Nationalist movement. His basic program was called "The Three Principles of the People." The first principle was "People's Rule," later rendered as "nationalism." This was initially a summons to the Chinese to overthrow the Qing dynasty, which he considered "foreign" because it was of Manchu rather than Han Chinese origin. But it also contained an unspoken appeal to make China strong enough to stand up to the West, even though Sun himself was a great admirer of the U.S. and Japan.

The second principle, "People's Authority," later

translated as "democracy," called explicitly for a republic in place of the imperial system. The third principle, "People's Livelihood," later translated as "socialism," was much vaguer, but it specified a restriction on private land ownership to prevent the accumulation of excessive wealth.

Sun was neither a skilled revolutionary planner nor a brilliant theoretician. He was above all a visionary whose dreams of a strong and united China found fertile soil among students in Japan, overseas Chinese communities around the world and followers in China of a secret society he formed in 1905 called the League of United Action (Tongmenghui). Several coup and assassination attempts organized by Sun's followers in the late 1890s and early 1900s failed ignominiously. But an army mutiny in Wuhan in 1911 provided the spark that ignited a nationwide movement against the Qing.

The last Emperor of China, Puyi, was only six years old when the revolutionaries finally triumphed, and his abdication was announced in 1912 by the Premier. From that year until the Communists came to power in 1949, China was officially known as the Republic of China (the name lives on as the official designation of Taiwan). Sun's followers in 1912 founded the Guomindang, or Nationalist Party, intending it to provide the political base for future democratic, constitutional rule. But between 1912 and the beginning of Communist rule 37 years later, there were few periods of true constitutionality in China. Sun Yat-sen, after being elected provisional President, had to resign in 1912 in favor of a military strongman, Yuan Shikai, who above all wanted to create a constitutional monarchy with himself as the monarch. Worse, regional warlords sprang up all over China, owing political loyalty to no one and seriously impeding the process of national unity and reform. It was not until 1928 that the Nationalist government was able to establish its authority over China from south to north, and even then it required the assistance of an uncertain ally, the Communist Party, as well as Soviet advisers of dubious long-term reliability.

If the Nationalists had been left in peace for several years after 1928, they might possibly have succeeded in bringing reform and modernization to China. The country, however, was not being left alone. The Japanese had long coveted the rich resources of Manchuria, in China's far north. In 1931 they turned a position of strong influence in Manchuria to one of outright control. Then, in 1937, with an ultranationalist militarist clique in power in Tokyo, the Japanese invaded north and central China and kept much of the country under military occupation until the end of World War II. Meanwhile, a far more dangerous threat to Nationalist control had sprung up in China's countryside, a rural-based Communist guerrilla movement.

As a system of ideas, Communism took root in China out of two main impulses among intellectuals. The first was the search for an all embracing world view that could provide the philosophical underpinnings for a new political order—but an order that would work in practice—just as Confucianism had provided the rationale for imperial China. The second was an emotional need for a system that was explicitly in opposition to the West, which, as many Chinese thought, had been the cause of most of China's woes during the 19th century.

Today, the influence of China's own version of its history as an unbroken path from anti-Qing revolution in 1911 to anti-Nationalist revolution in 1949 may indicate that no serious alternative to Communist rule existed once the party had come into being. But there was nothing inevitable at all about the course of the debate for the philosophical—and hence, eventually, political—soul of China that took place in the vacuum of early republican politics in the first three decades of the 20th century.

Ending the examination system in China in 1905 accelerated the introduction of foreign ideas. Confucianism was no longer even a serious contender for allegiance among those dedicated to institutional and social change. In fact, it came under almost universal attack by intellectuals in Beijing and Shanghai who were now trying to digest every current of Western thought, from libertarianism to social Darwinism and anarchism. The blast furnace for political debate was Peking University, known in common parlance then and today as Beida. There, scholars and students combined a passion for national self-reform with an open-ended examination of all philosophical alternatives. The pragmatism of John Dewey gained many adherents in China, and in general there was a rejection of religious or metaphysical viewpoints as irrelevant to China's condition. The New Culture Movement, a campaign for national literary reform, was led by the scholar Hu Shih, who championed the replacement of the old literary language of Confucian scholarship—as remote from spoken Chinese as Latin is from modern Italian—with *baihua* (common language), literally the written-down version of ordinary speech.

At first, the New Culture Movement embraced a wide variety of political viewpoints. Its principal forum was a magazine called *Hsin Ch'ing-nien* (New Youth), edited by Beida literature professor Chen Duxu (Ch'en Tu-hsiu), who selected as the motto for the magazine "Mr. Democracy and Mr. Science." All supporters of the movement were opposed to the continuing humiliations of China by foreign powers, particularly the Japanese, while Europe was tearing itself apart during World War I. On May 4, 1919, in fact, Chinese students and professors took to the streets of Beijing to protest the failure of their government to more vigorously defend Chinese national interests in the Versailles peace talks. The riot, during which several students were arrested and one died from a beating, was the starting point for the next 30 years of student political activism—initially called the

May 4 Movement. In 1989 the prestige of the movement remained so high that big-character posters in Beijing and Shanghai frequently referred to "Mr. Democracy and Mr. Science." What the May 4 Movement did for Chinese intellectuals was restore to them the same sense of participation in the national polity that traditional Confucian scholars had felt in imperial times.

Intellectuals like Hu, steeped in the Western liberal tradition, were unlikely to co-exist for long with Chen, who advocated moral relativism and economic determinism and wanted a much more aggressive China vis-à-vis the outside world. Hu simply wanted "good government" and improvements in society "a drop at a time." Though both liberals and economic determinists did cooperate during the May 4 Movement in 1919, the great divide that drew an increasing number of Chinese intellectuals to Marxism was the 1917 Russian Revolution. With their characteristically pragmatic approach to ideas, few Chinese had paid any attention to Karl Marx until the Bolsheviks actually seized power. The Communist Manifesto, first published in 1848, had not even been translated into Chinese until then. But as the Communists of Russia showed themselves increasingly antagonistic to the traditional Western powers and able, after three years of civil war, to defeat a Western military intervention, more and more Chinese intellectuals came to believe the doctrines of Marx, Engels and Lenin might actually work for China. The Soviets themselves contacted Chen and other Chinese in the summer of 1920 through agents of the Communist International, or Comintern. By 1921 enough Chinese interested in Marxism were aware of one another's existence to convene the founding congress of the Chinese Communist Party. The meeting took place in a girls' school in the International Concession in Shanghai. Of the twelve delegates, one of the most striking, in terms of physical appearance and intensity of convictions, was a young man from Hunan who had been assistant librarian at Beida. His name was Mao Zedong, and he was 27.

Mao was the only participant in that First Congress of the Chinese Communist Party in 1921 who had any direct experience with revolutionary activity. He had organized a small revolutionary group in Changsha, capital of Hunan province, and he was already convinced of the revolutionary potential of China's peasantry. His comrades in Shanghai were not so sure: classical Marxist doctrine called for revolution to be accomplished by the industrial labor force, the proletariat. Yet more than 80% of Chinese were not workers at all, but peasants, and the country's overall lack of industrialization offered little prospect for an urban-based revolution any time in the foreseeable future.

The Soviet advisers of the Chinese Communist Party saw this clearly. They also grasped that it would not serve Moscow's overall strategy for world revolution if the brand-new Communist Party pitted itself against China's Nationalist government. The Nationalists, after all, were already developing—under Soviet tutelage—in a promisingly anti-Western direction. To spare the Communists from government persecution, as well as to bolster the authority of the Nationalists, Moscow's Comintern agents thus advised the Chinese comrades to enter a United Front alliance with the Nationalists. Though the Communist Party would remain a separate entity from the Guomindang, Communists would enter the Nationalist ranks as individuals.

The approach worked well until 1927, when the Nationalist leader, Chiang Kai-shek, turned against his alliance partners and purged them from the Guomindang. In the subsequent anti-Communist crackdown, it was the urban-based party members who were hardest hit. In April 1927 in Shanghai, the organizational base of Chinese Communism, thousands of party workers and suspected sympathizers were disarmed or arrested, and hundreds were shot down in the street by Chiang's forces or gangster groups temporarily working with them.

These violent events helped propel to prominence the rural-based Mao Zedong. In his 1927 "Report on an Investigation of the Peasant Movement in Hunan," Mao dwelt glowingly on the revolutionary potential of China's peasantry, predicting a national peasant uprising in north, central and south China. "Without the poor peasants, there would be no revolution," Mao wrote, in a simple sentence overturning both orthodox Marxist theory that the urban proletariat would lead the socialist revolution and Marx's own prejudice that rural life itself could best be characterized as "idiocy." But in his report Mao stressed, in a way that was to foreshadow Chinese Communist thinking about political control for decades to come, the central role that political terror must play in the consolidation of Communist power in the countryside. "To put it bluntly," he declared, "it is necessary to create terror for a while in every rural area."

The Hunan rural uprising was, in fact, successfully put down by the Nationalist authorities. Mao and other comrades, as well as those who had survived the Nationalist crackdown in Shanghai, had to retreat to a remote area of Jiangxi (Kiangsi) province and build up a revolutionary base from scratch. Using the technique of encouraging poor peasants to denounce in public their own landlords and then witness or actually participate in their execution, the Chinese Communists slowly built up grass-roots political support that enabled their military forces to operate with the full cooperation of local peasants. Communist regular troops constituted the Red Army, and enormous emphasis was placed on their political indoctrination, strict discipline and full participation in organization and propaganda work. This put government forces at a great disadvantage, for the close Communist contacts with the rural masses in a given base area provided the Communists with an important intelligence advantage in discerning government-troop movements.

Meanwhile, Mao formulated the tactical principles of rural guerrilla war: retreat at all times in the face of superior force, but stay on the offensive whenever and wherever guerrillas could obtain local superiority. The combined political and military doctrine became known as "People's War." It characterized all Chinese Communist political and military action from the 1920s until the final civil war with the Nationalists, from 1946 to 1949, which required conventional military operations.

In 1931 Mao Zedong helped establish China's first permanent revolutionary base area, the so-called Chinese Soviet Republic, where the borders of three provinces meet, Jiangxi, Fujian and Guangdong. Since the Chinese Soviet openly challenged Nationalist authority, the Guomindang soon deployed intense military pressure to crush it. A series of five "extermination campaigns" from 1931 to 1934 eventually forced the Communists to break out of their base altogether in order to avoid total destruction by the enemy. Under constant Nationalist attack, and in the course of traversing hostile and geographically daunting terrain, the greatly reduced remnants of the Red Army finally straggled into Shaanxi (Shensi) province, in north China, in October 1935. The epic journey became immortalized in Communist mythology as the Long March. Most important for China's future, when it was over, the political ascendancy of Mao Zedong as Communist leader was assured.

The transfer of the Communist guerrilla base to north China was fortuitous, for it forced the Communists to confront the Japanese during the entire period of World War II. Unlike the Nationalists, who were compelled to try to defend China's cities against the superior Japanese forces, the Communists were able to implement land reform, indoctrinate the peasantry politically, and build up their political and military power behind Japanese lines, almost unmolested by the Nationalist government. Thus, by the time of the Japanese surrender in 1945, Communist political control in north China extended over perhaps as many as 100 million Chinese. Self-confident, hardened by years of guerrilla war and convinced that their moment in history had come, Mao and his Communist armies swept south after conquering Manchuria. Soon they overcame the better equipped and numerically superior Nationalist forces during three swift years of civil war between 1946 and Mao Zedong's proclamation of the People's Republic of China in Beijing on Oct. 1, 1949.

It may be one of the more tragic ironies of China's history that what most enabled the Communists to acquire political power least qualified them to govern the country. Even before formally becoming a Communist, Mao Zedong had been fascinated by what he considered the almost infinite malleability of human nature. The success of People's War in turning previously apathetic or browbeaten peasants into zealous crusaders against opium addiction, crime and corruption helped convince Mao that even Marx's definition of the word proletarian could be modified. The term, Mao believed, ought to apply as much to people's attitudes as to their actual class origins. Mao repeatedly attempted to implement this belief in a series of increasingly disruptive domestic policies during the 27 years he presided over China.

Once they were in control, the Communists at first confined their political terror to the countryside, killing hundreds of thousands—perhaps millions—of landlords and others whom they regarded as opposed to their rule. But after Chinese intervention in the Korean War in 1950, the climate of anti-Western, and particularly anti-American propaganda became more intense. A series of campaigns against corruption, waste, bureaucratization, tax evasion and other economic crimes from 1951 to 1953 became a nationwide witch-hunt against virtually anybody suspected of sympathy for or contacts with the U.S. and other "imperialist" powers. Characteristic of these campaigns were relentless efforts at "thought reform" of the guilty, a system of emotional coercion and harassment of an individual by his peers in order to force a confession and psychological contrition. The original rationale for such psychologically coercive tactics may have been to ensure a sense of participation by the peasantry in violent retribution against their oppressors. But in China's urban campaigns in the post-1949 period, the approach was resented by many who had otherwise sympathized with most of the declared Communist visions.

The Communist program to modernize China's economy, meanwhile, started initially along rational and predictable lines. It took some three years to bring the rogue inflation of the last few years of the civil war under control and to restore normal life as much as possible. By 1953 China felt confident enough to embark on its first five-year plan (1953-57), a program of extensive infrastructure development and industrialization deeply influenced by the experience and advice of the Soviet Union. Chinese feelings toward the Soviets were later to harden, but in the early 1950s the friendship and assistance of the world's most powerful Communist state was an important political and economic asset for the country. Had the first plan been followed by an equally pragmatic second one, China's industrial progress would have been impressive and living standards might have risen significantly by 1962. The country would still not have been "modern," but it would have moved significantly further out of its backwardness.

Instead, Mao seemed unable to wait for mere economic processes to bring about the proletarian consciousness he saw as indispensable for true socialism, and eventual Communism. One reason for his obsession may have been the rude discovery that, after years of Communist rule, many Chinese intellectuals still detested their new rulers. A political campaign launched in 1956 encouraged ordinary Chinese to express their true feelings about the party and its leadership, under the poetic rubric "Let a hundred flowers bloom, let a hundred schools of thought contend."

After initial hesitation and further official encouragement in 1957, a torrent of criticism and abuse of the party spilled out across the land. Shocked, Mao ordered an end to the dissident outpouring in June 1957, after only six weeks. He then called for a harsh crackdown on all who had rashly expressed their discontent. Under the operational direction of Deng Xiaoping, then a relatively new member of the Politburo, some 300,000 Chinese intellectuals were arrested, sent to prison or the countryside or in some instances executed.

Though Mao had once declared that "a revolution is not a dinner party," his politically more moderate critics in the party leadership had not suspected the extremes of policy he would adopt to dragoon China along the road of his revolutionary vision. From 1958 to 1961 China toiled in the throes of the Great Leap Forward, a crash economic "socialization" program that Mao believed would enable the country to shoot into the front rank of world nations within a mere 15 years. One aspect of the Leap was the total collectivization of Chinese agriculture into People's Communes, rural administrative units with almost total power over their members. Another was the belief that the normally unproductive rural labor cycle between the autumn harvest and the spring planting could be utilized for industrial purposes. Mao had peasants and city workers alike construct 600,000 backyard steel furnaces to turn pig iron into industrial steel. The frenetic activity was then punctuated with yet other campaigns, for instance the one to destroy China's sparrows because the unfortunate birds supposedly ate too much of the harvest.

Such constant hectoring and mobilizing took an appalling toll on the national health. Officially, 1959, '60 and '61 are known in China as "the three bad years." Starvation and malnutrition, seemingly banished during the quiet times of the early 1950s, roared back across the land. China's own official statistics reveal an absolute loss of population between 1959 and 1962 of 14 million, a figure that translates, with the anticipated natural increase factored in, as approximately 27 million starvation deaths in a three-year period. However heroic Mao's vision for the "New China" might have been in philosophical terms, economically it was a catastrophe.

By 1962 calmer heads had prevailed in the party, and Mao found himself relegated to a "second line" of leadership, with Chairman of the People's Republic Liu Shaoqi (Liu Shao-ch'i) and Vice Premier Deng Xiaoping taking over day-to-day administration of the country. Under their more rational control, in fact, China quickly recovered and by 1965 seemed to have returned to the clumsy, but at least safe and slow, procedures of detailed central economic planning.

At this point, however, Mao's pursuit of millennarial change in China came to the fore again. After plotting and preparing for months in complete secrecy in Shanghai during the autumn of 1965, Mao launched the Great Proletarian Cultural Revolution the following year.

On one level, the Cultural Revolution was aimed at purging from the Communist Party those who had opposed Mao at different times. Liu Shaoqi and Deng Xiaoping (who was referred to in wall posters at the time as THE NO. 2 PARTY PERSON IN AUTHORITY TAKING THE CAPITALIST ROAD) were clear targets, since they had never approved of Mao's extreme voluntarism in economic policy. On another level, the Cultural Revolution was Mao's last attempt to force the entire nation to become proletarian by changing its thinking. As millions of teenage Red Guards filled Tiananmen Square again and again in the fall of 1966, ordinary Chinese were instructed to study and memorize the contents of a pocket-size book,

Quotations from Chairman Mao, as though doing so would lead to a sort of religious conversion to proletarianness. Indeed, Lin Biao's (Lin Piao) introduction to the "little red book" described the thought of Mao Zedong as "a spiritual atom bomb of infinite power."

For nearly three years, as schools and universities closed down and bands of Red Guards roamed the country, China seemed to have abandoned normality. Millions of Chinese lost their lives in factional fighting or persecution as suspected "capitalist roaders," and the economy sank backward from the level it had reached in 1965. Whatever Mao's vision for China amounted to, it bore no relation to most people's notion of modernity. The devastation in China's economy was catastrophic. Living standards fell to starvation levels in some of the poorer provinces. In Gansu, in China's northwest corridor, some Chinese travelers reported seeing beggars at railroad stations so poor that they were stark naked. But even in China's previously Westernized cities, sloth and apathy infected economic life. TIME correspondent David Aikman was struck by how much Guangzhou in 1973 resembled from a high vantage point nothing so much as a daguerreotype of 19th century Paris. In education, science and technology, China lost an estimated 10 to 15 years' development.

The Cultural Revolution petered out as a day-to-day obsession in the early 1970s as Mao himself began to look for improved relations with the West, and particularly with the U.S. The visit of President Richard Nixon to China in 1972 dramatically underlined China's need to reduce its vulnerability to the Soviet Union, with which military hostilities had broken out early in 1969. But far-reaching as the U.S. connection proved to be in strategic terms for China, until Mao's own death in 1976, the economic policies of the country were dominated by an extreme left-wing egalitarian view of development that ensured stagnation or even retrogression in living standards. After the economic reforms of Deng Xiaoping began to be implemented in the early 1980s, the Chinese revealed startling statistics about housing and nutrition levels. The figures showed that by most measurements, the conditions of food and shelter for ordinary Chinese had actually deteriorated between the mid-1950s and a quarter-century later.

Deng himself had been disgraced and kept under house arrest during the early part of the Cultural Revolution. In April 1973 he surprisingly reappeared in public with the title of Vice Premier. Mao, who had been personally fond of Deng in the 1950s, evidently considered Deng's political and administrative skills essential for China's recovery from the Cultural Revolution. In 1975 Deng worked closely with Premier Zhou Enlai on a program called the Four Modernizations (overhauling agriculture, industry, national defense, and science and technology,) that was designed to double China's national income by the year 2000. When Deng firmly returned to rule China in late 1978, the program became the principal economic goal of China's development.

Before that took place, though, the most left-leaning of Mao Zedong's political followers and allies, the so-called Gang of Four, nearly succeeded in plunging China into another Cultural Revolution. The Gang consisted of Mao's wife, Jiang Qing, and the three most prominent Shanghai-based theoreticians and leaders of the Cultural Revolution, Zhang Qunqiao, Yao Wenyuan and Wang Hongwen.

Zhou died in January 1976 and was the immediate object of a vast outpouring of national grief. He was genuinely loved and respected as a voice of reason and moderation amid the vengeful insanity of Chinese politics in the 1960s and 1970s. But when hundreds of thousands of Beijing residents came to Tiananmen Square in early April to honor Zhou's memory during the annual Qing Ming festival, at which Chinese pay tribute to their deceased ancestors, the event became the occasion for raucous political outbursts against the regime itself. Deng had already disappeared from public view as a result of political efforts by the Gang of Four to turn China back from its Four Modernizations path. The authorities then suppressed the Tiananmen riot—later to become known as the "Tiananmen incident"—and embarked on a vicious persecution of any participants they could identify.

The new political witch-hunt might have taken China to the brink of real bloodletting, but in September 1976 Mao finally died. The Gang of Four attempted to organize a political coup of their own, using urban militias, but they were beaten to the draw by their political opponents, who had them arrested at pistol point in October. At first, political power was in the hands of Hua Guofeng, a Mao protégé who was nevertheless acceptable to the Gang of Four's opponents. Within a year, though, many Chinese were openly calling for the restoration of Deng to national leadership, arguing that this alone would enable China to return to the path of painful economic and political recovery. Skillfully deferring in public and private to Hua, Deng simultaneously orchestrated a public demand for his own return to China's leadership.

By the fall of 1978 he had outmaneuvered the inexperienced Hua and propelled himself back into national leadership. Three decades after China had first embarked upon the Communist path, the country once again began to look economic reality in the eye. In any ultimate sense, the new turn did not in itself constitute modernity. But at least it was a step in that direction. What the Chinese leadership did not realize, however, was that they were about to embrace a mistaken assumption that had characterized so many previous efforts at modernization— that China could attain the prosperity of the West without moving toward democracy, the basic political principle that made Western societies so dynamic. As generations of students would attest, China cannot have Mr. Science without Mr. Democracy.

CHAPTER THREE

THE ROAD TO REFORM

In a rice paddy in Yunnan province or a machine-tool factory in Nanjing. From the headman of a village in Sichuan famous for its rice liquor or from the country's top banker. The pat answer to the question of when economic prosperity began is always the same. Invariably, the reverential reply is that everything good stems from the decisions of the Third Plenum of the Eleventh Central Committee. In the annals of Chinese Communism, few meetings surpass the importance of that December 1978 gathering of the party's 333-member Central Committee. The Third Plenum completed the third rehabilitation of Deng Xiaoping. It also launched the first tentative stages of his economic-reform program. In addition, the plenum marked the beginning of the end for Mao's designated successor, Hua Guofeng.

For Deng, the plenum was his chosen battlefield for the crucial confrontations with Mao's heirs. Deng used two simple weapons in his contest with Hua, two powerful pieces of evidence against him. First, the China that Hua had inherited from Mao was, quite simply, a disaster. Although the worst excesses of the Cultural Revolution were merely bad memories by then, the country's economic, social and cultural foundations had been shattered. Second, like many other older party leaders, Deng had suffered greatly during the Cultural Revolution. He had been rehabilitated twice, but other respected comrades were still in Communist purgatory, and Hua was dragging his feet on returning them to the fold.

In his hurry to move his opponents aside and launch his vision of a new China, Deng resorted to a third, potentially more dangerous instrument: public opinion. In the weeks leading up to the plenum, his forces encouraged public discussion of the excesses of the Cultural Revolution. One outgrowth of that exercise was the creation of the Democracy Wall, a gray-painted brick barrier in Beijing's Xidan district. Beginning in late November 1978, the wall was plastered with posters demanding everything from better housing conditions to free elections and an end to corruption. But most of the posters were heart-wrenching descriptions of the personal tragedies of the previous twelve years. The Cultural Revolution was still being blamed on Mao's wife Jiang Qing and the three other members of the Gang of Four, and Hua got credit for having them arrested. But inside and outside the regime, it was commonly accepted that Mao shared responsibility for that national tragedy. Some Chinese even took to holding up five fingers when talking of the Gang of Four, a subversive way of indicating they considered Mao just as culpable. And Hua was nothing more than Mao's handpicked successor.

Hua and his supporters were swept away by Deng's tactics. Deng added four of his supporters to the Politburo. Though Hua kept his title as Chairman of the party and Premier, the policy pronouncements of the plenum made it clear to everyone that Deng was in charge. The wily politician from Sichuan was able to enlist the assistance of other old and revered comrades in pushing through the first stage of the economic-reform package. While the state would retain title to all land, peasants would be permitted to keep and sell any surplus food produced beyond the state output quota assigned to them. This became known as the "household responsibility system." As long as each family unit, or household, performed its state-assigned tasks, it was free to spend the remainder of its members' time as profitably as it wished. Although this may seem a small concession, the Maoist concept of total collectivization had completely banned any such private initiative.

As in any religion, the new departure had to be given a basis in past dogma. Deng had begun to lay the groundwork for this shift throughout 1978. In a series of speeches and articles, he stressed the paramount importance of reality. "There is only one true theory in the world," he told the People's Liberation Army's Political Work Conference in June, "the theory that derives from objective reality and is verified by objective reality." Other articles began to discuss Mao's own admissions of fallibility, stressing his long-forgotten admonition to "seek truth from facts." But the most important historical justification for Deng's apparent heresy was his mentor Zhou Enlai's concept of the Four Modernizations.

Zhou had advanced his vision for a new, more prosperous China at the January 1975 session of the National People's Congress, China's parliament, its first meeting in ten years. At the time, the concept of an orderly productive economy still ran counter to the ruling belief that the class struggle came first. But Zhou was a dying man with as much prestige as Mao himself. No one dared attack him. As Zhou's acknowledged protégé, Deng was able to hold up that goal of a modernized economy and defense as the ultimate justification for placing economic reality above ideological purity. Henceforth, class struggle and attempts to modernize through mass mobilizations like the Great Leap Forward would give way to rational, pragmatic approaches.

Whereas in Mao's days all economic directives came from Beijing, Deng's pragmatic approach would allow decentralization of decision making to take advantage of local knowledge and conditions. No longer would peasants in areas that could support only cultivation of barley be told they must plant wheat. Instead of everyone receiving exactly the same pay regardless of skill or effort, the new system would permit some economic incentives. At a minimum, hard work on the farm would be rewarded. Finally, the Maoist ideal of total national self-reliance was shed in favor of an opening to the West, with the hope that foreign firms would invest both capital and modern technology in China.

And in a country where no political statements are made casually, the ranking of the Four Modernizations by Zhou was important as well and was repeatedly reinforced by Deng. First would come agriculture, which had suffered greatly under Mao's mindless communalization. After the agricultural reforms were in train, reforms would come to improve the performance of Chinese industry. Only then would the military begin to benefit from the fruits of the reforms. (The People's Liberation Army had played a major role in Deng's rehabilitation and reaccession to power. But he had the stature, as a Long March veteran and as Chief of Staff of the P.L.A, to persuade his military comrades to await patiently the day a stronger economy could provide better armaments.) Finally, the list of priorities left science and technology to fend for themselves. Of the government funds at hand to advance China's modernization, few if any would be available for research and development—or even, as it turned out, to improve the country's lagging educational system.

The practical basis of support for the First Modernization, agricultural reform, was provided by one of Deng's protégés. Zhao Ziyang had made Deng's home province of Sichuan a laboratory for economic reform. Most of the key elements of Deng's rural reform program were first tried there between 1975 and 1978. The Sichuan experiment was impressive: in just three years the province went from being on the verge of starvation to becoming one of the country's most prosperous regions. That performance provided ample ammunition for Deng in debates with his peers. Zhao's reward was to be his elevation to the post of Vice Premier in April 1980, and Premier five months later.

In fact, the agricultural reforms were not that radical. Many of them had been advanced in the early 1960s, following the disastrous Great Leap Forward, by Deng himself under the guidance of Mao's then No. 2 man, Liu Shaoqi. In 1978 the old comrades had little problem approving changes that did not tamper with the basic tenet of Marxism-Leninism: state ownership of the means of production. Even conservative economists like Chen Yun, later to become a leader of the antireform forces, applauded the commonsense liberalization of the rural economy. But one of the most important administrative elements of the agricultural reforms was the abolition of the people's communes, Mao's nationwide system of rural collectives originally set up during the Great Leap Forward of the 1950s.

The benefits were quickly apparent. Coupled with a sharp boost in the prices paid for grain and other staples, agricultural production skyrocketed between 1979 and 1984. Foreign analysts scoffed in 1978 when the Chinese announced their intention to raise total grain output to 400 million metric tons by 1985. In fact, that target was reached in 1984. Meanwhile, per capita peasant incomes doubled, to $135 per year between 1978 and 1982. In addition to increased income from farming, peasants were allowed to engage in so-called sideline activities: crafts, construction and transport. Soon came the first reports of "10,000 yuan" households, peasant families with annual incomes greater than $3,000, or more than twelve times the national average. Soon peasants were building new houses and buying consumer durables like television sets and even videocassette recorders. The face of the Chinese countryside was changing at a breathtaking speed, although at the cost of enormous government subsidies, which reached more than $8 billion for food in 1981.

In the meantime, Deng was busily expanding his country's ties, political and economic, with the West, particularly the U.S. During 1978 China signed a series of huge bilateral trade agreements, the biggest a $20 billion deal with Japan. Just at the time of the Third Plenum, later that same year, China reopened diplomatic relations with Washington. A month later, Deng made a triumphal visit to the U.S., even donning a cowboy hat in Texas. The scenes of American prosperity and modernity that beamed back into the Chinese homes, offices and shops that had televisions were a revelation for the people and their leaders. Almost completely isolated from the rest of the world for the previous 20 years, China had no idea how far behind it had slipped. But the true epiphany came when Deng visited Tokyo. It was one thing for the fabled land of America to appear so advanced, but the Chinese believed they had defeated Japan almost single-handed in World War II. How could another Oriental race have come so far?

All of this strengthened Deng's hand in the internal battles over opening up China to the outside world. In fact, Deng made a practice of encouraging his fellow old revolutionaries to go abroad and see just how backward China was compared with the rest of the world. He wanted foreign investment and technology to be imported as quickly as possible, in spite of his belief that "when you open the window, some flies will come in." The flies were the social and cultural influences that he felt China could do without. The implication was always that if too many evil influences seeped in, the window could be shut.

One way to limit those problems was to create hermetically sealed areas of Chinese territory, where foreigners could set up shop while contaminating a minimum number of people. The four Special Economic Zones, established in 1979, had historical parallels in the treaty ports and foreign concession areas established by the Ming and Qing dynasties. Deng established S.E.Z.'s in Shenzhen, across the border from Hong Kong; in Zhuhai, next door to Macao; in Xiamen and Shantou, both across the strait from Taiwan. All four are coastal cities that could be easily isolated from the rest of the mainland. (Eventually, the government even built a security fence between Shenzhen and the rest of the country. The fence provided tighter security than that on the Shenzhen–Hong Kong border.) The theory was that the Chinese government would provide infrastructure and a cheap but well-educated work force. Foreigners, for their part, would come in with advanced-technology factories. The zones were also to be testing areas for social and economic experiments and bridges to the nearby Chinese communities of Hong Kong, Macao and Taiwan, which the mainland hoped one day to absorb.

The biggest problem in the early days of the open-door policy was that initially the door only seemed to swing inward when it came to trade with the outside world. A country that has been isolated as long as China was builds up an enormous shopping list. Quite simply, the Chinese needed everything the foreigners had to sell but had little to export in return. As a result, China wound up with a $3.9 billion trade deficit for the two-year period beginning in 1979. That was still relatively small for a country of China's size, but it was a shock for the old men used to practical autarky. As would happen several more times over the next seven years, Deng within a short time had to agree to a stabilization program that artificially restrained imports.

Some noneconomic problems were cropping up as

well. The Democracy Wall movement had soon got out of hand. Early in 1979, Deng was forced into the first of many tactical retreats. In order to fend off charges of revisionism (the Communist term for heresy) from old-line Marxists, he found it necessary to solidify his political position by formulating the Four Cardinal Principles, which restated China's commitment to socialism and set the outermost boundaries of political discussion. The four principles—socialism, the dictatorship of the proletariat, the leadership of the Communist Party and Marxism-Leninism–Mao Zedong Thought—were meant to assure Deng's colleagues that his reforms would not go too far.

By April the Deng-controlled official press had begun to condemn the nascent prodemocracy movement for advocating "bourgeois" freedom and an end to the leading role of the party. In October the security forces arrested one of the leaders of the Democracy Wall movement, Wei Jingsheng. Although said to be the son of a top official, Wei received a 15-year prison sentence. (By late 1989 he was still in prison. When Deng's advisers worried about world public opinion after repressive measures, the leader reportedly would point to the lack of foreign outcry over Wei's plight.) In December 1979 the government announced that the Democracy Wall in Beijing's Xidan district would be closed. A month later, Deng specifically criticized the practice of civic complaint through wall posters. The right to put up large-character posters was guaranteed in Mao's constitution, but Deng said the right had been abused by "ultra-individualists" and could cause instability. The right was removed from the new constitution in 1980. Within a year, all the top dissenters had been arrested, and all the underground publications that had sprung up were shut down. This was just the first of a series of cycles in which political liberalism under Deng yielded to repression.

But the economic picture grew rosier each year in the early 1980s. The rural economic reforms were succeeding far beyond their supporters' wildest dreams. In the countryside, the economy was booming. Not only were peasants growing more food, but they also had increasingly branched out into sideline activities. Collectives, composed of the members of what used to be called work brigades, created small holding companies producing everything from rice crackers to transistor radios.

The people of Qong Lai County in Sichuan province got something of a head start on the rest of the country. Qong Lai was one of the first four counties to experiment with the household Responsibility System. The village of Fenghuang had a total economic output of about $50,000 in 1977, mostly from growing rice. By 1984 the village's income was almost $1.5 million, and it was planning on doubling that in two more years. The village looked like one big construction site, with new houses and new factories crowding out the rice fields. Zhang De'an worked in the local still that made *Feifeng daqu* (Flying Phoenix rice liquor), but her family's main source of income was a sideline activity, the production of yeast for the still. With that additional $300 a month Zhang's family had gone on a consumer-spending spree. Her house was crowded with a color television set, a washing machine, a floor fan and an electric water pump. Zhang wanted a new refrigerator but decided to order one from the provincial capital instead of locally: "I will have to pay 900 yuan instead of 700, but it will be a much better refrigerator." A far cry from the days when a bicycle, a wristwatch and a transistor radio were the three wants of a Chinese household.

These new factories and sideline activities did more than raise the standard of living in rural areas. They also provided an important way of absorbing excess labor as higher prices inspired an increase in agricultural productivity, reducing the number of hands needed to grow the crops. By 1985 specialized households and rural collectives employed more than 70 million people. Instead of migrating to the cities, rural workers could find jobs at home. Although the government sanctioned this burgeoning second economy in the countryside, the concept of developing small rural factories arose spontaneously without the benefit of any major theoretical underpinning. The lesson of that success—that letting market forces and incentives operate unfettered by government meddling produced the strongest economic results—was lost on China's elderly leaders.

The government did increase incentives for peasants to develop their agricultural land by granting long-term leases, which could be sold or inherited. But the driving force behind that liberalization was the realization that the easy early gains in the farming sector had run their course. China did become a net grain exporter in 1985, but later that year the rice harvest came in lower than expected. For old-line conservatives like Chen Yun, China's pre-eminent economic planner in the years before the Great Leap Forward, a gradual decline in rice production was the worst heresy of all. Chen told a special party conference in September that "grain shortages will lead to social disorder." Although some senior leaders reportedly called for mandatory grain deliveries by peasants, the reformers managed to fight back that attempt to revert to central controls.

The success of the rural reforms paved the way for changes in China's urban economy. Beginning in 1983, the state began gradually to withdraw from the day-to-day operations of every factory in the country. The basic approach to enterprise reform was similar to that in the countryside. The new enterprise Responsibility System, the urban equivalent of the household Responsibility System, meant that state-owned firms that once had no control over any part of their production cycle could operate a bit more freely. Theoretically, they could set the size of their work force and the wages paid. Henceforth the state would take only a percentage of their production at the price set by the state. By the same token, the enterprises would now receive only a portion of their supplies at state-set prices. Thus, if a factory making iron bars was required to deliver 60% of its annual output to the state, it would receive 60% of its raw materials, including energy, from the state.

For the rest, the enterprises had to buy supplies on the open market and, just as importantly, sell their often shoddy products to increasingly discerning consumers. This meshing of free-market capitalism and a planned economy came to be known as "market socialism" or the "planned commodity economy." Somehow Deng believed China would succeed in doing what no other socialist country had before: merging the stability and equality of a planned economy with the efficiency of a free-market economy. In fact, China's top economists and political theorists had already made extensive studies of failed reform efforts in Yugoslavia, Hungary and Poland. They knew the fallacy inherent in partial economic reform, but the old comrades still held the reins of power, and none of them—including Deng—were ready to scrap the role of the state and the party.

The halfhearted urban reforms almost immediately ran into trouble. Decentralization led to another burst of investment and consumption. The country was flooded with foreign consumer goods as the government's decentralization of the banking system made it easier for enterprises to obtain foreign exchange. The newly autonomous enterprises, desperate for profits, found that, because of the artificial value of the yuan and the scarcity of luxury items, they could import consumer goods and resell them at three to four times their cost. Thousands of Japanese cars poured into the country. In 1984 Beijing had only a handful of broken-down taxis. A year later, 14,000 shiny new Toyotas and Nissans—all of them top-of-the-line models—were working the hotels for fares. The new status symbol became not a television set or a refrigerator but a Japanese color TV and a Japanese refrigerator. The results were disastrous for the balance of trade. If China's old men were concerned by the $3.9 billion trade deficit in 1979-80, they were horrified by the tab for the 1985 spending spree: a deficit of $15.1 billion.

Deng's Special Economic Zones did nothing to ease the foreign exchange problem. By 1985 there was widespread disillusionment with these supposed panaceas for helping China import technology while earning foreign currency. The biggest S.E.Z., Shenzhen, had thousands of square meters of empty factory space waiting for foreign investors who never came. Much of the "foreign" money that was invested there actually came from mainland-owned companies in nearby Hong Kong. Their primary line of business was importing consumer goods that could be sold in the flashy department stores of brash Shenzhen city. Shenzhen also developed some of the social problems that Chinese elders associated with contact with the West: gambling, prostitution and drugs. During a tour of this burgeoning capitalist haven, one old revolutionary reportedly asked with tears in his eyes, "Is this what we fought for?" In the face of such misgivings, Deng began to distance himself from what were essentially his creations. "We hope it will succeed," he said. "But if it fails, we will draw lessons from it."

Decentralization caused other problems in this traditionally fractious country. Individual provinces and cities began to go their own way, ignoring the directives that the central government did send out. In 1985 Chongqing, China's largest urban area, refused to remit a form of payroll tax to Beijing. At the same time, the *People's Daily* reported that half of all state and collectively run enterprises were cheating on their taxes. Provinces began to erect trade barriers against one another to keep out products that might threaten the jobs of local workers. In some cases, trade barriers were established to keep scarce goods available for the "home" market. Shanghai, for example, announced that it would restrict the sale of its beer to other provinces. At the same time, however, authorities in China's most important industrial city complained that under urban economic reforms their factories no longer had access to sufficient materials from outlying provinces. The connection between their beer and Shaanxi's coal never occurred to them.

In 1984 provincial banks rushed to lend as much money as they could after they were told that their future loan levels would be judged on the amount lent in that year. The resulting bulge in the money supply fueled a construction-and-investment boom that went far beyond the economic growth envisaged by the central authorities. Beijing was still providing "indicative" planning figures for the country, but some areas of the country saw annual growth rates of 20% to 30%, instead of the planned increases of 8% or less. All that economic activity put even more disposable income in the pockets of Chinese consumers, many of whom already had substantial savings accumulated during the years of scarcity.

Those inflationary pressures only exacerbated problems caused by the two-headed pricing system that was erected as a transition to a commodity market system. State-set prices for hundreds of goods remained artificially low, while free-market prices for the same items soared. Already in 1985, the first urban consumer grumbling was starting to be heard. In one poll of 2,500 city dwellers, more than half said that although they understood the need for price reform, they would prefer stable prices, even if it meant their wages would be frozen. It was common to hear housewives complain about the unconscionable price increases for items that a few years before were never available at all. Years of government propaganda had convinced them that there was no connection between price and availability.

Workers were also unhappy about how the urban reforms were changing their jobs. Part of Deng's reforms were aimed at breaking the "iron rice bowl" of lifetime job security, a Chinese worker's most prized perquisite. Although jobs in state enterprises did not pay very well, they were handed down from father to son, mother to daughter. They provided lifetime job security, subsidized housing and food, and free medical and child care. The urban reforms set out to end that system by forcing all enterprises to turn a profit. Since many of these factories produced goods that could not be sold for much more than the state-set price (and since the government tried to keep a lid on all price increases at the factory level), the only way for firms to operate in the black was to slice operating costs. Padded payrolls had to be cut back, while workers had to toil harder and had to pay more for some of the benefits they received.

Any enterprise that did not institute austerity measures faced that most capitalist of all fates, bankruptcy, putting all its workers out on the street. And the huge rate of underemployment in urban China—put as high as 50% by some Western estimates—meant that finding new jobs would be difficult. Although bankruptcy was tried only on an experimental basis in a few cities, the reformists made several attempts to pass a bankruptcy law in the National People's Congress, to no avail. One important reason was that the enterprises were never given enough autonomy to have a fair chance of succeeding or failing on their own. Another problem was that the dual pricing system made it practically impossible to determine which factories were making money and which were operating in the red.

Even on the simple level of providing incentives to workers, the reforms encountered major problems. Enterprises were permitted to award performance bonuses to their employees. As food and other prices continued to rise, managers were under great pressure to raise wages across the board. In the end, that is what most of the bonus funds were used for. In factories where managers did try to reward extra work, the recipients were frequently shunned by their colleagues. In other factories, impromptu strikes were called to protest implementation of incentive-pay schemes—even when those plans did not involve lowering base pay. In Beijing in the winter of 1985-86, municipal bus drivers, resentful of making less than cabbies even though cab work is harder, began driving their buses much more slowly than normal. But riders did not blame the bus drivers. They blamed the government's reform program. Mao's iron rice bowl had long outlived him.

The official press was unable to ignore the problems that kept cropping up in both city and countryside, but it chose instead to concentrate on peripheral ones—troubles that could be attributed to foreign influences. The generic term for these sore spots was evil winds, and a new one seemed to puff up monthly during 1984-85. One of the biggest gusts was the counterfeiting of products. Although advertising was still in its infancy, Chinese brand-name recognition was high, particularly for consumer durables like bicycles and watches. State and collective enterprises took advantage of that by turning out bogus Flying Pigeon bicycles with faulty parts. The government launched a campaign in 1985 to halt counterfeiting of products, but at the same time it seemed to sanction copyright pirating of foreign intellectual property like books and software, as well as foreign trademarks. The façade of the government's own Friendship Store for foreigners in Beijing sported huge neon signs featuring Mickey Mouse and Donald Duck look-alikes. Most evil winds were like that—they were evil only if the regime said so.

The ability of private enterprise to assist in unblocking some of the bottlenecks in the economy was severely limited. Entrepreneurs were permitted to hire no more than 15 employees. But urban collectives, like their rural counterparts, had no such limits. A neighborhood, a school, or even a group of workers from the same factory could launch a cooperative economic entity, called a collective. Initially, these new "work units," as the Chinese call their employers, engaged largely in service industries like restaurants and repair shops. But by 1984 manufacturing collectives like Beijing's Tian Qiao Merchandise Co., which produced cosmetics and clothing, had begun to spring up everywhere.

China's reform theoreticians used the urban collectives like test tubes, trying out economic policies on a small scale. As one government official put it, "We have a saying that 'a small boat can turn back more easily.'" Tian Qiao, for example, was one of the first enterprises in China to issue real stock with voting rights and variable dividends. But most important of all, the collectives provided the engine of economic growth for the country, while the fits and starts of the reform program for state enterprises tied them up. The collective sector of the urban economy grew at a rate of more than 20% a year in the mid-1980s. Collectives provided millions of jobs for city dwellers, particularly the millions of school leavers who entered the labor force each year.

Perhaps the biggest political problem from the half-hearted urban reforms was corruption, the unhappy consequence of trying to make a planned and a market economy coexist. The sons and daughters of top officials entered private enterprise. Some used their connections to obtain state-priced materials, which could then be sold on the open market at markups of 50% or more. Corruption has long been a part of Chinese life, as it is in nearly any country, but during Mao's time the country was so poor that graft was usually petty. The economic opening made malfeasance possible on a much grander scale. The problem was so broad and obvious that early in 1986 more than 8,000 senior party, government and military officials met in Beijing for a 2½-day conference and heard much stern talk about the need to stamp out corruption. There were even threats about executing top officials or their children.

By some counts, hundreds of thousands of party members have engaged in various forms of graft, from extorting free meals from a private restaurant to pressuring an American firm to send one's child to college in the U.S. But public skepticism about the thoroughness and evenhandedness of the 1986 campaign was accurate. Apparently none of the top leaders was completely clean. Zhao Ziyang's son set up a consulting business in Hong Kong, reportedly even mentioning his familial connection on his calling card. Even Deng Xiaoping's crippled son Deng Pufang was implicated in shady deals and was rumored to have a Swiss bank account. As long as the economy was neither fish nor foul—not centrally planned and not free market—corruption would be a natural, almost essential part of the Chinese scene.

Rather than swallow hard and proceed with the true liberation of prices, enterprises and the economy, Deng limited his aides to a variety of small-scale experiments in various cities. These included limited ownership of securities (they were called stocks but actually functioned as bonds, since they did not represent true ownership in the firm). The measures also included bankruptcy, but very few factories were ever allowed to go bust. Also, wage reforms were introduced in a few regions. But none of these gestures were tried on a large enough scale to reflect their chances of success. And repeatedly, the leadership shied away from the linchpin of economic reform in any other country: price reform. In retrospect it now appears clear why.

On the one hand, Deng still had to answer to conservative critics within the elderly leadership. Their concern that China was heading down the "capitalist road" increased with every new theoretical paper by a government economist about the need for more reform. On the other hand, public discontent over the price increases that had already occurred was so high that the regime was simply scared of its people. Instituting price reform might have been possible if Deng and his colleagues had been ready for political reform as well. By providing an institutional escape valve for the people, with free elections at least at the local level, it may have been possible to persuade them to accept necessary but painful measures.

But Deng insisted on keeping the ultimate reins of power in the hands of the party, at all levels, and that meant limiting the reforms. Deng is by nature a pragmatist. His motto was always that it did not matter if the cat was black or white as long as it caught mice. He could see that Mao's mass-movement approach to economic development had been a disaster. He could also see that the Soviet model of controlling everything from the center was better for a developing country, but that it had its limits for a country like China, which was ready to soar. What he could not envisage was a transcending alternative, short of a complete turn to capitalism. So he tried a little of this and a little of that. But the only reforms he felt truly comfortable with were the ones that provided some added incentives and freedom of economic action to peasants. Those were the reforms he had personally implemented in the early 1960s. They were the ones that had saved his home province, Sichuan, from starvation in the mid-1970s. But in both cases, the efficacy of the reforms was in large part a function of the disastrous situation that preceded them. Deng's reforms needed a bold second act, but he never found the strength to ring down the curtain on the first. As a result, his reforms never progressed beyond the margins of Marxism-Leninism.

The first thing that people who had visited China in the 1970s noticed when they returned in the early 1980s was the fashions. The sea of green and blue unisex Mao suits, which once stamped China as the world's largest anthill, had become a kaleidoscope of brightly colored skirts and blouses for the women, and jeans and T shirts with Western logos for the men. The fashions were not always, or even often, very well coordinated, but they represented a freedom of personal expression that had been denied for years.

The people's minds were also opened by foreign radio broadcasts, particularly those from the Voice of America and the British Broadcasting Corporation. China's rulers had sanctioned listening to these mouthpieces of the bourgeoisie so that people could improve their English. That they did, but they also learned about rock 'n' roll, love and sex, and the struggle for democracy waged by people in such nearby countries as South Korea and the Philippines. American music began to permeate the country. By the mid-'80s, even in a back alley in remote Yenan, Mao's headquarters after the Long March, a traveler could hear two different Chinese versions of John Denver's *Take Me Home, Country Roads* blaring from radios and cassette players. Cities and towns all over China sprouted "discos," which actually were more akin to ballrooms or polka palaces than to glitzy Western-style discothèques. Tame as they were, these Chinese versions—in which couples held each other close on the dance floor and snuggled in corners—were cesspools of shocking decadence to the old men who ran the country. Even worse, entrepreneurs were screening smuggled pornographic videos in their homes, charging the equivalent of a month's pay per viewing.

Western visitors found this ferment intoxicating. China experts extolled it. The world watched in fascination as a country that had long shrouded itself in mystery appeared to be opening up to the outside world and propelling itself into the 20th century. Coca-Cola came to China, along with Cadillac luxury cars, Kentucky Fried Chicken, the rock group Wham! and those ageless 1960s surfer–rock stars, Jan and Dean. It seemed that the Chinese were on the verge of becoming, as Western visitors would marvel, "just like us." In fact, most of these changes were restricted to urban China. The vast majority of the country's 900 million peasants were untouched by the trappings of Western pop culture. But it was the urban population about which the leadership worried, and worry they did.

In addition to the "bad" Western materialist influences that were on display for everyone to see, the keepers of China's ideological keys also fretted over some of the changes in the arts and literature. In the late 1970s, Deng and his colleagues had encouraged people to unburden their souls by writing "scar literature" about the injustices and injuries done to them during the Cultural Revolution. In fact, this was primarily a way of weakening the position of Mao's heir Hua Guofeng. But when some of these same writers continued to write about injustice as being an endemic, "darker side" of socialism, they were attacked for having a "bourgeois liberal"— Western capitalist—view of the world.

In the early 1980s several Chinese Marxist scholars discovered some of the German philosopher's earlier, more humanistic writings, which had been widely published in the West. The reaction of the leadership to this dangerous trend was the 1983-84 campaign against "spiritual pollution." Led by two elderly conservatives, Deng Liqun and Hu Qiaomu, the campaign was actually directed as much at literature as at ideological writings. Suddenly, short stories were being scrutinized for signs of spiritual pollution, which included romance, religion, admiration of things Western and criticism of the Communist system. Although writers who were caught in such errors were heavily criticized, they were not charged with any crimes. In some jurisdictions, however, local leaders used the ideological campaign as an excuse to attack disco dancing and the cosmetics and clothing worn by young women.

At the same time, an anticrime campaign sought to

frighten average people into obeying the law by staging public executions of thieves and embezzlers. By one count, 10,000 executions resulted. The regime was clearly concerned that it was losing its hold over the people. But just as the turn to the left seemed to be going out of control, word went out that spiritual pollution applied only to ideological matters, not to literature. Deng Liqun virtually disappeared from view in April 1984.

But he returned in May 1985, indicating both the strength of the conservatives and Deng Xiaoping's own belief that the country needed some sort of value system to keep it from going off the track. In June, just as people were beginning to recover from the spiritual-pollution campaign, the *People's Daily* quoted a speech by Deng Xiaoping in which he reaffirmed that China's eventual goal must be Communism. Declared Deng: "We must certainly not allow our young people and juveniles to become prisoners of capitalist thinking. That absolutely will not do."

Since the economic reforms could not go forward, an economic retrenchment was as necessary as the ideological one. And so, as happened in late 1980, a major clampdown on the economy and on the reforms themselves was planned to begin early in 1986. Wage and price reforms would be postponed for at least a year. In the meantime, the central authorities struggled to regain control over the creation of credit. The year 1986, the Chinese were told, would be marked by "consolidation, assimilation, supplementation and improvement."

But the theorizing could continue. Premier Zhao Ziyang, who had day-to-day control over the economy, created a string of think tanks, employing the best and the brightest of China's young minds. To these people the solutions were obvious: price reform, enterprise·reform, bankruptcy laws, change-of-ownership patterns. It was largely these people whom Westerners saw when they came to China, and that is part of the reason that the

Western prognosis for the reforms was so positive. Because of the resistance of the old men, the think tankers adopted a policy of continually pushing at the margins, taking two steps forward and then one or even two steps back. But they dreamed of bolder initiatives that would cut the knot that prevented the economy from breaking free of its ties to the party and the state.

In spite of the January admonition that no new reform initiatives would be undertaken in 1986, following the April session of the National People's Congress, these economic theorists let loose a swirl of sweeping reform theories that, if implemented, might have solved the problems created by Deng's gradualism. No longer content with calling for thoroughgoing price reform or an effective enterprise bankruptcy law, Zhao's think tankers began to question some of the very tenets of Deng's Four Cardinal Principles. Among the new proposals:

• Property Rights. Under orthodox Marxism-Leninism, the state controls the means of production through government ownership of industries and agriculture. The reformers now called for new forms of ownership, including individual holdings of stock in state enterprises. Liu Guogang, an economist at the Chinese Academy of Social Sciences, wrote, "The overemphasis on state ownership was a major factor contributing to the flaws in the national economy."

• Labor Market. One basic principles of Marxist dogma is that human labor should not be treated as a commodity that can be bought and sold like other goods. But in 1986 liberal Chinese economists spoke of the need for a more fluid labor market, in which employers could bid freely for workers, in order to facilitate the transfer of "skills and specialties where they are most needed."

• Venture Capital. An equally inviolate Marxist tenet is

that capital has no value in and of itself. It is, in effect, sterile. Yet 1986 saw the creation of a company called China Venturetech, a venture-capital firm that planned to invest in microelectronics and biotechnology startups.

While Zhao's think tankers were experimenting with the economy, some interesting developments were under way in the political field. In 1980 another Deng protégé, Hu Yaobang, had taken over as General Secretary of the party. With the final ouster of Hua Guofeng as party Chairman in 1981, Hu became the effective head of the party. Not much taller than Deng, the ebullient Hu was a somewhat comic figure in Chinese eyes, but he was perhaps China's most committed modernizer. Hu had come up through the ranks of the Communist Youth League, and he maintained his sense of what it takes to capture the imagination and cooperation of young people, an important talent in a country where some 60% of the population is below the age of 30.

Hu developed his own coterie of theorists, but their emphasis was on politics, not economics. Their high water mark also came in the summer of 1986. In an effort to convince China's intellectuals that this time the regime was serious about letting them think and speak freely, Hu's top aide, Hu Qili, helped launch a 30th anniversary celebration of Mao's ill-fated 100 Flowers Campaign. Mao had encouraged intellectuals to criticize the system, but a year later arrested thousands of them for being counterrevolutionaries. Persuading them to stick their necks out a second time would not be easy, but the bravest ones accepted Hu Qili's invitation to become "the think tank of the party."

Perhaps the most incisive and daring of the theorists who joined in the discussions of this period was Su Shaozhi, head of the Institute of Marxism-Leninism Mao Zedong Thought at the Chinese Academy of Social Sciences. Su published a series of articles in the summer of

1986 that called for a complete break with the past. Su went so far as to say that instead of ending feudalism in China, the Communist Party was simply continuing that long tradition and that only bold actions could change that situation. Wrote Su: "Reform is revolution." He also posited what was known in Chinese circles as the Hungarian conclusion, that economic reform could not succeed without political reform. "The crux of the matter lies in fully carrying out inner-party democracy," said Su. "Without inner-party democracy, there can be no people's democracy, and it will be impossible to make the best democratic and scientific policy decisions for reform."

But Su, like all the theorists who published articles that summer, stopped short of calling for full-fledged Western democracy or universal suffrage. Yan Jiaqi, director of the Political Research Institute of the Chinese Academy of Social Sciences, put it this way: "The ultimate purpose of reforming the political structure is to change the situation of a highly centralized leadership system and to establish a socialist political system with a high degree of democracy and a scientific decision-making structure. At the same time, this will strengthen and improve the party's leadership." Unfortunately, not everyone in the party saw it that way.

At the time, Hu Yaobang's calls for more political pluralism and Zhao's demands for price reform and a change in enterprise ownership dovetailed perfectly. After many false starts, it appeared that China was finally on the road to true modernization. But there were still a few clouds on the horizon, the biggest being Deng's succession. Although he had anointed Hu and Zhao as the "twin pillars" who would hold up the heavens when he retired, Deng never really removed himself from the scene. His lingering presence deprived Hu and Zhao of the stature needed to hold together such a disparate political system. More important, Deng was not able to groom Hu to take over his last job of importance, chairman of the Central Military Commission.

In retrospect, it is hard to see how Deng could have sold Hu Yaobang to his comrades in the People's Liberation Army. Although Hu was a veteran of the Long March, he did not have much real military experience. In addition, Hu was the man who announced in April 1985 that the P.L.A. would have to shed 1 million troops by the end of 1986, cutting the army to a "lean" 3 million. The P.L.A. had been slighted ever since the reforms began, and Deng had accepted the military's ranking as only the third of the Four Modernizations. Western intelligence agencies estimate that the P.L.A.'s share of China's total budget dropped from one-third in 1978 to one-fifth in 1986.

Thus the stage was set for the events of the winter of 1986–87. The economic reforms had reached a point at which they would begin sliding backward if bold action were not taken. Politically, the top leadership of the party had once again encouraged intellectuals to speak their minds freely on a wide range of topics, and official theorists had at last made in public the connection between economic and political reform. But Deng's succession was clouded by his chosen heir's inability to win the confidence of the military—or by Deng's unwillingness to help win it for him. The New Year would bring turbulent times.

CHAPTER FOUR

"LONG LIVE THE STUDENTS!"

One frigid morning in early January 1987, fleets of Mercedes-Benz limousines cruised along Beijing's Fuyou Street into the walled compound of Zhongnanhai, the official seat of the party and government. Behind the cars' tinted-glass windows were top Communist Party officials who had been summoned to an emergency Politburo meeting. The session had been enlarged to include Deng Xiaoping and half a dozen other semi-retired party patriarchs. On the agenda: assigning blame for the recently suppressed student revolt.

The meeting was acrimonious. Toward the end, someone moved for a show of hands to "accept the resignation" of party General Secretary Hu Yaobang, Deng's heir apparent, who had glumly sat through the session. All but two of the 20 or so participants present raised their hands. When Hu's two lone supporters realized they were outnumbered, they held up their hands in defeat. In the face of such an emphatic rebuke, Hu stumbled out of the room, distraught and brokenhearted.

Hu was allowed to remain in the 17-member Politburo, though without a specific area of responsibility. His main fault: being too soft on "bourgeois liberalization," that catchphrase for Western political ideas and cultural values. Hu was specifically blamed for failing to prevent the waves of student demonstrations that buffeted Chinese cities from December 1986 to January 1987. Upon Hu's resignation, Premier Zhao Ziyang took over, as acting General Secretary.

Chinese students, scholars, artists and journalists, intoxicated by the air of liberalism and tolerance fostered by Hu Yaobang, had been craving political liberalization since the early 1980s. Taking subtle cues from Hu and his allies in the party, these groups put forth a breathtaking array of ideas and concepts aimed at reforming the political structure. Government think tanks, notably the Chinese Academy of Social Sciences, became bastions of doctrinal heresy under the cover of "modernizing Marxism." By late 1986 murmurs of support for pluralism, democracy and *toumingdu* (transparency) in party and government affairs had built into a loud chorus.

Leading that chorus was Fang Lizhi, a noted astrophysicist who had become world renowned for his fearless advocacy of democratization. In 1986 Fang traveled around China to speak at several major universities. Instead of lecturing on cosmology, however, he electrified youthful audiences with critiques of one-party rule and the failure of socialism in China. On Nov. 15, 1986, for instance, Fang spoke to students at Shanghai's Jiaotong (communications) University. "Something bestowed from above is not called democracy," he bellowed. "It is called loosening up. If you were tied up too tightly, say, with a noose only a foot in diameter, and it was loosened up to five feet, the noose remains around you. And who is this noose? . . . democracy is a right we are entitled to. We can achieve it only by fighting for it."

Less than a month later, tens of thousands of Chinese students took to the streets to put Fang's words into action. In a sense, their protest launched the student movement that by 1989 would capture the imagination of the world, shake the Communist government to its foundations and precipitate the massacre in Beijing.

On Dec. 1, 1986 a *dazibao* (big-character poster) appeared on the campus of the prestigious University of Science and Technology in Hefei city, Anhui province. The U.S.T., where Fang worked as vice president for student affairs and helped reform the university's management structure, is China's training ground for aspiring scientists. The poster dismissed the National People's Congress as a RUBBER STAMP OF A HANDFUL OF PEOPLE and called on Chinese to FIGHT FOR GENUINE DEMOCRACY.

Four days later, more than 4,000 students in Hefei took to the streets shouting, "Down with feudal dictatorship!," "We want democracy!" and "Long live Sun Yat-sen!" On Dec. 9, some 10,000 student marchers brandished banners with angry messages like DEMOLISH THE BASTION OF FEUDALISM and FIGHT FOR GENUINE DEMOCRACY. They gathered in front of the provincial headquarters of the Communist Party to demand reform of the election system. Along the way, residents cheered them; some even displayed homemade placards on the verandas of their homes. One sign read, LONG LIVE THE STUDENTS!

Encouraged by these actions, the Hefei students wrote messages to young people at other universities, recounting their exploits and exhorting them to join the quest for democratization. Letters and cables were exchanged. Student couriers crisscrossed the country, mostly by train, to spread the news and exchange information. *Dazibao* proliferated, and their contents were picked up and spread further by the Chinese services of the Voice of America and the British Broadcasting Corp. A poster that went up on Dec. 11 at Shanghai's Jiaotong University asked rhetorically, THE U.S.T. STUDENTS HAVE MADE THEIR MOVES—THAT SHOULD WE IN JIAODA DO? From northeastern Changchun to southwestern Guiyang, from northwestern Lanzhou to central Changsha, college students were asking themselves the same question.

The ferment spread to other cities. In Shanghai, where the biggest demonstrations erupted, the issue that sparked them was alleged police brutality at a concert by a U.S. rock group. Seven students from Jiaotong and Tongji universities were beaten after they jumped onto the stage and danced to the music of Jan and Dean (Jan Berry and Dean Torrence), a surf-sound duo known for such 1960s hits as *Dead Man's Curve* and *Surf City*.

By Dec. 15 students at Jiaotong University, where Professor Fang had spoken only a month earlier, were still angry over the incident, demanding that the offending police officers be punished and asking for other reforms. That day, more than 2,000 students packed the school's auditorium for a meeting with university chancellor Meng Shilie and his four deputies. Students took turns demanding that mandatory political courses be discontinued and that the official student union be disbanded. They called for student participation in university management, for control of the student newspaper and for public disclosure of job openings to curb "backdoorism." They pressed school authorities to acknowledge that their action was reasonable and legal and to pledge that participants would not be subject to retribution.

The ferment at Jiaotong University was only the beginning. On Dec. 18, Shanghai Mayor Jiang Zemin, a Jiaotong alumnus, returned to his alma mater in an attempt to appease the restive students. In a meeting with 3,000 of them, Jiang denied reports of police brutality and called for calm and order on the campuses. When some students cited phrases from the U.S. Declaration of Independence, Jiang glibly recited entire sections of the Declaration—in English—and wondered whether the students really grasped the spirit of the document. The engineer turned mayor lectured them on the need for order, arguing that "there is no absolute freedom anywhere in the world."

In response, the students booed and heckled Jiang, who stormed out of the auditorium. That night 6,000 students from Jiaotong and Tongji marched downtown. The next day huge contingents of students gathered in front of the city government's headquarters along the Bund, the broad avenue whose German name dates from the days when major foreign powers each had their own quarter in Shanghai. The students shouted, "Jiang Zemin, come out!" Not until midnight did the mayor agree to talk with student leaders. He refused to accept two of their demands: access to local media and agreement that the pace of China's economic reform should increase. The impasse continued.

On the afternoon of Dec. 20, 1986, more than 30,000 students from over a dozen Shanghai schools, joined by workers and teenage youths, surged along Shanghai's narrow streets to demonstrate at the People's Square, bringing downtown traffic to a halt. At night thousands of militants staged a sit-in in front of city headquarters. Although the police showed remarkable restraint, local authorities tried an array of measures to contain the uprising. Family pressure was brought to bear on the students, and some worried parents fetched their children home. School authorities dangled the threat of bad job placements after graduation. On Dec. 22, Jiang announced a ban on demonstrations.

The turmoil shifted to Beijing, where dissent had been simmering for days. *Dazibao* went up on the campuses of Peking, Qinghua and People's universities, attacking government suppression of democracy and calling for a demonstration on New Year's Day. Thus on Jan. 1, hundreds of Beijing students, defying warnings by city authorities, outwitted the police by arriving in central Tiananmen Square in small groups. Ignoring the frigid windy weather, the students mingled with thousands of tourists and promenaders on the fringes of the sprawling square, which had been cordoned off since dawn by a human wall of police. As if rehearsed, the students then assembled into small knots, heading in different directions, singing the *Internationale* and unfurling placards and banners. Thousands of onlookers cheered when one column managed to breach the wall of police and make it into the square. But before they could occupy the Monument to the People's Heroes, burly policemen chased, tackled and roughed them up on the icy pavement; 53 students were detained.

When news of the arrests reached Peking University late that night, 4,000 students marched out of the campus in protest. Braving a storm that left two inches of snow, they plodded toward Tiananmen Square, bellowing, "Return our fellow students!" Midway through the twelve-mile trek, a university vice chancellor intercepted the march to announce over a loudspeaker that all the detained students had been released into the custody of university authorities and had returned to the campus. He urged the marchers to board the waiting buses hired by the school to ferry them back. It was 1:30 a.m. All but 400 of the exhausted, hungry and frigid marchers opted to go back. The stragglers pressed on, reaching Tiananmen at 3 a.m. They were taken back by Peking University buses at 5 a.m.

All told, more than 150 universities and colleges in 17 cities were hit by student activism from September 1986 to Jan. 15, 1987. The issues ranged from the mundane—bad but costly cafeteria food, cramped and dimly lighted dormitory rooms—to the philosophical: academic freedom and democracy. Many of the protesters had only hazy ideas of what they were agitating for, but they knew what they were against: corruption and nepotism in the party and government, unequal opportunities for jobs and promotions, outdated teaching methods, rising prices and inflation. Weeks later, a history lecturer at Peking

University observed, "Tactically, the students should have hammered away at the [issue of] rising prices. That way, they would have attracted angry workers, and urbanites would have greatly swollen their ranks." Moreover, the students' élitism lost them some popular support. Said the lecturer: "They shouted slogans like 'Long live democracy!' that were too nebulous for the ordinary workers. Besides, they appeared flippant and haughty by shouting 'Long live the students!' "

Ironically, the students' agitation for freedom merely curtailed what little freedom Chinese intellectuals previously enjoyed. A few days before Hu Yaobang was publicly sacked, three outspoken intellectuals—Fang Lizhi, muckraking *People's Daily* writer Liu Binyan, and Shanghai-based writer Wang Ruowang—were expelled from the Communist Party and publicly pilloried for spearheading the wave of "bourgeois liberalization." Conservatives subsequently launched a purge of Hu's followers in the party and state bureaucracy.

An ideological chill set in. Hard-line party apparatchiks seized control of the propaganda machine and ordered party-controlled media to hew more strictly to the canons of ideological purity and political uniformity. Literature and art turned turgid and predictable again. The writings of Freud and D.H. Lawrence were dismissed as "bourgeois liberalism," for instance, and exposés of social ills were criticized as "dwelling on the dark side of socialism."

Chinese universities reintroduced ideological indoctrination courses. To supplement book learning, the Cultural Revolution–era practice of sending college students to work on farms and factories for re-education through labor was initiated again, though students were sent for much shorter periods of stay—typically for one or two months. Authorities revived the long-discarded "Learn from Lei Feng" campaign, so named after an obscure 1950s and '60s soldier whom Mao had beatified as a paragon of Communist virtues. Under the campaign, Chinese were exhorted to be modern-day Lei Fengs, imbued with the self-sacrificing spirit of "a never rusting screw in the revolutionary machine." Indeed, the Four Cardinal Principles—socialism, the dictatorship of the proletariat, the leadership of the Communist Party, and Marxism-Leninism–Mao Zedong Thought—were revived and prescribed as an antidote to the virus of "bourgeois liberalization."

To remove any doubts that Deng Xiaoping himself was behind the anti–bourgeois liberalization campaign, the conservatives dusted off a 1984 speech by the leader lambasting advocates of "bourgeois liberalization" and had it published in the *People's Daily*. In the speech, Deng called for a protracted struggle against deviation from Marxist thinking.

Under pressure from the conservatives, Deng grew more cautious on the economic front. Price reform, which his government had characterized in a 1984 document as the core of urban reform, was suspended. Thus planners in cereal-producing regions were again allowed to set ceilings on the price of grain purchased from local markets. Authorities in big cities like Beijing and Shanghai reimposed ceilings on retail prices of major nonstaple food items like meat and eggs. Deng was afraid that soaring prices could spark urban revolt. During the crisis, he drew parallels between the Chinese student protests and the Polish Solidarity movement of the early 1980s, concluding that student ferment must be headed off before it spread among the working class. What he feared most during the unrest in Beijing and Shanghai was a possible alliance between the discontented workers and the intelligentsia—and thus a full-fledged urban uprising.

Zhao did his utmost to limit the scope of the conservative campaign. "Beyond the three intellectuals being criticized, no more comrades will be named," he declared in response to calls for more scapegoats. At the annual meeting of the People's Congress in March 1987, he warned against "stifling democracy on the pretext of opposing bourgeois liberalization." He assured Hong Kong and Macao delegates to the parliament that the anti-liberalization campaign would not last more than a few months. Indeed, as summer approached, the conservative chill started to dissipate. Zhao and his reformist faction appeared to be winning.

Deng Xiaoping, the ever pragmatic helmsman, was slyly tilting from the left back to the middle road. Obviously concerned that the conservative, or "leftist," revival was putting his reform program in serious jeopardy, the leader in May 1987 declared his opposition to both "deviation toward wholesale Westernization" and "leftist inertia." Deng gave his full backing to Zhao.

In the autumn of 1987, Zhao and his reformers made a strong comeback. He presided over the 13th Party Congress and established himself as Deng's likely successor. Deng and Zhao spoke about the need for political reform, for democratization and even for *toumingdu* in official matters. They skillfully maneuvered the retirement or semiretirement from the Central Committee of a cabal of staunch hard-liners, including veteran economist Chen Yun, State President Li Xiannian and People's Congress Chairman Peng Zhen. These old fogies were replaced by a group of reform-minded technocrats. Zhao was formally installed as party General Secretary and first vice chairman of the Central Military Commission. As a tactic to force geriatric politicians to step down, Deng himself retired from all his posts except the chairmanship of the Central Military Commission.

Despite Zhao's political coups, he was failing in his efforts to revive the economy. The nation suffered from stagnation in agriculture, mounting budget deficits and soaring inflation. In December 1987, Beijing reimposed rationing of pork, sugar and eggs in such major cities as Beijing, Shanghai and Tianjin, a move that shook public confidence in economic reform. In a survey conducted in Tianjin city in early 1987, residents were asked about their willingness to tolerate price reform. More than two-thirds of the respondents said price hikes had adversely affected their enthusiasm for work, and 56% said the "superiority of socialism" was only evident when commodity prices were stable. Many of them expressed a preference that wages and prices be left alone. In the words of a popular refrain: "We'd rather have the stable prices of Chairman Mao than the high wages of Deng Xiaoping."

Nearly a year later, the economy was still failing to show signs of recovery. As top party leaders met in the seaside resort of Beidaihe in the summer of 1988 to discuss inflation and price hikes, major cities experienced bank runs and panic buying of sugar, eggs, meat and even top-brand cigarettes and wines. Zhao's big gamble on price reform had failed. That summer, he was reportedly divested of responsibility over the economy. Conservative technocrats took over, men like Li Peng, 58, who formally replaced Zhao as Premier in November, and senior Vice Premier Yao Yilin, a protégé of central planning expert Chen Yun. Blamed for the economic mess, Zhao found himself in a precarious political position.

Zhao's setbacks on the economic front predictably compounded the seething discontent among dispossessed city dwellers—students and teachers, office workers, factory workers and retired cadres. On public buses and in barbershops, classrooms and offices, they complained openly about spiraling prices, nepotism, graft and profiteering—or *guandao* (official corruption), in the current parlance. Citizens expressed their discontent, cynicism and insecurities through wildcat labor strikes, work slowdowns, soccer riots, vandalism, absenteeism or by simply shouting at one another at the slightest provocation.

As in the past, Chinese campuses became cauldrons of dissent and discontent. At the top of the intellectuals' list of complaints was the near bankrupt education system. A college professor earned 200 yuan ($70) a month less than a taxi driver, who earns roughly 400 yuan ($140). Some teachers were forced to moonlight to make ends meet. Elementary schoolteachers in Shanghai sold ice cream to their pupils in class. A Chinese newspaper wondered whether "by doing so the teachers were forfeiting the pupils' respect." Yang Futai, an associate professor at Henan Teachers College in Zhengzhou, central China, solved his financial quandary by selling pancakes at the school gate right after his last class. His moonlighting brought him as much as $8 a day. Thus in five days, he could double his monthly salary earned as a professor. Even scientists who work in nuclear-weapons-production facilities earned less than vendors who sold *chayidan,* eggs boiled in tea.

As the economic crisis worsened, farmers began pulling their children from school to help out on the farm or to work as apprentices in factories and on construction projects. More than 40 million such pupils were reported to have "disappeared" this way in 1986-87. People no longer found educating their children to be a worthwhile investment. "Nowadays illiterates become millionaires," reported Shanghai's *Wenhui Daily* last April. "The Confucian saying 'Study to become an official' has now been revised to mean 'Study to become a pauper.'"

Meanwhile, a crisis of faith in Marxism gripped college campuses. Students complained that they did not find Marx's dictums relevant to their lives or their futures. Some even refused to attend mandatory Marxism classes because they were simply too boring and did not answer their questions about the relationship of the theory to their lives. What had filled the spiritual vacuum? Said Fang Lizhi, in a March 1989 interview with TIME: "The only thing for them is money, money, money. I think in a way this is good because it shows they have lost their belief in Marxism. But any good society should have some belief."

On the surface, students acted apathetic and even apolitical, dismissing any serious political discussions as empty talk. "This burned-out generation of college students learned the bitter lesson that politics is a dangerous game," said a graduate student in Peking University's philosophy department. "They are mostly junior and senior undergraduates who took part in the 1986 demos." In a clever play of words in Chinese, the graduate student categorized them into *pai* (factions)—the *tuopai*, who did little but study for their exams; the *mapai*, who fritter away their time playing mah-jongg; the *wupai*, who dance away the boring hours; and the *jiupai*, who simply drown their cares in liquor. "On the surface these students are politically passive," the graduate student noted. "But actually they are just as politically conscious as I am. Their passive protest is just the flipside of open activism."

In the first few months of 1989, Beijing's intelligentsia came out of hibernation. Fang Lizhi sent an open letter to Deng Xiaoping calling for amnesty for political prisoners and for the release of Democracy Wall activist Wei Jingsheng. A number of prominent dissidents gathered for a "neo-Enlightenment salon" at the Dule bookstore, the only privately owned book emporium in Beijing. Among those present were Fang Lizhi, Marxist theoretician Su Shaozhi and writer-theoretician Wang Ruoshui, a former deputy editor of *People's Daily* who was dismissed in 1983 for holding the view that alienation exists not only in capitalism but also in socialism.

At Peking University, a core of student activists kept up the ferment. History major Wang Dan, 24, presided over a "democratic salon." Participants would usually squat in circles on the lawn of a small park on the Peking University campus to hear speeches and discuss social or political issues. Speakers included Fang, his physicist wife Li Shuxian, then U.S. Ambassador Winston Lord and his wife, writer Betty Bao Lord. Wang Dan's group organized 17 democracy-salon sessions. Through student networks like Wang's, activists were planning a major demonstration at the university to commemorate the 70th anniversary of the May 4th Movement, the student-led protest against foreign domination and in favor of "Mr. Democracy" and "Mr. Science."

Peking University was typically placid on the afternoon of April 15, 1989. Because it was a Saturday, most of the students had gone home, and those who had not were taking their usual *xiuxi* (afternoon nap) in their cramped and dingy dormitories. "A classmate barged in our room and broke the bad news," recalled Jiang Liren, 18, a freshman in the economics department. Hu Yaobang, the former party General Secretary, had died that morning after suffering a heart attack. Jiang and his schoolmates had virtually worshiped Hu as a friend of the students and a champion of reform. "We were dumbfounded," Jiang said. "Someone suggested that we put up a poster, so we rummaged for paper, ink and brush and wrote down our thoughts."

The hub of ferment at Peking University was the *sanjiaodi*, or triangle area, a precinct surrounded by shops and dormitories. There, more than 100 *dazibao* went up on walls and bulletin boards. That night hundreds of students and teachers, some carrying flashlights, crowded in the dark to read the posters. Many laboriously copied the words on pieces of paper or in notebooks; others read them aloud into portable tape recorders, either for posterity or for mass dissemination.

Some of the *dazibao* were short and blunt. GRIEF, read a one-character poster written on a large white piece of paper. Others were solemn poetry, couplets in classical Chinese written in prescribed meters and rhymes. One striking theme in the posters was that the wrong leader had passed away. THOSE WHO OUGHT TO LIVE HAVE

DIED, read one. THOSE WHO OUGHT TO DIE. . . . Others expressed guilt that they failed to avert Hu's downfall in 1987. WHEN YOU WERE DEPRIVED OF YOUR POST, WHY DIDN'T WE STAND UP? read one. WE FEEL REMORSEFUL. OUR CONSCIENCE BLEEDS.

During the next few days, thousands of students, teachers and workers flocked to the *sanjiaodi* to read the posters and discuss what Hu's death meant for China's quest for democracy and modernization. On the evening of April 16, about 300 students converged on Tiananmen Square to lay funeral wreaths in Hu's memory, as police stood idly by. It was a precedent-setting breach of a government-imposed ban on demonstrations. Finally, the 160,000 students at Beijing's roughly 60 colleges and universities were beginning to awake from their ostensible apathy.

On April 17, a poster went up in the *sanjiaodi* announcing the plan by yet unidentified student organizers to procure a large wreath to lay at Tiananmen. The poster called for monetary donations to buy the wreath and black armbands. Minutes after it went up, an anonymous donor left two 10-yuan bills under the poster. More money poured into the donation boxes. At the nearby People's University, members of an obscure group called the New Thinking Society openly solicited donations at the school's main gate, where members set up a donation box adorned with Hu's funeral portrait.

That evening, just before midnight, more than 4,000 students from Peking University and the People's University marched out of their campuses and set off on a twelve-mile march to the square. Holding hands and linking arms, the young people walked through the night, chanting patriotic slogans and singing the *Internationale*. Hundreds of Beijing residents joined the procession on their bicycles. But police did not attempt to stop them.

The main attraction was a 20-foot-long white sheet of cloth held aloft by a dozen men as if they were pallbearers. Splashed on it in big black characters: CHINA'S SOUL. "I did the calligraphy," a Peking University lecturer and highly respected calligrapher volunteered proudly. "The style was meant to show sorrow and strength." When foot-weary mourners reached the square at 4 a.m., they surged triumphantly toward the Monument to the People's Heroes, around which they laid a dozen new wreaths (those left behind the day before had been cleared away by police). To the loud cheers of the marchers, four nimble young men scaled the monument to drape it with the CHINA'S SOUL banner. The sun was rising by the time they decided to leave the square and head back to the campus.

For the next five days, until Hu's funeral on April 22, the students continued making speeches, writing posters, staging sit-ins and marching. Their numbers swelled as students from other colleges joined in. At each turn of events, the indecision and successive blunders of the Beijing authorities served only to widen the movement.

Just past midnight on April 20, for example, a few thousand students moved from the square to stage a sit-in in front of Zhongnanhai, the official party headquarters and residence. "Come out, Li Peng!" they chanted in front the ornate Xinhua Gate. When a group of protesters tried to carry a wreath past policemen guarding the gate, scuffles ensued. The police charged on the hapless students, pouncing with sticks and leather belts. Eyewitnesses said scores of demonstrators were seriously injured and at least one was arrested. But the following day, the official Xinhua News Agency blamed the incident on student "troublemakers" and reported that four soldiers were injured. No student injuries were mentioned.

The students were furious at the report, and on the morning of Hu's funeral, tens of thousands of them gathered in Tiananmen Square. They carried huge streamers calling for democracy and for Hu's rehabilitation. A huge tapestry of Hu's visage, appropriately clad in Western suit and necktie, hung from the Monument to the People's Heroes. Inside the Great Hall of the People, 4,000 invited officials listened to party chief Zhao Ziyang deliver a glowing eulogy to the fallen leader. Deng Xiaoping attended the 40-minute funeral, which was broadcast live on radio and television. Yet it was clear to those in the hall that the effusive praise being heaped on Hu was a gesture meant chiefly for the protesters in the square.

But the students remained unassuaged. That afternoon, right after the memorial meeting, thousands of them surged toward the Great Hall, where Hu's body lay in state. Three student representatives went down on their knees on the steps of the Great Hall, pleading symbolically for a government leader to talk with them, specifically Premier Li Peng. The request was turned down. As a conciliatory gesture, the three were allowed into the hall to join Hu's wake, and a low-ranking official accepted a petition from them. The document asked for, among other things, Hu's formal rehabilitation and publication of the "real story" of the April 20 Xinhua Gate clash.

The latest wave of campus discontent in Beijing quickly spread across the country. Huge rallies erupted in Shanghai, Nanjing and Guangzhou in support of the Beijing students. In the city of Changsha in central Hunan province, Hu Yaobang's birthplace, 65 people were arrested after a demonstration by a motley crowd memorializing Hu turned into a rampage of looting and rioting. In the ancient capital city of Xian, Shaanxi province, a 24-hour curfew was imposed in the city proper after rioters burned vehicles and ransacked shops and offices.

Beijing's student activists, whom authorities expected to troop back to their classrooms after Hu's funeral, remained on the streets. Indeed, they had practically commandeered Tiananmen Square. They also captured the leadership of the "official" student union. Embryonic organizations clumsily called "student autonomous union preparatory committees" started to proliferate on local campuses. The students also changed their tactics: instead of merely mourning Hu, they now demanded a reassessment of the December 1986 student movement and the rejection of the conservative "bourgeois liberalization" campaign of 1987. But those demands were too politically sensitive to receive a fair hearing at this point.

The authorities continued their inflammatory ways. One major provocation was a *People's Daily* editorial on April 26 warning of a "planned conspiracy" by "people with ulterior motives" who wished to "poison people's minds, create national turmoil and sabotage the nation's stability." The editorial was lifted from a Deng Xiaoping speech at a Politburo meeting the day before. The warning, obviously intended to frighten the protesters, had the opposite effect. "The editorial was an outrage," a Peking University student said. "Its verbiage sounded like a Cultural Revolution tirade."

After lengthy debate, student leaders decided to call Deng's bluff by organizing a gigantic march the following day. On the eve of the action, many of the more energetic young rebels prepared for what they thought could be a final conflict. They wrote down their "last will," exchanged "farewell toasts" and shared a "last supper."

The next day more than 100,000 students descended on Tiananmen Square. They were joined by nearly 1 million Beijing residents. It was the biggest antigovernment demonstration in the 40-year history of the People's Republic. Singing China's national anthem, *March of the Volunteers,* and the *Internationale,* the students marched through the streets of Beijing for 17 hours, shouting calls for democratic reform, press freedom, *toumingdu* and an end to abuses by officials.

The students' persistence must have caught Deng by surprise. Several thousand police and army troops had been mobilized that day. But the security forces seemed helpless as people poured out of their homes and offices to root for the demonstrators. With the soldiers putting up only token resistance, the protesters broke through a series of police blockades, chanting victoriously, "The people's police love the people."

That night a poster went up in a Peking University dormitory: HISTORY WILL FOREVER REMEMBER APRIL 27! Recalled Jiang Liren, the freshman economics student: "The scene of our return to the campus was so unforgettably moving. We were welcomed with cheers and firecrackers." After a few hours of sleep, Jiang and his five roommates huddled in their dormitory room to talk about the day's events. "We were pooped and hungry," said Ruan Libing, 18, a lanky economics major. "But we were exhilarated. Breaching the police blockades was victory in itself."

Jiang and Ruan typified college students in China in 1989. They were in their late teens or early 20s, bright, fearless, brimming with enthusiasm—but, until recently, studiously apolitical. They were the cream of a small crop. Only 1% of Chinese high school students go to college. Every summer nearly 3 million high school graduates sweat through a rigorous national entrance exam, and only 25% of them qualify for a place in a university.

During the Maoist era, college students were culled from the ranks of workers, peasants and soldiers. They were chosen less for their academic potential than for their sound revolutionary background, rich social experience and high political enthusiasm. Not anymore. Today's students are mostly "three door" youngsters—those who have breezed through the doors of the elementary school, high school and college without stopping to gain work experience.

For the past four decades under the Communist regime, college education has been completely subsidized on egalitarian grounds by the government. Owing to tight state funding, however, even premiere institutions like

Peking University have suffered. China's equivalent of Harvard or Oxford and Cambridge, Peking prides itself on having the country's best teachers, the brightest students and the most beautiful campus, the centerpiece of which is a tree-lined man-made lagoon. However, Peking's classrooms, laboratories and dormitories are decrepit, dank and dirty. Jiang and his five roommates, for example, shared a tiny cubicle cramped with a table, two chairs and three double-deck bunk beds. A communal toilet on each floor was perpetually cluttered with laundry and stank of urine.

In principle, college education is free. Each student is even given a monthly stipend of 17 yuan ($5.60) for their food and other daily necessities. With the inflation of the 1980s, however, that was barely enough to cover two weeks of meals in the subsidized student cafeteria. Thus most students are forced to seek extra funds from their parents. "It's tough to study in this cramped environment," Jiang complained. "But what can we do? The state has no money."

For Jiang and his contemporaries, a more serious problem is the Chinese system itself. Jiang explained, "Our lives are determined by the college entrance exam and job placement after graduation." Jiang is fearful that he may be assigned for life to a job he does not like. On April 13, three days before the start of the 1989 unrest, the State Education Commission dropped a plan to allow college graduates to seek their own jobs.

Traditionally, Chinese students, and youth in general, have been looked up to by society as the "pillars of China's future." Considered to be more open than their elders to new ideas, they are praised by some for their boldness and condemned by others for their naiveté. Campus activism has a rich prerevolutionary history in China, and student movements are taken more seriously than those in many Western countries. Like many 1980s students, however, Jiang was hardly a militant.

"I was a happy-go-lucky boy," said Jiang, son of medical doctors in Inner Mongolia. "In high school I hated my classes and spent a lot of time watching video movies and reading kung fu novels." When Jiang enrolled at Peking University as a freshman in 1988, he was "a blank piece of paper," he recalled, "ignorant of a lot of things." Now he describes himself as "agitated by social discontent. Sometimes I do get carried away and do extremist things, but I've been maturing." Jiang insisted that his activism was not aimed at toppling socialism or the Communist Party. "I am a sincere admirer of the party," he said solemnly. "I idolize it just as Christians do their religion. If China must install an ideology, and we really need to reinstall one, we need not turn to any religion. We should rely on the party." He said he intended to fill out his application form for party membership as soon as the protests die down. "I think I'll qualify."

The day after the April 27 march, Peking University was awash in euphoria. "Everybody stood firm under extreme pressure, and that was quite an achievement," declared Chai Ling, 23, the intense young woman who went on to become the students' overall commander in Tiananmen Square on the eve of the June 3-4 massacre. "We also succeeded in forging close links with the city residents." An alumnus of Peking University and, at the time of the protests, a graduate student in child psychology at Beijing Normal University, Chai noted that "people have shown open support by clapping, cheering, flashing V signs and donating bread, drinks, candies and cigarettes."

Fresh posters in the *sanjiaodi* assured participants in the march that THE PEOPLE'S REPUBLIC WILL FOREVER REMEMBER YOU. Budding historians had already posted "A Road Map of the April 27 Peaceful Demonstration," tracing the route of the march. Beside it was a copy of the sheet music for a newly composed hymn, *Peking Univer-*

sity Pledge. A stanza reads, "Fear not, fear not, to shed blood for the people, fear not. . . . To demonstrate in our quest for people's rights, to oppose corruption and *guandao,* advance, fear not, fear not!"

Han Liang, graduate student in geology and a veteran of two previous student movements, in 1985 and in 1986-87, was more cautious. "We should move step by step," he advised. "Our main direction—achieving freedom, democracy and a legal system—remains unchanged, but we must have specific plans. Nevertheless, we must realize these can't be completely achieved in ten or even 20 years. That would be unrealistic. The weight of traditional ideas, especially of feudalism, is simply too onerous."

Despite such voices of sobriety, the bulk of the student movement was feeling a new aggressiveness as the long awaited May 4th anniversary celebration drew near. Seventy years earlier, the first Chinese student demonstration had burst from Peking University, aimed at pressuring the Chinese government to repudiate the Treaty of Versailles, which handed the port city of Qingdao to the Japanese, and to rid China of feudalism. By coincidence, on May 4, 1989, Beijing was the site of the Asian Development Bank's annual meeting at the cavernous Great Hall of the People. With so many foreign officials in town, the authorities would find it difficult to crack down on the students. So the government this time adopted a softer, more conciliatory line. "I hope there will be no mass demonstration," said government spokesman Yuan Mu. "I trust that those students will take conscious steps to maintain order and ensure the smooth progress of the A.D.B. meeting and the May 4th activities."

On the eve of the anniversary, Yuan and other government leaders held several televised meetings with the students but made no progress in resolving the crisis. Reason: they talked only with leaders of the moderate, government-recognized student union, which the protest-

ers had repudiated. Uerkesh Daolet (Wuer Kaixi), who
had just been elected president of an independent student
union, walked out midway through the session, declaring
that no dialogue was possible until the government recognized the legitimacy of his organization.

The *People's Daily* editorial had thrown Beijing into
an uproar, drawing fire not only from students but also
from the staff of the newspaper, high-level party cadres
and even the Beijing police officials who had been designated to suppress the demonstrations. Suddenly aware of
the wellspring of popular support the students enjoyed,
Zhao Ziyang, who had just returned from an official visit
to North Korea, proposed a change of tactics. "He was
the first to question the tone of the editorial, saying it was
too harsh and the conclusion was not right," said President Yang Shangkun in a secret speech to an emergency
meeting of the Central Military Commission. In public,
Zhao was also conciliatory. "Reasonable demands from
the students should be met through democratic and legal
means," he told a delegation of A.D.B. governors.
Leaked party documents later revealed that Deng considered Zhao's A.D.B. speech a "turning point" in that it
exposed different views within the Standing Committee
to the students. Zhao's tone, and the implied guarantee of
continued police leniency, effectively robbed the anniversary march of the lure of suspense and potential violence.
The pull of home and holiday likewise reduced the
marchers' ranks. Some parents forcibly brought their
children home for fear that the youngsters' careers would
be ruined if the students marched. Among them was Peking University's Jiang Liren, whose parents returned
him to Inner Mongolia.

When 60,000 students and supporters flooded back
into the Tiananmen area on May 4, the crowd was clearly
smaller and less spirited than that of the previous week.
The army and police again were unarmed and put up
only desultory resistance. "We've won!" exclaimed an

elated demonstrator upon reaching Tiananmen Square for the sixth time in three weeks. He joined other comrades in posing for souvenir photos against the backdrops of the Tiananmen rostrum and the Monument to the People's Heroes.

The students were joined by another group of marchers. Some 300 Chinese journalists from a dozen party-controlled media swelled the ranks to protest news censorship. DON'T FORCE US TO TELL LIES, read one banner. WE TOO HAVE OUR CONSCIENCE, said another. Students had earlier berated the press, especially the official outlets, for incomplete, inaccurate and distorted reports of student activities since Hu Yaobang's death. CCTV SAYS BLACK IS WHITE, read a poster at Peking University, with a drawing of an inverted TV set. A student chanted, "Xinhua News Agency makes nonsense!"

While the protesters invariably welcomed the foreign media, they shunned local journalists. "We'd go and cover an event, and the students would push and shove us, or even hit our cameras, as if we were plainclothes policemen," complained Che Fei, a reporter for the English service of China's national television. "It's very frustrating." Said Chen Zongshun, a correspondent for *Worker's Daily:* "We believe that truthfully reporting our problems is the best step toward solving them. We can't solve our problems if we can't even write about them."

During the first five months of 1989, two newspapers that wrote about society's problems were punished. Authorities impounded editions of the *Science and Technology Daily,* which carried extensive reports about the student movement during and after Hu Yaobang's funeral. In late May, Qin Benli, the editor of the liberal Shanghai-based weekly *World Economic Herald,* was sacked, and the publication was revamped by apparatchiks. Jiang Zemin, who had been elected Shanghai party chief, dismissed Qin for trying to run a six-page tribute to Hu. As a result of such actions, more than 1,000 journalists

signed a petition demanding press freedom and a "dialogue" with the leadership.

At the end of the May 4 march, student leaders Uerkesh Daolet and Wang Dan announced the end of the
two-week boycott of classes, partly in recognition of the
student movement's loss of momentum. "It's not over,
said one student. "We will do more public relations work,
but the stage of confronting the government is over."

A public relations opportunity quickly presented itself. With a big handshake in front of the cameras, Soviet
leader Mikhail Gorbachev and his host Deng Xiaoping
agreed on May 15 that "the problem of the past should
be gone with the wind." Thus as journalists from around
the world looked on, the two major reformers of the
Communist world ended 30 years of enmity between
their countries. For the students, it was an opportunity to
show the international press that new winds of change
were blowing in China.

In the days before Gorbachev's visit, student organizers began filling Tiananmen Square with increasingly
larger crowds of protesters. Foreign TV crews, on hand
for the diplomatic visit, could not miss them. On May 17
more than 1 million people took to the streets. Their banners, many of them now written in English and other foreign languages, paid homage to Western slogans. I HAVE
A DREAM, read one. WE ARE THE WORLD, declared a
banner hoisted by students of the Central Minorities Institute. A cruising Beijing taxi flew a huge white bedsheet
fastened to a bamboo pole and painted with perhaps the
only English word its driver knew: TAXI.

In addition to discovering the power of the international press, the students also discovered a powerful new
weapon to use against the authorities: the hunger strike.
Before long, 3,000 students in Tiananmen Square were

fasting. The square became a virtual field hospital as doctors and medical students dispensed glucose and tended to the increasingly weakened strikers. By the sixth day of the protest, more than 2,000 had collapsed from exhaustion and dehydration and were rushed to hospitals. In a move to escalate the crisis, a group of students from the Central Drama Institute refused to take even water. After 59 hours, doctors monitoring the health of students worried about how much longer they could last. Hysterical parents came to plead with their children to end the strike and to ask the government to meet the students' demands. Rumors spread that one of the strikers had died. Although it was soon proved untrue, student leaders began to be concerned that the protest might actually cost lives.

Wang Yan, 18, a freshman sociology major from Peking University, was among the hunger strikers. "The government stinks," said Wang, a young woman from central Jiangxi province. "Our demands are not excessive, but the authorities chose to resort to dilatory tactics. We have no other recourse." That afternoon Wang joined her fellow activists in reciting a hunger strike oath. In front of the Monument to the People's Heroes and within sight of Mao Zedong's Tomb, students raised their right hands, fists clenched, and pledged to "fast voluntarily with the aim of enhancing the process of democratization and the prosperity of the nation."

They vowed not to take any solids, and to desist from smoking. "We're going to stick to it right through to the end," they said repeatedly. Several minutes after the fasting commenced, however, a student marshal walked up with a pack of Marlboros; thereupon, several of the smokers among the strikers surged forward to take a cigarette or two. But what about their earlier no-smoking pledge? "It has just been revoked," replied a striker, matter-of-factly.

Meanwhile, the chaos on the square was giving way to rudimentary order. Using nylon packing string, student marshals cordoned off the hunger strikers and laid out a maze of roads for ambulances and delivery trucks to navigate the crowded square. The students also devised a system of passes to keep unauthorized people from entering *neibu* (internal) areas, such as those where leaders huddled over strategy and tactics or where they held press conferences.

To pre-empt government attempts to brand them as unpatriotic, the students repeatedly sang the national anthem and the *Internationale*. They hoisted banners proclaiming support for the Communist Party. They quoted Mao Zedong: "Whoever opposes the student movement will come to no good end!" They even recited a recent quotation from Deng to chide his obvious inconsistency: "A revolutionary party is a party that listens to the people, not one that keeps them silent."

Sympathetic workers brought in scaffolding and tarpaulins to put up makeshift tents. Around the Monument to the People's Heroes, students set up a battery-operated radio station, using several locally made Feiyue-brand amplifiers and speakers—donations from private enterprises—thus allowing amateur broadcasters and commentators to deliver their speeches. In one corner of the square, students turned out flyers from a rudimentary print shop. In another corner, a finance section handled contributions of cash and materials from home and abroad. At the height of the protests, the students said they were receiving tens of thousands of dollars a day.

The movement's most onerous challenge was to provide food, water and other daily necessities. Bread, pickled vegetables and soft drinks, largely donated, were distributed twice a day to protesters with student IDs. Olive-green and blue cotton-padded jackets and woolen blankets, some donated by sympathizers, others brought in by the city government, were issued to the protesters to shield them from the chill of late-spring nights.

Indeed, the scene in the square reminded some foreigners of Woodstock in 1969. Under the bright moon at night, weary, scruffy-looking students—some bundled in blankets and overcoats, other draped in plastic sheets—lay sprawled on the cold pavement, often in groups of eight and ten, curled close to one another. Those who remained awake read English textbooks, played cards or chess or sang Chinese pop songs to the accompaniment of a guitar.

Moved perhaps by the self-sacrifice of the hunger strikers, Beijing residents shook off their usual torpor and selfishness to show support. They flashed the ubiquitous V signs at the students, applauded and shouted slogans, dropped cash into donation boxes and tossed the students ice cream and cigarettes. Ice cream and soft-drink vendors around the square often declined payment from the strikers. Beijing taxi drivers, notorious for their greediness, reportedly offered to ferry stranded marchers to and from the square free of charge. The city's newly rich private entrepreneurs formed the "Flying Tigers," a 2,000-strong force of motorbikes that circled Beijing, delivering news to the residents and collecting intelligence for the student protesters.

Even the city's manners improved. Almost overnight, the generally brash and surly residents of Beijing became polite and considerate. In a mob of nonstudents crowded behind a roadblock in northeastern Beijing, a man unintentionally stepped on the foot of another resident. "Sorry, sorry," he apologized profusely. "I'm really sorry." But his victim gallantly intoned, "In this time of crisis, it's not necessary to say 'I'm sorry.'"

Seriously split over how to deal with the students, the Communist leadership dithered. Throughout Gorbachev's three-day stay in Beijing, feuding Chinese leaders dashed from protocol-imposed events, smiling and shaking hands with Soviet guests in front of 1,000 foreign and local reporters, into tense meetings to discuss the protest. Zhao Ziyang, still precariously clinging to his post, lobbied for a softer approach in dealing with the students. He suggested, for instance, that his Politburo colleagues renounce the April 26 *People's Daily* editorial. At an expanded Politburo meeting on May 15, however, the Old Guard voted down his proposal. "We cannot retreat," Deng said at the meeting. "One retreat will lead to another." Yang, perhaps Deng's closest ally at this point, chimed in, "We cannot retreat. Retreat means the dam will burst open. The entire front will collapse."

At a meeting of the Politburo's five-member Standing Committee the following day, Zhao again proposed taking a lenient approach toward the students, offering a dialogue with them and an investigation into reports of profiteering by top leaders and their families, including his own. Again, he was voted down, this time 4 to 1. Zhao offered to resign, but that move was rejected for fear of making him a hero and further shoring up his popularity. Later that day, Zhao met Gorbachev and deliberately took advantage of the live television coverage to reveal that it was Deng, not he, who was the top decision maker in the party by virtue of a secret resolution passed by the hierarchy when they accepted Deng's formal retirement in 1987 from all but the Central Military Commission post. "On major issues Deng is still our main helmsman," Zhao told Gorbachev. Deng's supporters resented the move. President Yang charged that Zhao's words were "designed to shirk responsibility by bringing comrade Xiaoping out in the open, as if to say all the wrongs came from him."

Gorbachev's flight home was barely off the ground when the Politburo Standing Committee convened another emergency session to decide how to end the student revolt. Li Peng advocated a crackdown. Zhao was the sole dissenter. When a second vote was taken, he was joined by party Propaganda Chief Hu Qili, with Qiao Shi abstaining. Nonetheless, Zhao was still in the minority.

Shortly after the meeting, Zhao, Li and several other top leaders made one small gesture of conciliation by traveling to two Beijing hospitals to visit hunger strikers. Lying in hospital beds, listless protesters reiterated to the officials that the students were not out to topple the Communist Party but merely hoped to hasten reform and curb graft and corruption. One student challenged the visiting leaders to fight corruption and to "start with your own sons." Curiously, the students asked Zhao, Li and the other leaders for their autographs.

After their hospital visit, the leaders were originally scheduled to meet with the student representatives, but Zhao inexplicably never showed up. That left Li Peng, who was already set to declare martial law, to preside over an acrimonious "dialogue." In the Great Hall of the People late in the morning of May 18, Li and a battery of Chinese leaders sat down with a dozen representatives from the illegal student union. The students were represented by Uerkesh, who came directly from the hospital clad in striped pajamas, and Wang Dan in a televised confrontation.

Li was obviously not happy to be there. Sitting nervously on a sofa, he delivered a long lecture on why the students should stop their strike. "Beijing is now on the brink of anarchy," he said, raising his raspy voice. He noted that the unrest had also spread to other cities. "We meet today to talk only about one matter: how to save the hunger strikers outside," he said curtly. Uerkesh cut in, "We don't have much time to listen to you, Premier Li. Thousands of hunger strikers are waiting. Let's get to the substantial points. It is we who invited you to talk, not you who invited us. We are just as eager to let students leave the square." But he stressed that the government must first acknowledge that the prodemocracy movement is patriotic and must retract the offensive April 26 *People's Daily* editorial. A few minutes later, midway through the talks, Uerkesh fainted, and white-robed doctors rushed to his aid, complete with an oxygen tank, while the TV cameras rolled on.

Although Li pledged that "we've always deemed your patriotism positively," he failed to give a clear assurance that there would be no retributions later. Hinting a crackdown, he boomed, "We cannot but defend the society, public property and personal safety." Agitated, he warned the students "not to misinterpret the action [i.e., the support] of the workers and other sectors." Li said, "I don't know their motives, but some of them are still encouraging you to continue the hunger strike, and I don't approve of that."

Wang Dan countered that the strike would not end until Li made a specific response to the students' demands. Peking University student leader Xiong Yan, one of the strikers, called on Li and the other leaders to stop "worrying about losing face" while searching for solutions to the crisis. "If the government admits its faults, people will support it," he said. But Li responded bluntly, "We have to defend socialism. I don't care if you like to listen to this or not."

Though Zhao wisely skipped that confrontation, he took his message to the students personally the next day. Just before dawn, he told fellow leaders that he planned to talk to the students in the square. He was warned that it would be unsafe to do so, but he insisted. After hearing about Zhao's plan, Li Peng—not wanting to be upstaged—also hastened to the scene. By then, scores of city buses provided by the Red Cross were parked in the square to shield the hunger strikers from the heat and rain. Li boarded one of the buses. He perfunctorily shook hands and asked the students inside where they studied, and then got off to wait for Zhao.

Zhao launched into a tearful confession to his young

admirers that he had come too late to be of help and that the government deserved their criticism. "I am sorry," he bellowed, his hands trembling. Speaking through a bullhorn in front of a Chinese TV camera, he told the hunger strikers, "I am too old, but you are still young. Live to see China's modernization." Hinting at his predicament, he called on the students to end their fast because "the problems are so complicated that it would take a process to solve them." Haggard students in the bus applauded Zhao's emotional ramblings and later mobbed him for autographs. Zhao solemnly signed his name on notebooks, headbands, visors, towels and even umbrellas that the strikers shoved at him. It was Zhao's last public appearance before the massacre.

Later that day, when Deng learned about Zhao's encounter with the students, he called for an expanded meeting of top leaders. They voted to call the People's Liberation Army into Beijing and to impose martial law. Although Zhao had been essentially stripped of his authority, the leaders agreed that he should attend a meeting late that night to make an official announcement of the party's decision. But Zhao refused, asking instead for a "three-day sick leave." The late-night meeting was delayed for him, but he never showed up. By the time the meeting began, troops had begun to move into Beijing.

Hours later, Li Peng, dressed in a black Mao suit, went on national TV to grimly announce the declaration of martial law. With Deng and Yang Shangkun sitting beside him, Li accused "a very, very small handful of people" of creating turmoil to overthrow the government. Raising his voice and punching the air to emphasize the point, he declared, "I now call on the whole party, the whole army and the whole nation to make concerted efforts and set immediately at all posts to stop the turmoil and stabilize the situation."

At midnight a full moon, shrouded in mist, gleamed over Tiananmen Square. Tens of thousands of students listened intently to Li's voice coming out of the government loudspeakers on the lampposts. Sirens wailed and blue lights flashed as another hunger striker collapsed and was carted off to the hospital. "Down with Li Peng!" the students shouted in chorus, "Li Peng, resign!" A strike organizer shouted over a megaphone that the army had been ordered to clear the square by midnight and urged them not to give up. Marshals immediately linked arms in a defensive wall. A "dare-to-die detachment" of about 50 men and women, including Peking University's Jiang Liren, snapped into formation and started to march double-time around the square, as if bracing to stop the assault with their bare hands.

In one corner of the square stood Zhang Gang (not his real name), chief of the marshals' detachment, a force that handled traffic, security and intelligence functions for the students. A tattered red flag in one hand and a battery-operated megaphone in the other, he gave orders to marshals posted along the fringes of the square. Wearing a faded jacket, a red headband and several days' growth of beard, the tall and emaciated-looking Zhang exuded toughness. Hoarse-voiced, he said, "We do not want violence, but we are not afraid of violence. If the government insists on resorting to it, we will answer with violence and show the power of the people. If the army comes, we'll resort to sit-in strikes. If they use force, we'll use the same. A tooth for a tooth. As Chairman Mao said, 'If you don't attack, I won't attack; but if you attack, I will certainly counterattack.' "

Zhang said he expected that the army would refrain from shooting at people. But he quickly added, "We too have weapons. We will topple anyone who is riding roughshod over the people. We are confident." Then he mumbled, "If this movement fails, please don't write about what I said because my parents. . . . No, no. Whether or not we fail, do write what I just said."

For at least the 100th time, a well-played tape of the

中央美院敬挽

何处招魂

Mourning Hu
Yaobang's death
ABBAS–MAGNUM

The demonstrations
grow
*FORREST ANDERSON–
Gamma/Liason*

Aiding student hunger
strikers
CHRIS NIEDENTHAL

Face-off at Zhongnanhai
JARECKE–CONTACT

Premier Zhao Ziyang visits the hospitalized hunger
strikers *Xinhua*

The Goddess of Democracy rises above the square
CHARLESWORTH–JB PICTURES

Displaying a stolen
AK–47
ANDERSON–Liason

APCs halted by bus blockade
HIRES–Gamma/Liason

How to halt an armor-
ed vehicle
HIRES–Gamma/Liason

As tension grows, violence erupts in the square
WIDENER–AP

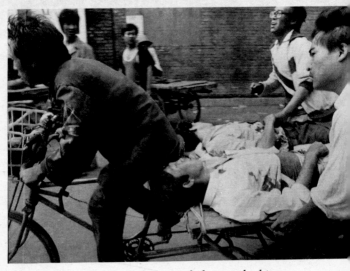

Shooting breaks out, and the wounded are rushed to hospitals
Liu–AP

A bloodied soldier is led to safety by students
CHARLESWORTH–JB PICTURES

Students overturn a bus to block attacking troops
CHARLESWORTH–JB PICTURES

Bodies of demonstrators crushed to death by tanks and
APC's *AP*

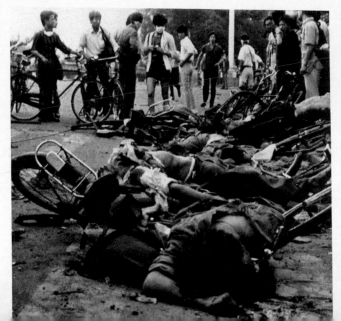

As bodies pile up, outrage deepens at the army's brutality
AVERY–AP

Internationale blared over the student's battery-operated loudspeaker system. A burst of jubilant shouts erupted from a cluster of protesters huddled on the cold pavement. "Civilians in the suburbs have been stopping the advancing P.L.A. troops!" a marshal announced over a megaphone. "Long live the people!" the students chanted, raising their clenched fists. "Long live [the people's] understanding!"

Along Beijing's elliptic ring road, city residents congregated near subway stations after word spread that the military would smuggle forces into the city using the subway. If so, the plan was blocked when sympathetic workers shut down the power supply. "We are fighting a force that is armed to the teeth," said a Chinese radio journalist at a makeshift roadblock. "We Beijing citizens are determined to topple this feudal rule."

Soldiers were moving into the city from several directions. More than 1,000 troops wielding AK-47 assault rifles arrived by train on May 22—just two blocks from the square—only to be surrounded by hordes of students. The soldiers, mostly in their teens, were from far outside the capital. They were also oblivious to what had been happening in the capital. For the past few weeks, they had been isolated in barracks just outside Beijing, where they were not allowed to listen to the radio, watch TV or read newspapers. Students immediately organized "propaganda teams" to meet the soldiers and win them to their cause. At the Gongzhufen (Princess's Tomb) traffic circle, 50 olive-drab trucks carrying about 25 artillerymen each were surrounded by students and local residents, who clambered aboard to bring them water and rolls. Two young journalists went from truck to truck to show soldiers color snapshots of the peaceful protest in the square. "Are these scenes of turmoil?" asked a woman. "Can't you see your brothers or sisters being among these idealistic students? You have been deceived." A plump, gray-haired woman interjected, "Please do not follow incorrect orders. We do not need you here."

When a small group of camera-wielding foreign journalists appeared in Shijingshan district, about eleven miles from Tiananmen Square, student marshals stopped them from taking pictures of a standoff between troops and residents. The residents objected. "We ought to let them show the outside world what is really happening here," said a woman in pajamas. "Why should we care about losing face?" But a student marshal later said that "we simply did not want the soldiers to feel provoked or humiliated."

The long-expected attack did not happen. More than a week after Li Peng imposed martial law, the army had yet to arrive in force. Most of the city appeared to be returning to normal. Except on Changan Avenue, which runs past Tiananmen Square, public transport resumed and traffic policemen returned to their posts. Some convoys of army trucks were allowed to turn around and encamp at nearby military bases or in roadside clearings. Others parked in the yards of government complexes. By this time, roadblocks by protesters had become smaller and irregular.

Yet there were ominous signs all over town. Troops moved into such strategic locations as Beijing's international airport and the compounds of the *People's Daily,* CCTV and Radio Beijing. Three men who were not connected with the student protesters threw paint on the portrait of Mao Zedong that hangs at the Gate of Heavenly Peace. They were apprehended by the students, who denounced the act and handed them over to the police.

In the closing days of May, the movement's early exuberance was beginning to flag, and exhaustion was setting in. Some 20,000 to 30,000 students remained encamped in Tiananmen Square. Around the perimeter, vendors were hawking everything from pancakes to soft drinks to cigarettes. Eating in the square took considerable fortitude. Even at some distance, the stench of urine was overwhelming. There was only one public toilet and a bus fitted with latrines.

Food, donated by work units and factories, often sat unrefrigerated in the morning heat. Heaps of fetid garbage stood nearby, sometimes next to first-aid stations. For the already weary demonstrators, life in the square was an invitation to sickness. A 23-year-old Beijing medical student found most of the students suffering from one minor malady or another, colds and diarrhea being the most common. A few people had hepatitis. Personal hygiene was limited to brushing teeth and rinsing the day's grime off faces and hands. But few students complained. As some noted, the appalling conditions of their dormitory rooms had accustomed them to it all. Some students spoke with a sense that their success was predetermined. "We are part of a trend now in the world toward democracy," said a student from Peking University's department of international politics. "The Communist Party will be forced to reform itself. It is inevitable. If not, it will be overthrown."

The students may have been unified in their determination, but their movement was not united. Rivalries between leaders were an open secret among protesters, and disagreements over tactics led to abrupt leadership changes. "Chai Ling was never a part of the Beigaolian [the independent student organization]," Uerkesh scoffed one day late in May. "She is good and dedicated, but she tends to be rather emotional in looking at things." Not that Uerkesh was immune to such criticism. A week earlier, he ended his hunger strike after he heard rumors that troops and tanks were moving in and that Li Peng had vowed to kill 2,000 people to clear the square. Uerkesh called a general meeting and ordered the students to evacuate immediately. When the crackdown did not come, he was ousted from his leadership role, and the students remained.

On the evening of May 29, with the movement at a low ebb, a magical figure entered the square. A procession of students from the China Central Institute of Fine Arts made their way 1½ miles from the school toward the city's center. With them, they brought on flatbed carts and trishaws a disassembled sculpture of plaster-covered Styrofoam on a wooden frame. This was the "Goddess of Democracy," a 30-foot-high figure whose flowing raiments and torch held aloft unmistakably suggested the Statue of Liberty and Western democratic traditions. Soon the crowd accompanying the statue down Changan Avenue grew to 20,000, and police blocked off traffic to accommodate them. The statue was positioned on a line between the huge portrait of Mao and the Monument to the People's Heroes—the "Celestial Axis" long sacred to the political and cultural life of China. As the art students assembled the statue on a platform, the crowd swelled to 50,000.

The regime wasted little time responding. On the evening TV news broadcast, an unidentified "local architect" was quoted as urging the municipal government to take swift action. "This is China, not the United States," he said. But while the authorities branded the statue "an insult to the national image and dignity," endless streams of bicyclists and pedestrians made their way to the square to catch a glimpse of the gleaming white statue that rose above the crowds.

Yet the movement was again losing steam. Protest leaders began to squabble. Some thought they should declare victory and leave the square. Others called for a new hunger strike. The ranks of the strikers dwindled to a few thousand. Litter proliferated, and discipline deteriorated. Hoodlums, drunks and undercover police were seen walking through the area at will. The press, now firmly under the thumb of the government, imposed a virtual blackout on the protest movement. Rumors began to spread through the city that troops were on the march again. The mood was grim.

Many of the Tiananmen Square leaders were ready to retreat. Yet fresh students were pouring in from the provinces. Thousands of them arrived in the capital every day, having used their student IDs to ride trains free of charge. After more debate, the leadership voted to remain in the square.

Indeed, they decided to stay until at least June 20, when they hoped that National People's Congress chairman Wan Li, who was thought to be sympathetic to their cause, would convene a session of the Chinese parliament to oust Li Peng. That proved to be little more than wishful thinking. Wan was returning from a trip to the U.S. and Canada. But his plane was diverted to Shanghai, and he disappeared from public sight, ostensibly for medical reasons but in fact under house arrest in a government compound in a western suburb of Shanghai. A few days later, the official press quoted him as supporting the imposition of martial law. With Zhao effectively removed from power, Wan had been the students' last hope among the leadership. As the weekend of June 3-4 approached, they were growing stronger in numbers, but otherwise they were running out of hope.

CHAPTER FIVE

A CRY HEARD ROUND THE WORLD

In the mid-8th century, with the once powerful Tang dynasty in chaos, the poet Du Fu wrote these lines far from the tumult of the capital: "I sit secure, yet feelings rise:/ the weight of distance on the heart." A similar pain struck at ethnic Chinese everywhere in the world as news of death and confusion arose out of the mainland. "We believed that China was gradually emerging from its long nightmare of war and repression," said I.M. Pei, the Chinese-born architect who with his wife moved to the U.S. about 50 years ago—and who designed the serene Xiangshan Hotel outside Beijing. "We worked in China, despite many frustrations, out of a love of that country, out of a sense that things were getting better. . . . Will we ever be able to work in China again?"

Now a resident of Paris, Jean Pasqualini, the French-Chinese author who was imprisoned in Mao's reeducation camps, thundered against Deng Xiaoping. "Remember when he first came to power?" said Pasqualini. "Everyone thought he was different. He was China's De Gaulle."

Around the world, usually fractious and quiet over-seas Chinese communities were united and vocal in their grief. Among the 40,000 Chinese who live in New England, sympathies had been split along generational lines, with older Chinese more impressed than their children by Deng's reforms. "Most people felt a great sense of hope," said Yon Lee, liaison to Boston's Chinese community for Mayor Raymond Flynn. "Many Chinese here still felt a sense of support for Deng. But that has changed completely now. People can't believe what the leaders have done. They despise them." Before the massacre, San Francisco's community of 150,000 Chinese Americans was clearly divided into Taipei and Beijing factions. But afterward, said San Francisco Supervisor Tom Hsieh, "the reaction was almost spontaneously and unanimously on the side of the rebellion." In a startling alliance, students from the mainland joined the wealthy, pro-Nationalist Chinatown organizations to form the San Francisco Bay Area Committee to Aid the Tiananmen Crisis.

In Southeast Asia, despite the silence of their governments, local Chinese communities began demonstrating against the brutality in the mainland. In Manila, where the overseas Chinese population has often kept itself politically disinterested, 300 ethnic Chinese rallied in front of the Beijing embassy shouting, "Long live freedom and democracy!" and demanding the resignation of Deng and Premier Li Peng. Other placards read: DOWN WITH FASCISTS! In Thailand folk singer Surachai Chanthimatorn composed a protest song titled *Tiananmen,* which featured, on backup vocals, Kraisak Choonhavan, son of Prime Minister Chatichai Choonhavan, who is also chairman of the Thai-Chinese Friendship Association.

In Toronto more than 15,000 members of the city's large Chinese community marched the day after news of the massacre reached Canada, which has about 360,000

Chinese residents. Similar protests were held in Vancouver, Ottawa and Montreal. In the British cities of London, Birmingham, Nottingham, Cardiff and Manchester there were outpourings of anger from the country's 200,000 overseas Chinese. "It is usually not a vociferous community," said C. Lem of the Chinese Association of Tower Hamlets in East London. "It is very important for the Chinese to show their anger and have the British public join in."

At the forefront of the demonstrations were students from the People's Republic. In the last decade, Beijing had encouraged its young people to go out into the world to master the science and technology required to uplift the motherland. China sent out its best, including the children of élite families. Among them were Deng Xiaoping's son Deng Zhifang, who studied physics at New York's University of Rochester, Qiao Shi's daughter Xiaoxi Qiao, who studied at Baylor College of Medicine in Houston, and Jiang Jemin's son Jiang Mianhang, a graduate student in electrical engineering at Drexel University in Philadelphia. After returning from their grandfather Hu Yaobang's funeral in April, Xu Kui and Xu Xiaopeng lent moral support to demonstrations at their school, the University of Massachusetts, Amherst.

By 1988 Beijing realized that its students were being ensnared by Western ideas and comforts, which was sometimes reflected in their decision to adopt Western first names and reverse the traditional order of surnames, relegating the family name to the end. Many stayed beyond their school terms and never went home. In response, the regime cut down the number of young people it sent out and prevented families from traveling together. But by then, only 25% out of the estimated 80,000 students who left for studies abroad had chosen to return home. About 40,000 of those students were in the U.S. Said Xiao Chuan Wang, a chemistry student from Wu-

han studying for her doctorate in Chicago: "I didn't
know anything about politics until I came to the U.S. I
thought China was the greatest country in the world.
Once I was here, and I saw how people lived, the freedom
they enjoyed, I thought, my God, what kind of life do we
have back in China?" Said Baoping He, a graduate student of engineering at Virginia Polytechnic Institute and
State University: "Here we learned not only high tech;
we learned democracy and freedom."

But high-tech skills came in handy when their compatriots back home took Tiananmen Square from the
government. While student groups throughout the U.S.
raised thousands of dollars to equip their Beijing friends
with supplies, including gas masks, and to contribute to
the Chinese Red Cross, many others set up communications centers to direct rumors and news in and out of
China. At the University of Michigan, Chinese students
purchased a fax machine and scoured old issues of *People's Daily* and other Chinese publications, clipping advertisements containing the fax numbers of government
offices and corporations. The machine was put to constant use, transmitting news stories and information to
offices in China. "We want to spread the news to other
cities and encourage them to back the demonstrators,"
said a spokesman for the group. The Michigan students
made use of Chinanet, a U.S.-wide computer network, to
keep other overseas Chinese students up to date on the
events in Beijing.

Similar tactics were pursued by other groups. Thousands of Chinese students, with access to computers,
tapped into two other nationwide computer networks,
Social Culture China and ENCS (Electronic News Chinese
Scholars). News and rumors—as well as more fax numbers—gleaned from telephone calls home were passed
along the computer channels. At Stanford University and
the University of California, Berkeley, students made certain that provincial offices were faxed their share of the

news. Said Huang Jingsheng, a Stanford graduate student in sociology: "In the provinces many people don't know what's going on." Said Lu Yin, a Berkeley doctoral candidate in biostatistics: "We have experienced waves of emotions. At first we were excited and surprised and even a little guilty that we weren't there. Now we feel we can play a special role."

Others believed they were playing major parts in the Beijing protests. In May 1989 Chen Jun, Mouren Wu and Shijin Wang set up a simple communications center in Elmhurst, in New York City's borough of Queens, composed of two telephone lines, one computer and a fax machine. They called it the Contact Office for the Chinese Democratic Movement. Linked up with other organizations in Los Angeles, San Francisco, Chicago and Hong Kong, they coordinated protest strategy and offered advice to student leaders in Beijing. "We are not just providers of information," said Chen. "We are actually involved in the movement."

A few could not stay away from China. The day before martial law was declared, Sanyuan Li, 32, a graduate student at the University of Chicago, returned to his apartment to find his wife Yu Cheng weeping quietly in a chair. "She was deeply moved by the students' fight for freedom," Li said of his wife, a doctoral student of education at the same school. "I shared her feelings. I understood." Yu said she was going back to Beijing to join the struggle. "From the look on her face," said Li, "I knew she was telling me, not asking me." But he made his wife, who was four months pregnant, promise not to join the hunger strike. Yu took their year-old American-born son Payton back to Beijing with her. They agreed that when she returned to Chicago, her husband would then fly to Beijing to take her place among the students. The couple spoke each night by telephone. "She told me she went to Tiananmen Square every day."

When the troops moved on Tiananmen, Yu's parents quickly took her and their grandson to the Beijing airport to catch a plane for San Francisco. But she was not among the people who disembarked. Li frantically checked for his wife's name on passenger lists but did not find her or his son there. "It's as if they've vanished," he said. "I believe she is being detained." In fact, she had been. "My son and I had cleared customs when several men in plainclothes took us away," said Yu, who was not able to leave China for nearly a week after the massacre. "They said I was a suspected activist of the rebellion. They searched all my stuff, went through my address book, everything. They didn't treat us badly, but they wouldn't let me call my family. After a few days, I think they didn't know exactly what to do with me, and they put me on a plane to Shanghai."

Other Chinese in the U.S. called local organizations to locate brothers, sisters and friends in the Tiananmen crowd. Chen Jun in Elmhurst heard through his group's channels that one of his friends was among the dead in Beijing. Others learned of the massacre from messages left for them on the computer networks. Said one student: "I sat there in front of my terminal for a while. I felt so sad for my country."

"There is no future for this brutal regime," said Jigme Ngapo, an ethnic Tibetan graduate student of international affairs at the University of Virginia and the son of a vice chairman of the National People's Congress. Ngapo did not even try to reach his father. "He would have to give me the official party line," said he. "It's difficult for them to say anything different." Other children of high-ranking cadres were not as vocal. One such student in Chicago begged his friends to keep his family connection a secret. Said a friend: "Because of what's happening in our country, he felt ashamed. He did not want to invite the derision of other Chinese students."

Before the massacre, sympathy demonstrations even

among students had been small, with participants numbering in the dozens. But protests blossomed after June 4. Replicas of the Goddess of Democracy were erected in Los Angeles, Boston, San Francisco, Hong Kong and New York City. In Manhattan, despite a steady rain, as many as 20,000 demonstrators gathered near United Nations headquarters, waving banners of black-and-red mourning the deaths in Beijing. The protesters demanded that U.N. Secretary-General Javier Pérez de Quellar convene the Security Council to condemn China's actions. In Bonn the sound of gunshots and screams echoed under the statue of Beethoven in the city's Münsterplatz as an audiotape recording of the carnage was replayed for protesters. Deng was long respected as a good emperor, said Lida Han, a language student in Bonn, "but we no longer need any emperors. We need a constitution that is recognized by the people."

In Paris French Maoists made the mistake of unfurling a brilliant red banner bearing portraits of Marx, Lenin and Mao at a gathering of 10,000 protesters near the city's grandiose Opéra. Enraged Chinese students trashed it, ripped the cloth from its wooden poles and chased the Maoists down the Rue Auber, shouting "Fascists! Assassins!" In Tokyo the Union of Chinese Students Studying in Japan gathered a crowd of 5,000 for a memorial Mass in a local church. Earlier, at the news of the crackdown, 2,000 people had hoisted protest banners in Tokyo's Miyashita Park and called on the Chinese embassy to lower the Chinese flag to half-staff. The embassy refused.

But though many students suspected them of keeping demonstrators under surveillance, Chinese diplomats were not entirely unsympathetic. At the U.N. protests in New York City, Chinese consulate officials were said to have surreptitiously supplied drinks to the demonstrators, provided masking tape for their posters and banners and offered transportation. In the weeks after the massacre, Chinese diplomats were reported to have defected in San Francisco, London and Canberra. By the end of June, Beijing had recalled all its ambassadors for consultation, presumably to deter further defections.

After the massacre, students in the U.S. continued to use fax and phone lines to subvert Beijing's intentions. When the regime broadcast telephone numbers that informers could call to turn in fugitives, Chinese students abroad took to jamming the lines. "What we've done is post the numbers on an electronic bulletin board accessible to anyone with a computer system," said Jian Ping Lu, midwest coordinator for the Chinese Students Association. "At first students who called said they wanted to report a counterrevolutionary. When asked who it was, the student would say 'Deng Xiaoping.' " Later, he added, the tactics changed. "Now we simply try to convince the person who answers the phone of the students' cause. Many people in China don't know what's truly happening, so they turn to the government." He said, "It's difficult to get through to China now, and the calls get expensive. But if we can change one person's mind or save one life, it's worth it."

Other students continued with the fax link. As the Beijing demonstrations turned bloody, the focus shifted from the capital to major cities such as Shanghai, Nanjing and Qingdao, from which news reports about the massacre were blacked out. For a while, the machines sent a daily stream of photographs and articles all over the People's Republic. But a week after the carnage, traffic began to slow. Fax lines would ring without being picked up. "People are afraid," said Lu Yin of Berkeley. "We think there has been some action taken against fax machines in China." The only alternative seemed to be getting information to the Voice of America, the U.S. government's radio service. Said Mouren Wu of the Elmhurst Contact office: "If 1,000 people were killed in Beijing, the people of Shanghai will never know if they do not hear it from the VOA."

From June 3, the VOA began transmitting eleven hours of news a day in Mandarin, nine hours more than the BBC provided. Chinese estimates gave the Chinese branch of the VOA an everyday audience of 60 to 100 million. With the crisis, the number of listeners may have risen three- to fourfold. After the Chinese government began jamming the service on May 21 for the first time since 1978, the VOA turned to a powerful 1-megawatt AM transmitter in the Philippines to overwhelm any attempts to cut its broadcasts. David Hess, chief of the China branch, told the Washington *Post*, "The only other medium more pervasive is rumor." Shortly after the crackdown, transcripts of VOA reports were tacked up on walls in Beijing.

For days after the massacre, the VOA not only broadcast news into China, it received information directly from the mainland. As part of its programming since 1988, the station had advertised a telephone number on which the Chinese could call collect to participate in radio talk shows. Immediately after the slaughter, the phone rang incessantly. "The calls were a wall of emotion," said Hess. "The almost incredulous expression of rage and frustration communicated by Chinese students exploding with anger was overwhelming." By June 12, however, Chinese long-distance operators told VOA officials that their superiors had forbidden them to place calls to the American radio station. Instead of anguished callers, the VOA began to receive obscene messages accusing U.S. radio of spreading lies.

Chinese Americans at the VOA in Washington had to fight back their emotions as they broadcast the news. Two days after the massacre, Richard Carlson, head of the VOA, passed a broadcaster at his typewriter weeping over the news report he was writing. Hess told the *Post*, "As the shooting started, people would have a piece of news that they just couldn't believe, and they would have tears streaming down their faces while they were translating the piece. It was disbelief. It was frustration. It was anger." Dah H. Lin, a veteran at the service, said he wanted to join the demonstrations. "I wanted to go, but because of my job, I can't demonstrate." Instead he encouraged his daughter Judy, a financial analyst, to join the protests.

Students from China did more than join protests and fax information home. Several renounced membership in the Communist Party, thus jeopardizing their careers if they return to the mainland. "We cannot do many things to protest. This is one thing we can do," said Pan You-fang, a graduate student in computer science at Indiana State University, who had been a party member for 16 years. John Shao, a Ph.D. candidate in finance at the Virginia Polytechnic Institute, said he had joined in 1983. "At that time, the party seemed to be advancing the country. Now I realize it is totally corrupted."

Meanwhile, other Chinese outside their country feared that such activities may have compromised them in the eyes of the authorities. Chinese intellectuals who were in the West at the time of the massacre feared they were being watched. Chen Kaige, director of such controversial films as *Yellow Earth,* which criticized the persistence of Chinese feudalism, and *The Big Parade,* which jabbed at the military, joined in demonstrations in New York City's Chinatown that he knew were broadcast on TV in the People's Republic. Many of his friends, he said, were in hiding in China, and he was afraid he was on a blacklist. "I would like to go back, but I am afraid it will not be possible." If he could not return, Chen said, he would make a movie about Chinese students in America. "They have been totally changed by something in the U.S.A. They know about democracy, so they can't stand the system in China."

While idealism motivated most of the student protests, some observers believed that self-interest played a part in the activism. Shortly after the massacre, the Bush Administration promised "flexible" consideration for extensions of student visas. But many of the visas were running out, and even under Bush's liberalized policy, most Chinese in the U.S. could stay only by proving they were in danger of persecution if they returned home. That was sometimes a difficult standard to meet, though radical antigovernment activity would certainly make a trip home perilous. Said Leo Orleans, China consultant for the Library of Congress and an authority on the Chinese student community in the U.S., "I think they're spoiled in a way and paranoid in a way. They're looking for any way possible to stay here." He added, "They know that the more noise they make, the less likely the American Government is to send them back." In late July, at the First Congress of Chinese Students in the U.S., a speaker representing the Immigration and Naturalization Service was hissed at by students.

A month after the massacre, so many Chinese student organizations had cropped up that accusations began to fly over who was and who was not truly antigovernment. At Washington University in St. Louis, one young man confessed that he had been sent by Beijing to spy on the local student organization. At Harvard, students accused Huang Jing, a fellow protester who once headed Cambridge's Beijing-approved Chinese student union, of being a lackey of the regime. Huang was said to have passed along spurious information, including the false report that Premier Li Peng had been shot in the leg by an irate policeman. Said Pei Meixing, another prominent student leader, speaking more from his heart than his knowledge of U.S. law: "Spreading these rumors is an offense punishable by death."

A sense of disarray seemed to plague the overseas student movement. A press conference in Paris broke up in near chaos because of a lack of interpreters and because there were rumors that Beijing infiltrators were in the crowd. Arriving at the scene by taxi, student leader Uerkesh Daolet took one look at the confusion and sped away as journalists rushed to corner him. Uerkesh's personal popularity also has been a distraction, making some members of the movement uneasy—including him. Mobbed by the press and by autograph seekers at the Statue of Liberty in New York City where he had given a speech, the 21-year-old activist pushed through a crowd, pleading with photographers to let him alone. Meanwhile, Beijing began to play on the students' nervousness about their immediate future. In the first week of July, it announced that it would not investigate Chinese students in the U.S. who joined antigovernment rallies "without knowing the truth."

In the aftermath of the massacre, China's overseas students seemed caught in the perennial dilemma of the exiled rebel: to reform the homeland they would have to return, but they prized safety and found it in distance. In spite of the abstract magic of electronics, they were driven by the fears and futilities of their desires. In that way, they relived the poet Du Fu's ancient trauma. Amid exile from the collapsed center of the empire, he wrote, "From several provinces now/ the news has ceased./ I sit here in sorrow/ tracing words in air."

Mikhail Sergeyevich Gorbachev was amused. For months, what would be the Soviet President's first visit to Beijing—indeed, the first by any of his country's leaders since 1959—had been heralded as one of the most momentous events of the decade: the reconciliation of the two most powerful Communist nations on the planet after decades of bitter rivalry. But by the time of his arrival on May 15, Tiananmen Square, the site of most official welcoming ceremonies, belonged to the protesters. The government had to move Gorbachev's reception to the airport. Unable to reach the Great Hall of the People through the packed 100-acre square, the Soviet leader's 30-car motorcade was detoured through side streets, past mounds of rubbish, into an obscure courtyard on the west side of the building, farthest from Tiananmen. His historic visit thus eclipsed by the protest, Gorbachev quipped to President Yang Shangkun, "Well, I came to Beijing, and you have a revolution!"

General Secretary Gorbachev's ambivalence about the protests was reflected in other utterances that week. Meeting with Zhao Ziyang, head of the Chinese Communist Party, Gorbachev said, "We have our hotheads too who want to renovate socialism overnight." But though he chose his words carefully, Gorbachev seemed infected by Beijing's spring fever. He could not fail to be moved by reports that he and his policies of *glasnost* (openness) and *perestroika* (economic restructuring) were inspirations for some of the reformist icons worshiped by the students. In fact, signs hailed Gorbachev as "the emissary of democratization" and "the initiator of political reform." The crowds in Tiananmen Square hung banners in Russian proclaiming DEMOKRATIZATSIYA—NASHA OBSHCHAYA MECHTA—Democracy, our common dream.

At a press conference in Beijing with Western reporters, Gorbachev was already subtly advising compromise, asking for "a sensible balance between the generations, combining the energy of the young in speaking out against conservatism with the wisdom of the older generation." When interviewed by Chinese television, Gorbachev seemed almost swept up by the enthusiasm of the students. "I liked the way the youth perceived *perestroika*," he said. "Maybe they want more than can be done right away." Then he added, "The youth will accomplish more than we were able to. It's not a fantasy. I deal in real policies."

Gorbachev was not the only foreigner won over by

the students. Even after Premier Li Peng declared martial law in Beijing, tourists ventured into Tiananmen to show support for the protest. There they found flattering references, beamed by satellite throughout the world, to democratic movements from their own country's past. Some banners echoed the American Revolutionary hero Patrick Henry: GIVE ME DEMOCRACY OR GIVE ME DEATH. Or Abraham Lincoln's plea for a government "of the people, by the people and for the people." A wall poster in Beijing paraphrased John Stuart Mill's *On Liberty:* BY LIBERTY WAS MEANT PROTECTION AGAINST THE TYRANNY OF THE POLITICAL RULERS. Students from the Journalism Institute in Beijing displayed a bilingual banner citing Lord Acton: ABSOLUTE POWER CORRUPTS ABSOLUTELY. Other signs sounded a pithy style worthy of Western pop: HUNGER STRIKE—NO TO DEEP-FRIED DEMOCRACY! Photographs of Corazon Aquino's "People Power" revolution were posted on campus bulletin boards. The Goddess of Democracy erected in Tiananmen Square reminded Americans of the Statue of Liberty. To Soviets it may have evoked the image of the statue of the motherland, raising her sword in Volgograd. Somehow, all this had been seen and felt before—in South Korea, in Poland, in the Philippines. The yearning to be free was infectious, addictive and welcome.

Western journalists, pouring into Beijing as the protests swelled, began to find themselves infected as well. "It was not possible to be dispassionate," said Charles Kuralt of CBS News. "The most cynical journalists could not help but be caught up." Confessed NBC News anchor Tom Brokaw: "I suppose the constant danger for a reporter is failing to separate head and heart, and we didn't do that a couple of times." Said Richard Wald, senior vice president of ABC News: "When these very appealing young people with their ideology seemed to speak directly to our history, remembering us as a revolutionary country, it made us feel good and good toward them. It

made us feel invincible, so we thought they were too."
Writing in the San Francisco *Bay Guardian,* Steve Stallone, a former student activist at Berkeley, pointed to stories in the New York *Times* and Washington *Post,* by normally unexcitable reporters, chronicling in detail the courage of Chinese journalists in resisting directives from above. Mused Stallone: "Were these reports a sly way of saying, 'Gee, we'd like to do this too?'"

In addition to journalists, many foreign sinologists wished the students success. Even with the declaration of martial law, Anthony Kane, director of the China Council of the New York City–based Asia Society, was optimistic. "They won't get Deng or Li," said Kane, "but the mutual restraint has been breathtaking." Michael Lampton, president of the National Committee on U.S.-China Relations predicted that "a collective leadership will emerge, and China will muddle around but head increasingly toward more pluralism and a less relevant Communist Party." Stanley Rosen, a professor of sociology at the University of Southern California, believed the soldiers of the People's Liberation Army would continue to take no action. "Otherwise," he said. "history would regard them as villains."

With the military sweeping around the edges of the demonstrations, U.S. Congressmen wanted Washington to try to guarantee the safety of the students. The Senate Foreign Relations Committee voted 19 to 0 to ask the Chinese government not to use violence against the students. That nonbinding resolution called on "the leadership of the People's Republic of China [to] take all necessary steps to establish a just and democratic society, with a free and open political system that will protect the essential human rights of all people living within that country." Earlier, the Bush Administration had released a statement saying, "We support freedom of expression. We hope the demonstrations will remain peaceful and that the authorities will continue to exercise restraint."

Many Americans, however, felt that even such muted hopes were unrealistic. One pessimist was Andrew Nathan, a professor at Columbia University and the author of *Chinese Democracy,* a study of the Democracy Wall movement. Said Nathan: "Something like this cannot go on forever. The demonstrations have to end someday. If some students on hunger strike die or the military should lose its cool, there could be violence." Others did not rely on reasoning. Speaking to the Washington *Post,* Sofia Chaureli, a Soviet actress who was part of Gorbachev's advance team in Beijing, said, "When I walked out of my hotel room, I saw my native Georgia." In the early morning of April 9, a week before the Beijing demonstrations began, Soviet troops had used poison gas to suppress a peaceful march by students and nationalists in the Georgian capital of Tbilisi.

The pessimists were proved right on June 4.

Among governments in the West, the massacre produced strong reactions of anger. Most major industrial nations, including the U.S., took disapproving action of some kind, typically a cutoff of military sales to China. "A regime that is forced to fire on the young, who protest in the name of liberty, has no future," said French President François Mitterrand. In Paris in mid-July, the annual summit of the seven leading industrial powers unanimously condemned the "violent repression" by the Chinese government and asked Beijing to "create conditions that will avoid [its own] isolation." However, the Group of Seven stopped short of imposing economic sanctions. The gaudy postmodern parade celebrating the bicentennial of the French Revolution also paid tribute to the student movement. Scheduled to be led off by Beijing opera performers break dancing on a gigantic red drum, the parade began instead with a solemn march of Chinese students, some with their faces masked, slowly pushing their bikes along a large banner that proclaimed, WE

SHALL CONTINUE.

In the U.S., President Bush announced a package of sanctions that included suspension of more than $500 million in weapons contracts. Said Bush: "It's not going to be business as usual." About $500 million of those contracts was concentrated with Grumman Aerospace, which in the week after the massacre blocked 40 Chinese officials from entering its Bethpage, N.Y., facilities to be trained under a nearly two-year-old deal on updating electronics systems for China's F-8 aircraft. Still, some members of Congress considered the President's measures inadequate. Stephen Solarz, a liberal Democratic Congressman from New York, and Jesse Helms, the conservative Republican Senator from North Carolina, joined forces to draw up legislation not only to cancel all military aid to China but to suspend high technology sales and Beijing's most-favored-nation status. Said Solarz: "I have to say that if the President doesn't take the initiative in changing American policy in this regard, Congress will do it for him." At the end of June, the House, by a vote of 418 to 0, passed a package that, among many stipulations, would expand the ban on arms sales to include equipment that could be used for police actions, and would deny U.S. Government insurance for private investments in China. Two weeks later, the Senate approved its own bill with similar measures by a vote of 81 to 10.

In the Communist bloc, the massacre produced a widespread sense of frustration. Sensitive about its newly mended fences with China, the Soviet Union officially asked only for "wisdom, sound reason and a balanced approach" in Beijing. But Foreign Ministry spokesman Gennadi Gerasimov said his government was "extremely dismayed." Said another Soviet official: "If you think we don't understand the situation, you're wrong. Not one Soviet, from the President down to a schoolchild, approves of China's use of tanks to repress the students."

During his July trip to France, Gorbachev called the crackdown "a tragedy." While reformist Hungary condemned the Tiananmen episode, East Germany and Cuba supported the Chinese government. The Italian Communist Party announced it would consider changing its name partly because of the stigma of the Beijing massacres.

Foreign aid and international credit also became scarcer for China. Japan, Beijing's largest foreign assistance donor, announced the suspension of its six-year $5 billion aid program. The World Bank postponed a $450 million loan. The European Community announced it was postponing consideration of any Chinese requests for trade credit. Among others, Chemical Bank in New York City put the brakes on a $120 million loan to Sinopec, the Chinese oil consortium.

Because of the People's Republic's remarkable decade of international economic integration, however, trade sanctions were much less easily imposed. Private businessmen were uneasy about giving up their investments. "You can't afford just to opt out of any world market, particularly one the size and potential of China," said Roger Sullivan, president of the U.S.-China Business Council, a Washington-based group representing 325 American companies with interests in the People's Republic. "For us to do that would be to just turn it over to the Japanese. These are the kinds of operations that already represent four and five years of time and energy to build up. You don't just chuck all that." Bush was convinced that commercial contacts "have led in essence to this quest for more freedom." Others joined him in arguing that staying in China would help boost proreform elements. "This government isn't going to last forever," said Sullivan.

The lure of profits kept many in China. Complaining that Japanese businessmen were "trying to make money like a thief at a fire" by heading back to the People's Republic, Japan's Foreign Minister Hiroshi Mitsuzuka admitted Tokyo could do nothing but recommend against such activities. Nike, an Oregon-based athletic shoe manufacturer with three factories in southern China, had no plans to pull out. "We've been in China for a long time," said company spokeswoman Elizabeth Dolan. "We've always felt that there's great potential there. There's a lot of feet in China."

Boeing, which had orders from China's national airline for 737s and 757s, as well as 18 contracts with Chinese partners to produce aircraft parts, announced that it planned "to maintain contacts in manufacturing and selling." Boeing Helicopters said it would be "business as usual" in fulfilling the $100 million contract it signed with the People's Liberation Army in January. The deal fell outside Bush's suspension of U.S. military sales. Even Grumman did not dismantle its F-8 program, which would have resulted in the layoff of 250 employees.

By August, Western travel agents were again hawking China to tourists. "Of course, there is a moral reason not to go to China," said Paticia Cunneen of EastQuest, a New York City based agency. "But I tell my customers that by not going they are cutting off what got the prodemocracy movement started in the first place: the Chinese talking with foreign visitors, the exchange of ideas."

Most of China's immediate neighbors were virtually silent on the incident. The military-backed regime in Burma, which had perpetrated a similar massacre on its people in 1988, blacked out all reports on the carnage in Beijing. In the Philippines, the government of Corazon Aquino, which had come to power by way of huge public demonstrations, issued a timid statement expressing "sadness" at the deaths in Tiananmen. Premier Chatichai Choonhavan of Thailand summed up the region's sentiments by declaring, "We cannot say too much about it because we are too close to China."

With China looking increasingly inward, key diplomatic processes began to stall. In Indochina, the Cambodian peace talks, in which Beijing supports the radical leftist Khmer Rouge, ground to a halt. India, which lost a brief border war and territory to China in 1962 and had recently tried to improve relations with its neighbor, speculated darkly about a more influential and adventurist People's Liberation Army. South Korea, meanwhile, worried about China's ability to rein in the unpredictable regime of its ally Kim Il Sung in North Korea.

In the past ten years, Asia has reaped political and economic benefits from a reforming China. Suddenly, the Napoleonic cliché about the Chinese giant awakening to astonish the world was being re-imagined into that of a somnambulant ogre, lashing out at its nightmares and crushing everything in its path. Living in China's shadow, many chose to seek safety in silence.

While others might afford silence, a duo of China's neighbors could not. Since 1979, Hong Kong and Taiwan had slowly bound themselves into an apolitical economic union with China. In October 1988, *Business Week* magazine was hailing the emergence of an entity called Greater China, a unit with total exports of $136 billion a year. That colossus combined Taiwan's noted scientific leadership and its $90 billion in foreign currency reserves with Hong Kong's status as the world's largest container port and fourth largest financial center, and with China's huge army of cheap labor. Hong Kong and Taiwan would no longer fear a military invasion from the mainland, which claimed both as its rightful territory. Trade and money would bind the three Chinas as one. In terms of economic muscle, Greater China would be second in Asia to Japan. That notion was pretty much shattered by the June 4 massacre.

The turn of events was most ironic for Taiwan. On the eve of the student demonstrations, President Lee Teng-hui had launched a new policy of "flexible diplomacy" toward the mainland, beginning a process of reducing tensions in the six-decade-old enmity between the Nationalists in Taiwan, who still claim to be the rightful rulers of China, and the Communists in Beijing. For its part, the mainland had been busy courting its rebel province, hoping to negotiate unity instead of threatening a military takeover. As part of Taiwan's new policy, President Lee sent Finance Minister Shirley Kuo to the 1989 Beijing meeting of the Asian Development Bank. Her arrival at that conference, two weeks before Gorbachev's visit, marked the first time an official representative from the Republic of China had come to the rival People's Republic. During the meeting, Kuo shocked her compatriots back home in Taipei by rising for the playing of Communist China's national anthem.

Two years earlier, Taipei had relaxed rules regarding travel to the mainland. As a result, Taiwanese ranked behind only Japanese in tourist arrivals in China. Battered by the appreciation of the New Taiwan dollar, Taipei businessmen had taken advantage of China's abundant labor by building manufacturing plants in Fujian province, across the Taiwan Straits. Earlier, any contact with the Communists would have been considered seditious. Now there was talk of fielding a joint team at the 1990 Asian Games, for which Beijing would play host.

The massacre changed all that. Beijing revived its old warnings against saboteurs and agents from Taiwan. In early July the People's Republic arrested a Taiwanese journalist for allegedly planning to help the fugitive student leader Wang Dan escape. Shortly after the crackdown began, Taiwan's former Premier Yu Kuo-hwa urged a return to the late Nationalist leader Chiang Kai-shek's tough anti-Communism, arguing that it was time to recapture the mainland. "We should immediately take more vigorous action," Yu was quoted in local papers. However, President Lee refused to consider military moves. Said he: "We must have the courage to face the fact that at this moment we are unable to effectively exercise the right to govern the mainland." Instead, the Taipei government prepared a worldwide publicity campaign to praise its own policies of free enterprise and political reform as the proper Chinese alternative to Communism.

Amid their prosperity, however, the people of Taiwan seemed to be gripped by guilt at their inability to do more for their fellow Chinese on the mainland. Millions of dollars in donations to help the wounded and their survivors poured into organizations that had no way of sending the funds to those who needed it. Blood drives lined up tens of thousands of donors, but the Chinese Red Cross refused to accept the donations. Sympathy demonstrations sprung up, but many were keenly aware of their futility. "Our sadness is caused, in part, because we feel that we can do so little," Young Yi-rong, a sociologist at the National Taiwan Normal University, told the *Asian Wall Street Journal*. Others reflected on the prosperous island's own dark history. Four decades earlier, the forces of Chiang Kai-shek had massacred 10,000 to 17,000 Taiwan Chinese after the islanders protested against the establishment of his refuge on Formosa.

Without any real options, Taiwan pursued a sort of reach-out-and-touch program. For the first time, the government opened telephone lines to the mainland so that people in Taiwan with relatives in China could keep them informed of developments. To help spread the facts in the face of Beijing's rewriting of the Tiananmen episode, local newspapers were bundled by the thousands and lifted by balloon over the Taiwan Strait to fall into the hands of people in the mainland who had not heard of the massacre. Taipei's diplomats abroad were told they were no longer forbidden to fraternize with representatives of Beijing. In addition, Taiwan's Premier Lee Huan, said that the government would continue to allow local businessmen to invest or trade with China, as long as transactions continued to be conducted through Hong Kong or a third country. Taiwanese with factories in China assured

Western partners and clients that there would be no slowdown in production or deliveries in spite of the chaos in Beijing.

Still, the indignation and sympathy masked one cold reality. Taiwan could try to reach out, but it would rather not have mainlanders reach back. In the wake of the massacre, the Taiwanese military was on high alert, not only against possible Communist attack but also to guard against an expected wave of refugees from the mainland. With 20 million people, Taiwan is by most standards overpopulated. One strong rumor that circulated in the weeks after the crackdown in Beijing held that military officers had turned back a young man claiming to be a prodemocracy student who had fled China in a rowboat. The government also began drawing up legislation that may mete out prison terms to Taiwan residents caught smuggling in Chinese citizens. Businesses that employ mainland refugees may also be penalized. In an interview with the *Asian Wall Street Journal,* Hu Fu, a political science professor at the National Taiwan University, said, "I believe this government has evaluated its own capability. Psychologically, as Chinese, we are all together. But politically, we need to be separate."

The British colony of Hong Kong and the nearby Portuguese enclave of Macao, also have the political luxury of separateness—but not for long. Britain's 99-year lease on Hong Kong will expire in 1997, at which time the colony will revert to Chinese rule; Macao will follow in 1999. But unlike Taiwan, with its activist policies toward the mainland, Hong Kong and Macao have long seemed largely apolitical, living life one day at a time. Hong Kong's business, as people said, was business. Macao's was gambling. In both places, the prevailing ethic was to squeeze out profits as quickly as possible—and to spend it well. Aware that they lived on borrowed time, people sought to eat, drink and be merry because tomorrow both places were going to be China. More cognac is said to be drunk per capita in Hong Kong than anywhere else in the world. And the Chinese have a saying about the Cantonese gourmands who dominate both Hong Kong and Macao: they will eat anything with four legs except a chair and anything that shows its back to the sun except a table.

In 1984, British Prime Minister Margaret Thatcher signed an agreement with Deng Xiaoping that guaranteed Hong Kong's capitalist system for 50 years after the colony's return to China. After some initial nervousness, many Hong Kong businessmen, encouraged by the economic reform process going on in China, grew more confident about the future. They came to believe that not only would Beijing honor its promise, but that the enclave's capitalist energy would somehow permeate the Communist mainland—allowing Hong Kong to profit even more. By late 1988, however, uncertainty had crept back into Hong Kong. In that year, an estimated 50,000 residents, mostly well-educated civil servants, chose to leave the colony. Most people saw no point in interesting themselves in the esoteric—and unpromising—negotiations with China over the Basic Law, the constitution that would govern the area after 1997.

In fact, Britain's guarantees of freedom and democracy for the people of Hong Kong were tenuous. Since the 1960s, a string of legislation made it progressively more difficult for foreign and commonwealth immigrants to settle in Britain. The most sweeping changes to the law were made in the 1981 British Nationality Act, which provided a multilayered system of citizenship. Under this act residents of Hong Kong were awarded Citizenship of British Dependent Territories status. Later, under the Hong Kong (British Nationality) Order of 1986, a person born in Hong Kong received a British passport as well as Chinese citizenship. These entitled them to visiting rights in Britain without need of a visa but provided for no residency rights in the country.

Thus, when student protests were met with conservative intransigence in Beijing, the people of Hong Kong were reminded of their uncertain fate and came out into the streets. At first, the protests seemed no more than extensions of the power struggle between liberal reformists and conservatives in China. Seventeen local college students began a hunger strike on May 15 in front of the Xinhua News Agency office in Hong Kong, Beijing's unofficial consulate in the colony. Two days later, 6,000 people joined them in a show of sympathy and presented Xinhua officials with 82,000 prodemocracy signatures. Soon, advertisements sympathetic to the Beijing students—perhaps placed by pro-reformist Xinhua staff members—ran in the colony's Chinese papers. On May 21, after Li Peng declared martial law, *Wen Wei Po,* one of the leading pro-Communist papers in Hong Kong, ran a four-character editorial—"*tongxin jishou*" (literally heart pain, head sick)—that poetically captured the range of Chinese emotions: anguish, anger, distress, resentment, heartsickness, confusion.

On the Saturday martial law was imposed, a typhoon struck Hong Kong, and the rain and gale-force winds kept most of the population indoors and glued to television programs. The news, however, focused on about 40,000 young people marching through sheets of water in support of the Beijing students. Many viewers were moved by the sight of the marchers, already drenched by the storm, shutting their umbrellas and sitting on the ground. When TV and radio broadcasters announced there would be another demonstration in central Hong Kong the next day at 2 p.m., the once politically indifferent citizens of the colony responded.

Even though the storm had subsided into light showers by then, the protest organizers expected only about 100,000 people. By 2:45 p.m., however, radio reports said 200,000 were crowding into central Hong

Kong. Then 300,000. By 9 p.m., police were estimating 500,000 to 600,000. Others applauded from alleyways, overpasses, rooftops, hanging out of apartment windows. Up to 1 million people, 18% of the colony's population, came out to support the protests.

Nine miles of winding, narrow streets were festooned with banners echoing the Beijing protests. The marchers, shouting "Down with Li Peng!" headed for the intersection in front of the Xinhua building, which was too small to hold such a big crowd. In a surprising gesture, the moneyed élite who control the Royal Hong Kong Jockey Club agreed to open the doors to the nearby Happy Valley racetrack. Images of the demonstration were thrown up onto the arena's gigantic video screen as the crowds filled the viewing stands and marched around the track.

The marchers came out not just for the Beijing students. They came out for themselves. "When I saw the students in Beijing going without food and sleeping on the ground in Tiananmen Square, I felt I had to march in the typhoon," said Frances Hung, a 24-year-old secretary at a Hong Kong trading company. "It was the least I could do to show my support." She added: "I am a Chinese British subject, with a British passport, but what does that mean? Nothing. I cannot leave Hong Kong!" For many, it was a discovery of their own Chineseness. No longer were they simply a microscopic promontory profiteering off the mainland. They had "brothers and sisters" in China who were struggling for historic reform, a change Hong Kong now wanted to share.

The colony responded with the element it loved most: money. Wallets and purses were opened and fistfuls of red-and-green Hong Kong dollar bills were stuffed into donation buckets. To avoid fraud, bank account numbers where contributions could be deposited were publicized in newspapers, on flyers, even on wall posters. Hong Kong's tycoons, some of whom had close ties to

Beijing, also offered their support. An aide to Li Ka-hsing, the real estate mogul, quoted his boss as saying, "It is the responsibility of the Chinese government to fight corruption and to give a just evaluation of the student demonstration." Briefcases full of cash were smuggled into Beijing to help the protesters defray the costs of the demonstrations—including the purchase of communication equipment such as portable telephones, walkie-talkies and fax machines. A contingent of Hong Kong students joined the strike in the Chinese capital, and colorful tents were donated to those living in the square.

The drafting of a post-1997 constitution for Hong Kong was halted as members involved in the Basic Law negotiations quit to protest Li Peng's martial-law edict. The deliberators issued a statement on the day following the demonstration saying, "We are temporarily unable to carry out our work as planned. We note that these events [in China] have done great damage to Hong Kong people's confidence in the Basic Law." People in Hong Kong—China's chief source of foreign currency, investment and credit—may have thought that protests and nervousness in the colony would effect positive changes in Beijing. China, they thought, must realize it cannot afford to panic Hong Kong. They were wrong.

After the massacre, the demonstrations in Hong Kong continued—but so did a search for a way out of China's clutches. On June 4, a protest against the crackdown drew as many people as did the May 21 demonstration against martial law. Again the marchers gathered at the Happy Valley racetrack, but the mood was different. The giddiness of political awakening had been replaced by silent grief. In Macao too there were large gatherings, though without much exhilaration. Instead, anger, desperation and a tremendous sadness pervaded both colonies. Said one Hong Kong protester: "The people here can no longer have faith in the Chinese government or in the future."

The Monday after the massacre, Hong Kong's usually frenetic property market, a traditional barometer of the enclave's economic health, began to stumble. Apartments that would normally have been snapped up within 24 hours of going on sale would not move. That was bad news for speculators who may have hoped to finance their own exodus from the colony through the profits from real estate sales.

The Hong Kong stock market went into a tailspin that rivaled Black Monday in October 1987. By the end of June, the Hang Seng index had fallen 25% from its level three months earlier. After recovering a bit, the market was again depressed by rumors in the first week of August that Deng Xiaoping was either dead or dying. The economy, however, received a much needed vote of confidence a week later when Citicorp announced it would arrange $667 million in loans to build two towers in Hong Kong. Still, local businessmen were wary of the potential of economic sanctions against China by the Western industrial powers. Many of Hong Kong's manufacturers had moved their factories into China's nearby Guangdong province, where the wages are lower than in the colony. Hong Kong businesses employed perhaps 2 million Chinese in these facilities, a number greater than the total work force of 850,000 in Hong Kong itself. Any tariffs slapped on Chinese-made goods in retaliation for the Beijing massacre would have a severe effect in Hong Kong. Said a spokesman for the Hong Kong and Shanghai Bank: "We view even the remote threat of trade sanctions as very serious indeed."

Their future in jeopardy, the people of Hong Kong turned to Britain in anger and desperation—and refuge. A deluge of demands from both inside and outside Hong Kong asked for safeguards to be built into the as-yet-unratified Basic Law draft to prevent the use of military force by China in the colony. The present draft, for example, stipulates two circumstances under which the

People's Liberation Army could be used inside the area. The first is if Hong Kong asked the Communist army garrison, which Beijing plans to locate within the colony, for protection. The second is in the event that China declares the existence of either a "state of turmoil" or a state of war in Hong Kong. After June 4 these stipulations were no longer being read as exceptions to the rule, but as ominous portents of seemingly inevitable doom. Responding to the colony's concern, a senior British official said that London would press Beijing for guarantees against such action, asking that it be underlined "in thick, thick ink."

Britain, however, was less than willing to become a refuge for worried Hong Kong residents. At the news of the massacre, the Thatcher government had reiterated its refusal to grant British residency to holders of British passports in Hong Kong. Instead, Thatcher promised only "more flexibility"—which residents of the colony assumed would be some scheme to allow selected Hong Kong civil servants to reside in Britain. Hong Kong politicians denounced that notion as "divisive."

Officials in London were terrified at the prospect of millions of Hong Kong immigrants flooding Britain, where nearly 5% of the population of 54 million consists of first- or second-generation immigrants—and where racial violence has flared sporadically in recent years. "We could not easily contemplate a massive new immigration commitment," said Foreign Secretary Sir Geoffrey Howe. In Macao, by contrast, the holders of Portuguese passports will have full rights as Portuguese citizens and can settle anywhere they wish in Portugal—or, because Portugal is a member of the European Community, in any E.C. country, including Britain, as early as 1992 when the Community is integrated.

The Thatcher government's refusal to admit Hong Kong refugees was seconded by the House of Commons' Foreign Affairs Select Committee. Instead, the committee suggested, people who wished to leave Hong Kong should be parceled out to other countries. While asking China for greater guarantees of Hong Kong's autonomy, the committee declared, "We believe the accommodation of even several million people from Hong Kong would be quite possible if shared amongst the international community." Hong Kong legislators complained that the move failed to recognize "that there is a confidence crisis in Hong Kong, which clearly calls for immediate action." During a three-day visit to the colony in early July, Howe was greeted by thousands of protesters, both Chinese and Western, and by signs that read HOWE CAN YOU SLEEP AT NIGHT? At a meeting with Hong Kong leaders, Howe repeated London's refusal to allow residents of the colony to resettle in Britain. He was loudly heckled, a response previously unheard of in the colony.

In the meantime, the very nature of Hong Kong may prove to be provocative to an increasingly conservative China. The colony's broadcasts reach deep into neighboring Guangdong. Western publications slip into the province as well, a flow that not even Beijing's post-crackdown ban on foreign newspapers and magazines could completely halt. Meanwhile, an underground railway of sorts was established to transport fugitives from China through Hong Kong to the West. Beijing may be tempted to make Hong Kong bend to its will—or at least heed its warnings. Some activists from Hong Kong caught ferrying cash to dissidents in China have been arrested by Beijing officials. When the prodemocracy Hong Kong daily *Wen Wei Po* continued to be critical of Beijing policy, its editor Lee Tse-Chung was fired. And while the Chinese government repeated that Hong Kong's capitalist system would remain intact after 1997, the *People's Daily* noted in late July that "we will not allow people to use Hong Kong as a base for subverting the central people's government."

In 1986 the Chinese government began erecting a

stunning symbol of its coming mastery of Hong Kong: the 70-story, I.M. Pei–designed Bank of China building, the tallest structure in the colony. From the start, the masters of *fengshui,* the ancient art of geomancy that many people in Hong Kong take seriously, had warned that the triangular theme and sharp edges of the building's architecture portended bad luck, directing evil spirits outward into the colony and inward toward the building's proprietors. Beijing officials paid little heed to the superstition. But bad *fengshui* is bad *fengshui.* After the Tiananmen massacre, Beijing's towering symbol of dominance and modernity had become a lightning rod for danger, threatening to draw ill fortune toward the entire colony.

CHAPTER SIX

THE CRACKDOWN

The first account that the sleepless people of Beijing heard from their government was sharply at odds with what they had seen and with the live television coverage that the rest of the world was watching. "A handful of thugs who crave nothing short of nationwide chaos stirred up a serious counterrevolutionary riot in Beijing," said Mayor Chen Xitong in a statement that crackled over Beijing Radio late Sunday evening, some 24 hours after the massacre. The army and police had rushed to the defense of the socialist system "with a courageous, dauntless spirit," the mayor added, but had managed to win only a "preliminary victory in the struggle to end the turmoil and smash the counterrevolutionary scheme." The People's Government, he concluded, had no choice but "to resolutely crack down on the rioters and severely punish them without mercy."

The student leaders of the democratic movement, who just two weeks before had attracted millions of people to their cause, were paid only cursory attention in the mayor's account, and their allies among the intelligentsia were altogether ignored. Mayor Chen's most glaring omission was predictable. He made no reference to the power struggle between Deng Xiaoping and the hard-liners represented by Premier Li Peng, on the one hand, and the liberal faction of fallen party General Secretary Zhao Ziyang on the other, which had paralyzed the leadership for the previous six weeks.

As reruns of old Korean War movies on the state broadcasting network gave way to selective replays of the mayor's message and other official statements that were even more farfetched, it became apparent that the government intended to cover up the brutality of its crackdown on the democratic movement. Although vestiges of a major military operation were everywhere in evidence, a clutch of latter-day thought controllers was hard at work behind the scenes to say it wasn't so. Tanks and armored vehicles were positioned not only in the square and other combat areas, but also at major points of entry outside the city and at most major intersections inside as well. The military had established a particularly heavy presence around the capital's foreign enclaves, where diplomats, journalists and businessmen worked and lived. The undulating wails of ambulance sirens and the sharp retort of automatic-weapons fire punctuated the silence of a city that was temporarily void of daytime civilian traffic. At night the alien groan of APCs navigating the gradual inclines of freeway flyovers made sleep difficult.

As word of the carnage that had taken place on the way to the square spread through Beijing on Sunday and Monday, tempers flared. One group of grieving students laid the body of a young Tiananmen Square victim out on ice and paraded it from campus to campus for all to see. At the University of Political Science and Law, the students arranged a grisly exhibition of dead bodies. Other students speeded up the distribution of posters and tracts, which had begun to serve as an alternate press during the heady days of the student demonstrations. A concise, 15-

point summary of Hong Kong press reportage of the Tiananmen massacre, which was posted in the middle of a busy shopping area, drew throngs of passersby. Likewise, a photocopied handbill identified as a "Peking University leaflet" and several photographs of gruesome civilian casualties, faxed from Hong Kong, were eagerly examined by residents of a *hutong* just behind Tiananmen Square. "Loyalists of June 3," read the document, "the 27th Army is a murderer and a slaughterer."

Many people who had taken up defensive positions on the barricades when the army moved in switched to the offensive when the major fighting ended. Surrounding stranded convoys wherever they found them on Sunday and Monday, they clubbed fleeing soldiers, broke open the gas tanks of their vehicles and set them aflame. In some cases soldiers beat civilians to the job, torching their own trucks after removing ammunition and supplies. By Monday the streets of the city were littered with the smoldering hulks of dozens of vehicles. Soldiers who approached the inevitable knots of bystanders that gathered near the wreckage were routinely jeered. Just as routinely they fired at those who taunted them, adding more casualties to the already overburdened hospital wards.

By then the propaganda campaign was well under way. Official party organs, which only weeks before had burgeoned to include actual news and photos of the student movement in the streets, were suddenly transformed back into the sort of shrill broadsheets that characterized the Antispiritual Pollution Campaign of 1983. Television, too, took several steps backward, dropping the usual news reports and substituting the texts of the proliferating martial-law decrees. TV newsreaders could not bring themselves to look the camera in the eye as they spouted the new government line. The broadcasters were warned that they would lose their jobs if they did not put a happy face on the revisionist statements they were required to read.

Among the most startling of that genre was one handed down by the party Central Committee and State Council on June 5, addressed to "all party members and the people of all China." The purpose of the counterrevolutionary riots, it claimed, was "to negate the party's leadership and the socialist system" by "killing all 47 million Communist Party members" if necessary. The masterminds of the plot, according to the message, were an "extremely few people who have doggedly persisted in taking the stand of bourgeois liberalization and have colluded with hostile forces overseas, providing party and state vital secrets to illegal organizations."

Given the outsize objectives of the propaganda campaign, it had to be at least as crude as the previous weekend's military campaign if it were to be effective. The target of the Communist Party Central Committee's leadership group for propaganda and ideological work was not primarily the audience that had witnessed the truth, either firsthand or through the lenses of foreign television cameras. Rather, it was the vast silent majority of Chinese, who it feared might have been infected by the same bourgeois liberal notions of free speech, independent association and government accountability that had animated the prodemocracy demonstrations. Chief among those the propagandists wished to inoculate were the 47 million party members who had been exposed to General Secretary Zhao Ziyang's assertions that political reform was an essential adjunct to economic reform.

Determined to eradicate any traces of such heretical thinking, party hard-liners had well before the massacre purged all Zhaoists from the propaganda group and even forced the hospitalization of one member of questionable zeal. The replacements the hard-liners chose were orthodox political thinkers like Shanghai party boss Jiang Zemin, who could work compatibly with the martial-law information units that had taken over newspaper editorial offices and the state broadcasting apparatus. The campaign that this newly constituted group unveiled two days after the massacre was couched in the only language every Chinese citizen understood: the language of fear.

"Maybe we underestimate the viability of Stalinism as a force today," commented a senior Asian diplomat as the government's campaign of intimidation quickly took on a life of its own. That campaign began with the broadcast of a segment of cleverly edited black-and-white video footage of the devastation wrought by protesters on the night of June 4. The tape was shot by the British-made remote-control cameras on Beijing's major thoroughfares. Purchased by the Chinese partly with development aid and purportedly installed to monitor city traffic, the system's cameras had been rolling throughout the six-week period of the demonstrations.

The cameras had a low-light feature that allowed them to record scenes at night, and their lenses stripped the protective cloak of darkness from the rioting near Tiananmen Square. They also homed in on individual protesters, like the one caught in the act of smashing the windshield of a military truck and hurling bricks at its trapped driver. The official voice-over of China Central Television (CCTV) reported that both the driver and his assistant had been killed. Both narrator and editor ignored the rest of the action depicted on the tape, which showed APCs roaring by the disabled truck in pursuit of the primary mission of the evening: to retake the square from the prodemocracy forces.

As that and similar tapes were played repeatedly on state television in the days following the massacre, the propaganda group, aided by 10,000 clerks, combed through miles of other footage previously recorded by the same cameras during the weeks of peaceful demonstrations in the square, looking for frames of key leaders. Once identified, their faces were frozen into individual electronic mug shots for display on the evening news. Not that the leaders were likely to elude the ever expanding police dragnet, which included university campuses, transport terminals, known dissident safe houses and those previous preserves of quasi-immunity, the foreign diplomatic compounds, which housed journalists as well as diplomats.

During the day or two after the massacre, student leaders, their intellectual mentors and their chief contacts inside the party ran for their lives. Those who had made contingency plans and secured exit permits were able, with the help of accommodating diplomats, to obtain foreign passports and visas. Among them was Marxist theoretician Su Shaozhi, 63, who was ousted from his post as head of the Institute of Marxism-Lenism and Mao Zedong Thought in the wake of the 1986-87 student movement. Provided with a Dutch travel document, Su was able to board an evacuation flight with a group of European students. An indifferent immigration official simply stamped his passport without questioning what a Chinese man of his age was doing in such company.

Others sought refuge inside embassies or prevailed on foreign friends to hide them and help spirit them to safety by way of a sort of underground railway to the freewheeling Special Economic Zones in southern China. There, sympathetic entrepreneurs and bureaucrats helped shepherd the suspects to freedom across the border into Hong Kong and Macao. One fugitive made his way onto a Chinese sightseeing boat and jumped overboard off Macao, where he was rescued. Several others, who are believed to have been smuggled out of Chinese ports in cargo containers, surfaced safely weeks later in France.

On the morning of Wednesday, June 7, several people who would figure prominently on the government's most-wanted list of alleged counterrevolutionaries were secretly hidden in the diplomatic compound of Jianguomenwai and the adjacent embassy row. Without warning, soldiers manning a checkpoint in the vicinity launched a series of terrifyingly puzzling maneuvers. Just before 10 a.m., thousands of foot soldiers and a convoy of scores of trucks loaded with troops belonging to the despised 27th Army left Tiananmen Square and rolled eastward. All night long the men of the 27th had been moving out of the capital, to be replaced by fresh troops.

When the trucks approached the Jianguomenwai overpass, several detoured into a side street on which the American and British embassies are located, firing shots into the air and yelling, "Go home! Go home!" as they passed. Meanwhile, the main column of troops proceeded down Changan Avenue, spraying the air with erratic bursts of gunfire, as if to ward off possible attack from unseen enemies. As bullets rained down on them, bicyclists and shoppers scrambled to escape the apparently trigger-happy troops by ducking behind hedges or hitting the ground.

To residents of the apartments inside the Jianguomenwai, which overlooked the street, and to employees in the adjacent thirty-story office tower belonging to the China International Trust and Investment Corporation (CITIC), the incident seemed anything but random. The bullets that crashed through the plate glass seemed to come from buildings of similar·height across the street, rather than upward from the soldiers on their trucks. In addition, the shots appeared to have been aimed at specific targets.

The small office of the Yugoslav industrial-engineering firm SMELT Global Project Management on the 27th floor of the CITIC building, for example, was left a shambles by eight shells, which shattered the windows, ripped the blinds and tore through the plasterboard walls and ceilings, dusting the desktop computers with shards of insulation. Ballistics experts who examined the flat trajectories of the bullets concluded that some of the shots came from the roof of the Chinese Academy of Social

Sciences, a hotbed of behind-the-scenes support for the student movement that had been occupied by the military immediately after the massacre.

SMELT's commanding view of the academy and Tiananmen Square beyond had made it a popular vantage point from which to photograph army maneuvers. Just before the attack, a Japanese TV cameraman had been warned by Foreign Ministry officials not to continue taking pictures from SMELT's windows. Afterward, an East European diplomat speculated that the attack was "a planned action to frighten away foreigners." Said he: "This is the sort of terror that does not cause any physical harm."

Minutes later, hundreds of rounds were fired into the nearby apartments of eleven American diplomats and numerous other foreigners. The firing was so intense that the U.S. Embassy lodged an official protest with the Chinese Foreign Ministry. The U.S. charged that the army had made a deliberate and premeditated attack on a building inside the diplomatic compound that had become a popular observation deck from which foreign military attachés could watch the tanks patrolling the bridge below. The embassy report challenged the official Chinese account, which held that the apartments were fired on by troops who were retaliating against a sniper. "There is no doubt in this embassy's opinion that certain apartments were deliberately targeted by the army," said the U.S. report, which was released a month later. It noted that one U.S. defense attaché's quarters had been pockmarked with 18 bullet holes.

One intelligence expert offered an explanation for why the Chinese fired into that particular embassy building. "The night before, the Public Security Bureau and the soldiers arrested 24 people and had them kneeling on the ground in the execution position while we watched from a balcony," he recounted. The security officers, aware that foreigners had trained their binoculars on their prisoners, moved away. "I am absolutely convinced that those people would have been killed if diplomats had not been there." He was quick to admit, however, that he had no idea what happened to the prisoners afterward.

Early the following morning at least one of the diplomats was warned by his Chinese counterparts not to remain in his apartment. By noon his flat was among those that had taken direct hits. Meanwhile, Chinese soldiers had sealed off the gates to the compound on the pretext that the mysterious sniper was inside. Residents were barred from leaving until plainclothes agents had removed an unidentified Chinese man. Witnesses reported that the man they removed was not looking especially worried, leading many foreigners to suspect that he was a plant and that there was no suspected sniper at all. In fact, some sources claim that the man the authorities were really looking for was Fang Lizhi. According to reports by the Hong Kong magazine *The Nineties* and Agence France Presse, Fang had been briefly hidden there after the massacre while waiting for the U.S. Embassy to answer his request for refuge.

The family and friends of Fang Lizhi and his wife Li Shuxian, a physics professor at Peking University who is as active a crusader for political change in China as her husband, feared for the couple's safety after the imposition of martial law. In late May their friend Perry Link, a professor of Chinese literature and director of the U.S. Academy of Sciences office in Beijing, who had been with the Fangs when police prevented them from attending a Feb. 26 banquet hosted by President Bush, inquired of an American diplomat whether the Fangs could seek refuge inside the U.S. Embassy, if the need arose. The answer he received was noncommittal.

The morning after the massacre, Link bicycled to the Fangs' spacious apartment near Peking University to check on the safety of his controversial friends. He found them relatively calm regarding their own condition, but fearful that the country's leaders had gone mad. Before they parted company, Li had agreed that if they needed Link's help, she would telephone him with a coded message: "Please bring the children here to play."

At 5 p.m. that day she called with the message. Link rushed back to find her nearly mute with fear. Friends had phoned to tell them that their names topped the government blacklist. This time it was Fang himself who queried Link about the possibility of seeking temporary refuge in the U.S. Embassy. Because it was Sunday, however, the embassy was closed. So Link drove the Fangs and their son to the nearby Shangri-La Hotel and booked them a room in his name.

On Monday Li's students called her to report that the military was preparing to take over the campuses located in the university belt in northwestern Beijing. They told her they were ready to die on the barricades, but urged that she and Fang seek protection. With that, Link drove the family to the U.S. Embassy, where they met with three ranking officials. Fang asked permission to hide in the embassy for a couple of days until the matter blew over. The diplomats explained that it would be impossible to keep his presence there a secret, given the large Chinese staff employed by the embassy and the likelihood of bugs. On the other hand, to grant him official protection as a temporary refugee was tantamount to sentencing him to a long confinement inside the embassy—not to mention the damage such a gesture would do to Sino-American relations.

Realizing that public disclosure of any attempt by Fang to seek shelter from Americans would discredit both himself and the democratic movement, he decided to abandon the idea and settle for a U.S. visa. That afternoon Link installed the Fangs in the nearby Jianguo Hotel. When he tried to call them the next day, June 6, he received no answer.

In Washington on the same day, a State Department

official said that Fang Lizhi and his family had been permitted to take refuge in the U.S. Embassy in Beijing. According to Agence France Presse, Fang was smuggled out of the hotel and into what was regarded as a more secure, hiding place inside the Jianguomenwai compound that afternoon. The following morning, shortly after the shoot-out in the streets, residents noted that limousines belonging to top-ranking American and British diplomats, which had been parked in the compound lot, departed just minutes before Chinese soldiers rushed in.

Before the day was over, the city was roiling with rumors that Deng had died, Li Peng had been shot by an assassin and civil war between rival army divisions was imminent. Anti-American rhetoric grew heated with the announcement on CCTV that Fang had indeed fled to the U.S. Embassy. A Foreign Ministry spokesman termed U.S. charges that the Chinese military had massacred students "flagrantly unwarranted" and called the Bush Administration's suspension of arms sales and military exchanges with Beijing "absolutely unacceptable to us." In a televised news conference, government spokesman Yuan Mu defiantly pronounced the regime "unafraid" of either "condemnation or sanctions." He also produced new official casualty figures for the June 3-4 fighting: no more than 300 people had died, only 23 of them students.

One diplomat felt he had witnessed it all before. "Everything we have seen in the past four days is preparation for a red Stalinist terror," he said. "What they are doing is attempting to drive out every foreign eye, so they can go about their executions." They succeeded in driving off quite a few foreigners. The shooting in the streets set off a stampede among expatriate dependents to join an evacuation effort that was already under way. Husbands with large attaché cases stood in long lines at the Bank of China's foreign-exchange windows, waiting to change renminbi bills that were nonconvertible outside the country. Meanwhile, their wives and children sat anxiously in a convoy of embassy vans, trapped inside the locked gates, until police completed their search for the alleged sniper. Hysteria mounted as they watched Chinese soldiers outside, pointing their guns at residents and forbidding entry to embassy guards who had been assigned to escort the convoy.

The scene at Beijing International Airport was chaotic even before that particularly besieged group arrived. Donna Anderson, an American, had been camped inside the terminal with her husband and three children for 24 hours by that time, waiting with hundreds of other foreigners to get on a flight to Tokyo. "We didn't know about the shoot-out until just before we boarded the plane," she recalled. "The report was that someone had fired rockets into the CITIC building." By then, said Anderson, "order inside the airport had broken down. The waiting lines had deteriorated, and people were shoving each other and tearing at the standby list. We were walking on the conveyor belts to get from section to section, and the employees, who seemed to be as scared as anyone else, were not telling us to get off. People were beginning to panic."

The panic was palpable that night, as an Asian diplomat watched an army supply convoy of 127 trucks pass under his balcony, bound for Tiananmen Square to the west. The lurid yellow-green glow of mercury-vapor lamps along the highway silhouetted the bayonets that protruded from the backs of the troop trucks escorting the convoy. Earlier in the day the 20 tanks and APCs of the 27th Army that had blocked the intersection below pulled out and headed east. That move fed rumors that the soldiers were preparing to defend themselves and their bloody conquest of the square from one of the rival armies that was said to be riding to the rescue. Ever since the massacre, Beijing residents talked wistfully about the prospect of civil war between the "bad guys" of the 27th Army and the "good guys" of the 38th, who had reportedly balked at orders to enforce martial law.

An Asian diplomat did not dismiss such speculation. For one thing, the presence of an estimated 250,000 troops in the Beijing region was a reflection of the political power struggle that was being waged there. Before martial law had been declared, many commanders had questioned the deployment of troops into what was essentially a political arena. A few commanders had reportedly refused, and they had been replaced. There were reports that more armies had been called up to prevent the dissident officers from pulling a coup. "The troops did not arrive here exclusively to deal with the students," a Western diplomat acknowledged. "There was a certain form of power play going on here, and troops were positioned against each other. One reason there were so many troops was that each faction was, in effect, showing its cards."

For another, wall posters in Beijing described "skirmishes" between several armies. Moreover, a segment of one of the ring roads that encircles the city remained littered with chunks of concrete road dividers well after street sweepers had begun cleaning up most of the city's streets. That was no accident, according to an Asian defense attaché. "Those chunks are standard antitank barricades that are designed to snarl the treads," he said. Two barricades had been erected at that particular junction, he explained. "The first barricade, which was made of buses, was erected by the people, but the second, the pieces of concrete, was laid out by the 27th Army." The 27th presumably wanted to stop some other unit's tanks.

Other evidence that Beijing-based diplomats and military experts had collected was more circumstantial, but no less intriguing. "Some of the troops that moved through Beijing on the night of June 4 were not issued any ammunition," said an Asian envoy. "Only Yang Shangkun's men were given ammunition. So for the first few days, Yang was saying, 'We have all the firepower, so don't move against us.' " His informants contended that although the Chinese military was indeed divided over the use of force against the students, its commanders were too loyal to Deng to bolt while he was alive. "According to one scenario, there are a lot of fence sitters in the military who are waiting for Deng to die, at which point they can switch allegiance," he said.

Given the uncertainty of the situation, it was no wonder that the government had been prompt to deny the report, first broadcast in Taiwan, that Deng was dead. Continuing headlines, in Hong Kong and elsewhere, that he was suffering from prostate cancer kept the level of tension high. "They are not sure where the threat is coming from, so the tanks swivel in all directions," the Asian envoy observed, "and the soldiers are very paranoid, very jumpy."

Yet reports of major clashes in the western hills or at the Nanyuan military airfield to the south of the city remained unverified. So did stories in the Hong Kong press describing divisions within the ranks. The independent newspaper *Ming Pao* alleged that because other armies had refused to clear the square, the tough 27th Army, which was loyal to Yang, had been given the job. As compensation, added the paper, all brave officers would be promoted one grade and courageous soldiers sent to military training schools. Other stories described the resentment that was building against the 27th by troops who did not take part in the massacre.

Soldiers from a Beijing military region unit that had chosen not to shoot their way through the citizen barricades were reported to be so distraught on June 5, when they learned about the violence wreaked by the 27th Army, that they ripped off their badges, abandoned their tanks and trucks and retreated into the nearby Military Museum. Protesters promptly torched the vehicles.

"They are not fighting it out," said an Asian ambassador about the curious behavior of some other military

units, "they are just maneuvering around each other."
The big question mark in the minds of most foreign observers was the Beijing garrison, which was believed to be
under the influence of Defense Minister Qin Jiwei, its former commander. A longtime ally of Deng, Qin was said
to have opposed the use of force against the students. He
was eyed by his fellow officers, as well as by foreign diplomats, as a likely candidate to lead a coup.

"Those élite forces, which have not yet been brought
into play, are sitting it out in the west of the city," said
the ambassador. His defense attaché had assured him
that rival forces were "trying their best to disengage and
compromise rather than use massive force against each
other." However, he remained uneasy. "You never
know," he commented. "One of my Chinese sources says
the army has gone mad. He warned me, 'The soldiers
have blood in their eyes.' "

On June 9, Deng Xiaoping broke the suspense by addressing a group of top military officers, Politburo Standing Committee members and party elders. It had been 24
days since the senior leader had made his last public appearance, his historic meeting with Mikhail Gorbachev.
The setting—Deng surrounded by top government leaders at a large oval table inside Zhongnanhai—was designed to show that he was not only alive, but in charge
and undaunted by world criticism of the massacre. As
television cameras panned the assembled guests, diplomats studied their TV screens carefully, preparing to note
any significant absentees.

One by one, the members of the Central Military
Commission and the general staff greeted Deng, who
walked under his own steam and stood unaided during a
silent tribute for the June 3-4 military "martyrs." Then
the group posed for a photo. There was General Yang
Shangkun, dressed in a sports jacket, as if to underline his
civilian role as President rather than his military role as
permanent vice chairman of the Military Commission

and de facto commander of the martial-law forces. There were his brother Yang Baibing, a member of the Central Military Commission and the army's top political commissar, and Chief of Staff Chi Haotian, another relative of Yang's by marriage. More interesting was the parade of officers who had been rumored to favor Zhao Ziyang. Defense Minister Qin Jiwei was present, as were Deputy Chief of Staff Xu Xin and Central Military Commission member Hong Xuezhi.

"Absolutely unified," declared a Western intelligence expert afterward. "Every element of the general staff was present, including the two members of the party's Central Military Commission who we believed were on opposing sides." The only glaring absence had been anticipated: Military Commission First Vice Chairman Zhao Ziyang. What had earlier looked like signs of civil war had probably been no more than "the usual sorts of arguments that a military man would use about calling in military forces to handle what should be a political situation," the intelligence expert mused. Despite such reservations, he argued, "the army will follow orders."

That was very much the message Deng delivered in his speech to the assembled leaders. He looked frail. His left hand trembled, his face was puffy, his eyes were ringed with dark circles. But as he spoke, his words grew in coherency. At one point he dismissed an unwanted bit of prompting from Li Peng, who sat in the seat of honor to his right, with a withering look.

"This storm was bound to happen sooner or later," he began. "As determined by the international and domestic climate, it was independent of man's will." He classified the problem as "turmoil," and had said as much in the vituperative speech to his inner circle, which was distilled into the notorious April 26 *People's Daily* editorial. Because some elements of the leadership had disagreed with his conclusion about how to handle the situation, he argued, events had got out of control and had provoked a "counterrevolutionary rebellion." At that point he had had to reach out to other elements of the party and to the military for support.

Gesturing to the top leaders and to the four members of the so-called Gang of Elders who surrounded him at the table, Deng said, "We still have a group of senior comrades who are alive, we still have the army, and we also have a group of core cadres who took part in the revolution." The leadership, he said, had been able to analyze the situation and detect that behind the students and the ordinary people who took to the streets there lurked "a rebellious clique and a large quantity of the dregs of society," who were intent on "overthrowing the Communist Party and the socialist system . . . and establishing a bourgeois republic entirely dependent on the West."

The army had stopped them. "This army retains the traditions of the old Red Army," said Deng with evident satisfaction. Noting that "there are not so many veteran comrades in the army, the soldiers are mostly little more than 18, 19 or 20 years of age," the old Long Marcher was all the more heartened by the troops' performance. "No matter how generations change," he said, "this army of ours is forever an army under the leadership of the party, forever the defender of the country, forever the defender of socialism, forever the defender of the public interest."

The show of unity by the military and the old revolutionaries under Deng certainly quelled speculation about impending civil war. Yet it also heightened anxieties that a clutch of paranoid old men would now have the power they needed to carry out a massive purge of all the individuals and interest groups whom they perceived to be enemies of the party. The performance also raised the question of what price Deng had had to pay for the Old Guard's support. Throughout his decade in power, he had played the role of master balancer of factions, seemingly belonging to none. Had he been forced by circumstances this time to sell out to the hard-liners? The events of the next two weeks led even his admirers to conclude that he had.

Ideological slogans that had not been widely heard in recent years suddenly seeped back into the public vocabulary. Two of the elders, former National People's Congress Standing Committee Chairman Peng Zhen, 87, and State Vice President Wang Zhen, 80, had been among the key architects of the 1987 campaign against "bourgeois liberalization." Zhao had managed to derail that campaign, and Deng had gone along with him. Now Deng himself laced his speeches with warnings against bourgeois liberalization. At the same time "class struggle," a Marxist concept that Deng had publicly tossed into the dustbin of history at the momentous Third Plenum of the Eleventh Central Committee in 1978, returned to vogue. That plenum, which launched China's historic process of modernization, also ordained for the first time that economic development and modernization must take priority over class struggle.

More chilling than the reactionary phrases were the images of repression that quickly bombarded the TV screens. On Saturday came the announcement that 400 "scoundrels" accused of attacking soldiers had been arrested in cities all over China. Footage that would be repeated on national TV again and again over the next week showed a sweating prisoner, his hands cuffed, his head bowed, being led into an interrogation room and questioned at gunpoint by police.

A student and a worker in Shanghai who had belonged to independent associations that supported the democracy movement in that city also figured prominently in the initial propaganda. The worker, Li Zhibo, had been beaten in the head by his interrogators and sported a puffed-up eye. Yao Yongzhan, a Hong Kong student activist who had been accused of heading the Shanghai Autonomous Union of College Students, looked to be in better physical shape. He had been grabbed at Shanghai airport while in the company of a group of British students and several consular officials who had provided him with a ticket to Hong Kong. He was detained for carrying restricted articles.

As if to caption the scenes of justice that were being meted out to this first group of prisoners, the authorities announced a nationwide ban on autonomous student and worker associations. Fearful from the start that groups without ties to the Communist Party might root themselves among the masses, much as the Solidarity labor movement did in Poland, Deng had warned intimates to beware of Chinese students' demands for an independent student union. Were independent student unions to crop up, he had predicted back in April, "we will have many Lech Walesas, not just in Beijing but in every province."

Throughout that weekend, CCTV repeatedly broadcast the first in a series of show-and-tell features: an attempt to persuade viewers to turn themselves and their neighbors in to the authorities, rather than wait to be hunted down. The 69-second video clip was identified as footage from an American television interview of a 40-year-old Beijing resident. In it he described the "massacre of students by the army" at Tiananmen Square, claiming that 20,000 people had died. Superimposed on the footage was the message "This man is a rumormonger," followed by instructions to denounce "those spreading false rumors" by going to the nearest police station.

In fact, CCTV had violated canons of international broadcasting behavior—and, probably, law—by snatching a sequence of raw video feed belonging to ABC News off a satellite during transmission from Tokyo to New York City. Moreover, CCTV had passed the sequence off as information that had already been aired on American television. It had not. On seeing the Chinese version, ABC correspondent James Laurie recalled, "I was extremely upset." CCTV had, he realized, aired footage that ABC had left on the cutting-room floor.

What happened was that the day after the massacre, Laurie had conducted one of many man-in-the-street interviews in Beijing with the Chinese man in question. In the 2½ minutes of conversation that Laurie's crew captured on tape, the man had touched upon several taboo topics, including the death toll in the square. Deprived of direct satellite transmission from Beijing since the imposition of martial law, Laurie shipped his unedited tape to Tokyo for transmission by satellite to New York. He then sat down in his hotel room in Beijing, wrote a script to go with the images, and read it, together with instructions on how to edit the tape, over a phone line to ABC in New York. What finally appeared on ABC's nightly news was a mere eight-second snippet of the man in the street with an English-language voice-over paraphrasing what he had said about bloodshed in the Chinese capital. "We are probably naive," says Laurie, "but we never thought anyone would do that." What is worse, the Chinese stratagem worked. Several days after the "rumormonger" was exposed on CCTV, he was identified and arrested in his hometown of Dalian.

The state network later showed the accused man, Xiao Bing, an aluminum-window maker, in police custody. Two women had spotted the "rumormonger" buying cigarettes. They had followed him to his hotel, reporting his whereabouts to the Public Security Bureau. "At first he refused to confess what he did," said the *People's Daily*. "But after the videotape was played, he confessed."

On Sunday CCTV went after Fang Lizhi and his wife Li Shuxian. "These two criminals are escaping to avoid punishment," read the government appeal for their capture, without mentioning that they had taken refuge inside the U.S. Embassy. "Once they are found, they should be immediately detained, and the Beijing Public Security Bureau informed." Under an old photo of Fang, the TV report offered this description of China's most famous dissident: "About 1.72 meters, a little fat, hair hangs to one side; long, square face, glasses; throws out chest and raises head when walking."

As the Fangs' photos and descriptions flashed before the eyes of viewers, the Chinese government stepped up its verbal attacks on the couple. Beijing Radio read an order from the city Public Security Bureau to alert border guards and airports throughout the country to prevent their escape. Meanwhile, the controlled press published ever shrill anti-Fang commentaries. The authorities even issued a pamphlet titled *The True Face of Fang Lizhi* to discredit him. "You've gone to hide inside a foreign embassy?" questioned an unsigned letter in *People's Daily*. "Exactly what kind of hero are you?" On the same day a signed commentary in that paper questioned Fang's patriotism and his continued usefulness to the prodemocracy movement. "Now he hides himself in the U.S. Embassy and has degraded his position to that of a beggar," said the commentator.

As the pace and quantity of arrests escalated early the following week, the nightly television news expanded beyond its usual 30 minutes to accommodate the proliferation of mug shots and the increasingly heavy propaganda. On Tuesday most of the extra air time was devoted to photos of 21 student prodemocracy activists wanted for leading the "counterrevolutionary rebellion." Most of the faces that flashed on the screen were frozen stills lifted from tapes made of the demonstrations in Beijing and other cities, or photos shot by the hundreds of plainclothes police who mingled with the demonstrators throughout April and May. Authorities had scrutinized the footage and matched faces with police records and other evidence, such as the license registrations of the countless bicycles that police had picked up at demonstration sites and confiscated.

The most charismatic of the student leaders, Uerkesh Daolet, was doubly honored by the showing of a separate short feature that was taken by a remote-control camera mounted on the wall of a dining hall in the Beijing Hotel. The footage was aired with a voice-over implying that the students at the table had been feasting when they were supposed to be fasting. Yet decipherable dates on the clip showed that the dinner actually took place more than a week after their hunger strike had ended.

By Wednesday the frequent replays of the list of most-wanted students began to pay off. Zhou Fengsuo, a 20-year-old physics student at Qinghua University in Beijing, was arrested in the central China city of Xian. Zhou was turned in by his sister, an employee of the Air Force Institute there. "Just after the evening broadcast of the arrest warrants on television," said the TV commentator, "Zhou's sister and her husband went and made a report to the local police after talking it over. Five policemen went and arrested him. He admitted he was a student leader."

Foreign residents were horrified at what they saw as his sister's betrayal of Zhou Fengsuo. But a Chinese viewer saw it otherwise. "She had to do it," he said, "there is no place to hide in China." Indeed, in a country where marital spats and birth control are the business of neighborhood committees, privacy and secrecy are at a minimum. Even in the best of times, Chinese citizens have been prisoners of their *hukoubu* and individual identification cards, which are necessary for obtaining jobs, housing and rationed food staples like grain and edible oils. Chinese travelers must routinely show their identification cards to buy train and plane tickets, and sometimes even provide letters of permission from their work units before boarding long-distance sleeper trains. Passports for foreign travel are good for one trip only. Chinese citizens who wish to go abroad must either buy foreign-exchange certificates on the black market, at a premium, or apply to the Public Security Bureau for coupons with which to buy airline tickets or limited amounts of foreign exchange.

During the first few days after the massacre, controls in train stations and airports were lax. Those fugitives who were lucky enough to possess the proper papers, forged or otherwise, could slip onto trains bound for distant provinces or even out of the country. However, those who did not get out early faced almost insurmountable obstacles. Once the crackdown came, soldiers stationed themselves in and around airline terminals and train stations, and special teams were mobilized to check the papers of arriving and departing passengers. Photo charts of the most prominent fugitives from the democracy movement were posted at airline ticket-sales counters all across the country. Travel restrictions were tightened in such a way as to render visas obtained before the massacre useless without an additional exit permit.

More ominous than the limits placed on travelers trying to leave China were those confronting people who had no choice but to stay. "My work unit has been assigned a quota of *baotu* to bring in," said a young Communist bureaucrat, who supported the student movement. So had his party branch. Although he could hardly be classified as a rioter, he had openly participated in some of the demonstrations. While he was unlikely to be detained, even a self-criticism would serve as a black mark against him in his dossier and would almost certainly hinder his career for as long as the conservative leadership remained in power. The party branch's quota concerned him even more. "Expulsion from the party is the worst thing that can happen to a Chinese," he said unequivocally. Loyalty to the party told him to confess and write a criticism, but adherence to his own ideals told him not to repudiate his support for democracy.

Students were in an even more precarious position than bureaucrats, since their actions had been so openly recorded, and since they were dependent on the state to assign them their jobs. Prominent leaders of the illegal student organizations like Zhou Fengsuo were in the most immediate danger. Even if they managed to flee to a distant province, they ran into problems when they tried to get jobs, housing or grain. "Even the pedicab drivers are organized," explained a Chinese official. Anyone applying for a job, no matter how menial, would have to present an identification card, as would anyone wishing to buy rice at the low, state-subsidized price. A fugitive risked discovery or starvation unless he had enough money to buy food and shelter on the open market, or he had had the foresight and the necessary Hong Kong connections to forge a new identity—and a new ID card—for himself and a new *hukoubu* for his family.

"In the new, open economy brought about by the reforms, the *hukou* did not seem so important," said a Chinese official. "People who could find part-time work in private or foreign companies and who earned enough money to buy their food and rent their housing on the private market could get along without one. Or, for a price, they could get their *hukou* transferred from their hometown to Beijing by a corrupt Public Security Bureau official." But the crackdown had momentarily changed that. "Many young people who had not committed serious crimes fled Beijing when the crackdown came," said a foreign resident. "They had been in technical violation of the law for staying on in the capital after graduation without a *hukou,* and they feared they might be picked up for that reason."

As the propaganda intensified and the number of arrests multiplied, it began to appear that workers were even more vulnerable to arrest and harsh penalties than students, intellectuals and bureaucrats. Whether they lacked the connections to obtain travel documents—passports, visas—or whether family responsibilities prevented them from fleeing quickly enough, workers constituted the bulk of those detained in the immediate wake of the crackdown. And, as a Shanghai court made clear in the first trial related to the democracy movement, workers were the first to draw the death penalty for their participation in the movement.

On June 15, three workers who had been charged, along with seven other people, in the burning of a train in Shanghai were sentenced to death. The incident stemmed from a June 6 sit-in on the railroad tracks to protest the Beijing massacre. An oncoming train had rammed the demonstrators, killing six of them. In retaliation, protesters attacked the train with petrol bombs, setting it on fire and beating some of the fire fighters who attempted to extinguish the flames. No further deaths were caused by the fire, but nine carriages, six police motorcycles and 900 bags of mail were destroyed, and transport on the busy Shanghai-Beijing line was halted for 50 hours. The court took pains to stress that the three accused had nothing to do with the student movement, but were "local hoodlums and thugs taking advantage of the disruption to cause trouble."

The tough verdict was intended as a warning that the government would not flinch in the face of hostile world opinion to eliminate what it regarded as the sources of domestic disorder. On the same day the Shanghai verdict was reported, *People's Daily* carried a front-page analysis of Deng's speech to the army. "If we give the impression of concessions or weakness, China will become a vassal of the imperialists once again," according to the paper. Analysts believed the death sentences also reflected the government's fear that the latent dissatisfaction prompting so many workers to join the student protests might flare into unrest and strikes later on.

As dramatic as news of the death penalties was, the proceedings in the Shanghai courtroom were no match for the performance that was playing itself out in a court in the Manchurian city of Changchun the same day.

There, 26 workers charged with the relatively minor crimes of instigating social unrest and spreading rumors were paraded at gunpoint into a packed hall. In a ritual that was reminiscent of the Cultural Revolution, the audience jeered as the detainees filed past, heads shaven and wearing placards around their necks imprinted with their names and crimes.

The manner in which the Chinese government and state media chose to flaunt the harsh public treatment of prisoners sparked a storm of protest in Western nations. The U.S., which had suspended arms sales early on to protest the mass killings in the square, had prepared a list of additional sanctions that could be brought to bear in the event that the executions proceeded. No sooner did the Shanghai verdict become public knowledge than U.S. Congressmen began lobbying for the enactment of those further sanctions unless the Chinese authorities granted clemency to suspects who had been sentenced to die.

The U.S. outcry did not daunt Chinese law-enforcement officials, who sentenced eight more people—workers, peasants and a jobless drifter—to death in Beijing for beating soldiers and burning vehicles on the night of June 3-4. In fact, the Supreme People's Procuratorate even moved to speed the wheels of justice by instructing judges that if the evidence was clear and sufficient, the courts "should not be hamstrung by details, and should expedite the process of arrests and prosecutions." Furthermore, as an official circular suggested, public sensitivities should not be spared. "It is necessary to pay attention to publicity," said the circular, "to increase the social benefit of the cases, suppress and deter criminals, and encourage the masses to struggle against counterrevolutionaries and serious criminal offenders."

No sooner had such instructions circulated than some particularly gruesome footage was aired on Beijing TV screens. It showed the charred and mutilated body of a dead soldier, slouched against the wheel of an army vehicle. As the camera tightened its focus on the dead man, one could see that his torso had been ripped open by a sharp object and his entrails pulled out and prominently displayed. The man accused of disembowelling the soldier, Zhang Jianzhong, was shown under interrogation by police. Zhang reportedly admitted to being a member of a "dare-to-die brigade" that had assaulted soldiers in Tiananmen Square. According to the voice-over, Zhang confessed to picking up a shard of glass from the pavement and using it to disembowel the dead soldier. Zhang was said to have described in detail how he tied a length of plastic rope to the man's intestines, pulled them out and displayed them prominently over his body.

Zhang's story proved to be a clever diversion on the part of the government. It increased viewers' awareness of the intensity of the violence that was unleashed in the streets on the night of June 3-4. At the same time it further compounded the confusion sown by the authorities as to which side had committed the worse crimes, the soldiers or the students.

As the symphony of propaganda swelled, analysts feared that a purge of major proportions was under way. Whether or not Deng could control it was a question that could not be answered, they agreed, until the party Central Committee finally met to determine the fate of Zhao Ziyang. Zhao had not been seen in public since his tearful visit to the hunger strikers in Tiananmen Square on May 19. Although it was a foregone conclusion that he would be replaced, the party leadership—like the government bureaucracy—was divided between the "dove" faction that supported Zhao's soft line on the protests and the "eagle" faction that wanted to smash the students and dump Zhao. As a result of that split, Deng had been unable to secure a consensus. "You delay a Central Committee meeting when you are not sure how it will come out," commented a Western analyst.

The hard-liners were not deterred by the stalemate.

They simply intensified their lobbying of Central Committee members. While Yang Shangkun briefed the Central Military Commission about Zhao's failings, Li Peng ordered the secretaries of all 30 local, provincial and regional party committees brought to Beijing, where he proceeded to meet separately with each one. After a full week of such dialogues in late May, he had built a core of support within the 175-member Central Committee for bringing a limited case against Zhao. It took him another month to secure enough votes to call a plenum.

Finally, on June 23, the Fourth Plenary session of the 13th Central Committee was secretly convened to take formal action on the matter. As a precaution against any unforeseen vote switching or any sudden surfeit of abstentions from resentful members, the army was called in to "protect" the meeting. "They used guns to force us to put up our hands in approval," one member confided to the Hong Kong magazine *Zheng Ming*. Fifty of the 285 members and alternates reportedly pleaded illness and did not attend.

With communication between Chinese sources and foreigners sharply curtailed under martial law, veteran diplomats and journalists fell back on the China-watching skills they had honed during the Cultural Revolution in an attempt to analyze the scarce data available. "It's just like the good old days," mocked one diplomat, on hearing the phrase antiparty clique for the first time in twenty years.

The only immediate source of information on the plenum was a picture taken by the photographer son of Yang Shangkun that ran on the front pages of the official newspapers the next morning. It showed Zhao and Hu Qili, the sole Politburo Standing Committee member who had sided with him, seated across a table from Deng during the meeting. Surprisingly, both appeared to be applauding Li Peng. "That's party ritual," said a senior Asian diplomat, who explained that the significance of the photo was not in the applause but in the fact that the two fallen members were present to hear the charges against them. "The picture is the party's way of saying, 'We have them under control and we are handling the matter within the party in our own way.'"

Although the verdict against Zhao did not go so far as to accuse him of counterrevolutionary activities, as rumor had predicted, it was harsher than that brought against either of his two ousted predecessors. "At the critical juncture involving the destiny of the party and the state," read the communiqué that was later made public, "Comrade Zhao Ziyang made the mistake of supporting the turmoil and splitting the party." More than that, it charged that the General Secretary himself had "unshirkable responsibilities for shaping the turmoil." The man who had, first as Premier and then as party chief, overseen the implementation of a decade of unprecedented economic reform in China, received only faint praise for having done "something beneficial to the reforms and the opening of China to the outside world."

The traits that had stood him in good stead when the economic reforms were popular and the rate of growth double-digit now weighed like shackles on him. He had, said his peers, taken "a passive approach to the adherence of the Four Cardinal Principles and opposition to bourgeois liberalization." Likewise, he had "gravely neglected ideological and political work." Accordingly, the Central Committee voted to strip him of all his posts—though not of his party membership. In a somewhat ominous compromise, the "doves" and the "eagles" also agreed to reserve the right to "look further into his case." Optimists observed that the prospect of further investigation signified that Zhao had not given his opponents the confession they wanted. Pessimists were worried that the Old Guard was trying to press more severe charges against him.

Even thornier than the dilemma of how strongly to

sanction Zhao was the question of who should replace
him. With Zhao's elimination, at least temporarily, from
the succession sweepstakes, the new party chief would
automatically vault straight to the head of the line of possible heirs apparent to the aged and ailing Deng. Each of
the octogenarians was playing kingmaker and pushing
his protégé for the job. Chen Yun supported the conservative Vice Premier and State Planning Commission
Minister Yao Yilin. The ambitious Peng Zhen championed Public Security Minister Qiao Shi. Known as "the
Chinese Andropov"—a reference to the late Soviet leader
Yuri Andropov, who was once KGB chief—Qiao was
widely perceived as the front runner for the post.

In the end, Deng imposed his own, more malleable
choice by winning the endorsements of former President
Li Xiannian and Li Peng for Shanghai party boss Jiang
Zemin, 63. Jiang was ultimately acceptable to the other
factions because, lacking a political base or appreciable
military support, he did not threaten any of them. "He's
manageable, and he'll serve as a place holder until this
power struggle is sorted out," said an Asian diplomat.

"Deng was looking for a carbon copy of himself
when he chose Jiang," said a Western diplomat, "someone who was for reform but at the same time tough on
nonsense." An engineer who worked briefly as a trainee
in the Stalin Automobile Factory in Moscow in the mid-
1950s, Jiang slogged his way up through the bureaucracy
from the state import-and-export and foreign investment
commissions. In those agencies, he was involved in the
establishment of China's Special Economic Zones. He
eventually became Minister of the Electronics Industry
and then mayor of Shanghai. Like Zhao, Jiang satisfied
Deng's preference for someone with hands-on experience
in the implementation of his precious reforms.

Not coincidentally, Jiang's easy manner with foreign
businessmen and his ability to speak their language (Jap-

anese and English, as well as Russian and Rumanian) figured heavily in his selection. Party liberals obviously hoped he would help restore the lost confidence of international investors and lenders and moot the cries for more sanctions from the West. A Beijing-based diplomat came away impressed after a first meeting with the beefy new secretary. "He seems like someone you could sit and drink a bottle of wine with," he said. At the same time the hard-liners looked favorably on the decisive measures he had taken to quell the unrest that roiled Shanghai in the wake of Hu Yaobang's death. Among other tactics, Jiang paid the people's militia, a volunteer brigade armed with clubs, 30 renminbi (about $7.50) a day to disperse student demonstrations. Although it seemed a crude tactic before June 4, it was subsequently judged a humane alternative to calling in armed troops.

The Central Committee also ratified the elevation of Jiang and two other Politburo members to the elite Politburo standing committee, making it a six-member body and therefore under the thrall of tie-breaking nonmembers Deng and the Gang of Elders. Significantly, none of the six Standing Committee members was named to replace Zhao on the party's all-important Central Military Commission. The Standing Committee was thus left without a direct line to the other major power broker behind the throne, the army. That gap left a convenient role for Yang Shangkun, the Military Commission's permanent vice chairman, to fill. China watchers pointed to a photo in which Yang was flanked on either side by three standing committee members as illustrative of the fragmented nature of the newly constituted leadership.

Backed by the military, in full control of the media and with a presentable new party chief in place, that leadership immediately set about trying to convince the world—and its own people—that life had returned to normal. Besides denying that a military massacre had taken place in Beijing, the state-controlled media began insisting that the worst was over and that nothing was substantially wrong with China that a strong dose of ideological education could not cure.

The return-to-normalcy campaign began the week after the crackdown with a photo on the front page of the official English-language *China Daily* showing two foreign tourists, two soldiers and a farmer all smiling together on the Great Wall. "Beijing is gradually returning to normal, with the tourist industry showing the most serious effect of the recent social unrest," the article began. But Beijing was far from normal, as a group of Japanese tourists learned some days later. Soldiers halted their bus and, citing martial-law restrictions, forced them at gunpoint to turn over films they had taken of Tiananmen Square under military guard. Two tourists who refused were taken into custody and briefly detained.

Foreign businessmen were treated with greater sensitivity. Those who had fled to Hong Kong or beyond were plied via phone and telex with promises of heretofore unattainable appointments or concessions on their return to China. "I expect all will be back very soon, since security is now no problem for them," commented Economic Relations and Trade Minister Zheng Tuobin at a press conference in mid-June. Those foreign traders who stayed on in Beijing were showered with invitations and publicly eulogized for their dedication. An official of the Italian automobile company Fiat was invited to meet a vice minister who had eluded him for months. During a reception at the Great Hall of the People, however, he suddenly found himself branded an "official friend" and surrounded by TV cameras.

That incident made other members of the foreign business community more wary of the hospitality of the Chinese. "There is great sensitivity on the part of the American business community not to be manipulated or ambushed for an interview by Chinese television," said a U.S. official. "Many companies are keeping their people out of China for that reason. They don't want to contribute to the credibility of the Chinese leadership."

That credibility had rested for a decade on the words and deeds of a government trying to convince the world it was dedicated more to modernization than to ideology. The perception that Deng Xiaoping's China was a more benign and pragmatic Communist society than its Soviet counterpart was destroyed on the night of June 3-4. Many foreigners underestimated Deng's obsession with stability and the primacy of the party, and thus felt shocked and betrayed by his sudden resort to violence. The subsequent propaganda campaign only deepened their revulsion.

The reality behind the rosy Chinese propaganda was that the economy, which had already been going through a painful process of restructuring aimed at cutting inflation and recentralizing state control, was in dreadful shape. Inflation had not fallen below the high 30% mark of the previous year in some cities. Indeed, it was expected to exceed that rate when the cost of keeping 250,000 martial-law troops in and around Beijing and the production losses incurred during the months of political unrest were factored in. "Some sources are already talking about 100% hidden inflation," said a European diplomat, who was concerned that the government was so preoccupied with its theories of political conspiracy that it was ignoring economic problems he considered even more threatening to its survival.

"I don't think they have had time to focus on the mess they are in," said a Western analyst. "They are putting most of their energy into re-educating people." Indeed, everyone from soldiers to party cadres to factory workers to graduating college seniors was required to spend several weeks studying "the important speech" delivered by Deng on June 9, in which he asserted that the student demonstrations had "developed into a counter-revolutionary rebellion." Once they understood the origins of the counterrevolution, the party ideologues contended, they would shed their bourgeois liberal tendencies.

Meanwhile, foreign trade and tourism—at once the cause of and the deliverance from their problems—were in the doldrums. Tourism, the country's No. 1 foreign-exchange earner, was expected to fall to half the nearly $2 billion it earned in 1988. The upheaval in Beijing had occurred during the peak spring travel season, resulting in the cancellation of some 300 tour groups, totaling 11,535 people, in the month of May alone. Similar losses during the fall season would reverberate far beyond the mirrored and marbled lobbies of China's luxury hotels. A month after the crackdown, there were so few tourists in Beijing that Rumors Disco, which catered to foreigners, waived its $13.50 entrance fee.

Nor was the prospect much better for 1990, when Beijing was scheduled to host the Asian Games. Although Chinese officials assured the organizers of the Games that they would go on as scheduled, only about half the necessary 27 stadiums and gymnasiums were ready. The government was still $58 million short of the $150 million it was expected to need for the event. Worse, if the political situation remained unstable, the Games might fail to attract enough spectators to be profitable or might be canceled altogether. That would only exacerbate the country's growing budget deficit. In a speech reported by the *People's Daily* in July, Finance Minister Wang Bingqian disclosed that state expenditures, including subsidies to money-losing state factories, had risen twice as fast as revenues during the first five months of the year.

Faced with the dreary outlook for tourism in general, joint-venture partners looking to cut their losses in unfinished hotels and convention centers grew increasingly quarrelsome. One particularly ironic tussle was over which side would pay damages for the 310 windows of the sleek new Beijing World Trade Center complex that PLA soldiers had shot out during their June 7 rampage down Changan Avenue. "Why would the soldiers do that?" questioned a Singaporean, whose firm is under contract to decorate one of the center's two hotels. "Didn't they know that it's not a foreign project, but one that is jointly owned by China?"

Bigger questions than that one remained unanswered after the crackdown. Foremost among them was why Deng, who had often said he wanted to live to see the historic raising of the Chinese flag over Hong Kong, had given orders that were so certain to destroy confidence in the viability of his "one country, two systems" concept for recovering sovereignty over the British colony. Beijing's new party chief Jiang Zemin tried to limit the damage when he met on July 11 with a small delegation of Hong Kong officials helping draft a new Basic Law for the colony. The officials were impressed with his style but far from reassured about his government's intent. "We practice our socialism, and you may practice your capitalism," the affable Jiang told the Hong Kong visitors, giving each a warm handshake and addressing the largely Cantonese-speaking group in their common language, English. Jiang added a bit of folk wisdom: "The well water does not interfere with the river water."

Not long afterward, Jiang's words rang hollow. Beijing fired Lee Tze-chung, the director of *Wen Wei Po*, the mainland-supported newspaper in Hong Kong that had denounced the massacre. Lee's removal made a mockery of the provisions for a free press that were enshrined in the 1984 Sino-British Joint Agreement on Hong Kong.

When the crackdown began, orders went out to party cadres and security forces to go after five types of counterrevolutionary elements. Guided by those criteria, several thousand people were picked up and questioned or detained, and at least 30 were executed. (This figure does not include secret executions.). On June 30, "Circular No. 3" was issued to party members. It doubled the types of crimes that could be labeled counterrevolutionary. Crime No. 10, for instance, involved people who take revenge on those who informed on them for any one of the nine other crimes.

The 25,000-word report, which Mayor Chen of Beijing presented to the 8th Meeting of the Standing Committee of the National People's Congress on the same day, added more fuel to the frenzied search for counterrevolutionary elements that was now going on nationwide. The report strung together a wealth of quotes, opinions and rumors lifted largely from the Western and the overseas Chinese press into one enormous paranoid conspiracy chronicling the rise and fall of the rebellion. "Some political forces in the West always attempt to make socialist countries give up the socialist road," the mayor began. These sinister Western forces, he said, plan eventually on "bringing these countries under the rule of international monopoly capital and putting them on the course of capitalism."

Chen's evidence was bizarre. First he cited a Sept. 19, 1988, meeting between Zhao and an American "ultraliberal economist," who turned out to be the American conservative economist Milton Friedman. The mayor intimated that the publicity given this tête-à-tête in Hong Kong newspapers showed that a plot was afoot between Zhao and the U.S. to "topple Deng." The essence of the plot was to "whip up public opinion for covering up Zhao Ziyang's mistakes and pushing on with bourgeois liberalization in an even more unbridled manner."

On that shaky foundation, the mayor proceeded to erect a leaning tower of innuendos and half-baked conclusions that embraced all the government's perceived enemies—from Fang Lizhi to elements of the U.S. Government, whom Chen implicitly accused of conspiring with Zhao and the students to overthrow the Chinese Communist Party. "The hard-liners are preparing to try Zhao," warned a disaffected senior party member. "Behind the scenes they are building a case that effectively accuses him of treason." He cited an unreported speech during the June Central Committee plenum in which Minister of Public Security Wang Fang, a longtime confidant of Deng Xiaoping, accused Zhao of being in cahoots with an American CIA agent, the Hungarian-born American anti-Communist philanthropist George Soros and several associates of China's best-known private enterprise, the Stone Corp., in plotting the overthrow of the Chinese Communist Party.

As if that were not enough, the hard-liners also made Zhao a target of the party's newly energized drive against corruption. In summarizing the lessons learned in the course of putting down the counterrevolutionary rebellion, Deng had stressed that many people had lost confidence in the party's leadership because of corruption. In no time at all, the new party leader launched an anticorruption campaign in which Zhao and his businessmen sons were offered up as convenient scapegoats.

"Our efforts in cracking down on corruption were not very successful in the past," state council spokesman Yuan Mu told a press conference in mid-July. "This was inseparably linked to the mistakes of Zhao Ziyang," he declared, explaining that the party General Secretary had taken a casual attitude toward corruption, brushing it off as an inevitable by-product of economic reform.

As shrewd observers of the situation were quick to point out, however, Zhao's enemies would prosecute the fallen General Secretary at their own peril. "If they want to be really stupid, they can try him," said a Western diplomat. Given his reputation as an economic reformer, many of whose programs would continue to be followed, and the fact that he had been ousted for siding with the students, he had the makings of a martyr. "They are treading dangerous ground," said the diplomat. "The leadership could make a real antihero out of him." No one knew that better than Deng, who had made a political comeback as a martyr himself and was therefore judged unlikely to hand Zhao such an opportunity.

Meanwhile, however, Deng did nothing to restrain the elders and their allies from their goal of "mercilessly rooting out" all the manifestations of "bourgeois liberalization" that had cropped up during the years they had been relegated to the political sidelines. They ordered the jamming of broadcasts by the popular Voice of America, planted vicious editorials against it in the press and secured the expulsion of two of its correspondents. Zealous followers in several cities even turned in a few unfortunate Chinese who were caught listening to it. They pressured foreign joint-venture hotels in Beijing to halve the number of satellite broadcasts of foreign news programs to their guests and banned the sale of foreign periodicals and a growing list of books.

As substitutes, they began promoting a patriotic line of audio and visual aids to understanding the counterrevolutionary rebellion. The official Xinhua news agency launched a TV ad campaign for sets of twelve "commemorative" photos of the "suppression of the counterrevolutionary rebellion" at the exorbitant cost, by Chinese standards, of $20. The captions were as memorable as the street scenes. "This picture shows hooligans inciting those masses ignorant of the facts to attack the enforcers of martial law," read the caption on a stock photo taken on June 3 of chanting students atop a barricade of buses, with helmeted soldiers looking on.

Newspaper ads promoted a cassette tape featuring ten top hits from China's early revolutionary years and the later Cultural Revolution, including *I Am a Soldier* and *Party, Beloved Mother.* A government-produced video titled *The True Story of the Turmoil,* which went on sale to foreigners at a seminar for overseas travel agents, bore a seal authorizing airport customs agents to exempt it from the confiscation prescribed for private photos and tapes of the June 4 violence or its aftermath.

"The conservatives definitely won this round," said a Western diplomat. "They are in full sway, and they don't need to worry too much about the balance between factions at this point." That made for a dangerous situation, he explained, because they were devoting so much energy to the purge that they were overlooking the ultimately more destabilizing problem of the economy. "They feel they are on a roll," he said. "They are saying to each other, 'Let's cure the country of Zhao once and for all'." Such madness was likely to continue for another three months, before the country's real problems intruded on their fantasies of a populace purged of its bourgeois tendencies and once again grateful to the Communist Party for all it has given them.

"The tragedy of China is that there is no system of retirement," observed an Asian ambassador to Beijing. "The people who took part in the Long March made a tremendous contribution to the building of this country. But these people, who are now over 80, and whose minds probably function for only two hours a day, are still making policy. For them the revolution is more important than anything else. In its name they shed blood in the past and are doing so again."

United in their age and the ties made in their young manhood, China's leaders had become so hopelessly isolated from more than 50% of the population born after the founding of the People's Republic that many younger party members who considered themselves good Communists no longer identified with them. "There is a mystical nature to the relationship between the octogenarians and the party," observed a veteran China watcher. "The threat they perceived from the students was a threat not to the country but to that mystical body, the party, as constituted behind the walls of Zhonghanhai." It was a threat not only to their power and privilege but to their theology. "Because what the leaders said was considered canon law," he added, "what the students were advocating could only be heresy."

The old leaders' remedy—large-scale ideological re-education—was being administered under the gun. Students tolerated it because it was a prerequisite to a diploma and a decent job assignment. Factory workers went through the motions rather than visit trouble on themselves by resisting. But after ten years of relative leniency, most Chinese chafed under the discipline of reciting the catechism.

Few relished the notion of forsaking the bourgeois pleasures just as they were on the verge of being able to afford them. And, like upwardly mobile groups everywhere, the concept of democracy appealed to their burgeoning sense of self-confidence and to their idealism, neither of which the party had properly addressed.

"It's too late for re-education," observed an American official. "In Beijing even the party cadres' kids were involved in the student movement. These are not the country bumpkins of the 1960s. Like kids in the U.S., they are more sophisticated than their parents in many ways. They have grown up on TV too."

If the elderly leadership had succeeded in suppressing the autonomous students' and workers' groups and their democracy movement for now, it appeared to have given little thought to how to solve the problems of official corruption, rising prices and untapped human potential, which had bred the discontent that ignited the protest movement in the first place. Nor had it been able to produce an acceptable successor. "The new party leadership is probably transitional," commented a Western diplomat on the selection of Jiang Zimin. "They need a supreme leader, but there is no one in sight."

Conventional wisdom ruled that when Deng died,

Yang Shangkun would replace him. However, given Yang's age, that was merely a temporary solution. "This is the only country in the world where an 81-year-old is running to replace an 85-year-old," joked the diplomat.

"Since June 4, China has entered a dark period," intoned the country's most prominent journalist, Liu Binyan, to an audience in Hong Kong one month after the massacre. "Perhaps it is not the darkest moment in Chinese history, but it is certainly the darkest in the past 40 years," he said. And yet Liu predicted that this period of repression would last no longer than two years. By then the country's economy would be in chaos, and discontented peasants would join students and urban workers in demanding change.

As he spoke, student leader Uerkesh Daolet, political scientist Yan Jiaqi and four other survivors of the Beijing Spring surfaced in France to announce the establishment of the Chinese Student and Democracy Movement United Association. For the first time since 1911, the government in Beijing was about to face a well-financed revolutionary movement in exile, not unlike the one that had succeeded in overthrowing the imperial system.

Time was on the side of these young activists. Deng's repressive policies, predicted Yan, would "quicken the end of the present regime." It was time for China to adopt a new political structure to end "thousands of years of the dynastic cycle." As an adviser to Zhao, Yan had hoped to point the way for the party leaders themselves to spearhead the political reform that he considered an essential complement to economic reform. His efforts and those of Zhao had failed, but his blueprint was still valid. As for the students, although scores of their number were now in jail on the mainland and many more were on the run or in hiding, their nascent network remained intact. And, as it had so many times in the recent past, the vast, extended family of overseas Chinese was ready to provide the necessary moral and financial support to perpetuate itself abroad until the day when it could reunite within a stable and prosperous nation.

On July 4 the leaders of the new movement issued from France a declaration "in the name of the students and masses slaughtered in the recent student and democracy movement as well as those who are now on the wanted list." Addressed to "all descendants of the Chinese people and the peace-loving people of the whole world," it proclaimed June 4 a national day of sorrow in China. The declaration also launched a campaign to obtain the 1990 Nobel Peace Prize for the Chinese students and the citizens of Beijing. "The progress of China's democracy movement is now uncontrollable, like the Yellow River breaking its dike," said the declaration. Announcing a break with the ideology on which it had been weaned, China's new generation proclaimed, "Modern and contemporary Chinese history has taught us sufficient lessons that fighting violence with violence and 'political power grows out of the barrel of a gun' will never guide China to genuine freedom and democracy."

CHAPTER SEVEN
CHINA'S FUTURE

During the summer of 1986, Deng Xiaoping appeared to be on the verge of accomplishing a feat unprecedented in modern Chinese history. Not only had he put his country firmly on the path of modernization, he had also secured what seemed to be a firm guarantee of political stability for the era after he eventually went on to meet Karl Marx and Mao Zedong in that worker's paradise in the sky. For much of the previous century, Chinese history had consisted of short steps forward toward progress, prosperity and stability, invariably followed by upheaval and a headlong rush backward.

Deng took great pride in the lengths he had gone to avoid repeating that pattern. He bragged once that after him the heavens would not fall because of his "two pillars," party chief Hu Yaobang and Premier Zhao Ziyang. They had been groomed as his successors, and they had in turn developed their own cadres of progressive, party and government officials. China did indeed seem to have finally learned the arcane art of modernization, a puzzle that had baffled the country since the early 1800s.

Even after Deng in 1987 jettisoned Hu, the leading candidate for his mantle, many Chinese and Western observers sympathetic to the reform program believed that somehow the second heir apparent, Zhao, would emerge as a natural successor. After all, he was the true architect of the economic reforms. Millions of party members and technocrats owed their careers to him, and millions more Hu loyalists had no one but Zhao to whom they could transfer their fealty. The country was facing severe economic difficulties, but those were considered to be transitional problems.

In retrospect, it is now fairly evident that Zhao was simply not up to the task. His political skills were particularly lacking. No good Communist who had studied the way Stalin had divided and conquered his opposition in the 1920s would have permitted his closest collaborator, Hu, to be ousted over something as minor as the student demonstrations of December 1986. And yet Zhao stood by and watched as Hu was humiliated by the party elders. The special "enlarged" session of the leadership that stripped Hu of his powers was a foreshadowing of Zhao's own downfall.

But it was not just Zhao and reform-minded officials who lost when the prodemocracy movement was suppressed in 1989. Gone too were Deng's hopes for the kind of political stability and economic progress that would make China a world power in the next century. Those goals were already in danger before 1989. Only a sound economy can create the environment needed for political stability, and the uncertainty of the course of economic reform during the past few years had led to uneven development. Reforming an economy is something like riding a bicycle. As long as it is moving forward, everything is fine. But when it stops, staying upright is difficult. The failure to push ahead with important but unpopular changes, particularly the removal of government controls over prices, had already jeopardized the advances of the

Chinese economy during the previous decade.

The dual pricing system, with some prices set by the government and some by the market, had led to distortions at all levels of the economy. Industries that produced basic industrial, agricultural and other price-controlled items suffered at the expense of industries that produced finished and semifinished goods, for which prices could more easily be raised. And in spite of government controls, inflation continued to soar, while the government doled out ever larger amounts to subsidize food prices. The government's own treasury grew so bare in 1988 that it was forced to pay some grain farmers with promissory notes. In many cases, it was not able to redeem those notes the following year in time to permit the farmers to buy the materials they needed for spring planting. In the wake of the May-June unrest, some local governments have reportedly found it necessary to force factories to pay their workers in part with savings bonds.

On a local level, the distortions have primarily benefited private entrepreneurs, particularly those with connections to high government and party officials. A July article in *People's Daily* asserted that 40% of the income of Beijing's 100,000 private entrepreneurs was illegal. That does not bode well for the 14 million private businesses elsewhere in China. Indeed, the regime will almost certainly launch a campaign against entrepreneurs, whose profits have already angered many Chinese.

That is not likely, however, to solve the problems facing Deng and the old men who banded together to dump Zhao. Somehow they and their chosen underlings have to keep the economy from slipping into a recession while reining in inflationary pressures; they must prevent profiteering while still maintaining incentives. Although some of the elderly leaders would like to solve these problems by returning to the Stalinist model of the 1950s, that option is no longer available. The past decade of economic reforms steadily dismantled the old central-control structure by increasing local autonomy and abolishing entities such as the huge agricultural communes. In addition, although many of the reforms are unpopular, the rights and powers granted to individual peasants under Deng's household "responsibility system" will aggressively be protected. China's rulers find themselves straddling an ever widening gap between two distinctly different types of economies, the free and the controlled.

The already impossible job of maintaining economic growth and stability will be made even more difficult by the fact that many of China's most competent economic policy officials were supporters of Zhao's and were purged along with him. Moreover, the disaffection of intellectuals—including white-collar workers as well as university students and professors—will also make economic advancement more difficult. Only about 10 million of China's 1.1 billion people are university graduates. Universities were closed or operated on only a limited basis for much of the ten years of the Cultural Revolution, leaving an entire generation without even the chance of a higher education. On top of that, about a third of the graduates China does have matriculated before 1949. As a result, many universities have been forced to retain elderly professors far past their prime. It is not unusual to find department heads in their 80s at leading Chinese institutions. This education gap constitutes one of the main barriers to progress in China, a fact not always fully recognized by the country's gerontocracy, many of whom came from poor peasant backgrounds.

Mao played upon the traditional antipathy of the masses toward educated people in many of his campaigns. It took Deng and his subordinates ten years to regain the trust of the intellectuals. Now all that work has been discarded. Although government propaganda after the massacre concentrated on reports of arrests of "hooligans" responsible for the chaos of May and June, the list of people who have been charged with actually fomenting the rebellion reads like a *Who's Who* of Chinese intellectuals. Not only will the regime lose the active help of the majority of China's educated class, it has also further reduced the percentage of Chinese students abroad who will return to "build the motherland." In addition, the government has taken step to shrink the absolute numbers of future university graduates. In July 1989 it announced that the usual incoming freshmen class of 600,000 would be cut by 10%.

In an interview with TIME in Paris in July, exiled student leader Uerkesh Daolet was asked how long it would take for a Communist regime to regain the confidence of Chinese intellectuals. "A very long time," he replied. "Perhaps 20 or 30 years." In other words, China has lost the input of its limited intellectual capital for another generation. It is hard to imagine any significant economic progress under those conditions.

The attitude of many of China's major trading partners will further damage economic progress. In the wake of the massacre, billions of dollars in foreign investment and loans were put on hold. China's foreign trade balance had already been swinging into the red before the political unrest began. The trade deficit was running at a monthly rate of almost $1 billion through April. China's foreign exchange problem will be further complicated by the collapse of its tourist industry. Although visitors will probably start trickling back, it may be years before they return in the numbers China needs.

Foreign businessmen will also return to China, drawn by the lure of the "world's biggest market" and some of its cheapest labor. Scruples will not override commercial interests for long. The Japanese government criticized some of its businessmen for the unseemly haste with which they rushed back into China. But those who return will not find the same country they fled in June. Official statements notwithstanding, the regime's open-door policy is in the process of a major reassessment.

China's leaders still face their age-old problem of how to import Western technology without Western values. The political turmoil of 1989 is being blamed on "bourgeois liberalization" imported from the West, and Deng has warned that China is becoming a "vassal of imperialism."

Again, the elderly men now running the country might like to return to the 1950s or 1960s, when China could go it alone or at least turn to the Soviet Union. But China is now too closely tied to the rest of the world economy. Importing Western technology is not a one-time event. It is a continuing process involving long-term imports of spare parts, semifinished goods and constantly updated versions of last year's technology. Very little of that could come from the Soviet bloc.

In order to keep the most advanced sectors of the economy from collapsing, contacts with the outside will have to be maintained. But the current regime will probably try to keep those contacts to a minimum. That is bound to compound the already formidable problems facing foreign businessmen. They will find that many of the officials and entrepreneurs who made things work before the crackdown have escaped or been purged. Those who remain will be reluctant to do anything that might be looked upon as accommodating foreigners at the expense of the motherland.

Business confidence in the economy of Hong Kong, China's other major source of foreign exchange, has also severely been damaged by the crackdown. That could ultimately cost Beijing millions in foreign exchange, since much of China's investment abroad is in the Hong Kong property market. In addition, Hong Kong is the biggest source of foreign direct investment on the mainland. The regime in Beijing has gone out of its way to try to reassure Hong Kong residents and investors that the crown colony will be permitted to retain its capitalist system after China regains sovereignty in 1997. But mixed with the soothing words are some equally unsettling ones.

Most recently, a *People's Daily* commentary warned that Hong Kong would be allowed to keep its system only if it was not used as "a base to subvert the central people's government." Perhaps more telling than those words have been the actions of Chinese authorities along the Hong Kong border. In recent years customs and immigration formalities had become surprisingly relaxed. A few weeks after the crackdown, however, the Hong Kong press reported that local businessmen who frequently cross into China were being severely harassed. In some cases returning Hong Kong residents suspected of assisting Chinese dissidents have had cash confiscated, while others have been forced to sign "confessions." Although Hong Kong will continue to be a major source of revenue for Beijing, its potential has gravely been reduced at a time when China can ill afford to lose any income.

In short, Deng's goal for China to quadruple its gross national product between 1980 and the year 2000 is almost certainly a casualty of the crackdown. And those reduced prospects will undoubtedly add to the social unrest already evident. China has always been a potentially violent country. During the Cultural Revolution, thousands of urban Chinese died in armed clashes in such major cities as Guangzhou and Chengdu. Even during the best years of the Deng era, reports filtered in from the provinces of violent confrontations between farmers and local authorities, between bus drivers and the police, between workers and factory managers.

In the first few weeks after the June 3-4 massacre, the official Chinese press carried accounts of several incidents that may have involved violent sabotage. At least two passenger trains were damaged by explosions in June and July. In addition, hundreds of weapons stolen from or abandoned by soldiers sent to Beijing before June 3 are still unaccounted for. But at this point, there are no signs that an organized, armed resistance is being formed. Although the Chinese system of social control has been diluted somewhat over the past ten years—urban Chinese, for instance, are no longer completely dependent on their places of employment for daily necessities—the ability of the police to lay their hands on malcontents and suspected malcontents is still impressive.

The people of Beijing who were firsthand witnesses of the June 3-4 massacre are relatively impervious to the government's propaganda efforts. But China's other 200 million urban citizens and its 900 million peasants are far more vulnerable to the government cover-up. Rural residents, who have access to little more than official media, have been the easiest to convince. But even more sophisticated city dwellers have apparently bought the regime's contention that the unrest was largely the work of hooligans and counterrevolutionary intellectuals working under the direction of foreign powers. Confusion in the Western media over what actually happened gave credence to the government line that more soldiers than civilians died.

The Chinese propaganda machine is not particularly deft. In fact, many top media managers have been purged in the wake of the uprising. But constant repetition of the official version of events will continue to fall on relatively willing ears. Chinese set great store in stability and harmony. When it seemed as if the prodemocracy forces had a chance of changing things for the better, they had popular support. That support rapidly dwindled when it became clear that the conservative forces were in complete control. It is probably also human nature to want to believe one's government is not a band of bloodthirsty, power-obsessed geriatrics.

For those citizens not so easily convinced, the forces of repression, while diminished over the past decade, still thrive. During the first three decades of Communist rule, police surveillance relied heavily on networks of old people who had nothing better to do than spy on their neighbors. In the past few years, those elderly snitches have increasingly been ignored. Even in Shanghai, a bastion of Maoist orthodoxy, the squads of traffic wardens consisting of elderly people with red armbands had disappeared. But within a week of the massacre in Beijing, the old folks on the street reappeared. The practice of informing on fellow citizens was rediscovered. For Chinese who even thought about resistance to the government, the most chilling message on the evening television news each night was not the number of people arrested but the high proportion who had been turned in by colleagues, neighbors and even family members.

It seems unreasonable to expect much organized resistance in a society that is so inherently repressive. That does not, however, mean that the millions of Chinese who spoke out during the spring of 1989 will meekly return to their previous state of political apathy. Over the past decade, because of Deng's policy of reforming the economy and opening China to the outside world, hundreds of millions of Chinese have been exposed to new ideas and concepts. The limited glimpses of the world made possible during the 1980s, coupled with modest political and philosophical debates in the official press, caused people to question the very basis of the Chinese political, economic and social systems. But even in the relatively open period of the past few years, most individuals kept their conclusions about Chinese society to themselves. Telling a relative or a good friend could turn out to be dangerous.

As in other Asian cultures, many people in China value harmony more highly than individualism, a tendency greatly reinforced by Communist rule. To criticize the collective was a step few Chinese were willing to take, and those few who did were viewed as sociopaths—even by people who secretly agreed with their critiques. But for a few weeks in 1989, millions of Chinese found the courage to speak out. In the process, they discovered to their surprise that they were by no means alone in disliking the Communist system. That revelation was liberating and exhilarating.

The intensity of the demonstrations, the willingness of ordinary citizens to place themselves between the army and the students are difficult to understand except in this context. Average people were motivated not so much by their hatred of the regime but rather by the relief and joy they felt when they found they were not alone in their despair. Although the government's propaganda and control apparatuses will probably be able to suppress public dissent for some time to come, Deng and his comrades have lost the battle for the hearts and minds of average urban Chinese. A whole generation in key cities is now aware that it is the old men in power, not the Tiananmen Square protesters, who constitute the "tiny fraction" opposing the will of the people. Ruling China will be more difficult for the next decade than it has been for the past ten years.

Further complicating the regime's problems are its own internal uncertainty and upheaval. Deng and the party elders, probably under the delusion that they were preventing a new Cultural Revolution, succeeded in routing Zhao and his reformist supporters. But there is little else on which they agree. About the only things the ruling elders have in common is their longevity and the fact that they were all abused by Mao at some point in their careers. Deng aided his return to power in the late 1970s by hastening the rehabilitation of these old comrades, all of whom had protégés distributed throughout the party.

They were not, however, his natural allies. On the contrary, Deng had waged bitter battles going back three decades or more against such rehabilitated veterans as Chen Yun and Peng Zhen. Those battles—based more on personality conflicts than on ideological differences—continued into the 1980s. As recently as 1987, Deng had moved to limit their influence over party matters by seeking to force them into total retirement. At the time, it appeared he had succeeded. But Deng found it necessary to reactivate the old comrades in order to unseat his own protégé, Zhao.

The old men share one other attribute: an almost total removal from reality. They live in walled compounds, rarely setting foot outside. Even when they go for a drive, they ride in sleek black Mercedes limousines with heavily tinted windows and thick curtains. In the West the rich and powerful may like to travel in anonymity, but they at least have some idea of what the world around them looks like. In China the isolation of the leadership, particularly the old revolutionaries, is almost total. That lack of contact helped make the Tiananmen massacre possible. Deng had no first- or even secondhand knowledge about the protests. His information came largely from the hard-line mayor of Beijing, who almost certainly colored the reports of his underlings to make the demonstrators appear to be advocating the overthrow of the system.

Beyond their isolation, the men running China today are old. The top five are all in their 80s. Even before the mid-1989 rumors about his failing health, Deng was reportedly able to work only about two hours a day. A few years ago, he liked to talk about the second and third echelons of top officials, men in their 60s and even 40s who were being trained to run the country. But with the fall of Hu and now Zhao, the logical progression to those next two tiers has been destroyed. The chosen underlings of China's gerontocracy do not have the look of eventual rulers of China.

Zhao's successor as General Secretary, Shanghai party chief Jiang Zemin, is clearly a transitional figure. A key *People's Daily* editorial about the Communist Party Central Committee meeting that stripped Zhao of his position never even mentioned Jiang's name. His major qualifications appear to be the quickness with which he brought the demonstrations in Shanghai under control in June, and his command of English, which should help reassure foreign investors. But Jiang is viewed as an opportunist who has almost no constituency of his own within the party. He will be easy to sacrifice at the first sign of trouble.

Another ready scapegoat is Premier Li Peng, the object of so much of the students' scorn during May and June. Li was the front man in the summer of 1988 for a group of elderly conservatives anxious to halt the expansion of the economic reforms. When they succeeded in truncating the reform program, Zhao ostentatiously turned over responsibility for the economy to Li. In the coming months, the Premier will have to bear the brunt of the inevitable criticism of China's economic mess. Li too lacks a major constituency of his own within the party, though he does represent a certain class of party official—those with high family connections. Li is the foster son of one of Communist China's few beloved former leaders, Zhou Enlai.

Further confusing the situation is Deng's reliance on the People's Liberation Army. In order to suppress the students, Deng found it necessary to throw in his lot with Yang Shangkun, President of the People's Republic—but more important, the No. 2 man on the Central Military Commission. That is the body through which the party controls the army, making the Military Commission's chairman in effect the most powerful man in the country. Mao held the chairmanship from 1935 until his death, and it is the one post Deng has never relinquished. Although Zhao was made first vice chairman of the commission in 1987, Yang—as the body's general secretary and as an army general—has held the more influential post.

Yang has used his position to promote his relatives in the military establishment, further adding to his influence. He has made no secret of his desire to succeed Deng as Central Military Commission chairman. But even Yang has his problems. Top military men are reportedly upset at the way his relatives and cronies have been catapulted over higher-ranking officers in the past two years. And senior party officials are wary of investing too much authority in a military figure. In addition, should the day come when the party and the army feel a need to distance themselves from the Tiananmen massacre, Yang could be sacrificed.

Perhaps the leading candidate to replace Deng is Qiao Shi, the party official in charge of China's security forces. The country's 1.8 million armed national police report to Qiao, as do the secret police of the State Public Security Bureau. As of late 1989, he was the only member of the five-man Standing Committee of the Politburo with a significant power base of his own. Qiao was widely rumored to be Zhao's successor in the early days of June. That he did not get the job is probably more a tribute to his political acumen than to any serious opposition. Clearly this is not the best time to take on the onus of being party chief.

But in the not too distant future, Qiao might find himself drafted into the job. If the party decides that to restore its credibility it must launch a credible attack on corruption and nepotism, no one would be better positioned to lead that fight than the relatively "clean" Qiao, who is the party's and the country's top cop. Qiao could also get the call if violent resistance emerges in the coming months. He has the added advantage of being something of an agnostic on the economic reforms, a stance that will give him great flexibility in any policy debate.

Still, neither Qiao nor any of his peers have the stature to step out of the diminutive Deng's massive shadow. Only Zhao or his predecessor Hu had the time and opportunity to develop support, both inside the party and among the public, to take over. With their downfall, the political maneuvering will continue in muted form until Deng's death. But when Deng goes, the succession struggle will begin in earnest, much as happened following

Mao's death in 1976.

In fact, many analysts compare the current political situation to 1976. TIME reporter Jaime FlorCruz, one of the few Western analysts to have lived in Beijing during both periods, sees remarkable parallels, especially in the demonstrations in Tiananmen Square. In April 1976, three months after the death of the beloved Premier Zhou, thousands of Beijing residents bearing memorial wreaths in his name packed the square on Qing Ming, the traditional Chinese festival honoring the dead. But the infamous Gang of Four, led by Mao's wife Jiang Qing, viewed this spontaneous outpouring of affection for Zhou as an assault on them. Indeed, some of the wreaths, which were piled 60 feet high, did carry oblique attacks on Jiang.

Similar events preceding the death of the Emperor pervade Chinese history. China faces the very unrest and instability that Deng feared would again disrupt its modernization efforts—and that he had spent most of the past ten years trying to prevent. Although reports of an imminent civil war in early June 1989 were probably gross exaggerations, it is clear that there is a serious, perhaps irreparable, split in the party and maybe even in the People's Liberation Army as well. In the coming months, hundreds and perhaps thousands of Zhao's supporters will be purged from their positions as the elderly conservatives and their protégés attempt to consolidate control. But the true struggle will begin only when Deng is no longer around to adjudicate the disputes.

One of Deng's great political strengths may turn out to be the major defect in his efforts to ensure an orderly transfer of power. In the highly personalized world of Chinese politics, Deng's role has been that of the pragmatic man in the middle. His prestige in the party and the army gave him the deciding vote in policy and personnel disputes. Particularly in the past decade, he has repeatedly shifted his weight back and forth between the reformist and the conservative camps. Most of the party hierarchy sits somewhere between the radical reformers who were ready to sell stock in state enterprises and the puritanical hard-liners who wanted to reassert party control over all aspects of Chinese life. When one or the other radical ends of the spectrum appeared to be going too far, Deng would step in on behalf of the other side. As a Chinese political scientist once said of Deng, "He does not win by too much."

While Deng's approach prevented major internecine strife during his reign—as well as serious assaults on his own position—it has left no single person or faction in a position to assume his mantle. In addition, it has left a large number of scores to be settled after his death. The suppression of the prodemocracy movement will increase those tensions within the party. The students who led the protests came from China's most prestigious universities. Given the role of connections in gaining admission to these schools, the protesters must have included a large sampling of top leaders' children. The number of high officials who lost sons or daughters or whose friends lost children may be high.

During demonstrations in Shanghai after the Tiananmen massacre, several protesters carried signs with the following lines from China's pre-eminent modern writer, Lu Xun (1881-1936): "Lies written in ink can never disguise facts written in blood. Blood debts must be repaid in kind. The longer the delay, the greater the interest."

Those words were written shortly after another Beijing massacre. In 1926 residents of the capital marched peacefully to petition the city government. Troops opened fire, killing 40 of the protesters. The carnage this time was much more severe. The prospect of repaying these blood debts, with interest, seems to ensure that once again China will find the road to progress and modernity blocked by its own tragic history.

For more than a century, this immensely talented

nation has struggled to find a way out of its bureaucratic and inward-looking past. Unfortunately, it has never been able to learn from previous mistakes. All the serious attempts have had two fatal flaws. The first has been a lack of confidence in the Chinese people's ability to take greater control of their lives. Most of China's rulers have lived in constant fear of chaos and disintegration. Although foreigners may view it as a homogeneous country, China is in fact quite disparate. The people of Guangzhou, for instance, have no more in common with the people of Shanghai than do Romans with Parisians. In both cases, the cuisines, cultures, personalities and spoken languages are vastly different. China often seems on the verge of splitting apart, much as Europe did 1,000 years ago. The limited local autonomy granted during the past decade, combined with the spontaneity of increasingly free markets and the rumblings of freedom of expression, created an explosive situation that the old men in Beijing could not tolerate. Their major worry was not ideological, that capitalism would overthrow Communism. They feared the disintegration of China itself.

The second flaw has been a belief, stretching back more than 150 years, that China should import from the West only technology, not ideas. The problem Deng and all his like-minded predecessors, including Mao, thought they faced was how to keep China "Chinese" while importing the technical know-how necessary for modernization. Make no mistake, Deng has always felt that the opening to the outside world was little more than a necessary evil. Premier Li once frankly told a French delegation that China wanted the West's technology without its values. Deng had a more backhanded way of putting it. He said that in opening up a door to let in fresh air, you had to expect some flies to come in as well. In the end, Deng apparently decided that the host of alien ideas swarming into China justified slamming the door.

China faces years, perhaps decades, of stagnation, all

the while watching its Asian neighbors stride briskly toward modernization. Amid their despair, perhaps the people of China can recall something else Lu wrote: "Hope can neither be affirmed nor denied. Hope is like a path in the countryside: originally there was no path—yet, as people walk all the time in the same spot, a way appears."

A CHRONOLOGY

1972
Feb. 21-28. President Richard Nixon's nine-day visit to China marks the official beginning of Sino-American reconciliation.
Sept. 13. Lin Biao, Minister of Defense and designated successor to Mao Zedong, is killed in a mysterious plane crash in Outer Mongolia.
Sept. 25-30. Japanese Prime Minister Kakuei Tanaka visits China and signs a joint communiqué establishing Sino-Japanese diplomatic relations.
1973
Feb. 22. The U.S. and China sign a communiqué agreeing to set up a liaison office in each other's capitals.
April 12. Deng Xiaoping makes his first public appearance after six years of exile, at a state banquet for Prince Norodom Sihanouk, with Premier Zhou Enlai as host.
Aug. 24-28. At the Tenth Party Congress of the Chinese Communist Party (C.C.P.), Deng Xiaoping is re-elected to the Central Committee.
1974
April 10. Deng Xiaoping, as chairman of the Chinese delegation to the United Nations, addresses the General Assembly, proclaiming China's place as a developing socialist country of the Third World, united against the world hegemony of the U.S.S.R. and the U.S.
1975
Jan. 8-10. At a plenum of the Central Committee (C.C.P.C.C.), Deng Xiaoping is elected Vice Chairman of the party and later appointed Chief of General Staff of the People's Liberation Army.
Jan. 13-17. Zhou Enlai, appearing for the last time outside the hospital, unveils the Four Modernizations, under which China will reform agriculture, industry, defense, and science and technology by the year 2000.
Dec. 1-5. President Gerald Ford visits China, meeting Mao Zedong on Dec. 2.
1976
Jan. 8. Premier Zhou Enlai dies of cancer at 77. First Vice Premier Deng Xiaoping delivers the eulogy.
Feb. 3. Public Security Minister Hua Guofeng is appointed by the C.C.P.C.C. to replace Deng as new Acting Premier of the State Council.
April 5. Mass demonstrations in memory of Zhou Enlai take place at Beijing's Tiananmen Square and in other major cities. Riots break out, scores are killed and hundreds of people are arrested.
April 7. China's Xinhua News Agency publishes the official report of the "Tiananmen incident," calling it the work of a "handful of class enemies" who used the "guise of commemorating the late Premier Zhou Enlai to organize . . . a counterrevolutionary political incident" in Tian-

anmen Square. At a Politburo meeting, Deng Xiaoping is blamed as the instigator of the "Tiananmen incident" and stripped of his official posts: vice premiership, vice chairmanship of the Communist Party and Chief of General Staff of the armed forces.

July 28. An earthquake in Tangshan leaves more than 242,000 dead.

Sept. 9. Mao Zedong dies at 82. New Premier Hua Guofeng is chosen to succeed Mao as party Chairman. Hua reads the funeral address, and Deng is not allowed to take part in the funeral ceremony.

Oct. 6. The Gang of Four is smashed, as Politburo members Jiang Qing (Mao's widow), Wang Hongwen, Zhang Chunqiao and Yao Wenyuan are arrested. The Cultural Revolution is declared to be at an end.

1977

July 16-21. The Central Committee names Hua to the country's top positions and restores Deng Xiaoping to his former posts as Vice Chairman of the party, vice chairman of the Central Military Commission and Vice Premier.

Aug. 12. A party congress confirms the new collective leadership of Hua Guofeng, Deng Xiaoping, Wang Dongxing and Ye Jianying, and adopts a new party constitution, replacing that of 1973.

1978

Feb. 26. The fifth National People's Congress adopts a new constitution.

Aug. 12. China and Japan sign a treaty of peace and friendship formally normalizing relations between the two countries.

Nov. 19. The first "big character" posters appear on Democracy Wall in Beijing's Xidan district, criticizing Mao, class struggle and the Gang of Four.

Dec. 15. The Carter Administration transfers its recognition from the Republic of China in Taiwan to the People's Republic of China in Beijing.

Dec. 18-22. The landmark third plenum of the eleventh C.C.P.C.C. convenes. Deng announces a new era of economic development and exhorts the party to shift away from class struggle to socialist modernization.

1979

Jan. 28. Vice Premier Deng Xiaoping arrives in the U.S. for a nine-day stay, the first official visit ever by a senior Chinese Communist leader.

Feb. 17-March 6. China invades Viet Nam, advances several miles into the country, and then withdraws after sustaining enormous casualties and claiming to have "taught Viet Nam a lesson."

March 29. Wei Jingsheng, editor of the dissident magazine *Exploration* and author of *The Fifth Modernization: Democracy*, is arrested as a counterrevolutionary. "Big character" posters and publications opposing socialism are banned by the Beijing municipal government.

March 30. Deng announces that China will continue to modernize but stay within the framework of the Four Cardinal Principles of socialism, dictatorship of the proletariat, party leadership and Marxism–Lenin-ism–Mao Zedong Thought.

April 10. President Carter signs the Taiwan Relations Act, reiterating that new U.S.-Chinese diplomatic relations will not preclude the sale of arms or commercial and cultural contacts with Taiwan.

July 1. Following the official republication of a 1962 Mao Zedong speech that signaled an earlier easing of censorship, "big character" posters begin to increase on the Democracy Wall.

July 8. The Chinese government adopts its first legislation on joint ventures between China and foreign countries.

Oct. 16. Wei Jingsheng is tried and convicted of selling "state secrets" to foreigners and "advocating the overthrow of the dictatorship of the proletariat." He receives a 15-year prison sentence.

Oct. 30. Addressing the Federation of Literary and Art Circles of China in Beijing, Deng calls for cultural workers to assimilate the best of all ages and all lands, a marked departure from the restrictions imposed on cultural expression during the Cultural Revolution.

Nov. 15. The first major local election for delegates to the National People's Congress in 25 years is held.

Dec. 6. Following a ban on posters, the Democracy Wall is officially closed by Beijing's municipal government.

1980

Feb. 25. Deng Xiaoping resigns as army Chief of General Staff to step up as chairman of the Central Military Commission.

April 16. Zhao Ziyang, a 61-year-old provincial party chief of Sichuan, Deng's home province, is appointed Vice Premier.

Sept. 7. Hua Guofeng resigns as Premier, and Zhao Ziyang is named to succeed him.

Sept. 10. Zhao's appointment as Premier is confirmed by the National People's Congress. That rubber-stamp parliament also abolishes Article 45 of the constitution, proclaimed by Mao Zedong, that had established the "four freedoms to speak out freely, air views fully, hold great debates and write" wall posters criticizing government policy.

Nov. 15-23. The trial of the Gang of Four and six other defendants takes place.

1981

Jan. 25. Jiang Qing and nine other leaders of the Cultural Revolution are convicted of "persecuting to death" 34,380 people during the Cultural Revolution. Jiang and co-defendant Zhang Chunqiao are sentenced to death. The other eight receive prison terms ranging from 16 years to life.

April 24. In the beginning of a crackdown, two dissidents—Xu Wenli and Yang Jing—are arrested on charges of taking part in the Democracy Wall movement.

June 27-29. Hua Guofeng resigns as party Chairman, and Hu Yaobang is appointed to succeed him.

June 30. The Central Committee officially acknowledges Mao Zedong's errors during the Cultural Revolution but concludes that his contributions to China "far outweigh" his mistakes.

Nov. 30. Premier Zhao outlines his economic reform program before the National People's Congress.

Dec. 25. The Central Committee declares that the Maoist principle of putting "politics in command" of industry is correct. The move suggests a split in ideology between reformers and hard-liners within the party.

1982

Jan. 19. Premier Zhao begins to streamline the government by easing out twelve deputy ministers from the State Council.

March 9. Zhao calls for a purge of radical Gang of Four supporters.

April 1. A revised criminal law imposes tough new punishments for "damaging the national economy" (smuggling, illegal purchases of foreign exchange, speculations, theft of public property, bribery, etc.). The penalties include death sentences, life imprisonment and a minimum of ten years in prison.

May 4. The government announces a major shake-up, eliminating 13 vice premiers and reducing by two-thirds the total number of ministers and vice ministers.

Sept. 1-11. A party congress adopts a new 168-article constitution abolishing the post of party Chairman and reviving the position of General Secretary. Hu Yaobang is named to that job. At the congress, Deng Xiaoping announces three national goals for the 1980s: modernization, reunification with Taiwan and an independent foreign policy.

Nov. 26. The National People's Congress ratifies the new constitution, in which many elements of Mao's programs are eliminated. The political role of the people's communes is abolished, and the ceremonial post of President is restored.

1983

Jan. 25. Jiang Qing and former Vice Premier Zhang Chunqiao have their death sentences commuted to life imprisonment by the Supreme People's Court.

June 6. Li Xiannian, a former Minister of Finance, is appointed President of China by the National People's Congress.

July 1. On the 62nd anniversary of the founding of the Chinese Communist Party, *The Selected Works of Deng Xiaoping* is published in Beijing. More than 40 million copies are circulated.

Oct. 12. The party adopts a plan to purge the party of extreme rightist and leftist elements—followers of Lin Biao, Jiang Qing and others.

Nov. 4. The party's propaganda chief, Deng Liqun, publicizes a crackdown on "spiritual pollution" and "bourgeois liberalization."

1984

Jan. 23. Deng Liqun's drive against "spiritual pollution" is halted by Deng Xiaoping.

April 26. President Ronald Reagan arrives in Beijing for a five-day visit. He signs agreements with the Chinese on taxation, nuclear cooperation and cultural exchanges.

Sept. 26. A Joint Declaration on the return of the crown colony of Hong Kong to China in 1997 is signed in Beijing by British Ambassador Richard Evens and Chinese Vice Foreign Minister Zhou Nan. The declaration provides that Hong Kong will retain its capitalist character for at least 50 years after China takes over.

1985

Jan. 1. Deng Xiaoping's speech advocating an open-door policy for China is published, encouraging foreign investments and introducing more changes to overcome "poverty, backwardness and ignorance."

April 22-29. Several hundred people who had been exiled to the countryside during the 1966-76 Cultural Revolution stage a sit-in demonstration in front of the Beijing municipal government and Communist Party headquarters.

Sept. 18-23. In a special session, the party Central Committee promotes more of Deng's supporters to the Politburo. Among them: Hu Qili, Tian Jiyun, Wu Xueqian and Qiao Shi.

Oct. 13-18. Vice President George Bush visits China and meets top leaders—Deng Xiaoping, Li Xiannian, Zhao Ziyang, Hu Yaobang and others.

1986

March 24. Premier Zhao submits the nation's ambitious seventh Five-Year Economic Plan (1986-90). The plan calls for a decentralization of industrial decision making, reduction of the gap between controlled and free-market prices and authority for domestic airlines, telecommunications and other state-owned enterprises to set their own rates.

March 25. Deng Xiaoping hints that he would like to retire from his party posts.

Aug. 5. China's first bond market since 1949 opens in the northeastern city of Shenyang. The experimental market begins by trading the paper of two Shenyang enterprises.

Sept. 25. The Central Committee affirms Deng's open-door policies.

Sept. 26. In Shanghai the country's first stock market opens on an experimental basis. Hundreds of people arrive to trade on the first two "socialist joint-stock" companies listed on the exchange.

Dec. 5. Students of the University of Science and Technology in Hefei, Anhui province, begin a demonstration that later spreads to several other major cities. The students' demands include better campus living conditions, freedom of the press and democracy.

Dec. 22. Shanghai Mayor Jiang Zemin, who would become party General Secretary in 1989, orders a ban on student demonstrations in his city and uses the police to disperse large gatherings.

Dec. 23-30. Students in Beijing demonstrate in support of marches that occurred in other cities calling for freedom and democracy.

Dec. 31. The government in Beijing announces that it has uncovered a plot to overthrow the Communist Party. It cites a Shanghai worker, Shi Guanfu, as an agent who distributed leaflets "inciting students to struggle against the Communist Party."

1987

Jan. 1. More than 2,000 students in Beijing stage a rally in defiance of new regulations limiting demonstrations.

Jan. 6-9. The official *People's Daily* and other state-run newspapers carry front-page condemnations of student demonstrations as harmful to the country and warn against "bourgeois liberalization." A 1984 speech by Deng Xiaoping attacking those who advocate "bourgeois liberalization" is published by the *People's Daily* at the same time.

Jan. 12. Astrophysicist Fang Lizhi is dismissed as vice president of the University of Science and Technology in Hefei, along with president Guan Weiyan.

Jan. 13. Deng Xiaoping singles out Fang Lizhi; Liu Binyan, an internationally known investigative reporter of the *People's Daily;* and Wang Ruowang, a prominent Shanghai writer and Marxist theorist, for special criticism in his public remarks on student demonstrations.

Jan. 14. Wang Ruowang and Liu Binyan are expelled from the Communist Party for their roles in setting off the December 1986 student demonstrations.

Jan. 16. The party announces the resignation of Hu Yaobang as General Secretary. Premier Zhao Ziyang is named acting party General Secretary. Hu retains his Politburo membership.

Jan. 29. Premier Zhao says the campaign against "bourgeois liberalization" will be limited and will not interfere with ongoing economic reforms and the opening of China to foreign investments.

Feb. 3. Party propaganda chief Zhu Houze, a follower of Hu Yaobang, is replaced by Wang Renzhi, a Marxist hard-liner.

March 25. Zhao warns that it would never be "permissible to stifle democracy on the pretext of opposing bourgeois liberalization."

March 28. Vice Premier Li Peng announces the State Education Commission's revival of the Cultural Revolution practice of sending college students to work in the countryside and factories to learn from peasants and workers.

July 5. More than 1 million students are assigned to compulsory work in the countryside during summer recess.

Oct. 1. Several days of Tibetan pro-independence demonstrations in Lhasa end in violent clashes. Six people are killed, and 19 police are reported injured. Chinese authorities claim that at least 50 foreign tourists were directly involved in a demonstration, and new foreign travel restrictions to Tibet are issued.

Oct. 25. Deng, 83, resigns from most of his key party posts—chairmanship of the Central Advisory Commission and membership in the Central Committee, Politburo and Standing Committee, retaining only the chairmanship of the Central Military Commission.

Nov. 2. Premier Zhao Ziyang, 68, is elected party General Secretary and named first vice chairman of the Central Military Commission.

Nov. 11. Li Peng, 58, First Vice Premier, is named Acting Premier.

Dec. 7. About 1,000 students march in Beijing to protest the death of Zang Wei, a student at the University of International Business and Economics, who was stabbed to death by local thugs at a campus store. Students charged Zang died because of university neglect and delays in getting him to the hospital.

1988

March 5. Nationalist riots break out in Chinese-controlled Tibet.

March 23. The Chinese Foreign Ministry revokes the passport of Hu Ping, a graduate student at Harvard University who has just become chairman of the New York City–based Chinese Alliance for Democracy and editor of the prodemocracy publication *China Spring.*

March 24-25. The Chinese government announces plans to reduce the number of students going abroad by about two-thirds.

March 25. The National People's Congress confirms Li Peng as Premier. During the same session, Yang Shangkun is elected to a five-year term as President of China, and Wan Li, Deng's ally, is named chairman of the N.P.C., replacing hard-liner Peng Zhen.

April 8. The Constitution is amended to approve private business and permit the sale of long-term rights to land use.

June 3-12. Hundreds of Peking University students march to Tiananmen Square to protest the murder of a fellow student by a gang of thugs near the campus. Wall posters criticizing the government's apathy toward education and democratization go up on campus.

June 15. *He Shang* (River Elegy), a controversial television documentary criticizing the backward state of Chinese civilization and culture, is aired for the first time. Weeks later, hard-liners attack the film as "nihilist" and "reactionary."

Sept. 15-21. Zhao Ziyang presides over a Politburo meeting that decides to postpone price reform for at least two years.

Sept. 26-30. The Central Committee endorses Premier Li Peng's new policy to slow the pace of economic reform, a severe setback for General Secretary Zhao Ziyang. Li also announces that for at least the next two years the government will not embark on new reforms.

Sept. 28. The Politburo kills the plan for price reform.

Dec. 10. Police open fire on pro-independence Tibetan demonstrators in Lhasa, killing at least three people.

Dec. 24-31. Racial riots flare up in Nanjing after a brawl between African students and local Chinese at a dance, which leads to race-related demonstrations in Nanjing, Beijing, Wuhan and Hanzhou.

1989

Feb. 1. Soviet Foreign Minister Eduard Shevardnadze pays a visit to Beijing—the first by a high-ranking Soviet official since 1969—to finalize plans for Gorbachev's visit.

Feb. 25-27. President George Bush's two-day visit to China is marred by the refusal of the Chinese police to allow astrophysicist Fang Lizhi to attend Bush's banquet. In his meeting with Bush, Zhao Ziyang sternly warns Americans to stay out of China's internal affairs.

March 4. Beijing imposes martial law in Lhasa, Tibet.

March 20-April 4. At the annual National People's Congress session, Premier Li Peng restates the need for at least two years of austerity and the tightening of central control over the economy.

April 15. Former C.C.P. General Secretary Hu Yaobang dies at 74.

April 16. Thousands of students march to Tiananmen Square to mourn Hu's death.

April 21-22. Defying government orders forbidding demonstrations during the official memorial ceremonies held for Hu in the Great Hall of the People, up to 100,000 people join the students at Tiananmen Square, demanding freedom and democracy.

April 26. The *People's Daily* publishes a controversial editorial denouncing student demonstrators as a "small bunch of troublemakers" and threatening a government crackdown.

April 29. After the government refuses to meet with student leaders, demonstrations are held in Beijing, Shanghai, Nanjing and other major cities, demanding democracy and freedom of the press.

May 4. A massive march commemorates the 70th anniversary of a historic student protest movement and coincides with an Asian Development Bank meeting in Beijing.

May 13. In Tiananmen Square, 3,000 students begin a hunger strike.

May 14. At a secret Politburo meeting, Zhao Ziyang's moderate line in handling the student demonstrations is reportedly adopted. The policy calls for a direct dialogue with student leaders and limited measures to implement democracy within the party.

May 15. Soviet President Mikhail Gorbachev arrives in Beijing for the first Sino-Soviet summit since 1959. Because of the hunger strike and continuing demonstrations, the welcoming ceremony is held at the Beijing airport instead of Tiananmen Square.

May 18. More than 1 million people take to the streets in Beijing to support the hunger strikers.

May 19. Zhao Ziyang makes an emotional predawn visit to the hunger strikers, pleading with students to leave the square. Li Peng warns that Beijing's turmoil has spread to other parts of the country and holds a televised meeting with a delegation of students led by Uerkesh Daolet (Wuer Kaixi).

May 20. Martial law is officially declared by Li Peng in "some parts of Beijing." Speaking to a selected audience of party leaders, Yang Shankun justifies martial law and the deployment of troops in the capital to "keep order."

May 25. Premier Li calls on the troops to "overcome difficulties and carry out martial law."

May 27. Some student leaders urge demonstrators to end the occupation of Tiananmen Square, but others escalate their demands for Premier Li to step down.

June 2. Unarmed troops try to enter Tiananmen Square and are pushed back by student demonstrators.

June 3. Armed soldiers begin to move to Tiananmen Square. Clashes between soldiers and civilians break out on the western and southern outskirts of Beijing.

June 4. Troops in armored personnel carriers and tanks crash through barriers and fire indiscriminately at students and city residents, killing thousands of people.

June 6. Protest leader Liu Xiaobo, later branded by Beijing as the "black hand" behind the unrest, is arrested while riding a bicycle in Beijing.

June 7. Prodemocracy Astrophysicist Fang Lizhi, his wife Li Shuxian and son Fang Ke take refuge in the U.S. embassy in Beijing.

June 9. Deng Xiaoping, who had not been seen in public since his meeting with Gorbachev on May 16, appears on national television to congratulate the commanders of the martial-law troops.

June 10. The Beijing municipal government announces the arrest of more than 400 people, including students, intellectuals and labor leaders.

June 13. The Public Security Bureau issues arrest warrants for 21 leaders of the Autonomous Students' Union of Beijing Universities, including Wang Dan and Uerkesh Daolet.

June 23-24. Following an enlarged Politburo plenum (June 19-21), the Central Committee meets in Beijing to endorse the crackdown and condemn Zhao Ziyang. Zhao is stripped of all leading posts and replaced as party General Secretary by Shanghai party chief and mayor Jiang Zemin.

June 27. The National People's Congress opens after a nine-day postponement. Chaired by Wan Li, the body endorses the crackdown of the "counterrevolutionary rebellion" and joins the call for tighter ideological control.

June 30. In a report to the National People's Congress Standing Committee, Beijing Mayor Chen Xitong details criticisms of deposed party chief Zhao Ziyang.

July 29. The *People's Daily* publishes a Politburo decision to 1) purge state-controlled companies, 2) prohibit children of high cadres from engaging in business, 3) stop the "special supply" of food to top party leaders, 4) strictly regulate the use of official automobiles and forbid luxury sedan imports, 5) prohibit the use of public funds for dinner parties or gifts, 6) strictly control foreign travel and 7) investigate cases of corruption, bribery and other crimes.

WHO'S WHO IN CHINA

Editor's Note: This book uses the now standard Pinyin system of transliterating Chinese into English. In the case of some historically familiar names, like Chiang Kai-shek and Dr. Sun Yat-sen, spellings using the old Wade-Giles system have also been given.

Bao Tong. Former personal secretary and a top adviser to Zhao Ziyang. In 1987 Bao was named head of the newly formed Research Center for Political Structural Reform and elected a member the Central Committee. He was reportedly arrested shortly before the June 3-4 massacre.

Bao Zunxin (1937-   ). Historian-philosopher and associate research fellow at the Institute of Chinese History of the Chinese Academy of Social Sciences. He initiated a signature movement to support the student demonstrations and helped form the Autonomous Intellectuals' Union. Bao was missing after the June 3-4 massacre.

Bo Yibo (1909-   ). Vice chairman of the party's Central Advisory Commission and a former Politburo member and Vice Premier.

Chai Ling (1966-   ). A graduate student majoring in child psychology at Beijing Normal University. She was a reluctant commander of the Tiananmen Square demonstrations and joined the hunger strike out of a sense of outrage against the leaders' insensitivity. She once pleaded with fellow students to leave the square before the massacre began. She was among 21 people on the government's most-wanted list after the massacre.

Chen Xitong (1930-   ). Mayor of Beijing. He has also been director of the Beijing Planning and Construction Committee since 1983 and a member of the Chinese Communist Party's Central Committee since 1987. In his "Report on Checking the Turmoil and Quelling the Counterrevolutionary Rebellion" to the Standing Committee of the National People's Congress on June 30, Chen delivered the strongest official criticism of Zhao Ziyang to date.

Chen Yun (1905-   ). Chairman, Central Advisory Commission. A member of the Communist Party since 1925, Chen was a longtime Vice Premier in charge of financial and economic work, as well as a strong advocate of orthodox Marxist central planning.

Dai Qing (1946-   ). A well-known *Guangming Daily* reporter who interviewed Fang Lizhi and other leading intellectuals. On June 4 she publicly resigned from the Communist Party in protest against the Tiananmen events. Believed to have been arrested.

Deng Xiaoping (1904-   ). Chairman of the Central Military Commission. Mao Zedong's comrade in the Long March, Deng became the archenemy of Mao's wife Jiang Qing during the Cultural Revolution. Attacked as a "capitalist roader," Deng was stripped of all his positions after the April 1976 Tiananmen Square demonstration. After Mao's death in September 1976, Deng gradually maneuvered his way back to power with the support of his surviving Long March colleagues and, ironically, a 1978-79 prodemocracy movement.

Fang Lizhi (1936-   ). Astrophysicist, dissident and former vice president of the University of Science and Technology at Hefei. Removed from his job and expelled from the Communist Party in 1987, Fang continued to speak out for democracy. Early in 1989 he wrote a letter to Deng Xiaoping requesting the release of Wei Jingsheng, a political prisoner. Fang's appeal was widely supported by other Chinese intellectuals both at home and abroad. After the Beijing massacre in June, he and his wife Li Shuxian were granted refuge at the U.S. embassy.

Hou Dejian. Songwriter who defected to Beijing from Taiwan in 1983. One of the prominent Tiananmen Square hunger strikers, he remained at the Monument to the People's Heroes up to the end. Whereabouts unknown.

Hu Jiwei (1917-   ). Former *People's Daily* editor in chief. A member of the Standing Committee of the National People's Congress, Hu initiated a letter-writing campaign among colleagues to convene an emergency session of the National People's Congress to resolve the country's political and economic crisis and possibly dismiss Li Peng as Premier. Hu was a close associate of Hu Yaobang and a supporter of Zhao Ziyang.

Hu Qili (1929-   ). Former Politburo member and former party propaganda chief. A onetime mayor of Tianjin, Hu was a close associate of Hu Yaobang and rose through the ranks of the Communist Youth League. He was dismissed from all his top posts in June.

Hu Yaobang (1915-89). Former party General Secretary. He was groomed by Deng Xiaoping as a possible successor but was forced to resign in 1987 after being blamed for the outbreak of student demonstrations and the spread of "bourgeois liberalization."

Jiang Qing (1914-   ). Mao Zedong's widow and leader of the notorious Gang of Four. She spearheaded Mao's Cultural Revolution and played a key role in removing Deng Xiaoping from office in 1976. Arrested later that year, she was expelled from the party in 1977 and convicted, along with nine other defendants, of "persecuting to death" 34,800 people during the Cultural Revolution. She received a death sentence, which was later commuted to life imprisonment.

Jiang Zemin (1926-   ). General Secretary of the Chinese Communist Party and a former mayor of Shanghai. Graduated from Shanghai's prestigious Jiaotong University with an engineering degree, Jiang was trained in the Soviet Union in the early 1950s. Fluent in Russian, he is also said to know English, French, Rumanian and Japanese. Jiang succeeded Zhao Ziyang as General Secretary shortly after the Beijing massacre.

Li Peng (1928-). Premier. The foster son of the late Zhou Enlai, a beloved former Premier, Li was trained in the Soviet Union as an engineer. He was named Minister of the Power Industry in 1979, Vice Minister of Water Conservancy and Power in 1981, Vice Premier and, concurrently, Education Minister in 1985. He joined the Politburo and the Party Secretariat in 1985 and the Standing Committee of the Politburo in 1987. He officially became Premier in 1989. A conservative, Li was despised by supporters of the prodemocracy movement, especially after he declared martial law on May 20, 1989.

Li Ruihuan (1934-). Politburo member and, since 1982, mayor of Tianjin. A son-in-law of National People's Congress Chairman Wan Li, he was a construction worker and became a manager in the building of Beijing's Great Hall of the People. His tough handling of student protests in Tianjin in 1986 and 1989 earned him high marks with his mentors. He was named to the Standing Committee of the Politburo in June 1989, in charge of propaganda and ideological work.

Li Shuxian. Fang Lizhi's wife, she was associate professor in the physics department at Peking University. She was also active in the democracy movement.

Li Tieying (1936-). Vice Premier and member of the Politburo and the party's Central Committee. Son of Deng Xiaoping's first wife and revolutionary veteran Li Weihan, Li Tieying is a rising representative of the "Princes' faction," made up of the offspring of top officials.

Li Xiannian (1905-). Chairman of the Chinese People's Political Consultative Conference, a largely ceremonial advisory body. He also served as Finance Minister and President of the People's Republic.

Li Ximing (1926-). Party secretary of Beijing and a member of the Politburo. It was his report that prompted Deng to conclude that the student movement constituted "turmoil."

Liu Binyan (1926-). A *People's Daily* investigative reporter who became famous for his exposés of party corruption. He was expelled from the party during the 1987 campaign against "bourgeois liberalization." Liu was allowed out of China in 1988 for a one-year stint as a Nieman Fellow at Harvard University. After the Beijing massacre in June 1989, he joined other dissidents to form a worldwide Chinese Democratic Front outside China.

Liu Xiaobo (1954-). Lecturer at Beijing Normal University. A prolific writer, essayist and literary critic, he was a visiting scholar at Columbia University in New York City before returning to Beijing in April 1989. Liu served as adviser to student leaders during the demonstrations at Tiananmen Square and took part in a hunger strike on June 2. He was arrested June 6.

Peng Zhen (1902-   ). Former Chairman of the National People's Congress and a member of the Politburo. He officially retired from all posts in October 1987 but still continued to exert influence in party and government affairs.

Qiao Shi (1924-   ). Member of the Standing Committee of the Politburo in charge of legal and security organs, Qiao has also served as Vice Premier, head of the powerful Central Discipline Inspection Committee and president of the Central Party School.

Qin Benli. Former editor in chief of Shanghai's *World Economic Herald,* a leading newspaper in the campaign for press freedom. Qin was dismissed from his post after refusing to print a retraction of accounts of Hu Yaobang's death and student demonstrations.

Qin Jiwei (1914-   ). Defense Minister. An army general, Qin was initially reported to have opposed martial law and suppression of the student demonstrators with military troops. One of Deng's trusted friends in the military, Qin has publicly supported the military crackdown.

Ren Wanding (1945-   ). Founder of the Chinese Human Rights League in 1979. He was first arrested in 1979 and served a four-year prison term for activities during the Beijing Spring democracy movement. In 1989 he made speeches supporting the student demonstrations. Ren was arrested again shortly after the massacre.

Rui Xingwen (1926-   ). Party secretary of Shanghai until 1987, when he joined the five-member Party Secretariat to be in charge of propaganda. He was dismissed from his posts in June 1989 along with Zhao.

Song Ping (1917-   ). A member of the six-member Standing Committee of the Politburo since June 1989, Song was head of the party's organization department. A former journalist, Song once served as Zhou Enlai's political secretary. He also was vice chairman of the National Planning Commission.

Su Shaozhi (1926-   ). A leading proponent of "modernizing Marxism" and democratizing the Communist Party, Su was dismissed as director of the Chinese Academy of Social Science's Institute of Marxism–Leninism–Mao Zedong Thought in 1987 during the conservative campaign against "bourgeois liberalization." He fled to the U.S. via Europe and in 1989 was a visiting scholar at Marquette University.

Su Xiaokang (1949-   ). Lecturer of broadcasting at a Beijing university and principal author of *River Elegy (He Shang),* a television documentary series critical of China's backwardness and explicitly supportive of Western-style political as well as economic modernization.

Tian Jiyun (1929-   ). Vice Premier and Politburo member in charge of economic matters, particularly agriculture. He was working in the provincial government of Sichuan when Zhao Ziyang brought him to Beijing and made him a Vice Premier. After Zhao's fall, Tian inexplicably retained his posts.

Uerkesh Daolet (also known as Wuer Kaixi) (1968-   ). Education major at Beijing Normal University and a leader of the student movement. An ethnic Uighur, he was one of the students who had a televised confrontation with Premier Li Peng during the May demonstrations and hunger strike. He escaped arrest, fleeing to France and then to the U.S., where he helped launch the worldwide Chinese Democratic Front with four other well-known dissidents: Liu Binyan, Yan Jiaqi, Wan Runnan and Su Shaozhi (q.v.).

Wan Li (1916-   ). Chairman, National People's Congress. A technocrat and Deng Xiaoping's close associate and regular bridge partner, Wan began his official career as Vice Minister of Construction in 1952 and was removed from office as Minister of Railways near the end of the Cultural Revolution. Reinstated the following year after the downfall of the Gang of Four, Wan became a member of the Politburo in 1982.

Wan Runnan. Chairman of the Stone Corp., a successful private computer firm in China, and a former son-in-law of Liu Shaoqi. Wan was deeply involved in the student demonstrations and named on the most-wanted list. He joined other escaped dissidents in Paris and helped organize the Chinese Democratic Front overseas, becoming the organization's secretary.

Wang Dan (1965-   ). Freshman history student at Peking University and a student protest leader. Wang first emerged during the April 1989 demonstrations of mourning for former party chief Hu Yaobang. After the massacre, he was No. 1 on the government's most-wanted list. Following an unsuccessful attempt to flee China, he returned to Beijing and was arrested in early July after asking a Taiwanese journalist to aid his escape.

Wang Zhen (1909-   ). Vice President of China. A veteran army general and party conservative stalwart, he was known for his hard-line views and played a key role in the student crackdown.

Wuer Kaixi. See Uerkesh Daolet.

Yan Jiaqi (1942-   ). Former director of the Political Studies Institute of the Chinese Academy of Social Sciences. He advised senior officials on political restructuring before the Beijing massacre. With his wife he co-authored the only comprehensive official history of the Cultural Revolution. Now in exile in France, he helped launch the Chinese Democratic Front.

Yan Mingfu (1931-   ). Son of Yan Baohang, a patriotic Kuomintang official who cooperated with the Communists after 1949. Yan studied in the Soviet Union in the 1950s and later worked as interpreter. He took part in the Sino-Soviet negotiations. In 1985 he was appointed Minister of the party's United Front, a body in charge of Taiwan-mainland relations. He was elected secretary of the Party Secretariat in 1987 and vice chairman of the National Political Consultative Conference in 1986.

Yang Shangkun (1907-   ). President of the People's Republic and permanent vice chairman of the Central Military Commission. A former army general, Yang played a key role in the military crackdown at Tiananmen Square by arranging the deployment of troops loyal to him. Control of the army was expected to pass into Yang's hands when Deng left the scene.

Yao Yilin (1917-   ). Close follower of Chen Yun and a conservative economist. Yao has served in leading posts in various financial institutions. A member of the Politburo Standing Committee, he was also a vice premier and director of the State Planning Commission.

Yuan Mu. A former journalist, Yuan has served as official spokesman of the State Council since 1988 and done much to discredit the Western press reports about the Beijing massacre.

Zhao Ziyang (1919-   ). Former Premier, Party General Secretary and first vice chairman of the Central Military Commission. After Hu Yaobang's downfall in 1987, Zhao was Deng Xiaoping's chosen successor. Blamed for the student protests, Zhao was stripped of his high positions, and his future remains cloudy.

A GLOSSARY

Antibourgeois Liberalization Campaign. A drive initiated by former propaganda chief Deng Liqun against those intellectuals who advocated more freedom of speech and democracy for both Communist Party members and people in general. It resulted in the 1987 expulsion from the party of astrophysicist Fang Lizhi, journalist Liu Binyan and author Wang Ruowang.

Antirightist Campaign. The first campaign launched by Chairman Mao Zedong in the late 1950s to re-educate those who were critical of his policies.

Antispiritual Pollution Campaign. A drive mounted by party hardliners from October 1983 to February 1984 with speeches and articles in the state-controlled press blaming foreign, especially Western, influence for crime, corruption, pornography and other social problems in China.

"Backdoorism." See *zouhoumen*.

baihua. A Chinese term for vernacular, or common language, as distinct from *wenyan,* or literary style, used in Chinese ancient writings.

baotu. Rioters, or the violent ones, a term used by the government to refer to people blamed for bloodshed in Beijing and elsewhere.

Basic Law. A legal document jointly drafted by China and representatives of Hong Kong to be adopted as a charter for the British colony after it reverts to Chinese sovereignty in 1997.

Beida. Contraction of Beijing Daxue, or Peking University.

Capitalist roader. A derogatory term to describe someone who has deviated from Communist orthodoxy and leans toward capitalism on economic matters. The term was most often used during the Cultural Revolution (q.v.) to refer to then President Liu Shaoqi and Vice Premier Deng Xiaoping.

CASS. An acronym for Chinese Academy of Social Sciences, where many intellectuals were associated with Zhao Ziyang's reforms and with the student demonstrations.

CCTV. An acronym for China Central Television, a state-controlled network.

Chin dynasty. See Qin dynasty.

Ching dynasty. See Qing dynasty.

CITIC. An acronym for China International Trust and Investment Corp., the quasi-official trading and investment organization set up by the government to deal with foreign trade and capital investments.

Cultural Revolution. A major political movement launched by Mao Zedong in 1966. Formally known as the Great Proletarian Cultural Revolution, it was carried out by the Red Guards (q.v.), young people who attacked all forms of bureaucracy and privilege in China. Led by

Defense Minister Lin Biao and Mao's wife Jiang Qing, the Red Guards destroyed careers, property and lives throughout the country. Only after Mao's death and the fall of his widow in 1976 was the turmoil finally declared a "great national catastrophe."

danwei. Literally, "unit." It could be a place for work or study or an organization with which an individual's livelihood and welfare are closely connected.

dazibao. Literally, "big-character poster."

Democracy Wall. A stone barrier in Beijing's Xidan district, where "big-character" posters making demands on the government and airing criticisms of it and its leaders were posted during 1978-79.

Feifeng daqu. A kind of rice liquor with the brand name Feifeng (Flying Phoenix).

Four Cardinal Principles. Also known as *sige jianchi,* or "Four Insists," a slogan promoted by Deng Xiaoping to uphold the principles of socialism, the dictatorship of the proletariat, the leadership of the Communist Party and Marxism–Leninism–Mao Zedong Thought.

Four Modernizations. A government program for development first advocated by Premier Zhou Enlai in 1975 and later implemented by Deng Xiaoping after the death of Mao and the smashing of the Gang of Four in 1976. They include the modernization of agriculture, industry, defense, and science and technology.

gaizao. To re-educate or reform a person's political thought.

Gang of Elders. The conservative supporters of the student crackdown, who, like Deng Xiaoping, are all in their 80s and former or current party leaders.

Gang of Four. The four ultra-leftist members of the Politburo who were accused of usurping power during the 1966-76 Cultural Revolution and of persecuting thousands to death. The gang consisted of Mao Zedong's widow Jiang Qing, Wang Hongwen, Zhang Chunqiao and Yao Wenyuan. All were tried and convicted after Deng took power.

Great Hall of the People. A building adjacent to Tiananmen (q.v.) Square, where major official conferences and receptions for foreign dignitaries are held.

Great Leap Forward. A slogan used for a crash socioeconomic program, implemented between 1958 and 1961, to catch up with the industrialized nations through mobilization of the masses and utilization of native resources, including the production of steel and pig iron in backyard furnaces.

guandao. Official profiteering or corruption.

guanxi. Connections, or personal relationships.

hukoubu. A household registration booklet issued by the government as a form of official identification of residence.

hutong. A Beijing term for a small street or alleyway.

Jianguomenwai. A compound of houses in Beijing where foreign diplomats and journalists live and work.

laobaixing. Literally, "old hundred names." A Chinese term for ordinary people or citizens.

liyong. To make use of (a person or thing).

Long March. A historic 1934-35 retreat by the Red Army under pressure from Nationalist forces during the civil war. Mao Zedong's troops marched about 6,000 miles from Jiangxi province in a roundabout way to Yan'an, Shaanxi province, in search of a sanctuary.

May 4 Movement. A political and cultural movement that began as a series of student protests in Beijing against concessions granted to Japan in China by the Versailles Treaty at the end of World War I. The date holds a significant place in the hearts of Chinese students. The prodemocracy movement in 1989 gained new impetus with the student demonstrations that marked the 70th anniversary of the May 4 Movement.

menhukaifang. Open door (policy).

National People's Congress. China's parliament, which meets once a year to hear top government officials' reports and rubber-stamp virtually all decisions recommended to it by the Communist Party's Central Committee through the Premier.

Qin dynasty (211-206 B.C.). A period when China was first unified by a powerful Emperor who named himself Qin Shihuang Di, meaning "the first Emperor of Qin." Among other achievements, he ordered construction of the Great Wall for defense and standardization of a system of weights and measures throughout the kingdom. The Emperor is also known in Chinese history as a tyrant who killed many scholars and burned numerous books in order to suppress dissent.

Qing dynasty (1644-1911). Also known as the Manchu dynasty, this is the historical period when China was ruled by the Manchurians.

Red Guards. High-school- and college-age Chinese, who were called upon by Chairman Mao Zedong during the Cultural Revolution (q.v.) to "defend the Communist Party" against all its "enemies," including anyone who did not follow Mao's orthodox guidelines and policies.

renminbi. Literally, "people's money." A general term for Chinese currency. The yuan is a specific monetary unit.

Responsibility System. A term used by Chinese reformers to emphasize the responsibility of families and enterprises for their own financial losses or gains in economic activities.

sanjiaodi. A "triangular area," specifically the one on the Peking University campus where students gathered to discuss their protest demonstrations before the crackdown.

Special Economic Zones (S.E.Z.). Established in 1979 as part of China's efforts to test economic-reform policies and attract foreign investments and technology. The most successful of the original four zones is Shenzhen, an area between Guangzhou (Canton) and Hong Kong.

Taiping Tianguo. Literally, Peaceful Kingdom, or the Heavenly Kingdom of Great Peace. Established in southern and central China between 1850 and 1864 by a rebel group led by a self-styled Christian, Hong Xiuquan (or Hung Hsiu-chüan). The period is also known in Chinese history as the Taiping Rebellion.

Tiananmen. Literally, the Gate of Heavenly Peace. It is actually the name of a building next to a huge square in the center of Beijing.

tiefanwan. Iron rice bowl. In Chinese parlance, it refers to state-assigned lifetime jobs that offer security regardless of performance or productivity.

Tongmenghui. The League of United Action, a secret society formed by Dr. Sun Yat-sen in 1905 among overseas Chinese communities to promote the revolution to overthrow the Manchu (Qing) dynasty.

tongxin jishou. A common four-character saying that literally means "heart pain" and "head sick." It was used as the entire text of an editorial by the normally pro-Beijing Hong Kong daily *Wen Wei Po* to express outrage immediately after martial law was declared in Beijing on May 20.

toumingdu. Literally, the "degree of transparency." The term has been used to refer to openness in official matters.

wanyuanhu. Literally, Ten Thousand Yuan Households, a term coined by the Chinese to describe the prosperous households that benefited from economic reform.

xiuxi. An equivalent for siesta, or afternoon nap, except that the Chinese have enshrined it in Article 43 of the 1982 Constitution. There is often a temporary stop in business transactions during the rest period.

zaigaizao. To re-educate once more.

Zhongguo. Middle Kingdom, or China.

Zhongnanhai. A sprawling residential compound in Beijing where top government and party leaders live and work.

zhongxue wei ti, xixue wei yong. Literally, Chinese learning as the core, Western learning for the application. An epigram often attributed to a Qing dynasty reformer, Zhang Zhidong (also known as Chang Chih-tung, 1837-1909).

zouhoumen. Literally, backdoorism. The term means using bribery or privilege, or both, to get what one cannot get through regular channels.

INDEX

ABC News, 211–212
Adams, John Quincy, 74
Adie, Kate, 40, 51, 54
Agriculture, 92, 100–102, 106
Aikman, David, 94
Anderson, Donna, 204
Aquino, Corazon, 179
Army. *See* People's Liberation Army
Arrests, 212–218
Asian Games, 226
Autonomous Workers' Union, 19, 30–31

Baihua, 85
Balance of trade, 103, 107–108
Baoping He, 164
Bao Ruowang, 161
Beijing massacre, 40–65; cover-up of, 193–198, 209–212, 242; fatalities, 23, 41–42, 55, 65–66, 68–69; foreigners and, 225; foreign reaction to, 161–163, 166, 167–172, 176–180; impact of, 12, 214–215, 236; military planning for, 31–40; sabotage following, 241–242; terrorism following, 199–204; trade sanctions following, 177, 178, 188–189
Boeing, 179
Bourgeois liberalization, 129–131, 210, 230, 240
Boxers, 79–81
British Broadcasting Corp., 115, 125
British Nationality Act, 185
Brokaw, Tom, 174
Burlingame, Anson, 78
Burma, 179
Bush Administration, 171, 175–176, 177, 179

Caccamo, Paul, 50–51
Cambodia, 180
Canada, 162–163
Carlson, Richard, 169–170
Central Military Commission, 32, 246–247
Chai Ling, 19, 22, 61, 142, 157
Chanthimatorn, Surachai, 162
Chaureli, Sofia, 176
Che Fei, 145
Chen Duxu, 85, 86
Chen Jun, 165, 166
Chen Kaige, 170
Chen Xitong, 22, 193–194
Chen Yun, 101, 106, 131, 132, 222, 228–229

Chen Zongshun, 145
Chiang Kai–shek, 5, 87, 182
Chi Haotian, 33, 34, 35, 208
China: dynastic cycles in, 73;
    modernization of, 235–236,
    250–251; opening up of, 94,
    102–103; West and, 73–81, 84,
    115–116, 250–251
China Central Television
    (CCTV), 23, 197, 211–214
Chinese Academy of Social Sci-
    ences, 124, 199–200
Chinese Communist Party: expul-
    sion from, 215; founding, 9–10,
    71, 86–87; leadership of, 3–6,
    231–233, 245–251; Nationalists
    and, 87, 89–90; students and,
    12–13, 148–156; support for,
    84, 86, 88–90; terrorism and,
    88, 90–91
Chinese Communist Party Cen-
    tral Committee, 30–31, 97,
    219–223
Chinese people; daily life of, 3–4,
    72; diplomats, 167–168; diversi-
    ty of, 250; impact of massacre
    on, 214–215, 244; overseas
    communities, 161–162
Choonhavan, Chatichai, 162, 180
Choonhavan, Kraisak, 162
Christianity, 72, 76–77
Collectives, 92, 99, 105, 111–112
Comintern, 86
Communist Party. See Chinese
    Communist Party
Confucianism, 72, 73–74, 80–81,
    84, 86, 133
Corruption, 112–113, 132, 151,
    229
Counterrevolutionaries, 198–199,
    226–231
Cuba, 178
Cultural Revolution, 5–6, 12–13,
    17, 71, 93–94, 116, 241
Cunneen, Paticia, 179

Decentralization, 107–109
Democracy Wall, 98, 104
Deng Liqun, 116, 117
Deng Pufang, 113
Deng Xiaoping: army and, 5,
    31–33, 100, 121, 246; economic
    reforms under, 5–9, 13–14,
    71–72, 93–95, 99–121, 130,
    131; foreign reaction to, 161,
    167; Hong Kong and, 184, 227;
    post-massacre leadership, 217,
    219, 225–227, 230, 235–238,
    240, 241–251; overseas Chinese
    and, 161–163; reappearance
    of, 207–210; reported death
    of, 188, 203, 206; repression
    under, 92, 104; rise to power,
    97–104; students and, 11–14,
    123, 134, 138, 139, 148, 153;
    successor for, 222–223, 233,
    245–249
Deng Zhifang, 163
Dewey, John, 71, 85
Dolan Elizabeth, 179
Drug smuggling, 75
Dual pricing system, 109, 110,
    237
Du Fu, 161, 172

East Germany, 178
Economic reforms: under Com-
    munists, 80, 91; under Deng,
    5–9, 13–14, 71–72, 93–95,
    99–121, 130, 131; impacts of,
    238; rural, 100–102, 104–107;
    urban, 106–113, 130
Economy, 94–95, 225–226,
    236–241
Education system, 133, 140–141,
    238
Enterprise Responsibility System,
    106–107

Fang Lizhi, 124–126, 129, 133,
    134, 201–203, 212–213, 228

Fathers, Michael, 59
Feng Guifen, 77
Feringer, Alexis, 67
FlorCruz, Jaime, 248
Foreigners, evacuation of,
    203–204
Foreign trade, 74–75, 102–103,
    107–108; post-massacre,
    224–226, 239–241
Four Cardinal Principles, 104,
    118, 130
Four Modernizations, 95, 96,
    99–101, 121
France: exiles in, 198, 233–234;
    reaction in, 167, 171–172, 176
Friedman, Milton, 228
Fugitives, 198, 211–215, 226–228,
    230–231, 233–234, 243

Gang of Elders, 209, 223
Gang of Four, 6, 95, 96, 98, 248
Gao Xin, 24
Gerasimov, Gennadi, 177
Germany, 78
Goddess of Democracy, 18–19,
    65, 158, 167
Gorbachev, Mikhail, 9, 146, 149,
    151, 172–173, 178
Great Britain, 74, 78, 184–185,
    189–190
Great Hall of the People, 25,
    27–29, 53, 62, 63
Great Leap Forward, 71, 92, 99,
    101
Great Proletarian Cultural Revo-
    lution. *See* Cultural Revolu-
    tion
Griffin, Nick, 52–53, 58
Grumman Aerospace, 177, 179
Guanxi, 7

Han, Lida, 167
Han Liang, 143
Helms, Jesse, 177
Hess, David, 169

Hong Kong, 180–181, 183–191,
    198, 227, 240–241
Hong Xiuquan, 76
Hong Xuezhi, 208
Hou Dejian, 23–24, 61, 62
Household responsibility system,
    99, 105, 238
Howe, Sir Geoffrey, 190
Hsieh, Tom, 162
Hsin Ch'ing-nien, 85–86
Hua Guofeng, 96–98, 116, 119
Huang Jing, 171
Huang Jingsheng, 165
Hu Fu, 183
Hukoubu, 214, 216
Hung, Frances, 186
Hungary, 178
Hunger strike, 23–24, 45, 61, 62,
    146–154, 158
Hu Qiaomu, 116
Hu Qili, 119, 151, 220
Hurel, Pierre, 44–45
Hu Shih, 85, 86
Hu Yaobang, 6, 10, 17, 119, 120,
    121, 123–124, 129, 135–138,
    163, 223, 235, 236

India, 180
Industrial Revolution, 74
Informants, 214, 243
Intellectuals, 6–7, 86, 129,
    132–133, 170, 198, 238–239
Italian Communist Party, 178

Japan, 71, 78, 81, 84, 89–90, 102,
    107–108, 167, 178, 179,
    239–240
Jiang Liren, 135, 140, 142, 144,
    154
Jiang Mianhang, 163
Jiang Qing, 95, 98, 248
Jiang Zemin, 126–127, 145, 196,
    222–223, 227, 232, 245–246
Jian Ping Lu, 168
Jigme Ngapo, 166

Journalists, 145

Kahn, Joe, 48
Kane, Anthony, 175
Kang Youwei, 79, 80
Karnow, Stanley, 12
Kuo, Shirley, 181
Kuralt, Charles, 174

Lampton, Michael, 175
Landy, John, 43, 44
Laurie, James, 211–212
Lee Huan, 183
Lee Teng-hui, 181, 182
Lee Tze-chung, 191, 227
Lei Feng, 129–130
Lem, C., 163
Leys, Simon, 71
Liang Qichiao, 81
Lin, Dah H., 170
Lin, Biao, 94
Link, Perry, 201–202
Li Peng: economic reform and,
     13–14; leadership of, 132, 220,
     222, 246; overseas Chinese and,
     162; students and, 8–9, 11, 17,
     39–40, 138, 151–154, 156, 157,
     159
Li Shuxian, 201–202, 212–213
Li Sunshi, 229
Liu Binyan, 129, 233
Liu Shaoqi, 93, 101
Liu Xiaobo, 24, 61
Li Xiannian, 131, 222
Li Zhibo, 210
Lu Xun, 29, 251
Lu Yin, 165, 168

Macao, 182–184, 188, 190, 198
Mao Xiangdong, 47
Mao Zedong, 4, 10, 13, 17, 28, 32,
     87, 88–96, 98, 99, 104, 114,
     119, 129–130, 148, 246
Market socialism, 107
Martial law, 153, 156

Marx, Karl, 86
Massacres, 1926, 249. *See also*
     Beijing massacre
May 4 Movement, 9–10, 85–86,
     143–146
Medical care, during massacre,
     53–55
Meng Shilie, 126
Military planning, 31–40
Mitsuzuka, Hiroshi, 179
Mitterrand, Francois, 176
Mouren Wu, 165, 168
Mueller, Michael, 55

Nathan, Andrew, 176
Nationalists, 82–84, 87–90, 181
News censorship, 145
Nike, 179
Nixon, Richard, 94

Old Guard, 4–5, 6, 8–9, 14
Opium, 75
Orleans, Leo, 171

Pan Youfang, 170
Pasqualini, Jena, 161
Pei, I.M., 161, 191
Pei Meixing, 171
Peking University, 9–12, 85,
     128–129, 134–140, 141, 142
Peng Zhen, 131, 210, 222
People's Armed Police, 25, 26,
     29–30
People's Daily, 139, 144, 150, 152,
     208, 213, 217, 226, 237, 241,
     245–246
People's Liberation Army: Deng
     and, 5, 31–33, 100, 121, 246;
     factions in, 205–206, 248; faith
     in, 50; government and, 209;
     Hong Kong and, 189, low mo-
     tivation in, 34; mobilization of,
     20–23, 31, 35, 153; post–mas-
     sacre, 194, 195, 198–200; stu-
     dents and, 18, 22, 155–156;

units of, 34; violence against, 41–42, 45, 48–49, 52, 56–58; violence by, 13, 22, 33, 40–53, 55–69; weapons bus and, 25–27
Perry, Matthew, 81
Police brutality, 126–127
Political reform, 119–120
Political terrorism, 88, 90–91, 199–204
Pomfret, John, 43
Presnick, Mitch, 68
Price reform, 109, 130, 132
Pricing system, dual, 109, 110, 37
Private enterprise, 106–107, 111–114, 237; foreign, 103, 108
Prodemocracy movement, 30–31, 104, 124–129
Proletariat, 87, 90
Propaganda, 223–226, 242–243
Puyi, Emperor, 83

Qiao Shi, 151, 163, 222, 247
Qin Benli, 145
Qing dynasty, 74, 77, 80, 82, 83
Qing Ming festival, 95, 248
Qin Jiwei, 207, 208
Quotations from Chairman Mao, 94

Red Army, 88, 89, 209
Red Guards, 17, 93–94
Reforms, 79–81. See also Economic reforms; Political reform
Repression, 104, 210–211, 243
Rosen, Stanley, 175
Ruan Libing, 140
Russian Revolution, 86

Sanyuan Li, 165–166
Schweisberg, David, 62, 68
Shao, John, 170
Shijin Wang, 165
SMELT, 199–200
Society of Righteous and Harmonious Fists, 79–80, 81

Solarz, Stephen, 177
Soros, George, 229
South Korea, 180
Soviet Union, 91, 94, 146, 177–178
Special Economic Zones, 103, 108, 198
Spiritual pollution, 8, 116
Stallone, Steve, 175
Student demonstrations, 17, 123–129, 143; ban on, 127, 136; Hu Yaobang and, 135–140; Gorbachev and, 146–150; impacts of, 129–130, 244; May 4 Movement and, 85–86
Students: autonomous union preparatory committees, 138–139; ban on associations of, 211; concerns of, 19; exiled, 233–234; elitism of, 129; foreign reaction to, 172–176, 185–189; post–massacre, 194–195, 198, 210–216; power of, 20; qualifications of, 140; rivalries among, 157–158; status of, 141–142; studying abroad, 163–165, 168, 170–172; Communism and, 133–134, 148
Sullivan, Roger, 178
Sun Yat-sen, 82–83
Su Shaozhi, 119–120, 13, 198

Taiping Tianguo, 76–77
Taiwan, 83, 180–183
Thailand, 180
Thatcher, Margaret, 184, 189
38th Army, 34, 204–205
Tiananmen Square: Hu's death and, 136, 138–139; hunger strike in, 23–24, 45, 61, 62, 146–154, 158; 1976 riot in, 95–96; student demonstrations in, 10–11, 18, 40, 127–128, 138–139, 142, 144–147, 154, 157, 159; Red Guard in, 93;

Zhou's death and, 95
Tian Qiao, 112
Tongji University, 126, 127
Tongwen College, 78
Toumingdu, 124
Tourism, 224, 226–227
Trade barriers, 108–109
Trade sanctions, 177, 178,
    188–189
Travel restrictions, 214–215,
    216–217
27th Army, 35, 39–69, 58, 59,
    195, 199, 204–206

Uerkesh Daolet (Wuer Kaixi), 19,
    144, 145, 151–162, 157–158,
    172, 213–214, 233, 239
Underemployment, 110
United States, 31, 94, 102, 115;
    anti-Americanism, 203,
    228–229; reaction by, 175–178,
    200–203, 218; Chinese commu-
    nities in, 162–172
Universities, 8–9, 129–130, 133,
    140, 141

Video cameras, 49, 197
Voice of America, 115, 125,
    168–170, 230
Voltaire, 72

Wald, Richard, 174–175
Wang Bingqian, 226
Wang Dan, 22–23, 146, 151, 152,
    182
Wang Hai, 34
Wang Hongwen, 95
Wang Ruoshui, 134
Wang Rûowang, 129
Wang Yan, 147
Wang Zhen, 210, 229
Wan Li, 159
Wei Jingsheng, 104, 134
Wen Wei Po, 227
Workers, 110–111, 211, 216–218

Wuer Kaixi, 19

Xiao Bing, 212
Xiao Chuan Wang, 163–164
Xiaoxi Qiao, 163
Xiong Yan, 152
Xu Kui, 163
Xu Xiaopeng, 163
Xu Xin, 208

Yang Baibing, 33, 208
Yang Futai, 133
Yang Jianhua, 33, 35
Yang Shangkun, 13, 32–33, 35,
    144, 153, 173, 205–208, 22,
    223, 232, 246–247
Yan Jiaqi, 40, 46, 120, 233
Yao Wenyuan, 95
Yao Yilin, 132, 222
Yao Yongzhan, 210–211
Yon Lee, 162
Young Yi-rong, 182
Yuan Mu, 143, 203, 229
Yuan Shikai, 83
Yu Cheng, 165–166
Yu Kuo-hwa, 182

Zhang, Gong, 66
Zhang Jianzhong, 219
Zhang Qunqiao, 95
Zhang Zhidong, 80
Zhao Ziyang: corruption and,
    113; economic reform and, 8,
    100–101, 117–119, 120; leader-
    ship of, 6, 33, 124, 130–132,
    173, 194, 196, 208, 210; ouster
    of, 12, 218–223, 228–231,
    237–238, 246; students and, 11,
    138, 144, 150–153
Zheng Tuobin, 224
Zhongguo, 74
Zhou Enlai, 5, 6, 9, 95, 99, 100,
    246, 248
Zhou Fengsuo, 214, 216
Zhou Tuo, 24

THE AUTHORS

NIEN CHENG, who wrote the Introduction, is the author of *Life and Death in Shanghai* (Grove Press; 1987), which recounted suffering during China's Cultural Revolution. The book was a national best seller, and Cheng was the subject of a 1987 TIME cover story. Born into a wealthy Chinese family in 1915, she met her husband in 1935 in England, where both were studying at the London School of Economics. A diplomat in the Kuomintang regime of Chiang Kai-shek, he served as general manager for Shell Oil after the Communists took power in 1949. When her husband died in 1957, his successor hired Cheng as his special adviser. She was imprisoned by the Communists in 1966, and after her release, 6½ years later, she immigrated to Canada. Cheng came to the U.S. three years later, and in 1988 became an American citizen. She lives in Washington, D.C.

DAVID AIKMAN, who wrote the first two chapters, "The Battle of Beijing" and "Mr. Democracy and Mr. Science," is a former chief of TIME's Beijing bureau. He joined the magazine as a correspondent in 1971 and is currently based in Washington. A specialist in Soviet and Chinese affairs and in Communism generally, he has also been the magazine's bureau chief in Moscow, Jerusalem and Eastern Europe. Born in England in 1944, he was educated at Oxford University and the University of Washington, where he received a Ph.D. in Russian and Chinese history. Dr. Aikman is the author of *Pacific Rim: Area of Change, Area of Opportunity* (Little, Brown; 1986) and the editor of *Love China Today* (Tyndale House; 1978).

SANDRA BURTON, who wrote Chapter 6, "The Crackdown," is TIME's Beijing bureau chief and former Hong Kong bureau chief. A graduate of Middlebury College, she joined TIME as a secretary in 1964 and became a correspondent in 1970. She was awarded the Edward R. Murrow Fellowship of the Council on Foreign Relations in 1986. Burton is the author of *Impossible Dream: the Marcoses, the Aquinos and the Unfinished Revolution* (Warner Books; 1989).

OSCAR CHING-KUAN CHIANG, who compiled the Chronology, the Who's Who and the Glossary, is a senior reporter-researcher for TIME. Born in Hubei province, central China, he moved with his family in 1949 to Taiwan. He holds degrees from the National Taiwan Normal University, Kansas State University, Columbia University and St. John's University (New York City). Dr. Chiang has written extensively about China for publications in the U.S., Hong Kong and Taiwan.

HOWARD G. CHUA-EOAN, who wrote Chapter 5, "A Cry Heard Round the World," is a staff writer for TIME International. Born of Chinese parents in Manila, he moved to the U.S. in 1979 and graduated from the Columbia University School of Journalism in 1984. At TIME he wrote the People section for a year and now specializes in Asian affairs. Chua-Eoan wrote TIME cover stories on the 1989 Beijing massacre. He is the author of *Corazon Aquino* (Chelsea House; 1988).

JAIME FLORCRUZ, who wrote Chapter 4, "Long Live the Students!," is a TIME reporter in Beijing. A native of the Philippines and a graduate of Peking University, he has been a journalist in China for nearly a decade.

RICHARD HORNIK, Chapter 3, "The Road to Reform," and Chapter 7, "China's Future," is TIME's National Economics Correspondent. He was previously the magazine's bureau chief in Beijing, Eastern Europe and Boston. He holds a B.A. degree from Brown University and an M.A. in Russian studies from George Washington University. Normally based in Washington, he was reporting from China in 1989 when the prodemocracy movement was suppressed.

DONALD MORRISON, who edited the book, is the Special Projects Editor of TIME In 21 years with the magazine, he has been a reporter in New York and London, and has written and edited in virtually every department. He was most recently the senior editor in charge of TIME's World section. He holds a B.A. degree from the University of Pennsylvania and an M.Sc. (Econ.) from the London School of Economics. He is the editor and a co-author of two previous TIME books: *Mikhail S. Gorbachev: An Intimate Biography* and *The Winning of the White House, 1988* (both New American Library; 1988).

The Research Staff

SINTING LAI, head reporter-researcher for the project, specializes in Asian affairs in the World section of TIME. Born in Hong Kong, she has a B.A. from Rutgers College and is a candidate for an M.A. in journalism at New York University. She has reported extensively for TIME on China and Japan.

BARBARA BURKE is a reporter-researcher in TIME's Nation section. She has a B.A. from Columbia University and worked for *Newsweek* for twelve years.

TOM CURRY, a reporter-researcher in the Nation section, has a B.A. in history from Haverford College and an M.A. in teaching from Reed College. He came to TIME after six years as a history teacher in the New York City area.

SALLY B. DONNELLY joined TIME as a reporter-researcher in 1985, after receiving an M.Sc. from the London School of Economics. Since coming to the magazine, she has specialized in Soviet and Communist affairs and has reported on events in Asia.

JOSEPH A. McGOWAN is a reporter in TIME's New York bureau. In 1985 and 1986 he taught European history and English in Beijing.

Foreign Relations. He is studying for a master's degree in international affairs at the East Asian Institute of Columbia University.

JEFFERY C. RUBIN is a reporter-researcher for TIME International and a former Sydney correspondent for TIME AUSTRALIA. A 1985 graduate of Kalamazoo College, he also studied at the University of Strasbourg in France.